11/23

CANDELARIA

CANDELARIA

A NOVEL

MELISSA
LOZADA-OLIVA

ASTRA HOUSE

NEW YORK

Astra House
A Division of Astra Publishing House
astrahouse.com

Printed in the United States of America

Library of Congress Cataloging-in-Publication Data

Names: Lozada-Oliva, Melissa, author.
Title: Candelaria : a novel / Melissa Lozada-Oliva.
Description: First edition. | New York : Astra House, [2023] | Summary: "A sweeping, mystical, intergenerational novel about mothers, daughters, and unsettled pasts, Candelaria is a story of predetermined futures and love that eats us alive"—Provided by publisher.
Identifiers: LCCN 2023011667 (print) | LCCN 2023011668 (ebook) | ISBN 9781662601804 (hardcover) | ISBN 9781662601811 (ebook)
Subjects: LCGFT: Novels.
Classification: LCC PS3612.O958 C36 2023 (print) | LCC PS3612.O958 (ebook) | DDC 813/.6—dc23/eng/20230421
LC record available at https://lccn.loc.gov/2023011667
LC ebook record available at https://lccn.loc.gov/2023011668

First edition
10 9 8 7 6 5 4 3 2 1

Designed by Richard Oriolo
The text is set in Century Schoolbook Std.
The titles are set in Century Schoolbook Std.

For Fransisca Villeda

"I ate the whole piece, desperate to prove myself wrong."

—Aimee Bender, *The Particular Sadness of Lemon Cake*

CANDELARIA

Boston, Massachusetts
CHRISTMAS EVE 2023

You are eighty-six years old and living in sin. Is it silly, living at the dusk of your life, with a boyfriend? Today you are making tortillas, clapping the masa back and forth, a motor skill as finely tuned as operating a steering wheel, which you don't know how to do, while Mauricio goes out to get more dish soap from the corner store. He would do anything for you, that man. ¡Y nunca te faltó el respeto! Ten years and he never even kissed you on the mouth. Now, that's a man! You were too precious to desecrate like that, Candelaria. Even when he made love to you, he'd cover his face with his hands, felt he did not deserve it, the sight of you. ¡Imagínate! He certainly could. You clap your tortillas and place them, perfect white disks, on the pan. All you could ask for as you run out of days before el Señor te lleva is company, somebody to feed, a familiar presence in the dark. Maybe it was destiny, maybe you were meant for each other. Maybe none of that has ever been true and you have just found yourself here, at a low-income, for-the-elderly apartment building in Boston's South End, on a day in December.

Your phone is ringing. You wipe your hands on your apron, searching throughout the apartment for the exact location of the buzzing, even though it's where you always have it, plugged in by the windowsill. "¿Aló?" you ask three times, even though Lucia, your youngest daughter, responded after the first.

"Mamá, qué haces?" You have Univision on in the background. A talking head is interviewing a man with a headlamp standing in the middle of a field of dirt. The man is holding up his hands and saying something that seems important, but you have the volume turned all the way down.

"Nada mija, saliendo a Revere con Mauricio."

"Did you forget what today is?"

"It's Tuesday," you say, narrowing your eyes at the screen. Some kind of alert is being broadcast, but these days there is always an alert being broadcast: some new disease, some weather warning. Still, the days remain for you more or less the same.

"I can't believe you. You're losing your mind."

You put your hand on your waist. Are you losing your mind? You've been feeling odd the last year or so, seeing things out of the corner of your eye, sensing a giant cloud approaching. But maybe it's just your corneas. You turn to your calendar of puppies in baskets, the one you bought at the dollar store.

"Noche buena," you say, gripping the plastic chair in the living room. How is it already Christmas Eve?

"Listen," she says to you, "Candy is in trouble."

"¿Qué pasó?" you say, trying to sound surprised. It was always something with those girls. Candy, the youngest, was always being bailed out of jail by her poor mother. The oldest one, Paola, ran away with some man, though your daughter insisted her disappearance meant death and even held a funeral for her (and for the love of El Padre Celestial, you still cannot figure out why), and the middle one, Bianca, who could've been a doctor, decided to dig up dinosaurs and never come home. But never mind about those girls. For now, this is about you.

"She didn't come to tamales. She hasn't answered my calls in a week."

You didn't come to tamales either, you're realizing. Did Lucia not make any at all?

"Well," you say, "where is she?"

"I don't know. Also, Bianca is back."

"¿Bianca? ¿No estaba en Guatemala? ¿Qué pasó? ¿Está mal?" *Perhaps she got salmonella*, you think. *She always did have the weakest disposition.*

"I'll stop by later."

"But I was on my way to the beach."

"Why were you gonna spend Christmas Eve at the beach?"

"Because the beach is nice." You hear Lucia sigh. You look out the window at the birds chirping on the building's roof. They are extra loud. Something in the air is stiller than it should be.

"Were you going to invite me?" It seems that your daughter feels left out. But it's because she keeps shutting people out of her life. That's probably why Candy didn't come to make tamales. Because she was sick of your daughter's shit. Pardon my language.

"Of course! You are welcome to come. You are always welcome with me and Mauricio. You are like a daughter to him. You can bring Candy and Bianca, too."

"I can't believe this. Didn't you hear me? Candy is in *trouble*. After all I've done for you, you still can only think of yourself. And on Christmas Eve. Sin vergüenza."

"Lucia, mija, that's not true . . ."

"You've always been like this. If I were Gabo—"

"You don't need to bring him up."

"If I were him you would drop everything and come to see me."

"Well, he's not here."

Your daughter hangs up the phone and you sigh. You know she'll stop being so mean once she has a little bit to cool off. Christmas can do that to people. All the pressure of those gifts. Your daughter gets so caught up in the spending. In the newness. In proving that she belongs here. She says that your old clothes bring bad luck. You watch her throw new things away every year. And you know they're not bad luck, they're just memories of the past. Of being hungry, and not having enough.

You place a dish rag over a basket and pile the tortillas into a soft tower. Como el tiempo pasa y pasa. How could she bring up Gabito in a fight? What if you don't want to think about him today? You never had favorites. But you think about him every day. Your handsome son is in each one of your prayers, in each count of a rosary bead, in each newly blooming flower. But him, and everything that happened, all of that feels like it was playing on the TV screen or sung about on the radio while you were in the room. Familiar lines, familiar faces, but they feel as though they happened to someone else.

We are in the season of your life that is Mauricio. You met him collecting dishes at the Old Country Buffet at the Watertown Mall; the job you picked up while the girls were at school, to have independence from Lucia, and to send some money back to Guatemala. It was the only job where you needed to know just a few lines of English: *My name is Candelaria. You all set? Very beautiful. Thank you so much.* And you would take the dishes: the disgusting pasta Americans love to drown in milk and cheese, the half-eaten chicken fingers, the chocolate cake—that one you actually like, the way the dark frosting and the moistness meet each other in one delicious bite. You'd have spoonfuls in the break room. ¡Traviesa! You made friends with a few coworkers, talking about your passion for Diosito Lindo to those who spoke Spanish, giggling with the ones who spoke Creole, always furrowing your brow at the Russians. The first time you saw him, he was a man alone, sitting in a corner booth, big hands folded, wearing a mechanic's uniform. He smiled at you all big and goofy. You said your *My name is Candelaria . . .* and he interrupted you in Spanish. *Una nombre divina*, he said to you. You took his plate, happy you'd painted your nails a vicious green, and left.

The second time you saw him, you were picking up your granddaughter from school, Candy, as they call her, the one who is in trouble. She was holding on to your hand and talking to you in Spanish, her curly hair bouncing the way it never does anymore because she spends her morning burning it con esa maquina. Poor thing. Something *has* been strange with her lately, but it's probably because she doesn't take care of herself. Or who knows, maybe she's on drugs again. Whatever she's doing, you still pray for her every day.

Mauricio was standing outside the auto shop in his bright red mechanic's uniform, chatting with the other mechanics. He saw you in your leopard-print jacket, put up that meaty hand of his, and walked over. He bent down to talk to your granddaughter and handed her a lollipop, then handed you a slip with his name on it. ¡Tan galán! You said you were a woman with a lot on your plate, and then you and your granddaughter walked away. You used Lucia's house phone to call him and did so in secret—she always yelled at you for making so many calls to Guatemala. She's always had such a temper. Sometimes you wonder—does she hate you? You sat in her bathroom, like some teenager in love, and used a veiny finger to dial each number.

It was quick from there. After a year you couldn't handle living with Lucia, the way she yelled at you for every little thing, treated you like her own daughter and not the woman who brought her into this world. All the cooking and all the cleaning! The way you maintained the house! If only she knew what you went through. You'd moved in with Mauricio but still took the 81 bus to Fenway and then the 57 to Lucia's, because of course you did—that's what a mother does.

And Mauricio, throughout these years, thought you were younger. You never corrected him. You really fooled him with all that hair dye and energy. Maybe all love is about fooling, about keeping your audience's eyes on one hand while you do the real magic, the kind that is all wit, no prayers or spirits or demons, with the other. Maybe he is a little stupid. But he is kind, gentle, isn't he? Do you think men can only be good if they are a little dumb? If they lack whatever it takes to want more out of life? That wanting more makes them forget their morals and the people they are tied to on this earth?

The door opens to your apartment and you are yanked down by the sound, away from your memories, back to this earth, wriggling your limbs in the present. There he is. Your man. He hangs his hat on the hook and nods at you, and something is wrong, Candelaria. The day, the news, the birds, and now, you cannot smell Mauricio. The thing is, he certainly looks like Mauricio. The beer-belly paunch stretching out a floral button down, tucked into beige pants, the wide glasses, the cropped hair and the mustache that you love. You shake it away. It's the food you are cooking. It's just a cold. And you are old now, admit it! The brain does funny things to you sometimes. You don't have to pay attention to every sleight of hand. Or perhaps you really do know better.

He comes closer to you and you ask him if he wants something to eat. He is standing with his hands by his sides. You breathe him in deeply, as if you're just giving another one of your sighs, the exasperated isn't-this-just-life-isn't-this-just-it sighs, but you're doing it just to take in his blue Old Spice bar and sweat.

There is no smell at all.

"¿Tienes hambre?" you ask him, breaking away and acting natural, another level of performance. You have been performing for eighty-six years, putting one foot in front of the other, moving the muscles in your jaw, exercising the flesh puppet assigned to your soul by los angelitos long ago. All to get to this moment. All your life, chugging your body through the air, a woman in motion.

"We're still going to the beach?"

"Claro," he says.

The two of you, this is what you do: collect his social security, watch the horóscopo on Univision, make instant coffee, and drive his beat-up Volvo to Revere Beach. You keep a healthy distance from the water with your scarf tied under your chin while Mauricio hands you slices of Wonder Bread, which you then break up into pieces to feed those disgusting seagulls. You and your birds. But will you make it today?

"I want to leave soon," you say. "Get ready." He shuffles into your room, where you each sleep in separate twin beds, and you hear him rummaging around, gathering his things. You grab your sharpest knife and hack away at a purple onion while it sits in your hand. From far enough away it might look like you're hacking into your own skin. You place your pan on the stove and light the burner with a match. Your hand hovers over the pan as you wait for it to get hot, and when it does, you unscrew your bottle of Crisco oil and gently pour the yellow liquid onto the pan.

You decide to test him.

"That man in 3C has been so rude to me," you say.

"Really, mi amor?" he says.

"Yes, he didn't open the door for me and he made a comment about my outfit."

"I'll talk to him, then."

"Vaya, pues," you say. The oil spits now and you sprinkle the onions in, watch them sizzle and steam. Cooking is second nature to you, the only other language you ever really learned. There is an unmatched literacy to the way you understand fats and heat and the precariousness of spices. How could you ever explain it to anybody, everything you learned because you had to? Everything you were never allowed to learn? How long did you get to be young? When was it, exactly, that you found out that the world was not big and endless, but small and suffocating? Outside, Mr. Chen's son takes out the trash, the clear plastic bag bloated with cans of ginger ale.

Mauricio sits at the edge of the table with its place mats in the shape of snowflakes. You crank open a can of beans, drain them into the sink.

"Candelaria," he says, "why don't we go to the beach now?"

"I'm not done cooking."

"I'm not very hungry."

You still haven't turned around. The beans join the onions in the pan, red fishes swimming through ice, and you wipe your veiny hands on your IHOP apron, courtesy of one of your daughter's old boyfriends.

"Well, I've already started, mijo." You called him mijo almost as a joke. A tender joke. The way some people say *Papi* to their husbands. But you almost meant it, saying *mijo*. You took care of him, after all. "Ten paciencia." Slow drumming on the table, Mauricio's sausage fingers padding the tablecloth. *Mijo.*

What else to do, to distract you from what comes next? Dishes in the sink. Hints of yellow grime on the counter. You spray Windex into an old shirt and wipe down the table. Mauricio's seat slowly scratches back and his body rises. From the window, you see Mr. Chen's son curse as the plastic bag rips open, and the cans of ginger ale break free. Mauricio gets closer to you. He is inches away from you and you cannot smell him. You must do this. You must.

Because it's not just Candy who is in trouble.

You all are.

Grabbing the steak knife, you tell him, "Nobody lives in apartment 3C."

He says, "My mistake, mi vida." He is getting closer to you now, and a tear escapes your eye, sinks into your lips, a bible lost at sea. His hand goes for your waist, and that's when you take your knife, turn around, and sink it into his belly. The small look of shock on his face. He was not expecting this from you. He stumbles and you take the pan full of lunch and whack it across his face. Blood leaks from his gut. He clutches his cheek, fumbles backward. You cry, Canda, you do, because he is leaving, and because it will all happen soon. Unless it's already happening. Quick! You are running out of time.

You hobble through your apartment, searching for your cell phone. You dial 6 and your daughter picks up.

"Mamá?"

The TV has just shut off. You hear sirens outside. Is it quaking beneath your feet?

"Hija," you say, "there's something you need to know." Your breathing is heavy. Stay calm, Candelaria, stay calm!

"What?"

"Meet me at the Old Country Buffet."

"What are you talking about? There is no buffet. It's a Chinese restaurant now. I told you that!" A beep comes from the other line, but you've never figured out how to make that work. Your phone dies, but how? You realize you unplugged it while you were cooking. There's a ringing going through the air, a song you've heard before. You take your purse off its hook on the wall. Lucia is always telling you to throw this purse out because it has faded into an ugly brown color. She says you look like a montañera when you wear it, and so what? That's who you are. That's who you've always been.

You fill it with what you can: a jug of water in the fridge—gracias a Dios, you've never trusted the sink; you empty the cabinets of the stray napkins you've been saving for years, the first aid kit from the bathroom, the ziplock bag of plastic forks, hydrogen peroxide, another ziplock bag to hold your dentures, the salchichas you made last night, cans of beans, tortillas and plátanos wrapped in tinfoil paper.

You snatch the pocketknife from the drawer in Mauricio's bedside table. You make to leave and then remember you forgot your insulin. Where is it? You toss things around, precious things, vases, toasters, coffee grinders, all fall to the floor. You find the insulin inside a packet of corn flour. Where has your mind been, Canda? You make to leave again, then remember the birds. The birds! How could you forget them? You open a cabinet and fill a chipped green ceramic bowl with water from the still-running sink. You carry it to the ledge, where you open the window with effort and leave the bowl sitting on the sill.

"¡Ya regreso!" you tell the sparrows, a lie, and their chubby bodies shake at you. Their chirping continues, loud and knowing. They know, as well as you, what is about to happen. You open your tinfoil and leave a tortilla on the ledge for them to share. Que pecado. The birds are ravenous, tearing the tortilla apart with their beaks. How will they eat without you? You grab the candle of la Virgen from your shrine and toss it into your bag. You will need her later. You take the last of the flowers and throw them at Mauricio's feet. A few good years together. Perhaps that is all we get. A few moments stitched together that you can throw over yourself to keep you warm. That is all we want, in the end: the nearness of somebody else to prove that you yourself are there.

There is no time.

You have to move.

Lastly, you grab your quad cane and walk with it, you are a mortal with three legs now, moving out the door.

You open the door to the stairwell with your hands, speckled brown with age. You have one orthopedic-sneakered foot on the stairwell and one hand on the banister, making your way down into the rest of your story, the remainder of your one precious life, when the walls shake, the stairs beneath your feet vibrate, the windows into the street crack, the screaming starts, and the groans of the earth begin.

I

ELASTIC

STRAIN

Earlier That Year

CANDY

Candy was on a table with her legs spread, an apple in her mouth, surrounded by men who all looked like her boyfriend, Garfield. They were circling around her holding knives, the Garfields, moving slowly like the hands of a clock. Surrounding her, there were plates and plates of food: plump grapes, various pearly meats and cheeses. Champagne. They were all going to eat her and the food and she could do nothing about it. She was frozen. The main Garfield, as was her impression, the leader of the pack, crawled over the table and spread her legs farther, a knife in his hand, his face without emotion.

Candy woke up, taking in the comforting realities of her room: the flecks of light peeking from her blackout curtains kissing the poster of *Rosemary's Baby* on her wall, the stand-up closet with its series of sportswear tops and bottoms, a photo of her and her sister Bianca at the New England Aquarium on her bedside table, and the outline of her on-again, off-again boyfriend Garfield asleep beside her. Of course it was just a dream, one of the same vivid nightmares that she had had periodically since her heroin-induced coma years ago. *Not to be dramatic*, Candy would tell her postrehab therapist, whom she had ghosted after the therapist concluded that the dream was some kind of PTSD reaction to childhood trauma. She didn't need to spend the $80 a week to learn that. Her mother had already gone into debt sending her to an expensive three-month stint of sitting in groups with other losers painting pictures of her feelings.

The people circling around her about to eat her varied. Sometimes they were the members of BTS. NSYNC. People running for office. Other times she was circling around herself. And while she would always wake up drenched in sweat, these days the dreams were more annoying than frightful. A nuisance to live through, like blood weeping from an ankle after shaving it. Waking up now, she was relieved that her life had remained exactly the same, and kicked off her satin bedsheets to open up her curtains. Light assaulted the room and Garfield groaned.

"Okay," she said, shaking him awake, and Garfield opened his eyes, frightened. "You need to get out of my house." She tried to ignore the stupid Snoopy tattoo underneath his dark nipples, her name emblazoned below. He had come to her the night before with a ceramic vase holding roses, crying about how he wanted to start a family. "How are we going to start a family, Garfield," she had said, placing the vase unceremoniously on top of her fridge, "if you don't ever have sex with me?"

Garfield pulled on a pair of jeans and a shirt with holes in it. "Will you think about what I said?" He tucked his shirt into his pants, as if that helped the state of the shirt.

"Yeah, sure," Candy said, taking off her underwear and bra without a sprinkle of self-awareness or sexuality, like Garfield was her sibling. "I will definitely *think* about it." She wrapped a large, black, fluffy towel around her body that she had purchased compulsively online. It was supposed to dry your skin in a less harmful way or something.

Garfield walked up to her and embraced her, the tattoos on his arms reminding Candy of pesky water bugs. "I love you," he said, which Candy responded to with a large sigh, as if to a canvasser for Amnesty International.

She broke away from him and fastened a shower cap over her head. "Bye, Garfungus."

There are ten crucial minutes after a heroin overdose that are essential for saving your life. When Julian, the boy Candy had convinced to get her drugs, found her passed out on Rebecca Polkinghorn's parents' bedroom floor, vomit caked into the plush gray carpet, one minute had already passed. When he called her sister Bianca, three minutes had passed. When her sister instructed him to rub her chest with his knuckles as she called EMTs, another minute had passed. When they arrived and administered

Narcan, five minutes had passed. And by then, enough of her brain had shut down that she was in a coma.

In the ten minutes it took Candy every day to get ready, taking an ice-cold shower (two minutes), washing her face (two minutes), violently rubbing herself in various lotions (one minute), pulling on a baggy black T-shirt and bike shorts (one minute), brushing her teeth (two minutes), tossing frozen bananas, almond milk, spinach, and collagen into a NutriBlend that produced a NutriSlop (another two minutes), she liked thinking about how she should be dead.

A decade ago, she wore the tightest clothes you could imagine, tiny, loud dresses that stuck to her like leeches, gigantic hoops swaying in her ears and nails always done. Now, she wanted to draw less attention. She would do her makeup at work still, wiping the sweat off after her bike ride and carefully distributing foundation and highlighter, applying expensive liner to her giant eyelids. Some things from the past remain. But she was a different Candy now. She was in control.

Chugging the NutriSlop as she went out the door, she saw a gray cat where her bike should've been, rubbing her body against the rusty gate, purring. The lock wasn't even there. It was taken clean off the gate, erased from the landscape.

"Fucking SHIT!" Candy screamed, causing a flutter of birds. The cat got on her back, exposing her white tummy and nipples that stuck out like little raw thumbs. She was, or had been, a mother. Candy scratched her small neck.

"Did you take my bike? Bitch?" The cat meowed, which felt insulting.

"I hate this," she said. The cat ground against her ankle, as if she was trying to burrow into Candy's leg. Candy lightly moved the cat away with her foot. She began to walk to the bus down Forbes Street, shoving her AirPods into her ears and blasting Mozart. She read somewhere that his music made you smarter, but maybe that was just for babies in the womb. It was also only the first four songs on the "This Is Mozart" Spotify playlist, on a loop.

Usually Candy would ride her bike all the way into Brookline, her speaker banging against her hip like a gun. Biking was a strong, rigid routine that kept Candy's head on straight. She had gotten into the habit of shaming her friends for taking cars and sometimes even public transit. She was intense about it, almost evangelical. *We're destroying the earth!* She would say to them, *There is going to be nothing left! And THAT IS WHY I BIKE!*

There was also the fact that she wasn't allowed to drive, had lost her license a few years back after zooming down the Mass Pike with a flask of Evan Williams in her hand screaming along to Rihanna. Her mother bailed her out of jail, disowning her as she always said, only with words and never for long.

Candy didn't have a lot of friends.

This interruption to her daily routine dumped tiny bugs into her psyche, and she felt the invisible creatures crawling and gnawing at her as she waited for the 39 on South Huntington. She turned up Symphony No. 40 in G Minor.

Her phone buzzed in her backpack. It was her mother, Lucia. "Hellooo?" Candy swiped open her phone to her mom's face at an unflattering, low angle. The bus was approaching, slowed by a row of cyclists ahead. She should have been one of them.

"Hola, amor. What are you doing?"

"I'm taking the bus to work. Somebody stole my fucking bike!"

"No usas ese lenguaje," her mother said. "What are you going to do?"

"Guess I have to buy a new bike." Candy let steam out of her nose.

"I would help you, but I am already helping you with rent."

Candy looked around, hoping nobody heard that through the phone. The bus doors groaned open and Candy squeezed herself inside, stuffing two dollars into the slot, but they kept spitting themselves out. The bus driver motioned for her to move to the back.

"Are you coming to dinner later?" Lucia set her phone against a vase on the dining room table and continued sewing the hem of a pair of beige pants.

"Duh." Candy clutched the germy pole as the bus lurched forward. A woman with long blond hair smiled at her like she knew her. She stood and motioned, with her hands, for Candy to sit down. Candy happily obliged, putting a leg up and hunching over her phone.

"Okay, pick up some scratching cards for Mauricio and Abuelita."

"Yeah, I will."

"You hear from your sister?"

"Uh . . . I think the service is really bad in Guatemala right now." Candy wiped a bead of sweat above her lip. That was the agreement she and Bianca, who had actually been back in New York for the last month, had come up with, if their mother ever asked: say the service was bad.

"She won't answer me. I'm getting worried. I had a dream."

"Again with your fucking dreams, Mami. I have dreams all the time and it turns out I just watch too many movies!" Candy noticed how some-times, when she was talking to her mother, she spoke in the idioms and phrases of a person who takes themself very seriously. It was a habit of children of immigrants to sometimes talk in an almost-accent so that their parents would understand them. It was also a habit to lie.

"Well, just call her, okay?" Lucia held the pants up to the screen, obscur-ing her face. Candy told her mother she loved her and hung up. Her mind was still on Garfield, and what she would do with *him*. They had had sex approximately four times in their two years of dating. The way he held on to her chest the night before as he sobbed made her really feel like a mother, and she was reminded of something her abuela said after her sister Paola disappeared: *Las hijas siempre se quedan con la mamá. Los hombres siempre encuentran otra.*

Her grandmother was always convinced that Paola was not dead, that she had instead run off with her boyfriend, but to Candy, that just seemed like a way of not dealing with the truth, which was that people just die. Paola never got the chance to be a mother, Candy was certain, because Paola was dead. Just like her dad. And now Candy had somehow become a skateboar-der's mother. Who knows. Her grandmother was always saying some shit.

The woman with blond hair waved at her as she got off the bus to catch the 66. Did she know her? She dialed Bianca, who picked up after three rings.

"Jesus, Bianca. Your whole face . . . it's getting worse." Bianca looked like a wet dog, as if she had either just left the shower or hadn't taken one in a week. Her curly hair was stuck to her forehead, yellow crust lining her red eyes.

"Thanks." Candy's face was lit up by the blue sky above Harvard Ave, whereas Bianca's was shrouded by the darkness inside her Brooklyn apartment. Candy stopped at the crosswalk as a truck full of men drove by. They all eyed her, one of them sticking his fingers in his mouth and blowing a whistle. One of them waved. Candy held up her middle finger.

"Anyway, my mom keeps asking about you. Are you going to tell her you're not in Guatemala?" Bianca and Candy often said *my mom* instead of *our mom*, the Spanish-language habit of saying *mi madre* sticking to them like faithful duct tape, often confusing their white friends, who had already thought they weren't related because they looked nothing alike.

"Not yet." Bianca sat up. She had been lying down on the floor.

"Did you at least call Mauricio today? You know it's his birthday, right?"

"Yeah." Bianca's eyes looked blank. "I knew that."

"You forgot."

"I've just had a lot on my mind."

"You said that you would come up, dude. Are you kidding me? You said you would tell her everything that happened then come up to Boston for Mauricio's birthday. Now it's just gonna be me, my mom and Mauricio, and the fucking ghosts of Dad and Paola. My life is so depressing, oh my *God*."

"I know, I let you down."

"Don't *I know* me. Fucking *call* my grandparents."

"I'm sorry, Candy."

"Pain in my ass."

"Miss you."

"I miss you, too. Pendeja." Candy could be as annoyed as she wanted to be with Bianca, but the thing about Bianca was that she had once saved her life. Basically. Candy kind of always thought she'd saved herself, though it was her sister who called the EMTs, but then how was it that she was able to wake up from a coma and be more or less okay? When she woke up from the coma, her sister's face was the first thing she saw, bespectacled and turtle-like—looking like an emotionless mess, if she was being honest. Actually, the first thing Candy said when she woke up was "You freak me out." Then, her mother weeping and kissing her hands, so happy she was still alive. And, eh, Candy didn't like to think about it too much. It was embarrassing.

"I woke up feeling so odd," Bianca moaned. She sounded like she was hungover. The 66 arrived and Candy got out her crumpled two dollars as a man wearing a red polo shirt and glasses cut her in line. He looked like some kind of businessman on vacation. No bags and no jacket. Just himself.

"Excuse me," Candy said, as politely as her personality allowed. The man turned and looked at her. His mouth parted slightly, in a small O shape.

"Jesus, move out of my way!" Candy climbed onto the bus, the doors shutting in the man's face. The dollars kept spitting themselves out. The bus driver once again motioned for her to go to the back.

"This city is full of trust fund kids and tourists, I swear to God. Sorry, what were you saying?"

"I said I woke up feeling so odd."

"Bitch, you're always talking like you're on the History Channel."

"But I do feel odd."

"Mom is feeling *odd*, too. It's probably something in the stars. Ask your wizard roommate about it. They probably, like, did a weird moon ritual last night." Candy saw her sister slowly pull open her curtains.

"They're not a wizard," Bianca said, shielding her eyes, "they're a professional perfumer."

"Whatever, whenever I visit, they're wearing, like, various robes."

"I have to go, Candy."

"Wait." Candy gathered herself, trying to be nice. "Do you think something bad is going to happen?"

"I don't know. Forget it. Just a weird feeling."

"That's so unlike you to have a *feeling*." When Bianca was fixating about her decision to move to New York, Candy dramatically told her, "You know what I'm always hoping? That one day I'll walk up to your door, be like knock, knock, hey bitch, and you'll actually just be gone. No hasta luego, no adios. Nothing. You'd have just left." It was a bastardized version of Ben Affleck's line from *Good Will Hunting*, which was obvious to Candy, but then she had to explain the premise of the film to Bianca, who thought it was a wildlife documentary.

"Bye. Stop FaceTiming when you're walking. You're gonna get hit by a car."

"If I do, I'll call you as it's happening so I can leave you with that trauma for the rest of your life, bitch."

Candy jumped off the bus and ran to the Coolidge Corner Theatre, where she had recently been promoted to assistant manager, something she was pretty proud of, despite the pang in her sister's voice that signaled that she wanted more for her. But shouldn't Bianca just be happy that she wasn't in a gutter or missing?

She sat at the ticket counter and began ringing people in for movies. It was a weekday, so the only people who really came were retirement communities, old people who fell asleep during their special showings of *Casablanca*. Then there were the teenagers who skipped school and the retail workers who didn't have real weekends, spending their wages on a basket of nachos and disassociating in front of the screen. Candy liked this job because she could see movies whenever she wanted. She didn't have the itch that her sister did, of thinking of time spent in the dark as wasted time. No, Candy loved being immersed in the darkness, becoming part of the seat as the screen opened up in front of her and freed her from the constraints of her physical form.

After Candy's break, during which she wolfed down a free burrito from Anna's Taqueria after silently handing over a free ticket for that night's viewing of *Paprika* to the girl behind the counter, a man approached the ticket stand. It was the man she had almost run into while waiting for the bus. He looked completely lost, but eyeing him, she felt like he knew exactly where he was supposed to be.

Men were always approaching Candy. The levels of approaching often led to injury: tripping over sticks, bumping into poles, getting slapped by their girlfriends. With the money she saved on free beers and coffees she could have traveled to Paris at least a few times. Candy had never been to Paris. Maybe one day, when she had figured everything out.

Silver hairs forked past this man's ears. A full head of hair, though. A thick mustache and round golden glasses. Something about this man was familiar, in the way same way as when you walk up the stairs and forget why you were there, then see a roll of toilet paper in your hand and remember.

"*Kung Fu Panda 4.*" The man put his arms on the banister, thick hairs sprouting across them. The way he said *Kung Fu* and *Panda* signaled to Candy *Stalker!* and *Give me your body NOW*.

"That's a children's movie," Candy said into the speaker, and put away her phone, on which she had been reading an interview with Korean actors. "It's ten dollars for children, and one hundred dollars for perverts." She folded her hands, staring him dead in the eyes. The man raised his eyebrows. He was chuckling at her, like they shared inside jokes.

"One hundred dollars."

"Yeah, we also do group discounts, but you're by yourself, so."

"I'm just . . . having a day for me."

"So you're spending it sniffing around kids?" The man put his hand to his chest and stared at her again, one corner of his mouth lifting up in a smile.

"Creepy." Candy took out her phone again. Maybe he would go away if she ignored him long enough. Employees were supposed to reach out

23

to their manager any time they thought they saw someone who would potentially jerk off in the seats, but she was the manager, so her decision was to give him the cold shoulder. Candy was trying to be tame. She didn't want to lose her job by punching someone in the face, though that was her instinct at the moment.

"What's your favorite movie?" The man had his nose pressed against the glass.

"Have you seen *Little Children*? Where the pedophile cuts off his own dick? Pretty spectacular." *Relax, Candy*, she told herself. She didn't really think he was a pervert, but nothing scares a man more than accusing him of being an abuser. How did she know him? She had met so many weirdos in her expensive, three-month stint in rehab, and sometimes they would find her on social media, even a decade later, leaving her long rambling voice messages about conspiracy theories or how she was the love of their lives. She always blocked them. Was he from NA? AA? Was he sent by one of the sponsors she ghosted? After alcohol and before her recent exercise kick, Candy had been on a lot of Tinder dates. Was he Ben Tinder or Larry Tinder or Mateo Hinge or Jennifer Lex or Patrick from O'Malley's Bar? Candy looked him up and down. Hapless finance bros, construction workers who hated finance bros, MIT graduates who wanted to prove that they could get laid or find a good wife to bring home to their fathers. It was like this for a few months until her sister told her she couldn't keep replacing one thing with the other.

Candy had had enough late-night trysts, enough scary close encounters and true up-close encounters—things she shut out of her mind the way you'd flick off a TV screen—that she was fine with someone who didn't want to have sex. Her sex life with Garfield wasn't exactly what she wanted, but Candy was afraid of the things she wanted and their consequences so she didn't let herself think about them.

Why was she thinking about all the sex she wasn't having with Garfield while looking at this man?

He looked like he was of Latin descent, which meant he probably recognized something in her, the baby hairs on her forehead, the slope of her nose, the fullness of her mouth, that he would eventually bring up so that they would have something to talk about. She looked exactly like her grandmother did when she was Candy's age, with a curtain of curly black hair parted in the middle that reached down to her ass and a naturally tight and muscular body that put gymnasts to shame; penetrative orb-like eyes that made people question her ancestry. Candy's looks held the particular genetic quandary that came with her particular Mestizx background: a bunch of violent shit in the past that she felt had nothing to do with her and made people ask her where she was really from, always in the context of trying to sleep with her, as if Candy's ethnicity was a travel manual to her pussy.

"Should I watch a different movie?"

"I don't know! I don't care!" Candy threw her phone down.

"Are you upset with me?"

"I don't *know* you. Go away."

"Tell me what to watch."

"If you pay now, you can catch *Godzilla Vs. Kong 2.*"

"Okay," he said, handing her a one-hundred dollar bill. Candy stared at the bill in disbelief and shoved it into her sports bra. He made his way closer to the ticket counter, so that a pane of glass no longer separated them, but a burgundy rope.

"Dinner." He folded his hands in front of him. Candy looked around at her employees covering their mouths from laughing. This wasn't the first time this had happened.

"No, thank you, sir," Candy said, a grimace on her face reserved for holding the bar of an X-ray machine in between your teeth at the dentist's office, trying to be the manager she was supposed to be. "Enjoy your movie." He nodded at her and turned away. She racked her brain—how did she know him? An hour and a half passed and Candy switched over to the concession stand, drumming her fingers on the counter. He walked down the stairs, slowly, sure of himself, and suddenly, the feral FaceTimes from Bianca returned to her, the screenshots, the photos, the call that she was coming back early from Guatemala because her professor Fernando Moreno had kicked her off her own site after spending two years sleeping with her.

"Dinner?"

"Get out of my establishment, you piece of shit!" Fernando Moreno smiled at her, nodding, like he had known her for years and years, like he would know her anywhere, like he knew it was exactly like her to be like this.

"What the hell is wrong with you?" She looked around and whispered, "My sister tried to kill herself." A lie, but she was trying to drive home the point.

"She did? Huh . . ." Fernando processed the information as if she had just told him that Amelia Earhart had died, but he had only just discovered who Amelia Earhart was. How dare he treat her sister like a second thought? As anyone but the Amelia Earhart of their lives?

"Sir, I am the manager here," she said in a raised voice, making customers and fellow employees turn their heads, "and I am kindly asking you to leave. If you do not leave, I will call the police." Fernando Moreno rested his thumbs on the outsides of the pockets, little confident nubs. He took a small card out of his pocket and stared at it. It was his card, but it was like he wasn't sure if it was his card.

"I'm giving you 'til the count of three," she said firmly. Fernando looked up at her and smiled again. He slid it across the counter wordlessly. Candy stared at it like it was a smear of pigeon shit. He walked out of the theater, his hands at his sides like a toy soldier.

"Men are not okay!" she said, moving her hands open as if she were revealing a magic trick, a particular hand of cards, a bunny still alive under a hat, and there was a small spattering of laughter throughout the theater lobby, a kind of relief that she had expelled a bad man from the vicinity, that ultimately, the strong woman in power had saved them.

BIANCA

Before things got really desperate and they dug up their dead to feast on their corpses, cut up their wives into salted little morsels after ripping their children out of their wombs, and only slightly after going through their leather shoes, the people at Jamestown turned to the dogs.

Instead of trying to understand trading, their captain had used strong-arm tactics with the Powhatan, and the Powhatan, in turn, began to attack any colonist who ventured near the woods trying to scavenge. When a drought rendered the colonists' soil infertile and their bellies empty, the horrors began. John Smith, arriving after hearing how bad it had become, wrote that he found a colony infected by lethargy. They were just lazy. They were just not trying hard enough. Really, they were suffering the effects of extreme malnutrition. They were just tired.

But the dogs. The colonizers were proud of these dogs. They had brought them from England on their ships, burly hunting dogs, the best of the best, and they killed them with hunting knives they didn't really know how to use, the dogs whimpering with confusion as their owners ended their lives. They prepared the dogs haphazardly, leaving brutish butchering marks on their bones which they later tossed into graves. Much later, after roads were laid, and the Jamestown Colony was turned into a historical site, and stores just for salads were built, these bones were unearthed. The archaeologists extracted mitochondrial DNA from the dog jawbones and saw the rough butchering marks around their bones made from the clumsy hacking. They extracted mitochondrial DNA that is only inherited from the mother, and discovered that these were not European dogs at all. In fact, they were most closely related to the ancient dogs of Ohio and Illinois, the Indigenous dogs who had been there for centuries and centuries.

Bianca worked on this study as a field technician as a part of her master's thesis at the University of Iowa, digging up the bones with a trowel shovel and cleaning them with a toothpick. The study was not hers, but

Bianca's work helped the team conclude that despite the feud between the colonists and the Indigenous tribes, as evidenced in the bones of their animals, those animals were actually able to cross freely from one settlement to the next. And despite this condition, they were still destined for the bellies of depraved invaders who were only a few more dogs, cats, and mice away from killing and consuming one another. The field was so excited about what this said about settlers, colonization. History. People glanced at it on Apple News, then got bored when they saw that it wasn't actually about people eating each other. Still, the sensation of this study helped Bianca get into NYU's archaeology PhD program, where she would study under Fernando Moreno and convince him to help her with her own study: unearthing the bones of the Tierra Nueva activists in the Candelaria Caves of Guatemala. Sleeping with him also helped.

Bianca was always a little self-conscious about the way the study turned out. Did it read too sentimentally? Were they arguing that the Indigenous tribes and the colonists were fused together through their dogs, a kind of rainbow ribbon holding them together? To her, it just seemed obvious that people think they are in control of things and often they are not. Despite all the walls they build, despite the places they swear they will never go, they end up there anyway. Obviously, Bianca lacked the self-awareness to see this in herself. She was not prone to myths, addiction, cults, or multilevel marketing schemes. Her mother had been in a few of the latter, pedaling vitamins and weight-loss drinks to her customers in the alteration shop below their house. Bianca usually found an excuse to leave a table of drunken friends when the conversation turned to the supernatural. Because she was an archaeologist, they would often turn to her and ask her if she saw anything on her sites, if any of her findings proved that something like this was possible. *Aren't there, like, fossils about this?* Bianca tried her best to be kind, but usually what came out of her mouth was blunt and slightly robotic. *The closest thing to a sea monster is a dinosaur. The only proof of God comes from the humans carving things into stone.*

Bianca continued organizing her roommate Blue's bins, color-coding trinkets for their jewelry business. Blue was a hairdresser and an all-around creative entrepreneur who occasionally did work in perfume therapy. During lockdown they started a jewelry business on Etsy to pay for their studio space in Williamsburg. Blue appreciated Bianca's bluntness, which came off as bitchiness, while Blue's high femininity, so different from Bianca's practical, muted wardrobe and appearance, reminded Bianca of her family.

Bianca hadn't left her two-bedroom railroad apartment in Bed-Stuy since she had returned, spending the last of her stipend on Uber Eats, leaving take-out trays of Indian food and pizza boxes scattered throughout the apartment. She slept on the floor when she arrived, waking up to a ceramic banana with a smiley face attached to a tiny silver hook from Blue's jewelry collection lodged in her cheek. Blue screamed when they found her, facedown on the carpet. She hadn't really let them know that she was arriving or that she had just been kicked off her site by her adviser and lover, Fernando Moreno.

Bianca didn't put too much effort into her appearance. She went for neutral tones and simple forms of fashion that weren't particularly trendy and could zoom in and out of any historical era from the seventies and beyond. She looked kind of like *whatever* in any year, with her hair pulled back into a ponytail and square glasses sitting on her face, straight-legged L.L.Bean jeans making her ass flatter than it actually was. She was focused on looking refined and put together, didn't bother with what she felt was saccharine, silly. Deep down, she wanted to show that she wasn't one of *those* Latinas, the ones who were too easily sexualized or deemed loud or crazy. She wanted not to be humble, but to be respected. She hadn't fought her way into a PhD program for nothing. But all of that refinement and self-respect had faded. She hadn't changed her underwear in a week. She'd been wearing the same sweatpants her mother gave her that said HOPE on them. She smelled like her natural self, untainted by soaps or detergents.

So, bad. Her curls were knotting and bunching up at the ends and moving to the center, giving her hair a mangled, atom-looking appearance. Her eyes were bloated from crying and her face blotchy and dried up from the calcium of tears.

Blue hadn't asked her to help with their jewelry business, but Bianca's state of hysteria led them to say, "Okay, sure, you can color-code." But Bianca did more than that. She applied all her research skills, all her right-brained, puzzle-putting-together skills that had gone into scaffolding and mapping out dig sites, into DIY jewelry construction. The earring business was something Blue had started during the pandemic, and it was mostly to give money to local mutual aid funds and fridges; something to keep themself busy that had leaked over into the world when it opened again. Bianca printed out every order and filed them according to zip code. To be an archaeologist, Bianca had found, was to put your hand in the pocket of clothing you hadn't worn in a while and find a dollar, then trying to find the story of the dollar, but also remembering the simple joy of the moment of discovery. Bianca wasn't discovering anything now.

Through the Jamestown study, Bianca found her angle for Tierra Nueva. What would the bones of her uncle tell her about Guatemala? About diet, the effect of stress from the war on the body? Was he holding anything when he died? Would her mother's sadness go away? She believed that if she found him, and other members of Tierra Nueva, she could reach self-realization, though she didn't think of it as that. She needed to know and had convinced an entire team of field technicians and the academy that they needed to know, as well. She needed to see straight into the past.

When once she was arranging the old dog bones buried by cannibalistic Virginia colonizers, now she was arranging jewelry trinkets by item: fruits, metal hands, small animals, tiny cars. There was a station for assembling and a station for mailing and a checklist to make sure everything had been done on time. After a few weeks, Bianca started getting territorial over the space, leaping up from the rug whenever an order would come in so that she could print out the postage label and begin to assemble. Blue started to dread when orders would come in, because then they had to deal with Bianca, who would bark at them if they forgot to check something off the list or didn't like the way Blue was arranging earrings because she started having a method.

Blue knocked on the door. "One sec!" Bianca said, turning on her phone, with which she started to record their conversation, a habit she had not kicked since she was a child, after her father died. He had given her a tape recorder for her birthday, and she had gone around recording sounds from the neighborhood: trucks delivering soda to the deli, dogs barking, neighborhood gossip. She also transcribed everything into notebooks, in case the recordings were ever lost, which they were. After he died, she read and reread every conversation she had with him in her composition notebooks, feeling him in the risen ink of their words to each other.

After his passing, she started recording everything. Even her sister's overdose and the drive to the hospital with that idiot Julian who was in love with her sister and sold her drugs was somewhere on the cloud and transcribed into a Google Doc. She had also once recorded her mother telling her life's story, detailing key information about the Tierra Nueva and her uncle. But her mother deleted the files before Bianca had a chance to transcribe them. And then she could never get her mother in an open enough, vulnerable place again. She had started becoming tight-lipped around her, afraid Bianca would record what she said. *Those are family things*, she told her. *This should be private.* Bianca opened the door.

313 PULASKI STREET, MARCH 26TH, 2023

BLUE: Hey.

BIANCA: You've had a few orders come in, but we're out of stamps.
   Can you go get some?

BLUE: About that . . .

BIANCA: What?

BLUE: I just want to check in really quick about the state of the
   house? Totally no pressure if you have no space right now.

Lately, everything was really hard to make sense of. Her mind was filled with mist, and if she took a wrong move, she could fall off a cliff. "Uh-huh?" Bianca said, holding an earring that spelled out ACAB and pressing the hook to her thumb. Blue took a deep breath. "Your takeout has kind of been living on the counter for a week now? And I just wanted to know if you have the capacity to get rid of it right now?" Takeout? A week? How long had it been? She shouldn't be here.

ZOOM PHD INTERVIEW, DECEMBER 10TH, 2020

FERNANDO: Saw your Jamestown work. Nicely done.

BIANCA: Thank you.

FERNANDO: Eres de Guatemala?

BIANCA: My mother is. My dad was Colombian.

FERNANDO: I'm also half Guatemalan.

BIANCA: I was wondering.

FERNANDO: Tell me about what you have in mind. Why do you
    want to study here?

BIANCA: I really admire the work you did in Mexico. I think you're
    not only an excellent archaeologist but also your politics are
    heavily aligned with mine, in that they are divorced from the
    origins of colonialist anthropology. You also treat your staff well.

FERNANDO: Thank you. Shame we can't meet in person. And what
    about your project? What are your goals?

BIANCA: It springs from something a little personal. My uncle was
    killed in an avalanche after the 1976 earthquake. He was involved
    in this radical group of artists called Tierra Nueva and for some
    reason, they all died in the same place, in the Candelaria Caves.
    Completely disappeared. I know that whatever documents or
    paintings, anything that they had there, are imperative to
    Guatemalan history, but also all our history. It can show us how
    artists react in times of turmoil and how our geographical
    landscapes always affect our political landscape. Obviously, the

earthquake only highlighted everything that was already wrong with Guatemala . . .

The mist in Bianca's mind was clearing into a field of embarrassment, a feeling she could hold on to because it was bright and achy. She felt bad because Blue was a professional perfumer and the smells from her take-out were cluttering their process. She had literally just talked on the phone with her sister about that. "I'll get to it," Bianca said. "I'm sorry, Blue." Blue tapped the door frame with their forefinger. There was something else.

FIDDLESTICKS BAR, SEPTEMBER 7ᵀᴴ, 2021

FERNANDO: Does your mom know you're looking into this stuff?

BIANCA: Not really.

FERNANDO: Do you go home a lot?

BIANCA: Not really.

FERNANDO: You just work all the time?

BIANCA: Yeah.

FERNANDO: She must be really proud of you.

BIANCA: I don't think about it.

FERNANDO: And you said your grandmother's name is Candelaria? And your uncle was crushed to death in the Candelaria Caves?

BIANCA: Yes.

FERNANDO: That's horribly ironic.

BIANCA: Just a coincidence.

FERNANDO: Have you ever been?

BIANCA: No.

FERNANDO: You make me feel bad.

BIANCA: Why?

FERNANDO: Because you showed up here with all these charts and maps, all this historical information, and all I have is a few notes about volcanoes.

BIANCA: I just really care about this.

FERNANDO: I love it. I wish I worked as hard as you.

BIANCA: Why don't you?

FERNANDO: Life's too short.

BIANCA: That's why I want to work hard. I don't want to be your age and full of regrets.

FERNANDO: Wow, okay! I mean, if I had your spirit all my loans would be paid off by now.

BIANCA: Why do you have loans?

FERNANDO: Because college is expensive.

BIANCA: I know. Why didn't you try to get a scholarship?

FERNANDO: I did.

BIANCA: Oh. Why are you laughing?

Blue was having trouble articulating themself. This always frustrated Bianca. Why not just come out with it? Everybody in the world was so worried about hurting one another's feelings, but what if we all stopped worrying and just said what was really bothering us, or just came out and said how we feel? Love was a pox for her family that she had quarantined herself from for years. Her mother was never the same after her father died, sleeping only a few hours a night for the decade following, walking around their house like a ghost. Her older sister Paola, presumed dead, had left in the middle of the night with her boyfriend, but only Bianca and her grandmother knew that. (She had never told Candy and didn't see a reason why she should have, and she always figured her mother knew but couldn't deal with the reason why a daughter would leave her own mother if it weren't for the next realm.) And that idiot Julian acquired Candy heroin because he couldn't say no to her, because he felt he was so in love. Bianca was determined never to lose herself in a person. She wanted to find herself in history. What if she had never given in to Fernando? Was she feeding off his attention the whole time, hungry for something she hadn't ever thought to be hungry for before?

34

NYU ARCHAEOLOGY OFFICES, OCTOBER 6TH, 2021

BIANCA: What's wrong?

FERNANDO: To be completely honest with you, I'm going through a
lot right now.

BIANCA: I'm sorry.

FERNANDO: Can I talk about it with you?

BIANCA: Okay.

FERNANDO: My wife's friends are all in journalism and media, so I
just feel like they're always, I don't know. They're always trying to
see why I'm *worthy of her*, or whatever. So stupid. They're also a
little, you know. White, I guess.

BIANCA: It's hard in those spaces.

FERNANDO: When you were growing up, did you feel different?

BIANCA: What do you mean?

FERNANDO: My wife never knows how to order when we go out
to dinner.

BIANCA: Does your wife not speak Spanish?

FERNANDO: I mean, she's tried to. But not really, no.

BIANCA: Frustrating.

FERNANDO: See, you just get me.

BIANCA: I do?

FERNANDO: Sorry, I'm talking your ear off. You can go if you want.
It's late.

BIANCA: No, I can stay.

FERNANDO: I've never seen anyone work this hard. You make me
want to work harder.

BIANCA: You do work really hard.

FERNANDO: I really want to make your project work. I think we can.

"So, rent is due soon," Blue said finally. Money. When she was in high
school, after all the drama in her family had passed, she asked her mom
to send her to an archaeology camp. It was as expensive as a semester at

college, but Bianca had gone through so much—that's what she wanted her mother to see, as she pleaded with her at the end of "a long day" of helping her mother sort orders and bag altered suits. So her mother borrowed money from one of her clients, Rhonda, the same one who helped send Candy to rehab, the one they were all in endless debt to though she never brought it up again. The camp in Western Massachusetts had given her a head start into archaeology; it elevated her resume and gave her the skill sets her colleagues were still learning in college. Without money from the academy and from an anonymous donor, they never would've made it to Guatemala. They wouldn't have had as big a crew as they did. They would've still been here in New York, pleading for it.

CHICAGO AIRBNB OUTSIDE ARCHAEOLOGY
CONFERENCE, DECEMBER 3RD, 2021

FERNANDO: That was amazing.

BIANCA: I'm worried I was too personal about the whole thing.
I don't know if I needed to mention how my aunt lost her leg.
Do you think I should've gone more into logistics?

FERNANDO: No, that's what they want! The personal. That's how
you get them.

BIANCA: Why are you looking at me funny?

FERNANDO: You have really narrow cheeks.

BIANCA: What?

FERNANDO: Sorry.

BIANCA: I'm not stupid. You have a wife.

FERNANDO: Yes.

BIANCA: You keep staring at me like you want something from me.

FERNANDO: Do you know what I want?

BIANCA: Yes.

Bianca shook her head, "Right. I think I have some of this loan left." Blue said the rest of what they needed to say in one sentence. They clearly had been practicing it for a while, afraid of Bianca's reaction. "Clove-is-moving-to-LA-and-now-I-don't-have-a-receptionist-and-I-can't-keep-covering-rent-so I-think-you-should-take-Clove's-position-at-the-salon."

Bianca ran her hand through her hair, which got stuck in a knot.

"I'm overqualified for something like that. I have a PhD." She was just telling the truth. She was the sister who made it, after all. Not the sister who disappeared or the sister who overdosed. Though that was a cruel thought. She shouldn't think that about her own sisters.

"Uh, I never went to college?" Blue said. "And now I run my own business and make more money than you so I don't know—" They started saying something else but then Bianca started hyperventilating. Why couldn't she look at herself? How did she get here?

NYU ARCHAEOLOGY OFFICES, APRIL 8TH, 2022

FERNANDO: You really see me. More than anyone else has.

BIANCA: I don't believe that.

FERNANDO: You don't feel the same?

BIANCA: I think we have good conversations. And we have similar goals.

FERNANDO: Come on.

BIANCA: No.

FERNANDO: I know you're feeling something.

BIANCA: Maybe. Hold on, I just got an email.

FERNANDO: Yeah? What does it say?

BIANCA: Oh my God. Do you think this is a virus?

FERNANDO: Holy shit.

BIANCA: That's so much money. Why is it an anonymous donor?

FERNANDO: People with money don't like to put their names on this kind of thing. It's embarrassing for them. They don't want to feel the stigma of being rich, but they also want to prove that they can do something good with it.

BIANCA: Are you speaking from personal experience?

FERNANDO: Hey, I don't speak to my parents.

BIANCA: Right. Which one of them went to Harvard again?

FERNANDO: Let's focus on this. You have to take it. You did this.
You proved that this project was worthwhile.

BIANCA: I can't believe this is happening.

FERNANDO: Believe it. This was all you.

Bianca threw the earring across the room and Blue flinched. "How about this," Blue said. "I'm gonna do you a favor and throw out your takeout. And you're going to take a shower, for as long as you want, and you just think about it." Bianca took a whiff of her armpits. There was a sharp, onion-like smell.

HOTEL CANDELARIA ANTIGUA, OUTSIDE CANDELARIA CAVES, FEBRUARY 22ND, 2023

BIANCA: So, it looks like we are still waiting on . . . two permits from the state. I'm going to talk to one of the tour guides tomorrow. They say they can lead us into the caves but are worried about something they haven't gone into detail about yet. Probably just want to make sure they won't lose money from having the caves shut down. But we're paying them, so it's okay.

FERNANDO: Yeah.

BIANCA: And then I'm going to meet with the crew to go over safety measures, stuff like that. Dos cervesitas, por favor. Am I missing anything?

FERNANDO: Gracias. Listen, Bianca.

BIANCA: I'm listening.

FERNANDO: My wife looked through my phone.

BIANCA: Even with that disappearing app? No, that's impossible.

FERNANDO: Well, I guess there's an app that finds disappearing apps.

BIANCA: What?

FERNANDO: So, I need to talk to you about how to proceed.

BIANCA: No. What? What do you mean?

FERNANDO: Well, she asks that we don't see each other anymore.

BIANCA: We're going to be here for the next six months.

FERNANDO: Bianca, I know this is hard. But I'm asking you
   to leave.

BIANCA: What? No. What? This is my site.

FERNANDO: Well, technically we did it together.

BIANCA: But I did all the research. I got us that grant.

FERNANDO: And you'll still get credit. You'll still be first author.
   But you can't be here.

BIANCA: What?

FERNANDO: She's threatening to leave me and the kids and go to
   the board. I could lose my job. Please, Bianca. We are so close.
   What we have together is so special. I need you to help me. Help
   me and I'll take care of everything here. You'll still get the credit.

BIANCA: The subject is here. Can we talk about this after? Hola,
   mucho gusto.

"Can I use some of your soaps?" Bianca asked.

Blue did a silent victory sign with their fist. "Please use all of them!
Hey, are you recording this?" Bianca nodded.

"Give me that for a second."

313 PULASKI STREET, MARCH 26TH, 2023

BLUE: Hi, this is Blue, it is one fifty P.M. in the afternoon. If you're
   listening to this, Bianca is crawling on all fours to the shower
   while I throw out her takeout from last Thursday. She just closed
   the door . . . Bianca? You gotta turn on the shower.

BIANCA: [inaudible]

BLUE: I am moving to the bathroom area. Bianca is in a ball on the
   floor. Come on. No, you have to stand up. There you go. Use the

soap I just made. Okay, Bianca is putting the soap into her
hand and . . .

BIANCA: Blue, I'm not gonna kill myself.

BLUE: Yeah? Okay, well, I'll just leave this on the sink, and if for
some reason you are thinking about it, I mean it's no judgment,
but just yell as loud as possible.

BIANCA: Fuck those people. Fuck history, fuck science, fuck the
academy, fuck reading, fuck words, fuck, fuck small animals, fuck
skeletons, fuck dirt, fuck love, fuck family, fuck souls, fuck me!

BLUE: If that is the energy you wanna harness right now, I completely
support it.

Bianca got out from the shower, a clump of hair in her hand, steam escaping the shower curtain like she'd just been created in a lab. She didn't think she was capable of this type of longing. She didn't know how powerful it was for somebody to acknowledge your physical form with their hands and words. How it sticks with you. How it leaves you in a never-ending emotional hangover when it's gone.

She hadn't checked her email in a month, not being able to deal with any updates from Fernando or pleadings from the academy or any reminder of how her life could've been if she hadn't been so stupid as to fall in love.

PHONE CALL WITH PROFESSOR FARUCH,
MARCH 1ST, 2023

PROFESSOR FARUCH: Are you sure there isn't something we can do
to make you stay?

BIANCA: It's really serious. I need to prioritize my health. I could
die. Fernando will carry out the excavation and I can work from
New York.

PROFESSOR FARUCH: It's a shame you can't be there on the site.
You're one of the best we've seen in a long time.

BIANCA: This isn't the last you'll see of me. Fernando will be in
touch with me soon and we'll carry on from there.

But he was never in touch. Every day she checked her email and
every day there was no response. She didn't dare write him again, because
she knew she would get him in trouble. Bianca heard her sister in her
head, cussing him out, and tried to keep that energy there, the anger, but
she couldn't. She sent Fernando the most professional, robotic emails she
could conjure, but there was no response. She sent emails to Professor
Faruch—nothing. They had all ghosted her. It was as if she had never
been to Guatemala or NYU at all. It was making her crazy. Sitting on the
floor in her towel, she began hyperventilating. Blue came in as she was
banging her head against the carpeted floor. Her towel was flopping everywhere and one of her breasts was out. Blue calmly wrapped the towel around
her and told her to breathe.

"I'm dying!" she screamed. "I'm having a heart attack!"

"Take one deep breath in and hold it in for seven seconds, then slowly
breathe out for seven seconds."

Bianca complied and eventually calmed down.

"Can you find my phone?" Bianca said, sniffling. Blue sighed.

313 PULASKI STREET, MARCH 26ᵀᴴ, 2023

BIANCA: They all abandoned me! They all forgot about me! And I
can't say anything or Fernando will be in trouble!

BLUE: You need to take this time to move on. You're smart and
capable and you need to pay the rent because I don't want us to
get evicted.

BIANCA: I'M SORRY! I'M SUCH A BAD ROOMMATE! AND
FRIEND!

BLUE: Listen, you're going to get up tomorrow and come to the
salon with me. And you're going to be the best receptionist there
ever was. Everything you do, you're good at.

BIANCA: Was I good at the earrings?
BLUE: Yeah, like, too good. It was annoying me.

Perhaps it was never too late to start over. *You aren't defined by your job,*
Bianca tried to tell herself. *You aren't defined by the choices you make or*
awards and titles or even how people remember you. You might not even be
remembered at all.

ZOE

Did you drink water today? Did you forgive yourself today? Did
you look inside the wound of your womanhood to remember that
every wound is an opening? That every opening is a door? That
only you can walk through it?

In a few hours, Zoe's husband would wake up without her there beside him.
He would assume that she had completed her usual morning tasks. Made
coffee for him from the Keurig, blended with hazelnut Coffee Mate and a
packet of sugar. Left last night's chili for him in the microwave. Done her
dyed blond hair up in a messy bun. Thrown on her leggings and oversized
Cubs sweater, her plastic rainboots from Walmart and driven her car to
her shift at the supermarket. She would already be gone.

And she was, but instead of bagging groceries in reusable bags that
were worse for the environment, she was at the border of Illinois with a
suitcase of her belongings in the back of her car, the sky slowly turning
from purple to blue.

She had stopped using a phone months ago, which angered Jared
because then he wasn't able to track her. She said there were too many
distractions on her phone and she just wanted to spend quality time with
him without the disturbance of Wi-Fi. But it was also so that nobody
would know where she was once he was dead. She followed directions on

her napkin, written out by Maria, but she didn't need to look at them. She already had them memorized.

It was only the second time Zoe had disappeared without a trace. After ten years of picking up and leaving in the middle of the night, opening the door softly to make sure she hadn't woken up her family, Zoe was driving back to Boston.

She chose the name Zoe because she thought it was cute and didn't have the burden and the foreign ugliness of Paola; the way everyone butchered her name, calling her *Paw-luh* or *POWLA*. Why did her parents want her to go through all of that? So much suffering when they could've just given her an American name. They were in America, after all. But all resentment regarding identity and politics slipped away from Zoe after she met Maria. All those labels became something that made her believe she was tied to her body, and not something bigger. Still, she was Zoe.

Zoe pulled up to a gas station and filled her tank. All the available food was encased in plastic, which was bad for fertility, so she ate pepita seeds and walnuts out of a repurposed glass jar. It was 6:00 A.M. She had been very careful. She extracted her savings in cash and closed her bank account. She had told her coworkers that she would see them tomorrow—saying that she was going on a trip would be too suspicious, make the police more inclined to look for her. When she didn't show up to work, her manager would ring her house a few times and figure that she was sick. And Maria said she would take care of the rest. Zoe didn't want to know what that meant. She didn't need to. Her various seeds resting in her stomach, she filled her tank halfway. The attendant asked if she wanted help, and she said no, thank you. She didn't need help. Not anymore. She climbed into her car and the tape began again.

Have you focused on the center of your throat chakra? Have you made yourself remember the child that you are? The Mother

wants you to remember. The Mother knows you have been trying
to forget.

Zoe brushed a strand of dyed blond hair, thick as the stem of a plant, behind her ear. Once, in high school, a girl sitting next to her picked up one of Zoe's stray hairs that had flown freely into her algebra textbook. She held it up to her wet eyeball as if the hair were some kind of bug. *Ew*, the girl said. That girl wouldn't recognize Zoe now. She had lost all her high school weight and, since meeting Maria, had become extremely trim and fit.

Zoe continued to drive down the highway as more cars entered her lane. The morning was here. The ride to Massachusetts would take approximately two days. She would stop in seven exits and drive to a hotel next to a waffle house, where somebody named Stella would greet her.

For Zoe's entire life, all she wanted was love all-consuming, wrapped around her like cellophane, tight enough around so that she lost a little bit of oxygen and was able to fall asleep.

She met Jared while working at Creations by Lucia, her mother's altering store. He was extremely skinny, with a face that looked like it had been pinched in, his nose, eyes, and mouth all sucking into the center. He was not handsome, Zoe could admit that now. She could see that clearly. He had come to get a suit taken in. As Lucia took his measurements, the yellow tape measure moving from inside his armpit to the end of his arm, he stared at Zoe. Zoe blushed. People didn't look at her that way. Nobody looked at her that way. She couldn't even look at herself. At seasonal trips to T.J. Maxx, she went into the dressing room and tried underwear on over her clothes. Hector, her stepfather, was the only one who didn't make any comments about her weight. In fact, he would often drive the two of them to Burger King and order two Whoppers for each of them and they'd happily sit in the parking lot, taking in the delicious, chemically altered taste of the smoked bun. But Hector was gone. Her only ally. *Perezosa. Gorda*, her mother would say, *Nunca encontrarás un esposo con este cuerpo*. It was always strange to her that in a world ruled by men, Zoe's mother couldn't find it in her to be a support system. Couldn't she see that it was them against the world? When she saw Jared looking at her, she felt salvation.

Remember that you are made of the stars above you. Remember that the only difference between you and the sun is desire, is longing, hatred taught to us by the men running our lives, that we can all make our hearts beat to the same chime if we just listen. If we just try.

Zoe pulled up to the hotel, where she parked and turned on her signal: making her car flash its lights six times, then beep. She waited for ten minutes until someone knocked on the glass window. She unlocked it and the woman entered. Her hair was odd—black and cut around her head in the shape of a bowl. Her teeth were abnormally large and her smile took up half her face.

"I'm so glad you came, Zoe," she said. "Maria said you were very bright." Zoe stared straight ahead of her. She had let herself cry a few weeks prior, when the decision was made. It felt like maintenance, bleaching the sink of her emotions, taking out of the trash of her guilt. And now she didn't have to worry about him anymore.

As the two of them entered the hotel, Jared was drinking his morning coffee. He was sitting at the dining room table, where he would spend dinners cutting up his steak and chewing the meat slowly, menacingly, while he interrogated Zoe about her day, watching her grow smaller and smaller as the meat turned to paste in his mouth. He was looking out into their yard, at the sign he had put up supporting a congressman who wanted to arm schoolteachers with rifles. He was feeling a little strange. He was clutching the tablecloth with his meaty hands, hands that had, a few times, been wrapped around Zoe's throat, and his vision was blurring as the untraceable poison Zoe had laced his coffee with was stopping his heart.

On the bed in the motel, Zoe found a letter from Maria Santiago. She opened it with her fingernail, which she had rid of paint a few nights ago.

You've made it this far. Your world has ended and a new one has begun. Come into the Mother's arms. Here. At the Woman's Stone.

The woman sat on the bed with Zoe and took her hands. "Are you ready?" she asked, smiling. Zoe nodded. A year before, after Jared had pinned her against the wall because Zoe had thrown away expired bread he hadn't had a chance to eat, she had started going to church. Her mother had raised her with religion, but they had stopped going to church once Hector died. You would think the whole thing would have made her more religious, but a loss like that, Zoe reasoned, surprised with the empathy she had for her mother, makes you stop believing in God. She drove to St. Andrew's. Sitting in the pews and opening the Bible, she found a pressed rose. A sign. She continued going to the same pew, and opening the same book, and finding more signs. Each time, there'd be a different flower. Signs. From God? She put the thought away. Maybe she was not meant to be saved. At the supermarket, stocking cans of beans, she found a grocery list on the floor.

BLACKBERRIES

EGGS

ALMONDS

THIS DOESN'T HAVE TO BE YOUR LIFE

The list worked like a spell. At breakfast she looked over at the man who had taken her away from the hell life in Boston and to Romeoville, Illinois, and saw a piece of bacon clinging to his blond beard like a tiny disgusting panda. His teeth were the color of pus and his hairline had receded to make his forehead look like a vampire's. She had wanted a baby with him so very badly. She wanted a version of them fused together in the world, their love incarnate. But she realized that, actually, she had just wanted a baby. And it's not like she didn't try. So many nights of Jared's thrusting, of tracking her period, and still, nothing stuck. Nothing formed. Nothing was made between them. And now she hated him with every fiber in her being. The first slaps were a joke, a silly greeting, a person imitating abuse like a jester at court, but then the laughter allowed for more imitation, and then that imitation became reality when she left her razor on the sink, when juice leaked from the garbage bag onto the floor, or when anyone would give her a second glance in public.

On a day off, she walked to a Niko's Breakfast Club and ordered a stack of pancakes with whipped cream on top. While Jared had initially said she was the most beautiful person he had ever seen, he had begun making comments about her shaking the car and laughing at her if she took another helping of food. At the diner, she could be alone with herself and her food. She poured syrup all over the cakes and happily cut them into triangles, letting the butter and whipped cream melt into her mouth with each forkful. She looked around, then closed her eyes and let herself feel every flavor. Every rush of glorious sugar on her tongue. When she opened her eyes a woman was sitting across the booth next to her. Zoe nearly choked on her food. The woman watched as Zoe gathered herself, chugging water and trying to get the morsels of food down.

"You're afraid," the woman said.

"No, I think it just went down the wrong pipe." She cleared her throat.

"I'm not talking about that." Zoe didn't want to look her in the eye. Her face was hot. She felt embarrassed of being in this situation. The woman knew somehow. She didn't know how, but she did. There was a bruise on her shoulder forming underneath her Mickey Mouse shirt from where Jared had shoved her.

"Sometimes," Zoe said. "It doesn't happen that often."

The woman reached for her hand, palm out. "This doesn't have to be your life." The person sending her messages. Some kind of angel.

"Who are you?" Zoe asked, taking the woman's hand and feeling her own hand grow sweaty underneath this stranger's grip.

"Someone who is here to help you." She smiled. "You can call me Maria." Maria told her to meet her there every Thursday at 2:00 P.M., which was coincidentally when Zoe had time off from the supermarket. At Niko's Breakfast Club, Maria helped her concoct a plan to leave Jared, safely and without a trace. It would take a few years' time. Zoe would have to be patient. On their third Thursday of meeting, Zoe asked why she was helping her.

"We are all part of something bigger than this," Maria said calmly. "When there is a wrench thrown in the wheel, we have to oil the wrench out, and make sure that it can never be thrown in again." She had eyes the color of Windex and honey hair that she wore long past her breasts. If you saw her from afar on the beach you would think she had the body of a teenager.

"Repeat after me," Maria told her, grabbing her hand. "I was made for this world."

"I was made for this world."

"And I will not let it undo me."

"And I will not let it undo me."

"Because I am the thread that keeps it together."

"Because I am the thread that keeps it together." Zoe was overcome. Nobody had ever cared about her this way, showered her in such affections, without judgment or the bias of their own life dictating the advice they gave her. She handed her some tapes she had made, a string of affirmations Zoe could listen to in the car. She learned Maria had started an organization called the Woman's Stone, a holistic health center where she trained doulas and ran an exercise studio. Maria had generational wealth; her dad was the son of somebody who invented a common kitchen appliance and there was a lot, a lot of money. When Zoe was worried about what she would do for work, Maria simply told her to work for her. "The only thing," Maria said, "is that I am based in Boston." Zoe furrowed her brow.

"I have a past there," Zoe said, "people who don't want to see me."

"There is no past," Maria said. "There is only now."

Despite all the chaos and the daily tasks we have to do every day and every year, know that you are here for a reason. Do you know how life is made? Do you know the circumstances of your birth? Out of all the millions of sperm one parent held, it was yours that made a fateful journey to your mother's womb, and survived its hostile environment and created life, and then survived another nine months, and broke into this cold world as one breathing, pulsing warm being, and now you are here, listening to me. Oh, it is a miracle.

Maria brought her to the Woman's Stone chapter in Illinois, a few towns away from Naperville. She had Zoe sit in on a spin class, where Zoe found herself out of breath, her heart racing. She thought she was about to die on that bike. But then Maria took her to the meditation room, where she brought out a bell attached to a white box. Setting the bell ringing and closing the door, Maria left Zoe all alone. Zoe was afraid in the dark. The bell was dinging ominously and felt almost like a call to the other side. Zoe began to cry. Shoulders heaving, gasping for air again, thinking of Jared's daily rampages. Then the bell seemed to grow louder and louder. It was coming from the walls and inside of Zoe's own hands. Zoe realized it was ringing to the tune of her heart. She was nowhere but in the room with the bell. She was the bell herself. She let it wash over her. She let herself be drowned by it. When she came out of the bell session, she was a new woman.

Maria had turned her body, starved of real nutrition and care, into the well-oiled and loved being that it needed to be with spinning and meditation and daily affirmations. After her shifts at work, Zoe would join Maria spinning, and she started to feel alive on the mounted bicycle, sweat meeting in a pool in the creases in her back, her thighs burning with life. She had never felt this held. Her mother had no space for her own daughter's complicated emotions, always telling her that she had been through much worse, always making her work, making her hate her body. When Maria asked her to lead a class, Zoe discovered that she was good at something. Up there on the bike, Zoe was new. She was in the present. She was leading women, cycling them away from everything bad, into a place where nobody could hurt them.

Zoe passed exit 127 and thought of her two sisters, and she wondered what they looked like now. If she wanted, she could go to her mom's house and all of this would be over. But what was she supposed to do then? Explain that she wasn't kidnapped and possibly murdered, but had just wanted to make a choice that was her own, with someone who chose her? She didn't even know if they all still lived in the same place. They wouldn't find her. They wouldn't even recognize her.

Creation and destruction make love under the moonlight. We don't choose which side we are on. We are in the middle of the thrust, back and forth, until something breaks open.

The Charles River stretched out in front of her, the modest buildings stacked together in the distance forming a proper city. She rolled down the window. The cassette tape ended and nostalgia flooded the car. Nostalgia is dangerous, Maria had taught her. It makes us long for things that are no longer here, instead of dealing with the present, instead of preparing for the future. Still, she thought of trips to the ice-skating rink on Charles Bank Road, and how tight the skates were on her ankles, how she found it easy to glide over the ice while her sisters needed to hold onto crates and the sides. But Zoe had always been graceful. She had found the grace within herself, finally. The guide that was within her all along. Her car reached the tunnel now, and she was zooming and zooming, getting closer to the opening and all the light bursting at the end of it.

CANDY

Candy shoved open the glass doors to the spin studio.

"Welcome," the woman at the front desk said. She had long, sinewy hair and a beef jerky kind of body, "How may I help?" The studio was typical of

Boston's many new-development buildings that had been forming the city into a glorified strip mall. The walls were white, the atmosphere clinical—it was as if she were inside a home for AirPods.

"Yeah, I would like to sign up for *Zoe's* spin class?" Candy said her name with quotation marks, her fingers turning into hooks slicing through the air. After the shift where she had to be humiliated by the fucko who broke her sister's heart, Candy had walked by a sign on a new spin studio with a familiar-looking face.

"Are you a member?"

"Can't you just do a one-time thing?" Candy brushed her hair behind her ear, suddenly self-conscious about the drama of the air hooks. It didn't help that the woman smiled at Candy like she was a small child showing her a handful of bugs she had just found in the rain.

"Of course," the woman said, handing her a clipboard. "We don't force things here."

Candy wrote down her email address, her phone number, and a fake name, for safety purposes. "What is this place, anyway?" she asked, picking up a candle called Yonic and giving it a sniff.

"This is the Woman's Stone," the receptionist said, her eyes narrowing slightly, as if she were staring into the sun.

At the spin class, Candy took a seat in the back. She wondered if the bikes could be hooked up to the electrical grid, if all of these women pedaling could somehow power a building or an entire city. She thought this whole thing was kind of a scam. The lights dimmed and the beginning of "Till the World Ends" by Britney Spears began to play on repeat: the drum machine and the fake piano crashing into each other, lit-up party buses on the highway driven by no one. The sudden dark and the booming music gave Candy panic. She felt trapped inside somebody else's pulse. She was considering leaving when the door opened and a woman with brown skin and a blond ponytail strutted to the stage. Applause came from the other women on bikes as she took the center. There she was: a ghost in a sports bra.

"How are my warriors today?" the ghost said, adjusting her headpiece and settling on her bike as if it were a horse. The warriors around Candy screamed.

"You've been at your jobs all week," the person who had renamed herself Zoe said. Candy couldn't believe it. She remembered the dress in the coffin, with no body, her mother not crying, simply hardened.

"But this should be the one thing you're really working for. Turn your knobs all the way to the right." Candy followed the instructions, though she felt as though she was about to have a seizure. The beat finally dropped and Britney was howling. Everyone's bodies mimicked Paola's as she rose and fell with her ass to the beat, her legs pumping the machine. This wasn't difficult for Candy—she was a cyclist, after all—but the immediacy of being in the air and then not was making her break into a sweat. She found herself in competition with her sister.

"I WANT YOU TO THINK ABOUT SOMETHING THAT SCARES YOU," her sister bellowed, like a preacher, "AND LIFT UP THOSE WEIGHTS!"

Candy complied.

"ALL OF THAT FEAR AND PAIN ISN'T IN THIS ROOM RIGHT NOW!" If Candy didn't know who this was in front of her, she would have found herself giving in to this the way the women around her were. She heard someone behind her crying. She cracked up when Paola lifted up her arms with her weights, eyes closed, light shining on her like she was Jesus Christ incarnate, and yelled, "RISE UP!" Tears in her eyes from laughter, Candy finally caught her sister's eye, and something small in her face faltered. She stopped laughing then.

For a while, Candy had walked by posters of her sister's disappearance, until the weather turned Paola's face blue and they eventually tattered and dropped to the ground like leaves. When Bianca came back in the fall, she searched Paola's room for clues, looking through notes and photos and AIM messages. But her sister had found nothing. Candy heard her mother call her sister over and over again, leaving frantic message after frantic message, each one getting more deranged and hysterical than the last. It was after this series of calls that Candy started hanging out in the alley behind school where all the teens smoked. It was after this that she overdosed and almost died. Fury ran through Candy's knuckles as she gripped the stationary bike's handles. Her grandmother was right. Paola had abandoned them. And then what? Candy became an addict loser with no one to help her and her mother got meaner and her sister got obsessed with being Indiana Fucking Jones. Paola could eat shit. Fuck Paola.

When the session finished, Candy was in a puddle of her own sweat. She grabbed a towel that was folded in a basket at her feet and wiped herself off. The music stopped and Paola elegantly dismounted her bike. She was almost floating in the air.

"Until next week," Paola said, uncapping her giant metallic bottle and elegantly sipping from it. She packed up her bag slowly with her back turned, as if she was waiting for Candy to approach her. And Candy did.

"So," Candy said, cutting to the chase, "*Zoe*, huh?" Zoe-Paola looked up at her sister and Candy took in the way the years had and hadn't taken hostage of her face. She had one almost elegant wrinkle, a dip that separated the canvas of her forehead, and her face was slightly thinner, but mostly she looked exactly the girl who left her family a decade ago.

"Did you enjoy the class?" Zoe put her hands on her hips, talking to Candy like she was a customer and not her youngest sister. Candy played along, feeling as though they were both acting, and if their performance stopped the audience would come out of their seats and kill them both.

"It was kind of psycho, but yeah. I needed a workout. Somebody stole my bike."

"I'm sorry to hear that." Zoe made her s's sharp, like a snake's, the way Candy remembered her doing when she was ordering food or spelling out her date of birth for a pharmacy over the phone.

"Why are you back?"

Zoe took a step off the stage and walked toward the break room, motioning to Candy to follow her. "Community," Zoe said, taking out a chart behind the desk and writing something down. A giant painting of a pregnant woman hung behind her. She was holding onto her belly and there were small animals dancing around her stomach, as if the stomach were the globe, earth itself.

"Is it just this spinning thing?" Candy wondered how many more questions she had in her until the wall broke.

"There's other things. I'm also training on how to be a doula. Maria will be by soon if you want to speak with her. Are you looking for a job?" Zoe-Paola shuffled the papers together and put them back in the desk.

The question bit her hair follicles and nestled into her dead skin. Candy reached deep inside herself to find patience and not lunge at her sister, tear out her dyed blond hair, take the pens in the cup, and stab out each of her eyes.

"Can I have your number or something?" Candy asked. She felt it, the seats flapping up as the audience members stood up, knives in their hands. "We shouldn't be strangers."

"I'm always here, every day if you need anything." Zoe cleared her throat, correcting herself: "The Woman's Stone is always here."

"Right," Candy said. "Okay." The audience was on the stage now, the wall had been broken, the curtains fell on each and every one's body. "Where do I put this?" she said, holding up her soaked towel. Zoe pointed to a bin at the end of the room, and Candy followed her directions, tossing the white towel in, hearing it land on a pile of other white towels. They made a mountain. They held everyone's dirt.

BIANCA

"Hey," Candy said, "you outside? You leave the house finally? I hear cars and people screaming."

"Yeah," Bianca said, almost getting hit by a Kraft truck. "I got a job, actually, and now I'm picking up some beer." Bianca didn't need to tell her what the job was, and that it had nothing to do with the PhD she never earned.

"Wow! And to think back to this morning, when you looked like shit."

Bianca walked up to the bodega, where a cat flicked by her next to an empty can of Fancy Feast. "Yeah." She ignored her sister's jab. "Why'd you call?"

"Dude, I'm having the most fucked-up time." Candy sounded like a little girl again, the way she did when she had done something bad, like when she had knocked over a jar of cookies as a kid and stepped in the glass, almost on purpose, so that her mother would be more focused on the shard in her foot then the mess she would have to clean up.

"Yeah? What's going on?"

"My bike is gone, so that fucked everything up, and Bianca . . . I just saw Paola?"

"Oh. What do you mean?" Bianca knew the day would come when Candy found out their older sister wasn't dead. She was afraid of telling her sister, but also, she wanted to hold on to the information as a know-it-all, the same reason someone would read *A Game of Thrones* all the way through: just to prove that you knew, before anyone else, what was going on.

"Like our long-lost sister is in Boston and alive."

"She's in Boston?"

"She's teaching a spin class, she's going by *Zoe* . . . I don't know, it's fucking *odd*! I can't believe she's alive?"

"That's crazy," Bianca said, trying to shove the guilt out of her mind. The cat got on her back and wiggled.

"Then this morning that guy Fernando asked me out."

"What?" She knelt down and tickled the cat's stomach. Fernando-Fernando?

"That guy you were porking? Kicked you out of Guatemala? Technically, that was before I saw Paola. Sorry to be confusing."

"Yes, I'm aware. What do you mean he asked you out?" Bianca tried to keep calm and steady but felt like she was going to topple over. She sat down on the bodega floor with her legs crossed and took a few deep breaths.

"He just, like, showed up at the theater and asked me *out*. Psycho shit."

"Do you think it could've been someone else?"

"You calling me a liar?"

"He's not in Boston right now so I don't know how he would do that." Somebody stepped over Bianca and yelled at her for being on the floor— didn't she know how disgusting it was? The cat kept purring at her, almost violently. She needed to be touched and held. Bianca remembered her mom's voice shrieking over the phone, telling her she had just bailed Candy out of jail, again. She was so glad to not live at home. It was like this all the time.

"I'm telling you *he is* and so is Paola, who happens to be alive."

"You don't have to tell me again that Paola is alive. I've known for years." Bianca stuck her know-it-all knife in.

"Well"—she could hear her sister try to imitate her tone that signified it wasn't a big deal, a dead sister not really being dead—"where has that bitch been, then?"

"Illinois. There was an entry in a diary that I kept going back to. I had a hunch and I followed it. But I never made contact."

Her sister huffed over the phone. She had gotten to her. "So . . . why didn't you tell me this?"

"It wasn't worth it. Like how maybe there's life way out in the universe, but it's so far away, we might as well just be alone."

"This isn't aliens, bitch! This is sisters. You should have told me."

The cat playfully bit Bianca's hand. "You also weren't stable."

Candy breathed in and out, as if into a paper bag. She knew that rage was coursing through her sister's arms now. That she felt extraordinarily light and could fly into the air, burst into a million Candys that pelted pedestrians and burst through car windows.

"What did you say to me?"

"Just like how right now you're not being stable." Bianca stood up and the cat followed her. The cat wove in between her legs like an infinity symbol. The man behind the counter told her she could take it home if she wanted.

"She seems to like you," he said. Bianca took a deep breath and said nothing to him, which might have made the man behind the counter think she was rude.

"You're being a fucking cunt right now," Candy said.

"Candy, I need you to be honest with me. Are you using again? I'm not going to judge you, you know I am never going to, but I want you to get the help you need." Bianca grabbed a six-pack of Blue Moon and walked to the counter, where the cat was waiting for her.

"This is so unfair."

"Candy, I just want you to be honest with me." Bianca took out her card.

"I AM BEING FUCKING HONEST WITH YOU AND YOU WON'T LISTEN TO ME! YOU'RE THE ONE WHO KNEW PAOLA WAS ALIVE THIS ENTIRE TIME AND YOU NEVER EVEN TOLD ME!"

"I can't talk about this right now, Candy, okay?" Bianca's throat felt tight. This was just like the past. Like everything she had escaped from.

"YOU THINK I'M ON DRUGS WHEN YOU'RE THE ONE WHO WAS ADDICTED TO THIS FUCKDICK! I WISH I WAS ON DRUGS RIGHT NOW! I WISH I WAS HIGH OUT OF MY ASS! ARE YOU KIDDING ME?"

Bianca hung up on her and paid for her beers. The cat had jumped onto her tote bag. "I got litter," the man behind the counter said. Bianca considered, briefly, a life with a cat. How she would watch it age. How her apartment would smell like chicken guts and piss. How it would need her to be around constantly, or it would die faster.

"Everybody needs a companion," the man grinned, "Her mom gets pregnant all the time. Come back next spring and there will be even more of these!" Bianca tried to move her face around into something polite but was struggling.

"Thanks," Bianca finally said, flatly, the bell on the bodega door chiming as it let her out into the night air.

You hold on to the banister like a tree in a storm. You clutch your heart, a cruel drum, and cry out. Is there anybody out there, Candelaria? Are you all alone? And then it stops. The quake lasted thirty seconds tops and it could've cost you your entire life but somehow you are still alive.

Something moves above you and you skip down two steps. A piece of ceiling crashes where you were standing. You hop to each step as the building crumbles around you, making it just in time to open the door. The December light is shining on your face, Candelaria! Do you smell that in the air? It's Christmas! The spirit of the holidays all around you and Mr. Chen's son's body strewn against the pavement, gasping for air, blood gushing from his chest where a stop sign pierced it. Púchica. You make your way to him and he reaches out with his left hand, his wedding band shining in the winter sun.

You never had a first love. You were always barefoot and wore two dresses, one for the outside and one for inside. There was the old man, Jaime, your parents sold you to in exchange for a cow. You left your mother sobbing, your virgin shoulders shaking, and all she said was that she was so lucky that you were so beautiful. Jaime—was that his name? Or was it Alvaro?—had a giant gut covered in white hairs. He had most of his teeth because he had money. Yours, at fifteen, were already feeling loose and stung when you sipped hot coffee. Now you have sophisticated dentures with two fake gold teeth! Eres guapa! Una belleza.

The first night with Jaime-or-Alvaro you stared at a candle burning in the corner, your nightgown hiked up to your waist, him jackhammering inside your new body. Your mother didn't teach you about love, she taught you obedience. Love was a task, crumbs to wipe off the table. A month of this every night and you became pregnant with Gabo. Jaime-or-Albaro still wanted you even when you were pregnant and would hit you when you turned away. You asked him to teach you how to read and he laughed in your face, saying that would never be necessary for you. You took his books off the shelf, ones with long titles and maps inside. You traced your finger along the green and blue masses of land and tried your best to match the letters to the photos, but never could. You were doing this one day, in the stable on a stack of hay, when he caught you and shoved your face into manure. You left in the middle of the night, heavy with Gabo. It was you and Gabo against everything. This company in your belly. Together you would go find those green and blue masses and start a new life. You couldn't go home, so you went to the city, where you started working at a grocery. When Gabo came, you weren't surrounded by family but by coworkers. You remember the man who delivered him: his mustache and the towel draped over his shoulder. You couldn't believe another man was looking at your privates. You can't remember any of the pains in your life, just the atmosphere around them. The stench of your sweat, the noise of a plate shattering.

You take out Mauricio's pocketknife and use your cane to balance. You kneel next to Mr. Chen's son, because it feels like the proper thing to do. He says something to you that you cannot understand, and you say, "Yes, very beautiful," and slice his throat. "Thank you so much," you say, and wait with him until he stops breathing. Very beautiful. Thank you so much. Then you stand up, wincing as your knees crack. The cortisone shot is wearing away and now the deterioration of your knee is making itself known. You think of the latest X-ray, and the blackened bits of your knee that should've been bone.

But you must get going. You must get to the Old Country Buffet.

The bus you usually take to your daughter's house is lying on its side and you look away from the arms and legs poking from underneath it. Children from the preschool who were out for a walk holding onto a rope when the bus tumbled. Their little backpacks with the cartoons on them. Their small sneakers and hands. They all belong to the earth now. But you don't have time for everybody's mercy right now. Or more memories. The Old Country Buffet! The Old Country Buffet!

When Gabo died, a part of you left your body and your soul. Ripped it right out. But along with whatever left was the fear. Because the worst thing possible had happened, and now you were no longer afraid. And of course you worry about Lucia, and seeing her go through pain after pain. History repeating itself.

The church has tumbled. You walk to the wreckage and realize you are not the only person left alive, unfortunately, because esta perra Altagracia is somehow stumbling about, walking toward you. You walk away to avoid her, catching yourself as you almost trip over spit-up sidewalk. She sees you anyway.

"¡Candelaria!" Altagracia is from the Dominican Republic. She once told everybody at church that your tamales were subpar and still has the gall to talk as if the two of you are close friends. On top of that, she's always talking about her son the doctor, and all the money he makes, and how he takes care of her. You never see the son around, or at least haven't in months. She thinks she is better than you.

"¡Canducha, que suerte! ¡Diosito Lindo ayúdanos ya!"

"Que la Virgencita nos salva," you say, eyes narrowed.

"¿Camino contigo?"

You sigh and Altagracia takes that as a yes, and you begin to walk together. Candelaria, you were never really one to have friends. You believe that anybody can betray you at any moment, because they have, and you tell your granddaughters this. Whenever they'd bring their little friends over for those cursed sleepovers, you would tell them the only people they can trust are El Señor and their own mother. And sure, when Lucia heard this she gave you a dirty look, but she didn't correct you because she knew that the best way to keep the girls safe was to scare them, and for the most part, that worked. Except for the granddaughter who did drugs. And the other one who left for a man. And the other one who is busy digging up bones. You shake your head. Those girls need so much help. You wonder where they are right now, and if they're okay.

You do not trust Altagracia, but walk with her anyway. And she won't shut up.

"My son is waiting for me. He is going to help us. He is a doctor."

"Uh-huh, I know."

"Where is your family?"

"Waiting also," you say diplomatically. You do not reveal what you know. You walk through the rubble, one orthopedic shoe in front of the other, slowly, because you could trip and fall if you aren't careful. You don't want Altagracia to hold you up. She can be pretty chatty. Every minute is precious. In this walking, you almost trip over a body. Altagracia stops and gasps. So dramatic.

"Ay, no," she says. "El sacerdote." She begins to gag, "It's too much, no!" Your priest, Padre Hernandez, must have been on the way to the grocery store when the quake happened. His head has a piece of wire from the grocery store's awning pierced through it. Altagracia makes the sign of the cross. The sole of your foot smashes a dirty, heart-shaped box once held by a bear tossed a few yards away. The both of you pray for him. For his soul.

The priest, I mean. Not the bear.

Alta leans down to close his eyes with her fingertips. But then he stirs.

"He's alive!" you say, helping Altagracia move his body, helping him up. He opens his eyes and air starts to leak from his nostrils and then his mouth. Is he just burping?

No, it's a miracle. And with the awning wire sticking through his head? Now, how is that possible? Altagracia is nearly jumping out of her skirt, she's so thrilled, for there is hope now, and you feel it too, but then you remember Mauricio's body in your kitchen and how it didn't disappear, like you thought it would, and how maybe you are not right about all of this.

"¿Padre?" Altagracia says, as he begins to sit up straight. "¿Padre, te sientes bien?" His eyes are clouded. You look behind you. No, that can't be. You've never seen a person come back to life before, have you? You've never done a double take as somebody who knew you very well came walking toward you, the sun hitting their flesh, when they well should have been dead? No, no. Push that thought away for now, Candelaria. We can think about that later.

Because Mr. Chen's son is walking toward you, dragging his foot behind him and still holding on to the bag of recycling, the blood from his neck still leaking from where you ended his life. And the children's hands under the bus are twitching, their bodies wriggling, as the bus topples over. And those aren't moans coming from the children as they begin to crawl toward you.

"Alta," you say, pulling her closer to you, "we have to move." The sacerdote starts to moan, too. Something in his stomach is signaling what's left of his brain.

Altagracia understands, which surprises you—to you, she has as much brain capacity as this newly alive priest. You start to run. The newly animated bodies come to you slowly, slowly enough for you in your old age to outrun, though it is suspicious how fast you are running, given your knee problem.

The both of you dash into what was once a Flour Bakery + Cafe. Candy liked going there sometimes and bringing you back an almond croissant, which you aren't supposed to eat because of your diabetes. Those were delicious treats! You wonder if there are any in here. The people in here are all still alive, but they look confused. Why were they spared? Why were you? But really, there is no reason. For now, it's just right place, right time.

They are all frozen with terror, so you bark orders at them in Spanish. Motioning to barricade the glass door with tables. A man and a woman in scrubs (they probably did a semester abroad in El Salvador) understand you and obey, pushing the table forward and setting it against the glass. This will only buy you time. Altagracia grabs a pastry from the rack and bites into it.

"Pay attention!" you tell her, taking a bite yourself. Delicious! All the tables and chairs are up against the glass doors, and the dead are approaching slowly. Altagracia is cowering behind you, and you feel bad for her, you know that she hasn't experienced much sorrow or pain in this life. You can smell it on her. Her gentleness. The way she is so very afraid. But you—you are ready. You toss her a broom and tell her to get ready to fight.

Now the bodies are throwing themselves against the glass windows, trying to get to all of you, and you have no choice, this is not the end, you know the end, you can feel it in your bones, plus, I need to see you still, so you wield your cane, and people follow you, you are their leader and you are going to get out of this, and the doors break, the newly animated bodies, they crash in, glass all around, taking people and biting into their necks, and you don't know how you know to do this, or where you found this strength, but you are dándoles pijazos with your cane, making them fall away from you, and you keep going, forgetting your body, remembering the old man hammering inside of you when you were just a small bird, just a quaking criatura, all the choices you didn't get to make are these eyes, and the knife you grabbed from your bag is your might, and they squelch and bleed, and Altagracia, she is moving too, screaming like crazy, but one of the undead just bit into her, and one is about to come for you, the last of your strength zapped when his head is smashed in with the green shovel she always carries in her car, and as it clears you see her, in all her fifty-five years and those eyes that are just like yours, you see her. Lucia. Your daughter.

"Mamá," she says, battering another undead with the shovel. "Hold on." Alta is losing blood on the floor. The life is leaving her eyes. Well, you think, it was nice knowing her. I mean, I really thought she was gonna be your end-of-the-world pal. But what do I know?

You try to drag her away from all of this, give her some peace in death, maybe you'll slit her throat too, she deserves the mercy, she was nice! But the things start to shake again, and the bodies all fall around you, and you grab your daughter's wrist, and she shields you from whatever is coming with her arms, but then there is nothing, just blood all around, just the aftermath of the fight, just wondering what exactly the two of you are going to do next. But you know what you need to do. You've always known.

II

DILATANCY

CANDY

Candy considered going into Blanchards and sending Bianca a picture of ten nips of Fireball with the caption *BUTT CHUGGING THESE TILL I PASS OUT.* But then she decided against it. She wouldn't prove her sister right. She cooled herself off on the four-mile walk to her mom's house. There, they blew out candles for Mauricio's birthday and tried not to think too hard about the empty seats at the table.

"You talk to your sister?" her mother asked, collecting her uneaten Stop & Shop cake.

"She's really busy," Candy said, looking into her lap. Despite their fight, she still had a promise to keep. Her grandmother looked out the window, peeking behind the blinds.

"Is your friend picking you up?"

"No," Candy said. "Why?" She joined her grandmother at the window. The two of them peered through, where there was a woman whose face they couldn't make out sitting in a blue Hyundai.

"I thought she was one of your friends."

"No, Abuelita. I don't have friends." But then the woman started the car and drove away.

"You have to be careful," her grandmother said, wrapping her hand around her wrist. "You can't trust people these days. You never know who is going to come in and steal. Kill us in the middle of the night. Tu no pones atención. No ves las noticias. Your mother has the business. And you know her, she can't protect herself. You should be here with her. In case anything happens."

"Mamá," her mother yelled from the kitchen, "basta con los babosadas. Nobody is coming to hurt us! Stop scaring everybody!" Candelaria looked at Candy and made a cuckoo sign with her fingers. Candy laughed and a frightening snore came from the couch, where Mauricio had fallen asleep before they joined him on the couch.

"You didn't bike here?" her grandmother asked.

"No." Mauricio almost choked on his own snore. "Alguien me robó mi bicicleta."

"Why do you live in that bad neighborhood?" Her mother came in with a cup of étol. Her grandmother took a sip.

"It's always best to stay inside and with your own mother where it's safe. Lucia, this tastes like chalk."

Candy rolled her eyes. They were all so problematic. What did they mean, *safe*? Her grandmother stood up again and went to the window.

"Mamá! Can you sit down? You're making everybody nervous."

"Me siento rara," her grandmother said, touching the back of her neck and peering through the window again. She turned around.

"Voy a prender una vela."

The next morning, Candy went for an angry jog through her supposedly bad neighborhood. She wasn't an addict. She wasn't seeing things. Candy, who wasn't an addict, pulled on her running shoes and tied her hair up in a ponytail. Candy, who wasn't an addict, strapped on a pedometer and began stretching. She pulled back her toes and pushed her foot against her ass. Then Candy, who wasn't an addict, began to run. She ran down Forbes Street, past the houses that looked like crayons, zipping in and out of recycling and compost bins and the same stray cat who kept looking at her funny. She put Mozart on again and felt her brow furrowing. Fuck Bianca. She began sweating. She ran around the park next to the train station thinking about how much she hated her family and how much she didn't need them. Maybe she would move. But to where? There would always be movie theaters. Or at least retail. She could start over. She could be anybody she wanted.

At the Stony Brook train station, she saw two white Jamaica Plain yuppies pushing a stroller. They had probably unhoused a few Black working-class families in the process. Something Candy had also done, if she was being honest with herself. *Fuck me, too*, Candy thought. Another reason to get out of here. HONK! Fest was happening and a chubby Latino kid was playing the trumpet at the station's entrance. Candy stopped to watch as his family cheered him on with their phones out. His father embraced him, gave him a kiss on the cheek, and the kid looked shy but proud of himself. Candy was jogging in place and she found that she couldn't stop. Maybe she could go like this for an hour. Maybe two hours. Maybe she would die like this, and then what would her family think, when they found no drugs or alcohol in her system at all, just pure adrenaline? How ironic would that be? Dying just like her father? Candy sat down on the ledge, endorphins pumping, drowning the thought she was having in the bathtub of her mind. The stray cat ran toward her and jumped on the ledge.

"What is up with you?" she said, reaching her hand out and scratching her neck. The cat stared at her with big yellow eyes and purred hysterically.

"What?" Candy demanded. And the cat continued to make her rattling sound.

"Freak bitch." She pulled out her phone. She had memorized Fernando's number already and dialed it. When she answered all she heard was breathing on the other side.

"Hello? I'm calling because I was sexually harassed yesterday at the movie theater."

"Really?" He was so extraordinarily calm.

"Yeah, by some pervert named Fernando?"

"Oh."

Candy wiped some sweat from above her lip. This man wasn't fazed at all by her.

"Anyway, if that pervert wants to, like, take me out to dinner or something, that would be cool." She sucked her breath in through her teeth.

"I'll take you."

"Fine, um. How about Grendel's?" Harvard Square was far enough away from her apartment so she wouldn't run into anybody she knew.

"Grendel's." She could hear him trying the name out in his mouth like an Airheads mystery flavor. When was it going to be, Candy wondered, that she would get this out of touch? Farther away from her, the trumpet family was making their way into a small car.

"Yeah, Grendel's."

"I'll find you," Fernando said.

As Candy was getting dressed for her date, she was thinking, *I deserve to be wanted and cared for in unexpected ways, I deserve nice things.* She took the Orange Line and switched to the Red Line at Downtown Crossing. She would have to get a bike soon. The train made her anxious. There, at Grendel's, he was waiting for her, at the end of the bar.

"You," he said.

"Yeah." She turned to the bartender. "Can I have a Shirley Temple? And some fries?" He passed over the drink and Candy sipped with glee like a child. Fernando stared at her curiously.

"Tell me about yourself."

"Well I'm Bianca's *sister*."

Fernando did not react to that at all. Candy burped. "I like movies. I work at the movies. My boyfriend never wants to have sex with me. I did drugs as a teen, then kind of went down a notch and started drinking heavily, then having sex heavily, now I'm a boring loser going on a date with an older loser." The fries arrived.

Candy began shaking her leg up and down. Fernando smiled at her, very friendly. She knew, popping the fries into her mouth, that this man was not the love of her life. Gazing at this older man who had obliterated her sister's career, Candy did have a familiar feeling, one of power and control. There is something that happens when a man looks at you like you are something more, or perhaps less, than what you really are: like you are an answer, a salvation, the living and breathing embodiment of something that can finally free you from your mortal coil. Candy pictured herself surrounded by flowers and light and Fernando below her on a field, crying.

"Please forgive me for saying this," Fernando said, "but when I look at you, time stops."

"Oh."

"It is like I forget what age it is. It's like I am here and there. Everywhere I've been, there you are. Buildings can rise up and fall down, species can die out and be made again. But you? You will have stayed the same."

"I don't know if anyone has ever called me beautiful by trying so deeply hard not to at all."

Fernando looked baffled but also like he had never met a woman like Candy before, or ever met a woman at all.

"Let's go," she said, sucking her Shirley Temple dry and chewing on the ice.

Fernando took out his wallet and laid it on the counter. Candy looked at him.

"Are you going to pay, or . . ."

Fernando smiled and nodded, unbuckled his wallet, and shuffled through cards: IDs, museum passes, coffee stubs. He stared at the credit card for a long minute until Candy snatched it and slammed it down onto the counter, where the bartender collected it. They left without signing.

Walking awkwardly side by side, they took in the Boston spring air. The trees were slightly budding, new life threatening to burst. It had rained while they were inside and everything looked especially green and vibrant, even at night.

"Really tell me about yourself," Fernando said.

"I already did."

"Tell me about yourself." What was up with this man? But also, had anyone ever been this into knowing what she was *about*?

"Okay, you really want to know?" Fernando nodded. He was an empathetic newscaster, and she, a woman recently rescued from a deserted island.

"My dad died when I was a kid. It was really unexpected. Just like, a heart attack that had no explanation while he was out one day on a run.

Um, my mom made me and *Bianca*"—Candy paused again, to see if there would be any rise to his face—"go upstairs while she and my older sister figured out what was going on. And those few hours, or maybe it was just half an hour, I don't know—time!—were the longest of my life. Because my sister was freaking out and I didn't know what was going on. And she didn't want to tell me what was happening because it would make me feel bad, but the more in the dark I was, the more my imagination got worse. I felt this trapped kind of panic that wouldn't go away."

They reached Harvard Yard and sat in one of the chairs that were bolted to the ground. Fernando took her hand. It was a little nice, Candy thought, thinking of Garfield and his mommy issues, to seek out comfort instead of being the one who was doing the comforting.

"And the panic continued. And I guess I tried to quiet it with drugs and whatever. I mean, I've already figured this out in therapy, but I don't talk about it with a lot of people because it's humiliating to have feelings! So."

Fernando nodded his head. "I'm sorry," he said to her.

"Another thing is my older sister disappeared after my dad died and everyone just, like, thought she was dead, but I just saw her and it's like everyone is lying to me. And Bianca, you know, she just does whatever she wants. She just left. I guess that's what everybody fucking does! I'm the only one who ever stays."

Fernando nodded, putting his hand to his chin.

"I don't mean to be so *drama-drama*."

Fernando just kept staring at her. He took his hand away from his chin, but the hand stayed stuck in that position, as if it were holding an invisible plate.

"It's my own fault," Candy said, "I mean I have . . . issues."

Fernando's hand eventually returned to a normal position, slowly, like a memory foam pillow.

"You are many things," Fernando finally said, and Candy thought she saw something ripple across his cheek. She blinked.

"Why do you talk like Robert Frost?"

"Who?"

Candy's leg kept shaking. It made her, somehow, feel more still. She was thinking about leaving. This man was clearly an idiot.

"Candy?" A low, familiar voice. A man had approached her. Again.

"Yes?" Candy took in his blue baseball cap that read RELIEF, the shoulder-length hair underneath it, the J.P. Licks ice-cream cone he had clutched in his hand, the stick-and-poke tattoos littering his brown arms.

"Sorry, um." The man jerked around like he was part of a LEGO set. "I'm sorry, this is . . . maybe I should go."

Candy narrowed her eyes.

"No way." The ice cream started melting onto Julian's hand. He had his mouth hovering above the cartoonish ball of Oreo cake batter but seemed to be afraid to continue licking it because having his tongue out or acknowledging food at all felt impolite.

"I just was over there, saw you over here, and I thought I would say hey, it's been a while, hope you're well and healthy, was the pandemic weird for you? Um . . ." Candy felt bored. Julian was a flight attendant demonstrating safety measures before takeoff. An acquaintance excited to show her a YouTube video where a child says something heinous. Her sister hated Julian, but Candy was never mad at him.

Rebecca Polkinghorn wasn't even really her friend. She had just wanted to show up. To be part of the wrong crowd and interrupt the right crowd, who all put UMass Amherst as their safety school while gunning for Ivies their parents would pay for through legacy or credit card. It was exciting to show up as the high school druggie, makeup plastered on like an old sticker, tiny and fuckable, walking through the crowd buzzed. She had told Julian she would be right back, though really she was just trying to get away from him. She had made him go there and now was escaping him. Bitch hours. Cunt vibes. She was looking for a bedroom, a quiet space to try what was wrapped up in the cellophane in her pocket that Julian had gotten threatened and beaten up for. She liked that she could make him do that. Prove himself. He said he'd wait for her downstairs. She was just going to be right back. She found Rebecca Polkinghorn's parents' bedroom and settled down on their plush gray carpeting. Yes, she had idealized the drug. She had heard from new friends and old movies that nothing was ever the same after trying it, and she wanted to know if that were really true. What would it be like, she wondered, to never be able to recreate a feeling, but to have at least known it once? What sucks is they were all right. All of them. The movies. The songs. They were right. The brief flood of rapture. The pleasure. The wind of the hole inside of her, quieted. All of that was true, and then she woke up in a hospital bed. All that happened to get her there, she liked to block out. The entire ordeal of rapid knuckles to her chest, her breathing that was almost undetectable, Julian's speeding car, her screaming mom, the debt to that Rhonda woman for rehab, all of everything it took to save her life. She wanted to be locked inside a necklace and haunt it until everyone she knew during that period of time was dead. But maybe she could at least be polite for now.

"Hey, Julian," she said, the corners of her mouth bouncing around like a frantic cursor as the computer freezes. "This is Fernando." She pointed a thumb over at her date. Julian leaned over clumsily, his ball of ice cream threatening to fall off the sugar cone.

"What's up, dude, nice to meet you, man . . ." She felt Fernando tense up, and she almost liked his protectiveness. Fernando held out his hand and shook Julian's, stiff as a mannequin at a theme park. Candy wasn't sure what to say to him and wanted him to understand that sometimes there is nothing to say to anybody except for *Hello, you're still alive, goodbye.* They looked at each other again and Julian seemed to hear her say that, and she was thankful for it.

"Kay. Nice to meet you. See you. Have a good life." He put his mouth to the ice cream, finally, and walked away. Candy, of course, thought of her sister, and her protectiveness of her, and how she made Julian feel horrible, and she felt angry. What did her sister know about anything? All she wanted to do was control.

"Did he mean something to you?" Fernando asked, snapping Candy out of her trance. His hair looked grayer underneath the university lights. Could she see his scalp? Was it red?

"Not really."

"Okay," he said, fixing his gaze on her again, as if Julian had never been there and she were the only person in the world. He coughed suddenly, and a tooth came out in his hand. He kept his gaze fixed on her. There was no blood on the tooth.

"Uh, do you want to take care of that?" Candy was used to this. Garfield had a lot of dental issues. She almost found it endearing. He set the tooth on the bench.

"You're kind of nasty," Candy said, a smile forming at the corners of her mouth.

"What do you like in this world?" Fernando asked. His eyes were very dilated.

"Like, in general?" Fernando took in the word *general*, trying it out in his mouth.

"Yes."

"I guess movies?"

"Movies."

"I love every movie. Even the bad ones. I went into this YouTube hole a while ago looking for this movie called *The Leaf*. It's a nineties horror flick, but instead I found a movie that's also called *The Leaf*, but it's made by this independent filmmaker somewhere in Idaho and it's probably the worst thing I've ever seen."

"The worst?"

"Yes, it was amazing. There's a leaf that lands on this guy's face and there's blood on it, and obviously it's a metaphor for his dead son, and he takes the leaf off but it keeps haunting this guy, who also obviously wrote and directed it, so pathetic, and then the leaf starts torturing him? Somehow it cuts off his legs? And then at the end, he turns *into* a *leaf*."

Candy was delighted talking about it, clapping her hands together, her eyes glossy with tears, "I love stuff like that. It's just so bad. Maybe I'm sick."

Fernando nodded his head, completely serious.

"Thank you for sharing that with me." One of his eyelids were closing, like he was falling asleep or winking at her.

"Yeah . . ." Candy crossed her eyes and made the sign of the horns with her fingers. It was impossible for her to be sincere and he was embarrassing her slightly. What was wrong with him? "It's just funny because it was like one movie was cosplaying as the other." He nodded. She started feeling disappointed. She wanted something to come from the night, instead of this extremely boring bust. She wanted to reach him somehow, even if it took drowning in her own words.

"But what do I know?" she said. "I've never written a movie or even tried. I always say I'm going to and then I never get around to it because, well, I work full-time, and I have all this trauma that I got to deal with, so it's really important for me, to rest in a radical way, I guess, but also I'm a piece of shit who can't do anything because I never technically finished high school. I mean I have my GED and I'm always consuming things. I'm, like, a person of *culture*. I'm pretty smart, actually. You don't need to be educated to be an intelligent person. Everyone's like, *Oh, Bianca's the smart one*, but actually Bianca is the most selfish one. And being selfish gets you places, I guess. And look at her. She isn't even happy doing what she's doing. I'm totally fine staying here. I'm pretty happy just kinda doing whatever."

Fernando took her hand and Candy let him. Maybe this man wasn't so bad, she thought. Maybe, like Julian, he was someone who had made a mistake. Maybe Bianca got hysterical and couldn't see what was actually happening, that he just wasn't into her anymore. It was probably Bianca who kicked herself off her own site.

"I like listening to you," he said, leaning closer to her. And she felt it, whatever it was, the power that she had over him or that he had over her, interlocking and making a decision.

"Listen. I know this is weird, considering, you know." Candy took her hands away from him and moved them around as if she were juggling the words *Bianca* and *lover*, two pieces of fruit nobody was going to eat anyway. "But do you want to get out of here?" she asked. Fernando grinned and stretched out his hand to her again.

For Candy, there had always been consequences to feeling good. Trauma for her family. Jail. Shame: shitboats of it. But she thought she had finally found a way to feel good enough without the aid of drugs, or alcohol, or sex. To fill the hole she had been trying to fill forever. And that was with regimen. With exercise. She gave herself endorphins by moving her body extremely, sweating from one place to another. It was the most moral thing to do, riding a bike—you use the food inside your body to move a machine that isn't leaking any gas into the world. It's not taking away carbon, but it isn't adding it, either. The best thing you can do, as a person, is to be neutral. But her bike was gone.

Was this neutral? Candy thought, as she led Fernando into her room and he took off her clothes. Bianca had lied to her. This made it even. This made it neutral. Fernando lowered her onto the bed and Candy felt herself giving into neutrality. *At least I'm not on drugs*, she thought, the walls around her body falling. *At least I have a say in what's going on.*

"You smell good," he said, his nose against her neck, his hand drifting up her thigh.

"You don't smell like anything," she said. And he didn't. Candy figured she had allergies. It was spring. He held down her right hip with his hand and she felt as if she were merged with the bed, and she liked it—the acknowledgment that she was really there. Briefly she thought about how her sister had once been in her place, but she dodged the thought like a speeding car, focusing instead on her own breath and the gooseflesh raising on her arms. Fernando, with his hands on both her thighs, began eating her out, and she was not present, she was everywhere. She was on her doorknob, she was wherever the hell her bicycle ended up; in a blond wig in an old car taking a long drive to a motel that would ruin her life; a montage of blood oranges and old photos, bursts of light and darkness, a song she heard in a supermarket while holding a sack of sugar; away from herself. She clawed at Fernando's back, turning over his shoulders and having him enter her. He was remarkably stiff and it made Candy feel like she was fucking a silicone doll of a man, which was amazing because it was almost like being alone. She could barely see him in the dark. And if she did, she would've seen that his ear had fallen off.

Then it was over and Candy let herself feel the loss of it, the reckoning that something this good must end, and then she fell asleep. She had the same dream, about the table, and the people who wanted to eat her, and this time she was the table.

Candy woke up suddenly around 3:00 A.M. to a slurping noise. Turning, she saw Fernando sleeping next to her. His cheeks rustled like trees, his chin elongated. His face was stretching until it reached his shoulders. His body began contorting and melting until it was the shape of silly putty ready to be molded and packaged into a cannister. She backed away from the bed, nearly falling down as Fernando's body took over it. Candy ran to the bathroom, rubbing her eyes, certain this was just a dream. When she returned, Fernando was gone. There wasn't even the shape of him left on the bed. She climbed back in. A dream. He had left. There was no evidence of what she had just done. She had felt amazing and then deeply afraid, and both of those things canceled each other out, didn't they? She didn't feel good. She didn't feel bad. The sheets were just cold. She was just alone.

ZOE

"Do you think this is okay?" Carmen spun for Zoe. She was wearing a blue, flowery dress with a sweetheart neckline that accentuated her cleavage and waistline; the skirt rustled at her freshly shaven knees.

"It's great," Zoe said. Carmen looked in the mirror hanging from Zoe's room, putting her hair up and then down.

"I feel a little nervous," Carmen said. "Do you think he'll like me?"

"He will." Zoe put one hand on her cheek and Carmen held it there.

"I'm sorry that you can't do this." Carmen stroked Zoe's finger.

"I wasn't meant to," Zoe said, wrapping another hand around Carmen's face. Carmen broke away and sat down on Zoe's bed. Zoe lived in a complex owned by the Woman's Stone close to the Charles River. Carmen was just down the hall with other members and would often visit Zoe. They were close. Carmen took a thermometer out from her purse. She placed it under her tongue, waited for it to beep, and then checked something on her phone.

"I'm ready," Carmen said.

"Good," Zoe said. She was looking through something in her closet, not wanting to look at Carmen. The Woman's Stone's doctors had confirmed with her what she had always feared: that she wasn't able to conceive and wouldn't ever be able to. That's not everybody's purpose. That's not everybody's role. Still, she longed for it when she went to sleep at night. Imagining her belly growing, feeling the increased blood flow to her vulva, feeling connected to every living part of the earth.

She picked up a spinning cleat and blew some dust off it, slamming it together with its pair and placing them in a neat line. There wasn't much in her room. She had adopted, from the Woman's Stone's ethos, a sense of minimalism. Clarity of space and mind. Her room was for decompressing, and any mess would cling to the impurity of her own thoughts.

"Where are you meeting him?" Zoe said, moving her legs underneath herself.

"This pub downtown."

"No illness? You had him screened?"

"Of course." Zoe sat down on the bed with Carmen.

"He's tall. Full head of hair."

"If it doesn't work this time, don't be hard on yourself." The light was fading from Zoe's room. The room was washed in pinks and reds, now.

"I have a feeling it will." Carmen hugged Zoe. "You've been such a good help." Zoe held on to her hand. She couldn't help but feel worried. The Woman's Stone, she had learned, was everywhere, and Carmen would be safe, in case the man turned out to be bad. Carmen would always be in control, because she had a net of humans ready to catch her. She was free to make any decision she wanted, inside this net.

BIANCA

The salon was simple enough work. She answered phones and made appointments, swept up dyed hair and dumped it into the trash. Blue was particularly talented, and after a local influencer shared the shag they gave her on her socials, they were flooded with appointments to get the same kind of shag. Bianca admired her friend's work ethic, the pride they took in it, the second nature in their hands as they snipped and brushed somebody into a better mood. It reminded her of her mother's hands with needle and thread. One day, after Blue found Bianca looking through PhD programs, they took her aside and told her she needed to not do anything archaeology-related for a while.

"But this is what I love to do."

"But what you love to do hurts you."

"But I can do it again. Better. I can find some other school and some other professor. I can do it better."

"What if you just relaxed for now? You can figure it out some other time." Blue was so calm about these things. And deep down, Bianca knew they were right. They managed to convince Bianca to let them give her the shag they had been giving everybody, but she still wore it in a low ponytail. Bianca's demeanor fit into the coolness of the salon. Customers began to think that because she had such a specific, judgmental affect, the experience they were getting with Blue was worth their money. The worse the bedside manner, the better the haircut. It worked for the salon very well.

It was this bedside manner Julian encountered one day in the fall, when he came into the salon hunched over and sweating. She didn't recognize him at first. His hair was much longer and underneath a yellow beanie, the thick strands peeking out like an upside-down blackened spider plant. His brown arms were littered with stupid tattoos and his socks were both different colors. He came to the front desk, grabbing onto it like a sailor lost at sea, and asked, "Can I use your bathroom?"

"What are you doing here?"

"Hey, how are you?" He let out a tremendously smelly fart. The last time Bianca had seen him, it was outside a hospital room, where her sister had just miraculously woken up from a coma. She had told him to never contact her or her family again. You're dangerous, she told him. What had he been up to since then? She had heard that he dropped out of school, but she had no idea what became of him. She and Candy sometimes brought him up, but so much time had passed, he had become mythical, a town specter.

"The bathroom is for customers only," she said, her face as emotional as a can of seaweed.

"Listen," he said, adjusting his posture, "I work next door at the plant store? I think we've given you guys plants? This pothos dangling right here, I'm pretty sure that's ours." He looked over at Blue, who was bleaching someone's hair. "I mean y'all plants? Sorry, what are your pronouns these days?" Another fart.

"I'm sorry," Bianca said, "those are the rules." She was done up and wondered what he made of her. "Is everything okay?" Blue asked, pleasantly, but still wrinkling their nose at the smell.

Julian self-consciously turned around. "Okay," he said, "You know, I guess I'll get this." He handed over twenty dollars cash in exchange for a hair cream called Suffuse that Blue had made in their kitchen sink. Bianca rang it up and then he ran to the bathroom. "Don't you want your change?" she called. But he was already exploding in the bathroom. The sink ran for a long time. Another flush. Some light scrubbing sounds. She and Blue exchanged glances. He opened the door and quietly closed it, and walked away with his head down, away from the salon. Blue put down their scissors and walked to the bathroom.

"Well," Blue said, "he didn't leave a trace, at least. Who was that shit-boy anyway?"

"Someone from high school."

As Bianca was walking home, Shitboy trailed behind her. She walked with purpose, her culottes swishing and her Keds stomping on the pavement and her tote bag bouncing against her hip.

"You don't have to respond to me at all," Julian said, completely lurking, "but I wanted to say that I'm sorry. That's it." Bianca kept walking, her head slightly turned toward him. She turned at the end of the street, stepping over bags of trash that were leaking fluids. He followed. "It was such a messed-up time, not that that's an excuse." She realized he wasn't talking about exploding in the bathroom. "I put your family in a really . . . chaotic, harmful position. I can't even imagine. I just wish I could change this. I haven't gone a day without thinking about all of it." Julian gulped. He stopped walking and Bianca walked a few paces but then paused. She turned around and walked toward him slowly. She peered at him, eye to eye. They were the same exact height. He hadn't grown at all, but he was more muscular, with visible tendons in his neck and triceps taking shape underneath his band shirt.

"It's not all your fault," Bianca found herself saying, to her own surprise. "Candy can be . . . really manipulative."

"I don't think it matters. No matter what, I was always in a position of power."

Bianca didn't have the energy for this. "Maybe," she sighed. She continued walking and Julian took that as a cue to follow.

"How is she, anyway?" Julian said. "I actually saw her a few months ago in Boston. Actually, I have been doing a lot of harm reduction work since the last time I saw you."

Bianca glared at him sideways and adjusted her tote bag. "Yeah?" she said. "What was she doing?"

Julian scratched his head. "She was with some guy named Federico or something on a date."

Bianca stopped walking again. Julian did the same.

"What did he look like?" Bianca asked this accusatorily, as if she were asking a small child where all the Hershey's Kisses were.

"Like, white Latin guy, I guess," he said, and Bianca felt sick. "Kinda looked like he was in Jurassic Park?" Julian added, searching Bianca's face for an answer.

"Fernando," Bianca said, his name a prayer and a curse, a winning lotto number and a noisy garbage truck the morning of a hangover.

"*Fernando*, that was it. Do you know him or something?" And that is when Bianca slapped him across the face, a delayed reaction, some might call it, and Julian held on to his cheek, the pain turning into a prickle, a hint of spicy sauce, a limb waking up from a deep slumber.

CANDY

Candy spent the next three months occasionally masturbating to her tryst with Fernando. She'd replay the moments in her head and feel herself transported, her hands becoming his. It was exciting to masturbate to a memory. Porn got boring after a while and the threat of becoming addicted to it loomed. Candy didn't want to be an incel, eyes red from staying up all night jerking it to some underage girls sucking dick. This was better.

Every Sunday Candy would go to her mom's house, where her abuelita and Mauricio would sit and talk about stuff that didn't matter while her mom went on about how her hands and her back hurt. Candy would look at her phone and the sun would set, then she would make her way back home, where Garfield would be waiting with a frozen pizza, making jokes that he ripped from the internet as they watched movies. She was slowly getting used to the train and the bus and walked everywhere with defined calves. She'd accompany her abuelita to her doctor's appointments and translate, however poorly, the effects of the cortisone shot on her knee and how she should keep away from things that cause high blood sugar. She'd help her mom dye her abuelita's hair while

Mauricio would sit on the couch, drinking a beer, watching *Seinfeld*. Meanwhile, no calls from Bianca. *This is it*, Candy surmised. *I am the last one left.*

One afternoon, checking tickets at the door, Candy felt a strange wave come over her. Not nausea or dizziness, but an uncanniness, a feeling of melancholy perversion; a feeling she had done something very, very wrong. The lights around her felt extra stimulating. "I'm gonna do rounds," she said to Jenny at the counter, a forever employee who sometimes bothered Candy simply because she was old, who gave her a thumbs up. She entered theater three, where *La Jetée* was playing. She needed the darkness of the theater, the calmness of a dark room. It was like opening a freezer door and feeling cool, mechanical air on her face. She breathed in and out. She grabbed onto the railing and concentrated on the images changing on the screen. Her hands felt like they were buzzing. Was her hair lifting up with static? Her heart pumping fast, she clutched her chest and kneeled. She was just panicking. Breathe in and out. Think of things that are warm. Think of a happy memory. She looked up, and there, on the screen, instead of *La Jetée*, was herself. She heard something in her ear. A voice, narrating. Her own, but not her own.

> *Meet Candy. She's a hardworking girl on her own.*
> *Just kidding. You know who you are. Look at you.*
> *You're there. On the screen. That's you.*
> *Look at your own face.*
> *Staring at yourself and touching your own face.*
> *But how? Who is recording this?*
> *A wave.*
> *A wave back. Hello.*
> *Hi.*
> *Behind you, a figure.*
> *You turn around.*
> *Nobody.*

Scattered heads turn toward you.
"We know what you did. And with who."

A few customers were standing over her.

"Oh, thank God," one of them said, holding her hand up. "Seems like you fainted."

"After you vomited," another said, pointing out paper towels that were covering up her puke.

"Gross," Candy said. The nausea that she felt in her stomach before the vision, or whatever the hell that was, had turned into something different: an emptiness that needed to be filled. She let one of the customers lift her up and she looked at him, a man in his fifties there with his wife, who was looking at Candy with wide, worried eyes. She glanced at the vein pulsing in his neck and the muscles stretching against his T-shirt. She could hear his heartbeat. It was so loud.

"You wanna go wash yourself up?" he said, gently, putting his hand on her shoulder. "There's some stuff on your mouth." He motioned to his own lips. Candy touched hers, that were wet with saliva.

She felt her insides rattle inside of her, each organ shaking like hard sweets in a jar.

"I need to step out," she said, walking away from the man, because for some reason, she wanted to put her mouth on him. She marched to the concession stand.

"Going home," she said to Jenny. "Have the flu." She began to walk home. She continued to walk, putting in her headphones trying to let the same four Mozart songs drown out this new pain in her stomach. She took out her phone and there she was again, on the screen, in her hand, looking at herself. She stopped and looked around. The girl in the phone stopped and looked around too. The voice began again.

The park bench wobbles.
And all around you it is night.

You dart your head back and forth.
The street light flickers, like a pair of wings.
You stand up, head toward a whirling noise.
There is a hole, pulsing in the air.
It spins and spins. Calls to you. It wants you.
You reach out to it with your hand.

It was daylight again and a pickup truck was honking at Candy, who was in the middle of the street. "The fuck is wrong with you!" the truck driver yelled, swerving. A league of cars was waiting for her to get out of the way, like she was a goose with her ducklings making her way across the road. She held her hand out and said sorry. Her mouth was still watering. She worried she would faint.

She called a car, afraid of what would happen if she went on public transit. When it arrived, she closed her eyes, breathing in an out. "You drunk? You gonna do that again?" the driver asked, pointing at the vomit on her clothes. "Because that'll be a hundred-dollar fee." Candy shook her head, breathing into her hands and trying not to look at the driver or the sweat on his neck or the tendons underneath his tank top.

"Someone puked on me," she said. "Retail, you know." She put her head in her lap, continuing to breathe in and out, counting to ten and then backward from ten. When they arrived at her apartment she practically rolled out of the car.

Outside, on her doorstep, was the same cat who had been following her. She opened her door and the cat sprinted inside. She watched her rub herself against her furniture and lie on her back. She could hear the cat's heart beating underneath her fur. It was so loud in her ears, she almost wanted to cup them so she couldn't hear anymore.

No, no, Candy thought. *Not that.*

She opened her cabinets and grabbed a jar of Skippy, using her fingers to scoop a dollop, then sucking on them. It wasn't enough. She looked toward the cat. The cat was looking at her like she knew what Candy was thinking, almost daring her to do it. No.

She found herself inching closer, but the cat ran to the fridge and started rubbing herself against it ferociously, as if she were in heat. Candy opened the fridge, remembering the steak she had bought a few days earlier from Whole Foods that she had planned on cooking but probably would never cook because she could never follow a recipe or stick to a plan.

She ripped the door open and saw the raw steak encased in plastic. It was a topless woman on a rock at sea, her fingers beckoning to Candy's sailor mouth. A moan escaped her. Her head hurt so much. The cat meowed.

She kneeled and scooped the packaged meat and yanked away the plastic and put her nose to it, taking in its wet, iron smell. Her legs began to shake. She found herself moaning. She let her mouth hover over it until her teeth sunk into the triangular piece of meat while the cat continued making noise, almost cheering her on, and Candy's eyes fluttered and Candy's entire body vibrated as the juices of the steak that would never be cooked dripped down her face and all she could think was that she didn't want it to stop, she didn't want to get to the end of it, she wanted to be filled all up with it, she was on her knees, all at once worshipping the flesh and destroying it, and then before Candy knew it, the meat was gone and she was licking the liquid off the yellow packaging, until all she could taste was Styrofoam. She tossed it aside, the plastic that had covered the steak rolled up next to Candy's foot like a tossed aside condom. Her dizziness had faded. Her breath was regulating. Her head was clear. She took in the kitchen around her and rested her head against the fridge. It had been just right, but not exactly what she needed. It was a snack before the meal. But she couldn't think of it now. She was afraid of herself suddenly. And ashamed. The cat leapt over her legs and began pawing at the door.

"What do you want, bitch," Candy stood up and let the cat out, and as the cat ran down the steps and into the neighbor's yard, Candy tried to remember the last time she got her period.

BIANCA

Bianca took the familiar route to the archaeology office, up the grungy elevators and into the room with medically blue carpet and the canned-pea office walls. She knocked on the administration's door.

"Come in!" a familiar voice said. Bradley Faruch, the head of the archaeology department, was very surprised to see her.

"Bianca," he said. "I am very surprised to see you."

Bianca lingered by the door. He motioned her to sit down in a plush green love seat. She had sat there a few times, with Fernando, making compelling arguments for funding and giving progress reports on their research, the lint on their jeans bravely flying from one thigh to the next.

"I want to get straight to the point," Bianca said, folding her small hands together.

Bradley looked weary, confused. He took off his glasses and cleaned them. "Sure, sure," he said, "Go ahead, Bianca."

"Fernando and I were having an affair," she said. "There were never any allergies. I am actually not allergic to anything. I can eat whatever."

"Oh," Bradley said.

"And when his wife found out, he told me that I had to leave the site because his career could be jeopardized," Bianca said, realizing how stupid she sounded. How much backbone she did not have. "So I'm here to report him. And to take accountability. We were both consenting adults," Bianca said with a sigh, "so I'm also reporting myself."

"Bianca," he said, "It's interesting to hear that."

Interesting? That was the last thing she wanted; to be the subject of gossip.

"I bring this up because he was seen outside the country in March, when he should've been in Guatemala. I think he's leading the site into shambles because he's addicted to sex. He's irresponsible and cannot be trusted. So, if you'll have me . . ." Bianca really thought that showing accountability would make her seem more trustworthy. "I'd like to come back on board."

Bradley took a sip of water. The color was leaving his face. "Please let me know of any steps I can take moving forward." It felt good to confess, to let the years of affair off her chest. She was ready to repent. To make things right.

"Bianca," he said, looking down at his hands, dry and cracked with age. "Has no one told you?" Told her what? That Fernando won some kind of award? Had risen all the way above her on the back of all her hard work?

She shook her head. "Nobody's told me a single thing, actually. For months."

"Fernando died on March twenty-first."

The world ended. The world began again. Creatures rose from the water and grew legs. Wars. Famine. The world ended again. Cracking open forever and enveloping itself in its vitellus.

"What?'"

"I'm so sorry," Bradley said. "He died in a small avalanche. They don't know what happened. It went under the seismologist's radar. Completely random. Pretty sure it made the news." He went onto his computer, putting on his glasses and squinting. He muttered under his breath and narrated as he typed. "Fernando Moreno earthquake." He pursed his mouth and cocked his head. "No . . . NYU . . . professor." He continued to type. "Tragic death. . . . Guatemala. . . . Earthquake." He pressed the backspace. "Earthquake . . . Guatemala . . . news . . . professor . . . dead."

"You can stop," Bianca said. "Please." He sat back in his chair.

"I guess nobody picked it up." He took off his glasses. "But there's been a lot going on, so. It is a tragedy, for sure. And . . . the project's been disbanded for months. It's just too dangerous in those caves. I'm sorry, I thought you knew. I thought somebody told you. Surely someone must have reached out?"

"No," Bianca said, her chest tightening. The love seat was an entire green continent, filled with nobody but her. "Nobody said anything."

"Well. I'm so sorry about that, Bianca." Bradley's head moved up and down like a Zoltar machine that had expelled an unhelpful-but-sinister future to its customer and was about to ask for another coin.

"Oh!" Bradley the Zoltar Machine said, "As for that first thing you told me about?"

"Our affair."

"Right. I would just keep that to yourself for now. It . . . well, it doesn't look good for the university."

She was making weird *glub glub* sounds. A fish on cement. A monster melting into water of bucket that was thrown on her. She stood up, hearing her knees crack, nodded at Bradley, and left.

"Sorry for your loss!" Bradley called out pathetically.

The attendant wearing fake red horns over his beanie wasn't startled by Bianca, who slapped a fake cobweb that was hanging over the counter away. There were Halloween decorations everywhere. Monsteras were half off because of the name.

"Where's Julian?" she demanded.

"Welcome to Crest Hardware," he said, almost sarcastically. "Can I 'help' you?"

"Show me to Julian."

"Are you family or a friend or?"

"Family," Bianca said, lying, in case the plant store had some strict rule, like a hospital. He showed her to the back of the plant store, where Julian was in a green oasis wearing a vampire cape, next to a giant parrot that kept chirping up iPhone sounds. He lit up when he saw her.

"Bianca! Hey, what's up? Are you looking for anything in particular? By the way, anything you want is on the house. Except for this guy." The parrot squawked a car-alarm sound.

"You said you saw Candy with Fernando." Bianca said, almost an accusation. Julian scratched his head.

"Pretty sure. I mean, I know it was your sister. No idea who that other guy was." Julian's eyes grew wider. "Oh, no, is Candy okay? Listen, I can't be a witness to anything because I'm on a lot of watch lists—"

"When did you see them together?"

"I dunno, like . . . end of March, I guess? I was doing a small tour and one of our stops was at the Sinclair so I was just walking around. Then I ran into her and this dude."

"When *exactly* was your Sinclair stop?"

"Uh, I have to look it up."

"THEN LOOK IT UP!"

A few customers turned their heads. Julian looked genuinely afraid of Bianca and took out his Android.

"Not technically supposed to be on my phone right now."

Bianca glared at him.

"I don't put anything in my calendar because then the state has access to everything that I'm doing."

Bianca slammed her hands on the table. "I NEED YOU TO FIND OUT NOW!"

"Fuck, okay! My band has an Instagram, I think there was a flyer?" But then he had to redownload Instagram. And then he had to reset his password. And then his phone died.

"Uh, sorry," Julian said, clearly panicked. He asked a customer pushing a stroller if he could use her phone. She eyed him but handed him the phone, shaking her head about this generation.

"We're almost there, hold on. All right. Yeah. We played on March twenty-second. See? Right here. Sinclair. Cambridge, Massachusetts." Julian seemed pleased with himself, though he was beginning to understand that he was confirming something Bianca didn't want to hear.

"Look up Fernando Moreno, archaeologist, PhD."

"All those words in a row?" The picture loaded and there was Fernando's face, handsome and recently shaved. Bianca remembered this photo. She had taken it.

"Is that what he looked like?" Julian peered at the photo.

"Yo, yes! That's him." Bianca placed the tips of her fingers at the bottom of her eyes and pulled. She was a boogeyman. She was a great big scream.

"Is that bad?"

The customer was still waiting for her phone back.

"If I fucked up somehow, I want to know."

"It doesn't make any sense!"

Julian handed the phone back to the customer with a stroller and thanked her. She rolled away with her baby, muttering something about why this is why she didn't come to Williamsburg.

"Can you fill me in here, Bianca? What's going on?" Julian said, the parrot quacking back. "What's going on?" Bianca was frozen with anxiety. She felt herself floating above herself. She needed to swim back. Julian cupped his hand over her wrist and led her over to a slew of outdoor patio furniture.

"I was working on an excavation with him in Guatemala and then I had to come back," Bianca said, avoiding his gaze. "Anyway, he couldn't have been there that day, because he *died* that day in Guatemala."

Julian gave her a look. They were shrouded by plants but he could still see the top of the head of the woman with her stroller. He took Bianca's wrist again and led her to another corner, a more discreet one stocked with shovels. He whispered to her.

"Okay, you can be honest now. What's really going on?" he asked, both of his hands on her shoulders, which Bianca shook off.

"Nothing. Why are you being dramatic?"

"I'm not," Julian whispered again.

"You don't need to whisper. We aren't in a play."

"Sorry," Julian said, still in a low voice. He was slightly embarrassed but still sticking to his guns. "Just trying to be careful. What were you doing in Guatemala?"

"I was trying to uncover the bones of this revolutionary group. I wasn't, like, on vacation." She wanted to remind him that she was making something of herself, that she was earning her *PhD*. Julian looked at her funny and then stepped back.

"Bianca. Stop recording this."

"How did you—"

"You have your hand in your pocket and I see a little light."

"Why do you care if I'm recording this?" Bianca sounded like she had just been caught holding a gun.

"Let me see that." Julian held out his hand, and what was Bianca to do? She had been found out. She handed her phone over.

"Do you upload it anywhere?" Julian asked. "Somewhere that's encrypted?"

"Just the cloud."

Julian gasped. He really was so dramatic.

"Bianca, everything you do on your phone can be traced by the government. Everything. It can be subpoenaed in court. It can be used as evidence against you."

Bianca was silent. *Or,* she thought, *or it can be for the archaeologist of the future to use in their studies and for me specifically so that I feel like I can never forget anything again.*

". . . And if your sister was the last person to see Fernando alive, and you were doing something questionable the government didn't want you to see . . ."

Bianca switched off her phone. He had a point, maybe.

"It wasn't questionable. Everything was totally normal."

Julian ran his fingers through his hair. "Why don't we meet later? We can go over everything together. I want to help."

She got a look at him in his black cape: his stockiness and his broad shoulders moving them out so that he was in the shape of a short spooky triangle. Was he really trying to help her?

"We're all supposed to dress up," Julian said, self-consciously, moving the cape to the side as if it were long hair. "It's supposed to help sell plants, I guess."

"No," Bianca said, "I'm fine."

What she really should do, she thought, was call her sister and ask her what was going on. But she was embarrassed at how she had reacted, how willing she was to put a man over her family. She walked past the front desk, where the man with horns thanked her for visiting. She walked down Union, in a daze, past the Walgreens and down Broadway, trying not to think about the lead from the J train invisibly raining down on her. She stopped for a slice of pepperoni pizza. At a certain point, in the right kind of weather, with not enough food in her stomach, she knew she would have killed for him. She hated that. And now he was dead. And she was a little girl again, holding open a notebook with nothing written inside of it, only flat blue lines cutting across the white pages.

You step over the bodies that have collapsed as your daughter leads you outside. There is a slight chill in the air.

The dead could still wake up at any moment. You don't know what has quieted them, or if they will rise again. For now, they've stopped, and people behind you are cleaning their wounds and screaming for help. But you don't have time to help. You must keep going. You limp down the street with your daughter's arm around you, your cane moving both of you forward.

"Your knee?" Bad, but it could be worse. Honestly, you're probably fine.

"¡Me esta matando! Mire, hija, temenos que ir a—"

"You should've worn a hat. Always con estas putas bufandas." She motions to the one you have wrapped around your neck. You do not answer. There's nothing wrong with your scarf! It's keeping you warm! You look like an old actress. Not too old, though! Outside, some Christmas lights are still blinking, but if things keep going this way, that won't be for long.

"What is happening?" Lucia says under her breath, and you could tell her what you know, but what you know is starting to change. You were not expecting people who eat people. You were not expecting more shaking, and those people collapsing. Still, maybe you should tell what you know. But what if she leaves you? What if she gets so upset and then you're all alone again, at the end of the world?

"People are crazy!" you say, shrugging, and your daughter rolls her eyes.

"Where are you going?" a young girl who worked at Flour asks, blood splattered on her apron. You and Lucia look to each other.

"You knew how to kill them," one of them says, one of the doctors who helped with the tables. "We all saw you. You were fantastic." You think you were just angry. You were just trying to survive. But you don't understand what they're saying, anyway.

But I want you to know that. They all thought you were fantastic.

"Do you know what's going on?" he says, and luckily, you can say, "No English." You and Lucia turn. She yells something at them and they all look like they are saying sorry.

"¿Que dicen?" you whisper to your daughter. "Just let them follow us," you say. "We need protection. It couldn't hurt." You hope she's still mad at you for earlier and that it can last until you can tell her what's going on and what happened with Mauricio, because, luckily, she still hasn't asked.

The land has shifted in the last hour. It is Boston but it is not Boston. The smell of burnt flesh is in the air. This isn't an ordinary earthquake. And you've seen a few. No, something is alive. You can feel it in your blood. This feeling that nowhere is really safe. Lucia yells something at the group and a young person offers you water.

"Gracias, mijo," you say, taking a swig. They are all looking at you for direction. Finally, you think, some respect. Lucia starts to slow you down and you realize she is taking you to her car. Her car is small, but you could fit a few more people in the back.

"Mamá," she whispers in Spanish, "I can't bring anybody with us." You look to her. Why not?

"We do not know who will turn into whatever that was, we cannot risk it. We have to act fast." You nod. You are proud of her. This is what you have given her: this ruthlessness. Some of that is inside of you. She says something to the young one, the one who gave you the water. You always have to guess at what's going on, but you can tell what she is going to do. She rummages for something in her pocket. The car is feet away from you. She nods slightly, just so slightly, a motion you can see only because she is your daughter, because you know her face and her wants and fears, all of that culminating in the slightest nod that makes you bolt for the handle as she clicks the car open and you leap inside, slamming the door shut.

"¡Eso, mamá!" she shrieks, she's laughing, you like to see her happy, there have been so few moments since Hector died and Paola disappeared, when her face breaks open like an egg full of healthy yolk and she laughs her full-belly laugh, the laugh of a woman in pain, one of the most beautiful laughs because it means they know how truly funny things are because of how bad everything else is, and that is the laugh you hear come out of her just now, as she turns on the car and hits the breaks as the people following you hit the back of the car and window with their fists, but you can't look back, you just have to keep going, even though, truthfully, and perhaps you will find this out soon, you could have used the help, and truthfully, nobody had been bitten, they really were safe, but sometimes, when things seem dangerous, it is because you are remembering danger, and driving faster and faster away from your memories. But anyway, seems like you two are having fun.

"Faster!" you tell Lucia, clapping your hands because that end-of-the-world-and-I-don't-know-if-I'm-going-to-live-or-die adrenaline is running through your veins. "You must go faster!" You're zooming down Mass Ave and you're so happy that you got away, the bodies in the distance, merely figures now, something that happened a little bit ago, and now, now! Now!

"Now we can go to the Old Country Buffet."

"What? Why?"

"Because I need something there." You look at the fuel gauge. Oh no.

"It's flashing red." You point at it.

"Mamá, me haces un gran favor y te callas con esas babosadas." So, seems like she also knows it's flashing red. You both know that once it stops flashing at all, you're in real trouble.

It is starting to snow so hard. It's like the sky has opened up. There are still people around, struggling, trying to move through the snow, but toward what, you don't know. You're approaching the Charles River when it happens, the car sputters and comes to a halt in the middle of the road, where other cars have stalled. That didn't take much time.

"That's why it's always important to fill your tank up with gas," you say, folding your hands.

"You don't even know how to drive!" she says, and you know that you've gotten to her.

"Well, you better figure out something soon, because we need to get to the Old Country Buffet. It's important." She ignores you. The snow is all around you, all you can see is white. You glance out the window and you see a face, large and green with yellow eyes, and a mouth growing larger and larger, but then it is gone.

What was that, Candelaria?

Did it scare you?

Be honest.

"We have to keep going!" you say to her, trying to shove the face out of your mind.

"I am *trying*," she snaps at you, slamming the wheel with her open palm.

"Relax!" you say to her, but that makes her even more angry. You open your purse and hand her a tortilla.

"I DON'T WANT A TORTILLA RIGHT NOW!"

Okay then! you think. *Sorry for asking! Always so angry.*

One night in 2002, she called you, her voice clouded and weak over the phone, a strong tea left overnight in water and made bitter with time. Her husband, Hector, who you had only met on the phone, had collapsed on the side of the road during a run. He had shown no signs of stress but had suffered a sudden heart attack. Now she had nobody to help with the girls. There was contempt in her voice that was overshadowed by a pleading and a helplessness, and while that was what won you over, you were always going to go. Your own mother, despite her faults, which included selling you to your first husband, was still your mother, still the person who brought you into this world. You wouldn't exist without her, after all.

The security measures were out of control. The towers had just fallen and customs berated you with questions, you, a woman of sixty-five years holding a bag full of Pollo Campero. The three granddaughters greeted you at the gate, all of them excited to finally meet their abuela, while Lucia gave you a sullen nod. You were surprised at the girls' Spanish, a mangled net of Colombian twang, Guatemalan-isms and English words. You were disappointed at how free they all seemed, with American hobbies and fascinations. None of them ever made their bed. Lucia hadn't really cooked for them at all. She had no time, with the business downstairs and all of this and that, you never really understood what there was to be so busy about. They were on a diet of chicken nuggets and frozen tacos, cereal, and yogurt. Factory things. Forgetful things.

But you changed that for the girls. Lucia took you to the market and you gathered all the ingredients that were missing. You made them elaborate omelets in the morning with cilantro and jalapeños, your soft homemade tortillas with refried black beans and queso fresco you had rolled out by hand the night before for lunch and pepían de pollo for dinner. Those girls have never eaten so well, adapting to the spice intake you had enforced on them with all those jalapeños. It was good for them, you thought, as tears rolled down their faces after they bit into a tortilla chip they had scooped into one of your sauces. It made disease run away from their noses and out of their lungs. Cleared everything up. Kept them healthy. Safe.

Lucia opens the car door, and you worry slightly that she is about to leave you out there, but she comes around and opens the door for you and helps you out with her hand. You are at the bank of the river, which is frozen. You can't believe that just this morning you were going to the beach to feed bread to the seagulls on the sand with Mauricio, who was now dead on the floor, probably about to eat somebody or be eaten. It's just too cold for that.

"Where is Mauricio?" she says. There it is. She was just waiting to ask.

"He didn't make it," you say, folding your gnarled knuckles in front of you so that you are holding your stomach.

"Are you lying to me?" Now, how did she know that?

"No, no. Nunca. Se murió," you say, narrowing your eyes and shaking your chin into a sob, and looking up to the sky, but she knows this move.

"Enough. You left him behind, didn't you?" Well, at least she gave you an out. You say nothing. You neither confirm nor deny.

"Of course you did." She shakes her head, and while her silence hurts you are glad that is all. You try to change the subject.

"Where are the girls?" She shakes her head. You can see that she is crying. Oh, Lucia. She had arrived on the hottest day of the summer, and you were in the house you had moved into, the house that your husband swore he would fix up when he came back from his trips but never did. The walls were made of wood and let in a draft during the night. The stove was a hole in the floor, but you were used to that. You weren't ever fancy, but you always had class. You were in your late twenties and your body was still spry. You weren't ever worried about putting on weight because you were always dashing back and forth. There was always somewhere to go. Giving birth to Lucia wasn't glorious. It was a task you needed to get to the end of. Painful and familiar. Your mother helped you. Held your arms as you crouched down and screamed. Your nose is cold. Your hands, too.

"At least we are together," you say, touching her shoulder. She shakes you away.

"We need to find the girls." But the Old Country Buffet . . . Maybe there still is time. Maybe you can have the best of both worlds. You sniff the air. Snow is falling and falling all around you. A white Christmas. Your granddaughters have always felt romantic about the snow, standing outside with their tongues out and wriggling their bodies on the dirty ground. They would push over each other to get outside and have to be yelled at to shovel. You always felt like it was a sign that illness was near, that the colder your face felt, the more likely you were to be sick for Christmas. Watching the flakes come down and fall on dead Christmas lights, you worry about the girls and their American wits. Maybe you do need to find them.

"There's something I need to tell you," Lucia says, looking into the river. Hopefully, we'll be even here—in the secrets department.

"¿Si, hija?"

"Paola is alive."

"I knew that. I told you that!" You purse your lips. You had. You had! Many times. She was the one who insisted with the funeral. All of that weirdness. The dress in the coffin that didn't even fit her, poor girl. You didn't understand what was wrong with her. You told her many times that she should just get up and go for a walk, but she always took it the wrong way. And then, all of a sudden, she had left with that ugly man and Lucia didn't care enough to chase her.

"Don't start with me." The snow falls down a little harder. You wrap your scarf around your head a little tighter and fish around in your pockets for gloves.

"No," she says, winter in her voice, "the police said . . ."

You decide to double down, slipping on the red gloves you had purchased at CVS with Mauricio's social security.

"You heard what you wanted to hear, Lucia. You didn't even try to look for her."

"You didn't even try to look for *me*." Her eyes are wild, she looks like she could bite off your head. You stare at her back, fumbling with your scarf, and then you look away, pretending that you just didn't hear her, or entering a realm of the universe where she never said that. Remarkable the way you can do this. Peel away time and feed it into the garbage disposal. *Anyway. Moving on. What lovely weather we're having.* Speaking of—the snow around your ankles grows.

"So, what are we going to do?" you ask. "Because the Old Country Buffet is that way." You point east.

"Do whatever you want, Mamá." Lucia turns from you and walks back to her car, where she retrieves her shovel and her own bag of things, "I'm looking for my daughters." She walks away from you and the snow falls and falls, and you let her get a few yards ahead of you before you follow.

"¡Espérame!" you say. You hobble to her, your bloody cane making red markings in the snow. She turns and waits, and lucky for you, in the distance, into Cambridge, there are army tents, and about two miles behind you, sniffing the air and salivating, are the people you stepped over who have risen again, as something different, biting into those poor souls you left behind.

CANDY

"Having a barbecue?" the woman at the register said as she eyed the ten packages of raw steak Candy brought up. Candy took out her card and jammed it into the reader.

"You're really fucking nosy," Candy said, piling the meat together, the packets of flesh squelching against each other in a little meat tower, and refusing to put them in a bag because it was bad for the environment. "Has anyone ever told you that?"

"We have a sale on barbecue sauce—"

"I don't care."

Surprisingly, Candy had never had a pregnancy scare before. She had always believed she was infertile because she had been so irresponsible in the past with no consequence. She thought condoms felt like plastic rods inside of her and she popped Plan Bs like Tic Tacs. That sticky feeling of jizz on her stomach was just part of the experience! Plus, she exercised a lot. Additionally, she was hairy, so didn't that mean she had PCOS? In conclusion, her grandmother had diabetes and her blood sugar was probably just super low.

Balancing all the raw steaks in her arms, she walked out of the Whole Foods to the CVS and purchased three pregnancy tests and Vitamin Water. She had blown half of her paycheck already on this bullshit.

In her living room, she paced up and down, making the floor shake below her, as she waited for the results. She sat down on her IKEA futon and stared blankly at the TV screen on her black childhood trunk from Target. She was thinking about how she always meant to decorate her place more, really make it hers, when the voice began again and the TV turned on.

There is a porch in the southwest.
You sip lemonade and are wearing a yellow dress with a pair of
white Keds.

Lovely out. Morning.

You grab your belly and smile.

Looks like a storm is comin'!

Your belly grows bigger.

Your face, grayer.

You collapse.

The baby bursts from your belly like a bug.

The skin on your stomach peels like an orange.

You expire. Goodbye.

The baby crawls out with a piece of cake in its hand.

The alarm ringing woke Candy up. She tore open the packaging of the steak and bit into it like a slice of pizza.

If she had a girl, she would have to keep her safe from the dangers of the world: white vans and eating disorders and sexual predators. And if she had a boy, well, what if he became an active shooter? Or a DJ? And of course, either way her body would explode. Disgusting. She picked up the stick, sucking the meat juices off her other finger.

"Fuck my life."

She was putting together that her symptoms only happened around screens, and that they were saying something about her fears around being a mother. It must have been psychological. But then what about her new cravings? Her mom used to tell her that she craved jars of olives when she was pregnant with her. Pretty similar, right?

She was just pregnant, that was all. Whatever. No big deal. And being pregnant was a nightmare that was normalized to keep women as second-class citizens. So obviously, she was going to take care of it.

Candy paced. How much was an abortion in Massachusetts with insurance, anyway? She was still on her mother's Blue Cross Blue Shield plan until next year, even though her job offered her health insurance. Her mother insisted that Candy use hers until she couldn't, always inventing some (statistically probable) circumstance where Candy had to go to the ER or get her stomach pumped. They could cover her, but then it would appear on her mother's monthly bill and actually, she would rather throw herself in front of the 57 bus instead of having that conversation.

But then how the hell was she supposed to pay for it?

Candy checked her bank account. Enough for rent, but barely. Fucking hell. She heard small, desperate scratches coming from outside. She opened the door and there was that cat again, sitting stoically with her tail flicking. "I'm going," Candy said, kneeling so that she was eye-to-eye with the cat, "to KILL MYSELF!" The cat meowed in response. Candy slammed the door on the cat's emotionless face. She tossed everything around in her room. All her things crashed to the floor. Her sportswear and eyeliners, scattered. The lamp on the floor came unplugged from the wall. There was still one person she could talk to, Candy realized, taking another bite out of the raw steak; maybe someone who felt she owed her something.

ZOE

"What's up, bitch." Candy's mouth was a raw, flaky wound. She looked extraordinarily pale. Zoe had watched her stomp into the studio wearing giant sunglasses and remembered that nothing is urgent in this life. That we don't have to do anything but die as we choose who we let into our lives. "What time do you get out of work?

"Three."

"Wanna get coffee or something?" A bloody fingernail tapped on the counter.

"I don't consume caffeine." Her sister's hands were twitching. She had bitten each nail down to the bone, hangnails like plastic peeling away from her grayish sausage-link fingers.

"Please," she said, and she saw how painful it was for Candy to ask her this. To beg. "I need you." And all her training, all her reasoning about family and choosing, melted away. Maybe because she loved her sister. Maybe because she loved being wanted.

"Okay," Zoe said, lowering her voice. "Cornucopia down the street?"

"Sick," her sister said. "See you there." She slammed the glass door behind her, though it was designed to shut softly and soundlessly. Maria opened another, her essential-oil smell wafting in.

"Who was that?" she asked, one hand on Zoe's shoulder.

"A client," she said.

"I'm proud of you for how many people you've already brought to us," Maria said. Zoe beamed. Since she started working here, she had acquired a small following. There was a waitlist for her class now. Maria was planning something "exciting" that she had yet to tell her about because it was entering its final stages, but she had told Zoe that she had an important part in it.

"Thank you, Maria. I'll try my best." Maria squeezed Zoe's shoulders and left. When her shift ended, Zoe packed up her things and walked to Cornucopia. She was starting to get used to Boston again, or at least its bougier outer edges. Naperville, Illinois, had been something of a desolate Republican land, not that she cared much about politics. She and Jared only went into Chicago a handful of times, but otherwise he would complain about the stinkiness of the city, the crime, the Mexicans. "Don't look at me like that," he would say, when Zoe tilted her head, her mouth slightly open, like a cat who had just smelled another cat on the lint of a sock. "I'm not talking about you." If she were ever able to have a child, she wondered what they would look like, if Jared would hate them or make some kind of exception, the way he did for her. She wondered, briefly, if he had felt any pain in his final moments. Then she shook the thought away, a cobweb she had accidentally walked through. She left everything up to Maria and the Mother. Opening the door to the coffee shop, she saw her sister sitting at the back, shaking her leg up and down, a childhood habit she had never seemed to get rid of.

"Hey," Candy said, a giant cup of coffee in her hand. "I know you said you don't drink coffee. Do you want this croissant?"

Zoe shook her head. "I stay away from gluten," she said, taking a seat in an unfriendly metallic chair. The two sisters sat uncomfortably with each other.

"So . . . how is work?" Candy raised her eyebrows underneath her sunglasses. Her skin was dry, too, the look of leftover flour on a board after dough had been rolled on it.

"Rewarding," Zoe said, her back straight.

"Cool. Do you make okay money?" Candy scratched at her neck and bit a piece of skin off her lip.

"Are you looking for a job?"

"I'm just wondering if you're, like, financially okay." Zoe eyed her sister as she began tearing into the croissant, the flakes flying everywhere.

"Do you need help?" Zoe was waiting for her to just ask for it, to finally be of use in whatever way. She took her hand away from the other's grip and began swirling the QR code housed in hard plastic.

"I'm pregnant," Candy said, as if she were calling in late to work or letting a roommate know that there was no more toilet paper.

"I see." Zoe felt something she thought she had long banished away: jealousy, propelling itself out of the pit of her stomach. "Do you have health insurance?"

"I'm on mom's still," Candy said, munching on her lip.

"Can you ask her for help?"

"I don't want her to see the claim. That bitch is so Catholic."

"I'm glad we're finally talking about this. She's an abusive narcissist." Maria had helped her unearth so much about her childhood. But it was against the ethos of the Woman's Stone to gossip. Plus, Candy would never understand what it was like to be the oldest of a young immigrant mother, the way faults and expectations projected onto her felt like wearing many linen dresses in the heat, all at once, and none of them ever fit her.

"Okay, *Catholic* does not mean *terrorist*. She's just traumatized. Sometimes she tells us shit and it's like, okay, of course you're kind of cooked."

Zoe didn't want to talk about it. Jared was so awful to her about her eating, but every toxic thought she had before him she could attribute to what Maria had called her mother's emotional incest. But she was over it now. She had not forgiven, she had not forgotten, she had simply accepted that this was who her mother was.

"And what about Bianca?"

"We're kind of in a weird fight right now. And she's broke, anyway." The coffee table moved as if a malevolent spirit were being called forth, but it was just her sister's knee shaking it.

"You two were always so close," Zoe said, trying to sound as neutral as possible.

"Bianca saved my life and you what? Made us all believe you were dead? Of course we're going to be close. Are you kidding me?"

Zoe stiffened. The QR code stand was still doing small back flips with the help of her hand. She stopped, thinking of how close it was to not having composure.

"I ran away with a man. For love. But then he hurt me. And Maria helped me. I owe everything to her." That's all she needed to say.

"Dang."

"Would you consider keeping it?"

"You think I want to host a shitty little parasite to grow up in this shitty little world with all of our shitty little generational trauma?"

"What if I had a child one day? Would you call them that?"

"Would I have the privilege of meeting it?"

"Maybe. It depends."

"Would you bring it with you to your weird yoga-studio cult? Would it be in the back doing sound therapy?"

"So what's your plan?" Zoe asked, ignoring her.

Candy sat up now and folded her dry fingers and bleeding cuticles together, as if she were about to present Zoe with a business proposition. "I'm getting an abortion."

"When?"

"Tomorrow. I need you to drive me to it. And, like, take care of me maybe."

"Why tomorrow?"

"Because it's, like, the last day they can do a last-minute abortion. It's the one where they suck it out with a vacuum. I need to get hoovered."

"Candy, please."

"So can you drive me?"

Zoe took a deep breath. This wasn't breaking the rules, and were there any rules in Maria Santiago's world? She always said she could come and go whenever she wanted. And maybe one day Candy would want to join the family at the Woman's Stone. Yes, maybe she could recruit her. This could all be so good.

"I can."

"And can you give me eight hundred dollars? Cause I can't pay for it."

"Who did this to you?"

"Did this to me? Pao, there is no *rapist* involved. Jesus."

"It's Zoe."

"Oh, God. It was just this one-night stand kind of thing. I don't remember who he was. Whatever, he doesn't matter." Candy was practically vibrating, shaking her leg up and down. Zoe had access to funds from the center, only to be used in emergencies. She could just ask Maria. She would understand.

"Okay." Zoe looked up at her sister, who was so filled with relief that she bent over the table and hugged her. Zoe was startled but let herself give in to this: a simple embrace from somebody who used to know her.

Zoe picked Candy up from her apartment on a normal Tuesday morning. Candy was wearing those same large sunglasses again, the ones that practically covered up her entire face.

"Hi," she said, putting her sneakers up on the dashboard.

"Please take your feet off." Something had crawled between them, a spider that had made its way out of the bathroom sink drain while nobody was home and realized that it was safe. Zoe started the car and they made their way through Jamaica Plain.

"Do you have an aux cord?" Candy asked, tapping her gnawed finger nervously on the car door handle.

"No."

"Okay, can we listen to something? I don't care what it is. I feel anxious with all this silence." Zoe pressed in a cassette.

Have you realized your greatest strength is being grateful? Have you asked the Mother for forgiveness and grace?

"What the *fuck* is this?"

"It's Maria Santiago's tapes."

"I can't listen to this, I'm sorry."

"Fine." *Patience and gratitude*, Zoe thought, *peace and light.* Candy turned on the radio and began flipping through channels. Magic 106.7. Kiss 108. She flipped frantically, in a way that would make anyone want to jump out the car. She landed on a Spanish radio station where some old-school bachata blasted.

"Aw, Dad used to love this song, let's go!" She turned the volume all the way up, grinding her ass into the passenger's seat. This made Zoe turn off the radio.

"What the fuck?"

"I don't want to listen to that."

"Okay, Miss Republicana."

"What?'"

"Are you an anti-vaxxer, too, or something?"

"I don't do politics."

"Well, what *do* you do? You're in some kind of weird spinning cult, you're calling yourself Zoe, what the fuck is going on?" Zoe felt her sister's penetrative stare through her sunglasses.

"I'm allowed to start over." Zoe looked ahead, her eyes almost glossy. "Your mom wanted me to be something that I'm not. And I can choose to be whoever I want to be." Her sister shifted in her seat and crossed her arms. She rolled down the window and then opened it again.

"Look at these assholes," Candy said, pointing with her chin to a group of children holding a rope passing by them at a stoplight.

BIANCA

LUCIA_CASTILLO1: Good afternoon, Julian.

REDJUMPSUITAPPARATUS1993: Good afternoon, Ms. Castillo. Is everything okay?

LUCIA_CASTILLO1: This isn't Lucia. This is Bianca, her daughter. I'm using her AIM.

REDJUMPSUITAPPARATUS1993: ??

LUCIA_CASTILLO1: I find internet culture devalues the way we digest information and shortens our cerebral lifespans.

REDJUMPSUITAPPARATUS1993: k

LUCIA_CASTILLO1: Question.

REDJUMPSUITAPPARATUS1993: whattup

LUCIA_CASTILLO1: I would like to lose my virginity to you. We don't have to date one another and you don't even have to talk to me about it later. I just ask that we're safe and you kiss me on the forehead once. I guess this isn't really a question and more so, a proposition.

REDJUMPSUITAPPARATUS1993: 4 real?

LUCIA_CASTILLO1: I don't want to assume anything about you but given our age you are most likely also a virgin. This way you'll no longer be a virgin and you'll have more experience for someone you really like.

REDJUMPSUITAPPARATUS1993: u seem to have this all planned out haha. I mean y not? I guess as long as we promise not to tell anybody

Bianca put back the printed-out AIM convo between her and Julian into her manila folder labeled TEENAGE ACCOMPLISHMENTS, which also held certificates for various camps and scholarship awards for college.

Everybody had already thought they were related because they were the only other Guatemalans in the school. Though they didn't look anything alike. Julian was a boy of Indigenous Mayan heritage adopted by white academic lesbians who decided to befriend Bianca's parents when she was in elementary school so that he could feel less alone. He hadn't grown past five foot five by junior year of high school and never would. While Bianca was paler, there was something undoubtedly foreign about her; maybe it was in her slight mustache or sideburns, or something in the shape of her eyes, or the smell emanating from her lunch box. Whatever it was, Julian didn't want to be associated with it as they grew older, often ignoring her in the hallway and instead paying attention to Candy, who had just entered high school and wore her Latinidad, or whatever it was, the way it was meant to be worn: like she had peeled it off a magazine sample and found a way to dab it on and off forever.

Bianca told her mother that she was doing work with science club and that she would be dropped off by Julian, who she knew her mother trusted. If only she knew that Julian was the high school drug dealer, a fact that Bianca put together with her expert sense of investigation (she saw him handing a bag of something to a theater kid, and when nobody was around and she asked what he was doing, he said, "Dealing drugs"). The deed took place in the back of one of his mother's minivans on Cabot Field. Bianca recorded all of it.

Bianca sighed as she listened to the recording in her headphones. Something about the vulnerability of their teen bodies clashing together had made Julian defensive and self-conscious, but maybe Bianca was just being mean.

CABOT FIELD, NOVEMBER 11TH, 2006

BIANCA: Our legs are kind of the same length.

JULIAN: Are you calling me short?

BIANCA: Well, I'm short. So yeah.

JULIAN: That's so racist against Guatemalan people.

BIANCA: I'm Guatemalan.

JULIAN: But you're not *really*. Not the way I'm Guatemalan.

If she did think about it, this tiny, stupid moment was when she began spiraling about her identity. She'd gone to bed and tried to list all the ways that she was Guatemalan, panicking when she realized exactly how American she was. Her grandmother would always call Julian "el indito," lovingly, but looking back, she started realizing how fucked up that was. Or was it? Was her grandmother just saying what he was, in relation to what her family was not? Was it honest? But exactly how far back did her family go in Guatemala? That was the other thing about the caves. She wanted to prove that she wasn't all colonizer. That her uncle was doing something good.

The day after, of course, Candy overdosed, and who called Bianca to let her know but Julian? If she had died, Julian would have been in jail. Bianca would have made sure of it. But Candy, to the doctors' shock, woke up somehow with full brain capacity. So Bianca felt perfectly okay with telling Julian never to speak to her or her family again. And perfectly okay with withdrawing from social circles, focusing on her studies and Guatemala, and doing whatever it took to become who she was today. And she rose up. Bianca rose and rose and rose, becoming a prime PhD candidate at NYU. And yes, maybe the entire time she was secretly trying to prove something to Julian; that if she knew enough about something, then she truly *was* that something.

A few minutes after their awkward first time, Julian suddenly had the gall to show her a love song that he had written not about her, but about Candy. Bianca had no opinions about the song. Bianca hated music. All she could think about was how art is only ever really about the person who makes it, not the person it's about. *That's not love*, Bianca thought, as her phone died, which was strange since she never left the house without charging it to one hundred percent.

. . . .

"Good afternoon," she said to the barista, who had a very wide smile and whose dark hair was cut in a mushroom-like style. She hated asking things of people. She was suddenly very aware of how stoic and mean she seemed all the time, how instead of sounding like a warm and kind person, she sounded like she just sucked up a helium balloon and was constipated.

"Hey, girl." The barista was so cheery, and when she spoke, she was still smiling.

"Do you have a phone charger?"

The barista held out her hand and plugged Bianca's phone in next to some beans. "You work next door?" she asked, smiling.

"Yeah."

"I've been thinking about getting my hair cut there."

Bianca looked at the barista's hair. "What were you thinking?"

"I don't know, I want to try something different."

Bianca nodded and slowly turned away, unsure how to exit the conversation. She sat back down. The barista kept smiling wide, her teeth like a piano.

Bianca still wasn't sure if she wanted Julian's help or not and wasn't sure if she could trust him. She decided to spend her lunch break thinking it over.

Bianca looked outside. Despite all the signs of autumn, it just wasn't cold. Bianca could see it very clearly: the slow deterioration of the earth, how it would happen so slowly that nobody would even notice or have enough time to get used to it. How it would get so hot that people would spend less and less time outside. How being outside would require a heavy face mask because of pollution and dust bowls. The city she lived in would eventually be underwater. And all of it thanks to the headless giant that was the corporations that ran the world, the ones that were also responsible for the plastic that wrapped the takeout she ordered for dinner, the phone she used, the glasses fixed on her nose.

She and Fernando would talk about it often: every which way the world was doomed because the people in power didn't know how to unplug themselves from the machine they believed ran it. They often spoke about why it was so good they were never going to have a child together. They never discussed it. It was a reason to keep putting on a condom or for Bianca to get back on birth control, even though it made her breast tissue stretch painfully against her skin and fed her intrusive thoughts. She didn't buy when people said that birth control was Big Pharma's problem. That was paranoia. That was hippie business. Bianca trusted doctors and science, though she immediately stopped taking her pills after Fernando broke up with her.

Still, sometimes she hoped for a small mistake she would have to contend with. She would feel fuzzy about the parasitic problem they would have to deal with together. But to Fernando and Bianca, it was selfish for people to bring children into the world. It was biological, socially acceptable narcissism. Now she was mourning a mistake that could never happen. Bludgeoned by a giant eraser. Dusted off into a palm and thrown into the trash.

Fernando would never see the world end, but Bianca might. And how lonely would that be? She might as well enjoy this day, she thought, and the way it didn't make her sweat or shake.

What time was it? Bianca needed to get back to work. She returned to the barista.

"Hey. Can I have my phone back?"

The barista looked at her for a few moments with a huge grin, as if what Bianca said came at her in a delay. "Yes," she said. "Have a good day."

Bianca felt uneasy. She really wasn't sure if she was smiling or if her face was just built like that. Had she said something weird? She would spend the next hours of her shift going over what she said to her and how she said it.

Well, Bianca thought, stepping into the warm air and checking her phone, *if the world is ending, what do I have to lose?* Maybe she didn't need to take it so seriously. Maybe there wasn't that much at stake. She texted Julian. **Hey**, she wrote, **this still you?**

Bianca opened the door and Julian held up the pack of Modelo he'd brought as a courtesy.

"What's up," he said, nodding and moving his lips around his teeth, his eyes darting around Bianca but never looking directly at her. She stood by the door, face blank. She looked Julian up and down.

"You didn't have to bring those."

"Oh. I'm sorry. You don't drink?"

"No, I do."

"So, is it okay that I brought them?"

"Yeah, I'm just saying you didn't *have* to." Julian was still holding the carton of Modelo up. She made him feel like a silly boy with a bag of candy, but she wasn't aware of that. The valleys of Bianca's intonations always plateaued into a cold, abrasive road that made you feel like you were somewhere you shouldn't be. It wasn't bitchiness. It seemed like Bianca was almost being nice: *You didn't have to bring that.* You didn't have to, but you did. Bianca moved aside so that he could come in.

Julian took a seat on a blue chaise lounge that Blue had been gifted from a sugar daddy and crossed his legs, a bare toe dancing freely in the hole of a sock, opening a Modelo with ease, like he'd been here before and would keep coming back.

"Can you put your foot away?"

"Okay, sorry." The beer sat between them, a dewy reminder of all that had happened. Blue came out and sat next to Julian, eyeing him.

"Hi," they said.

"Nice to meet you," Julian said, holding up his hand. Blue did not take it.

"You're the one who almost destroyed my toilet?"

"Julian is here to help me with the Fernando stuff."

Blue shook their head. "Are you sure you wanna go down that hole?"

"Yes, I'm sure." Bianca said, almost snapping. Julian was sitting stiffly, then interrupted the tension.

"Uh-oh, roommate fight!" Julian said, and then sipped a beer when nobody answered him.

"All right, let's think," he said, recovering from the awkward silence. "Why would Fernando be in Boston?"

"Because he's a creep," Blue said under their breath.

"That isn't helpful."

"What's your deal with this guy, anyway, Bianca?"

Bianca picked a nail and told Julian everything: the affair, the kicking her off her own site, the potentially him fucking her sister.

"So this guy honks."

"He doesn't *honk*. He just never had a chance to be sensitive or vulnerable. Everybody makes mistakes."

"Honks?" Bianca sat down in a red chair with gold trimmings that looked like a throne. Blue had found it on the street on the first of the month and had fallen in love with it.

"Yeah, you know. It blows. But it honks. Like a *womp womp* sound that's a person."

"This is kind of a big mistake," Blue said, reaching over to the table and cracking open a Modelo.

"Yeah, I mean"—Julian put one socked foot over the other, suddenly self-conscious—"I also don't believe in carceral solutions to dealing with abusers . . . but fuck this guy."

"He's not an abuser!" Bianca's voice was raised. "He just messed up, okay? And he's dead, so there's not that much more we can do about him anyway." Bianca's eyes welled up and she looked away. Julian and Blue looked at each other. Suddenly they had something in common: hating this man.

"Okay," Julian said. "Have you been in contact with the university at all?"

"Yeah, but they just told me not to tell anyone about this."

"Your recordings," Julian said, putting the Modelo down on the table. "When is the last time you spoke to Fernando?"

"When he broke up with me, I guess."

"Well," Julian said, sheepishly pursing his lips, "Do you want to listen to them?"

At that moment Blue stood up, wrapping their blue silk robe around them. "Listen," they said, "I need to speak honestly right now. Bianca, you can't keep coming back to this hole that this man put you in. It's just gonna lead to you being mean to yourself and not growing at all."

Julian took out his phone politely, so the roommates could talk.

"I'm an adult, Blue."

"All right," Blue said, turning around, their robe swishing. "Then I'm going to treat you like one."

"*Thank you.*"

Blue walked into the kitchen. Bianca took Julian over to her desk, where she pulled out her laptop and found a file labeled FERNANDO.

"We were about to interview this guy named Sylvester, whose dad was in the Tierra Nueva, but he was being weird."

"Wait, and what is the Tierra Nueva?"

"The political group in Guatemala? The group of artists who wanted to rebuild Guatemala through art and mutual aid? Pay attention."

"Sorry. That's kind of sick, though, if your uncle was doing that. Big props to him. I actually would love to start something like that here. I actually kind of have been, with grocery deliveries, installing free libraries across Bed-Stuy, that kind of thing."

Bianca ignored him. She was having trouble finding the file.

"Do you know if your block has a community fridge? I think you could easily hook it up through your window." Bianca was furiously clicking. She searched Fernando again and opened the file, and it was blank.

"No, no, no, no," Bianca said, pounding on her computer. She started it up again and searched the documents once more. They were still gone. She searched her other documents, the transcripts of all her recordings.

Everything was gone now. Every conversation she had recorded with Fernando, every win from the academy, the interactions at the bodega, everything. Her memories. Her entire life. They had disappeared.

CANDY

"I have to pee," Zoe said. Candy opened a bloated *People* magazine from 2016. They had just walked arm in arm into the Planned Parenthood in Allston, past a group of protesters who held signs that read things like *WHAT IF MARY DID WHAT YOU WERE GOING TO DO?* There were photos of fetuses in petri dishes, women holding their gray, lifeless babies.

"Okay, do you want permission or something?"

"No, I'm just letting you know."

"Go." Zoe got up and walked down the hallway of the clinic, looking behind her and then to her left, and her right, like she was scared or something. *Absolutely cooked*, Candy thought. She shook her leg up and down. When Zoe didn't come back for five minutes, Candy started to wonder if she actually had diarrhea. After fifteen minutes, she wondered if she had just left her.

Twenty long minutes passed by when Candy was called into the room by a nurse who had a small bump underneath her scrubs. The room was the same room where she had met with the abortion doctor a week ago.

"Isn't there, like, a surgery room?" Candy said, the paper from the bed crinkling underneath her.

"Yup," the nurse said pleasantly, washing her hands in the sink.

"Is it weird to work at an abortion clinic if you're pregnant?" Candy blurted out. The nurse turned off the faucet and spun around.

"No," she said. "It's a gift."

"Ehh," Candy said. She just wanted to get this over with. The nurse handed her a surgical gown.

"Do I need to take off my shoes or anything?" Candy asked. "My rings?" The nurse didn't respond, shuffling around the room, opening and closing cabinets until she took out a vial of something.

Candy was thinking about abortions of the past and how much harder or easier it was to excavate life. Was it even life? Or was it a bunch of cells smacked together? Kind of just an idea? *Does that make everybody just an idea?* Candy thought, looking up at the fluorescent light on the ceiling. *Am I just an idea?* There was a lot she wanted to do once this was over. Maybe she'd move. Maybe she and Bianca would stop fighting and she could move to New York and work at some pretentious Brooklyn theater. Did Bianca even know how good she had it in Brooklyn? Boston was so classless. Or maybe she could save enough money to go to Spain for a month. She loved Pedro Almodóvar. Maybe she'd do a *Todo Sobre Mi Madre* tour. The nurse handed Candy a surgical gown and a cap.

"How are you feeling?" the nurse asked, brushing a strand of hair away from Candy's forehead. It was very tender.

"Normal," Candy said, flinching away from her. "Like running an errand." The nurse smiled. Candy was expecting a *Have you done this before?* Like she was a waiter at an experimental fusion restaurant, but the nurse asked nothing. It was respectful. It was rudimentary. The nurse handed Candy a pill.

"What did you have to eat today?"

"Uh," Candy said. A raw steak out of the package, a fat sparrow sitting on her windowsill. "Oatmeal. Where's Dr. Linden? I kinda thought she would come in and give me a sentimental pep talk."

"She'll be in soon. Take your antibiotic." She handed Candy some water in a glass.

"*A glass!*" Candy said. "Fancy."

"There are too many BPAs in plastic," the nurse said. "Just to let you know." Candy popped in the antibiotic and swallowed it with the water.

"Put your feet in these stirrups."

Candy complied. She had painted her toenails for the occasion—was that insane? They were bright red. They stared back at her, bloodred many-eyed creatures blinking. After this, there would be no more weird symptoms.

No more raw steak five times a day. No more neighborhood birds. She wouldn't be in danger of hurting anybody. The nurse held out Candy's arm and tied a blue cord around it, but Candy was already feeling sleepy. When would the anesthesia come?

"Count down from ten, Candy."

Candy began. As she fell asleep, she began to dream. In the dream, the voice spoke to her.

It's dinnertime. Hungry, hungry, hungry.
There's a table set.
Your sisters all around.
Are you full? Is there room enough in you?
Your sisters grow and grow into large things, tall and stretchy.
They start to tickle you.
Stop! you say.
Stop!
Stop it!

Interlude

As a child, Gabriella Linden received her flu shots in the kitchen, from her mother, an ear, nose, and throat doctor, while her father, a renowned dermatologist, read the newspaper at the kitchen table. Her family did not expect her to become a doctor. They encouraged theater, reading, sports.

They had both class-jumped after finishing their residencies and hated the suffocative nature of their close-knit families, the way tradition was worshipped and intellect was frowned upon. Gabriella's parents were told enough by their family that they thought they were better than everybody else, and while it offended them, they started to internalize it. To them, Gabriella was a human they created for whom they needed to be responsible until she could be responsible for herself. Their duty as parents was to raise their daughter in a safe environment and give her the tools to be successful in the world. They had her later in life: her mother was forty-two, her father forty-five. When Gabriella turned eighteen, they sat her down and said that they wanted to transition from a parental relationship to a "relationship between adults." "So," Gabriella said, "you're my friends?"

Gabriella moved to study medicine at Boston University, three thousand miles away. Gabriella was absent in relationships, not knowing what to say when men complimented her, and often felt crowded as they spooned her. Two years into the program, Gabriella's dad was diagnosed with stage-three colon cancer. "There's treatment," her mother said over the phone. "He's hopeful. But we want you to be prepared." Gabriella bought a flight to Palo Alto as soon as she found out. Her father had just had surgery and completed his first round of chemo and was, surprisingly, feeling energetic. They walked a mile together and her father was extraordinarily sentimental. It was disturbing to her, how much he was caring for her, how much he wanted to hold on to her elbow, how he kept bringing up mundane moments from her childhood, how he even seemed childlike and full of joy. What kind of relationship between adults was this? As she was on the plane back to Boston, her father suffered a heart attack and died. At the funeral, her mother made a joke about traveling the world without him complaining all the time. And she did, sending Gabriella photos from Russia and Belize. Gabriella felt proud of her mom for being independent this late in life. A relationship between adults. Gabriella graduated with high honors, with only her mother at her ceremony, tanned from her travels and taking one blurry photo of her daughter on her phone. Gabriella was placed at Tufts for a gynecology residency. There, she met Eli, a sculpted boy from Connecticut. When her mother died from a flu she contracted on a cruise ship, Gabriella panicked to Eli about what she should do: she had no family now. Eli proposed to her then, struck by the romance of his girlfriend's new orphanhood. They were engaged for six weeks and then Eli was placed in another residency in New Mexico. She encouraged him to go, as in, break up with her, and a week after she dropped him off at Logan, him leaving slobbery wet marks on her shoulder from tears, she discovered she was pregnant.

She weighed the pros and cons of having a child. She didn't tell Eli. She was far enough into her career, but she didn't have enough money. But after a week of wondering if she should keep it, she received a letter in the mail about life insurance. Her parents had left her a breathtaking amount of money. They had thought of her after all. So Gabriella bought a small house in Cambridge just as her belly started sticking out underneath her shirts. A friend from her residency encouraged her to get a job at Planned Parenthood, and while Gabriella was never particularly radical, something about a baby growing inside her and her newfound fortune made her want to give back in some way. She started shortly after Quinn was born and began taking solace in being the face women would see before being put under, the person they think of when they finally win that award, publish, or get a raise. And Gabriella wanted to be different with her daughter. She wanted to give her love and affection. She wanted to tell her every day that she was extremely smart, that she was very worthy, that she could be whoever she wanted to be, and that her mother loved her more than anything.

Quinn turned thirteen and chopped off all her hair after being inspired by a scene in a movie where a girl did the same, to prove something. Quinn didn't really have anything to prove, the image just reverberated so much in her mind that she wanted to re-create it herself, watch her hair falling to the floor defiantly, pushing against something invisible. Quinn listened to Juliana Hatfield and Bikini Kill. She made TikToks with lyrical analyses and histories of the bands. She started her own band and played at Girls Rock! Camp, and at showcases her mother would be in the front row, with her phone out, bunions stretching against her sandals.

Because of her mother, Quinn was often the one who gave her friends access to condoms, told them what to do if they ever had unprotected sex. Gabriella's house was a place of solace for Quinn's friends whose parents were a little stricter than Gabriella. She kept a warm abode, with yellow walls and blue tables and books everywhere. She would pick Quinn's friends up from parties when they were drunk and let them sleep on the couch with two ibuprofens and a glass of water. Gabriella disclosed a lot to her daughter and Quinn did the same. Quinn talked to her about her crushes and her anxieties. Sometimes her friends were jealous that a mother and a daughter could be so close. Other friends thought their relationship should be more mother-daughter, and less friend-friend.

One day, Gabriella told Quinn about a strange email she'd received of a doctored video that showed her saying abortions should especially be provided to Black and Latina women.

"In, like, a eugenics way?" Quinn said in the hallway with a towel draped over her shoulders and blue dye in her hair. Her mother turned off her monitor and went to her daughter.

"I guess so. Weird, right?" The timer on Quinn's phone went off.

"What do they want you to do?" Quinn went to the sink and her mother turned on the warm water as the blue spiraled down the drain.

"To not perform any abortions next week." She turned the water a bit to the colder side and Quinn winced.

"You think they're gonna, like, bomb you or something?" Gabriella grabbed a towel and dried her daughter's hair.

"It's a bluff," she said. "I'll be fine. Don't worry!"

But two days later, Gabriella received another email, offering her $20,000 not to perform any abortions the following week. She marked the email as spam and continued on with her day.

"Candelaria—did I say that right?"

The young woman sat in front of her, shaking her leg up and down. Her backpack was still on and AirPods were lodged in her ears. "It's Candy." And Gabriella smiled at her.

"Right, so, Candy, you *are* pregnant." Gabriella had trained her tone of voice to make it sound like a very easy situation: you're pregnant, the same way that you have a leaf floating in your hair, a booger hanging from your nose, an eyelash stuck to your cheek.

"About eleven weeks along. Does that sound right?" Candy gave her a thumbs up. "We'll be performing a late-term surgery, totally normal, nothing to be afraid of." And Gabriella demonstrated, as she always did, how she would go into Candy's uterus and gently excavate the fetus with a suction tube.

Every day, Gabriella walked past a group of protestors in a prayer circle and through bulletproof doors into the clinic. In her office, she'd look through her mail: letters from past clients updating her on their accomplishments, thanking her for saving their lives during ectopic pregnancies. There were, of course, letters from conservatives and religious fanatics politely and lovingly informing her that her soul was in peril, and Gabriella always laughed at those.

She would see her clients twice: once to counsel, and once to administer the mifepristone pill or a surgical abortion. Sometimes they were there in secret, sometimes a partner brought them, sometimes they already had children, sometimes there were a lot of tears from fear or pain, other times they felt nothing but relief.

When Gabriella came in the morning of Candy's abortion, past the protestors and up the stairs and into her office, a pile of mail waiting for her on her desk, she was ready to go about her day as she always did. But there were two people waiting in her office when she arrived. One was somebody she had never seen before, with a strange bowl haircut and a giant smile, and the other was a taller woman with brown skin, dyed blond hair, and a muscular body.

"You've received our messages?" Her smile stretched from ear to ear, taking up her entire face.

"Excuse me?" How did they get past security?

"The video," the tall, perhaps Latinx (was that the right word?) woman said, with her arms crossed, trying to assert herself. "The email."

"I got those weird messages. Is this some kind of joke?"

"All we asked is that you perform no abortions this week," the smiling woman said. Her teeth were so shiny. "And yet here you are."

"It's legal in Massachusetts."

"You have a client in the next hour." The Latinx woman swallowed her spit, "Candy."

"How do you know that?" Gabriella felt her heart racing and her bowels seizing, the fight-or-flight instincts that statistically make you die faster kicking in.

"We cannot let you kill that child," the smiling woman said, and Gabriella realized they were talking about the fetus.

"It's not a child yet. And this isn't up to you."

"You're right. So much isn't up to us." The woman with the bowl cut took out a phone, where there was a video of Quinn sitting in a chair.

"What is this?" Gabriella whispered. "Where is she?" The video played. Quinn was sitting in a chair in a white room.

Hi, Mom. Listen, I'm safe, I think. They're not allowed to tell me why I'm here but they're asking me to tell you to please not do what

you're about to do? They won't say what that is, but, um, please
don't do it? I don't know if they're gonna like, kill me, but it's
definitely . . . like maybe they would kind of vibes? Okay. Uh,
I'll be here, I guess. You don't have to worry about me. I'm an
adult. I love you!

Gabriella steadied herself against a poster that showed a graphic of contraceptives.

"What are you going to do to her?"

"Your child? Nothing, if you cooperate."

"The girl I'm about to operate on."

"We will take care of it. Aren't you more concerned about your daughter?" The woman's teeth were too overwhelming. Gabriella threw up in a trash can on top of the wrapping for a falafel sandwich she had eaten the day before. The woman with the huge smile and the maybe Hispanic woman went for the door.

"She doesn't need to know. We aren't using an anesthetic on her. It's something more organic. From the ground. From the Mother." Gabriella began to cry.

"What the hell does that mean?"

"Your daughter will be home tonight. Thank you for your time, Gabriella. You're making this world open."

III

AN INFLUX OF WATER

You need to take a break in the middle of the bridge, where you've been climbing on top of the cars. That's how bad the snow has become in the last hour. You can barely see in front of you. Your daughter has a beard of snow on her face, which is why she would've benefited from a scarf, to be honest.

"¿Estás bien?" she says, spitting snow out of her mouth.

"Si, mija, no te preocupes, mi amor." You are milking this a little bit, though the pain in your knee is real. But you like to make her feel a little bad, admit it, because then she feels all that generational guilt rattling inside her. You are petty like this, sometimes. She waits with you as you do your little exercises on top of a car: kicking your knee out and then in, doing a two-step back and forth, pushing your arms out and doing heavy breaths. This goes on for five minutes when she starts to yell.

"I'm gonna let you get eaten by those things if you don't move now." So, you continue, Lucia taking your arm as you move from snowy car to snowy car. You see a smattering of the tents in the distance, you had both spotted them a few cars back, but weren't sure if it was a hallucination. You still need to find the girls. And you still need to tell Lucia what happened, and you still need to get to the Old Country Buffet, but you can't do that if you're dead, can you? You thought you heard some snarling behind you but figured that was just Lucia's heavy breathing.

"We have to hurry up," you say, as she helps you onto another car.

"Too bad I'm with the slowest person in the world," she says, really looking like Santa Claus at this point. As you inch closer, you start to wave and yell. If you squint, you can see the CITGO sign far enough in the distance, but it's disappearing before your eyes. Probably from snow. Right?

Finally, you've made it over the bridge. You scream and wave your cane, begging to be seen and rescued. Your daughter waves and yells, too. You untie your red scarf and begin to whip it around in the air, yelling,

"¡SOCORRO!" Then, what is that? Are those two men getting into a jeep? Is that it revving up? "¡SOCORRO! ¡AUXILIO!"

The truck gets closer and closer, you can smell the gasoline, and you are thanking la Virgencita for saving you. You take out your candle and give it a kiss. The truck doors open and two soldiers jump out, heaving you by the armpits and legs into the giant truck, and your daughter too, and oh, what a relief! It isn't just you and your daughter at the end of the world anymore.

Fifty years earlier, you and Lucia carried Sandrita to the tents the Americans had set up, hoping they could fix her leg. The Americans were thick, well-fed humans, pouring food into bowls for people. You and your daughter were sure they could help Sandra. Lucia was asking for Gabo. *Have you seen him? Have you seen my brother?* There were mattress frames tossed all around, dust flying through the air. Children were coughing and crying, begging for their mothers. An American woman, una canchita, found you and took your family into the tent, where they sat her on a cot and undid the bandages you had given her, your daughter. She was careful about showing her expression, blank-faced and clinical, like you were small animals who might attack her at any moment. She spoke to you in broken European Spanish, making a slicing motion with her hand, and you understood. You kneeled and your daughter gave her a towel to bite on as the woman poured antiseptic over her legs. But there was another screaming you heard. Gabo's girlfriend, Mirna, was running and running to you. And the screaming felt like it was coming from everywhere but mostly it was from inside you.

Here, the army tends to the damaged once again. Inside, there are heat lamps going and aluminum jackets being passed around. A soldier wraps one around you. You thank him.

"¿Todo bien, mamita?"

"Oh! ¿Hablas español?"

"Un poquito," and he smiles at you, so bashful. How kind men can be. Sometimes you wish Lucia could have had a boy. Just one boy! They're so much easier. Carefree. Like your Gabo. An angel. Rest his soul! Girls break into this world and there's too much to protect them from. Too much watering and then not enough.

"Mire, hijo, I really need to get to the Old Country Buffet. If you could, please, we would like to borrow your car. We will bring it back!" The soldier looked at you, confused, and then to Lucia.

"Don't listen to her," your daughter says, sipping hot cocoa, her face blotchy from the cold outside, "The cold and the snow made her a little . . ." She makes a twirling sign with her fingers against her head. You scowl. The soldier laughs. He starts talking to Lucia, and you examine their facial expressions to try to determine what's being said. Things are always happening without you. Are they going to let you borrow the car or not? Your daughter furrows her brow and the soldier smiles at you and walks to the medics.

"They think we were attacked," Lucia says. "Los Russos. Una bomba. We're waiting for Washington."

"Did you tell him about . . ." The people eating each other.

"I asked if he had seen anything weird, and he said no, no. But who knows."

"You can't trust the government."

"Cállate, Mamá. This isn't Guatemala. The government isn't corrupt."

"Ha! Remember when you dated that cop? And I told you it was a bad idea?"

"Enough."

"Because if he got mad at you, he could just kill you." You make a pistol with your hands. "With his *gun*."

"You were about to tell that soldier everything about your life. I could see it in your eyes. Don't act like you're better than everybody."

"Can't you ask him if we can borrow the Jeep?"

"Why do you think they'll let us borrow the Jeep? When all these other people are here?"

"If you just ask . . ."

"All so that you can go to the Old Country Buffet, which by the way, is a Chinese restaurant now, if you even *remember*, which you probably don't, because you're losing your mind. What do you need so badly there anyway?"

Luckily, before you can muster up an answer that would have too much to do with the truth, a man across the tent who had brought Christmas lights is plugging them into the generator. They light up and his family cheers. His son hugs his leg. You look over at Lucia, who cries. Your hand goes to her knee.

"I don't know where they are," she says, her shoulders shaking. "Why didn't I try to find them? Why did I get to you first?" You don't know what to say. For all you know the girls are with Diosito Lindo Celestial, or eating people up, but that's probably not something she wants to hear, so instead you ask, "How is the chocolate?" She sniffs.

"Watery." You reach into your purse and grab a ball of tin foil, opening it up carefully to reveal the maduros you had fried this morning. They aren't serving *this* in the tent. She rolls her eyes, but you think you see a glint of something in her eye. A small, smile.

"I don't have a fork," she says. And you rummage around in your purse again for the wrinkly ziplock bag of plastic take-out forks.

She shakes her head. "Unbelievable," she says. There is peace for a few moments as she chews.

"I'm sorry about Mauricio," she says, swallowing, "Did you know he was going to propose? I was going to help him with the ring."

You look away from your daughter, shifting around on the cot, and you cry. She pats you on the shoulder.

"You're right," she says, "At least we are together."

"We need to leave soon," you say, looking at the exits.

"You burned these." Lucia passes you back the fork. Malcriada. Outside the wind howls. The snow gets deeper. The father and his family begin leading everybody in some American Christmas song. Your daughter sings along like she knows the words, but looks like one of those vacero movies you love to watch that are dubbed in Spanish, the cowboys shooting wildly in the desert and another man speaking for them. The soldiers talk into their walkie-talkies, but nobody is talking back. They look to the other, turn around, whisper.

And somewhere a few miles away, your granddaughters are realizing they're all in the same place.

CANDY

Candy woke up feeling refreshed, rejuvenated. She was a white woman in a yogurt commercial. A smiling photo on store-brand UTI medication. She wasn't going to eat anybody anymore. Or have visions. Or hear a strange voice in her hand that sounded like her own but was not her own narrating her life as if it were a movie. And? She wasn't going to have a fucking baby.

Calling out of work, she was excited to spoil herself with a movie. Zoe was in the kitchen, making her some tea, and Candy felt oddly comforted and loved by this. Like Zoe was always supposed to be there in the kitchen and Candy was always supposed to be on the couch and somebody was always supposed to be getting taken care of. They were hopping into their roles one leg at a time.

"Here you go," Zoe said, setting a slightly chipped pink mug down, "and I just put fresh flowers in that vase on top of the fridge."

"Oh. Thanks. What's in this?" Candy asked, taking a sip.

"A chamomile ginger thing I like to make."

Candy scrunched her nose and put it down. "Do you want to watch *Forbidden Planet* with me?"

Zoe looked uncomfortable.

"Come on, sit!" Candy took out her Apple TV remote—she happily paid for this herself—and went to the Criterion Channel. Zoe sat tentatively next to her.

"This movie's fucked," she said, shaking her head. "Do you even like movies?" Candy was so relaxed. Zoe sat upright like a rod.

"I haven't had a chance to watch a new movie in a while. All my time's spent at the Woman's Stone."

"Why do you like it there so much?"

Zoe lit up.

"First of all, there's a profound sense of community," she said, as the men on screen landed on a strange, new planet. "Everything that's missing from our healthcare system is there. If you're sick, or unhoused, or can't get out of something . . ." She glanced at Candy, then glanced back. Candy knew what that meant but tried to ignore it. " . . . the Woman's Stone is there to help you."

"Cool!" Candy said, clearly not meaning it, like she had just heard Zoe try to sell her a new useless contraption for ten easy payments for $29.99 that she could find later at Bed Bath & Beyond.

"It would benefit you a lot," Zoe said. On the screen, a doctor was telling the men not to come to the planet. It was dangerous. Candy smiled, her top lip curling inward, only the fronts of her teeth showing. She looked a little bit like a chipmunk, or a goofy meme of some young girl. It was the face she made when it was too much effort to smile or be genuine. Irony that had turned into habit.

"Yeah," Candy said, "I think I'm good!" Zoe was put off by the face, and Candy could tell.

"Really, you should stop by again. You could be part of it. This could be easy." Zoe was being very insistent. Easy? It was the most Candy had heard her talking. She was so passionate about this. It was kind of sad.

"Zoe, I'm glad you have like, found your thing, but that stuff kind of freaks me out." A beautiful woman entered the screen. She was blond and had long legs and was barefoot. The men were all around her, trying to claim her for their own.

"How do you mean?"

"I don't go into AA because it's culty," she said snappily, matter-of-factly, giving it a name, finally. Then she shrugged, because that was that. "No offense."

Zoe folded her hands and took a deep breath, then said nothing. They watched the rest of the movie in silence, found out that the villain was really the girl's father's sleeping ego, that he had awakened while messing with alien technology. Whatever comfortable feeling Candy had earlier had now faded, like the heat in the tea Zoe had made her.

"You know, I feel fine," Candy said, as the credits rolled. "Like, pretty okay. I feel like because I don't drink alcohol my body is like, really good at recovering from things." Candy nodded. "Uh-huh."

Zoe stared.

"I think I'd be . . . totally cool if, like, you left," Candy said, showing only the top of her teeth again. She didn't know how else to say it. Could she please just go? This reunion stuff had run its course. They could go back to pretending they never knew each other again and that Zoe was dead. Zoe patted her blanketed knee.

"Sure," Zoe said, getting up and grabbing her bag, giving Candy a curt nod.

"I put my number in your phone." Zoe headed toward the door, "in case you need anything." She had come into her life at exactly the right moment, and now she was leaving. Should Candy say something more ceremonial? Should they embrace? Pass something deep and familiar from one body to the other with one strong hug? Nasty.

When her sister's hand hit the door knob, she called out, "Thank you!" And then, "Thank you, Zoe."

She watched her sister turn slightly, feeling pulled by this fishing line of affection. She met Candy's gaze. Candy tried one more time, and this was the last she would say, to show her just how thankful she was, and then she would be free from the guilt of it, of someone helping her out, doing her a favor. She took a deep breath.

"Thanks for staying as long as you did."

ZOE

These days, Zoe was never bloated and she was never tired. Her new life in Boston had been churning smoothly, one day leading into the next, perfectly measured and scooped out into peaceful regiments of time. She slept seven and a half hours each night, waking to meditate with Maria and the rest of the Woman's Stone, the bell ringing to the beat of all their hearts, a synchronized rhythm that technology could not re-create. Hearing the scared bell in her body, she felt in touch with the secrets of every woman ancestor there ever was, dancing their way into freedom.

Zoe wasn't focused on the past anymore. There was no past. There was no Paola. No controlling mother. No abusive husband. There was only now.

This is what she told her students in spin class, the next day, as music blasted over her outstretched arms. Be here now. Yes, this session is timed. Yes, this is a structured environment. But this is for you. Don't think about me. Or your wallet. Think about yourself. When you think about yourself, you're able to give in to a greater cause. We are all in this together individually, but when we finally meet, we turn into something unimaginable, our bodies and minds coming together into a powerful Goddess. Like the Mother. We are so strong. We can do anything.

"I'm so proud of you all," Zoe said as she dismounted her bike, "I'll see you next week." The women all filed out, thanking her, thanking *Zoe*, and Zoe luxuriated at the name as they all chatted among themselves, exhausted and full of endorphins, as if they had all just made love.

Today was the day she was going to see the new additions to the Woman's Stone. She was nervous, but mostly just excited. Maria had never failed to impress her. Zoe locked the door to the studio once the last student filed out. It was important that this was kept secret. That only official members of the Woman's Stone could see the new additions and plans. Zoe was still working on getting her students to become members. She had been successful here and there, but a lot of the time people felt uneasy committing to things. They had their lives: car payments, pets. Children.

She had to find people who seemed like they needed guidance. Who felt like they needed to be found. Like Carmen, who had started weeping during a spin class. Zoe had connected with her at the end of class, and it turned out she was heartbroken and looking for a home. The next day, Zoe had set her up working in the kitchens and Carmen was doing her part, happy, belonging to something, no longer heartbroken over some man. Men cause suffering. Men should only be used as tools, as they had used women for centuries.

Zoe walked over to the last bike at the corner of the studio, the one that was always out of service. On Maria's instruction, Zoe mounted it and turned it on, making the bike whir as her spiked shoes moved the pedals. Maria said things would "open for her" about a mile into a ride but did not say what that meant. So, Zoe kept going, waiting for some kind of sign. She pedaled and pedaled, and once she hit a mile, the floor beneath the bike opened up like a mouth. She gasped as the bike began to lower itself down. She let herself feel frightened. Reactive feelings eventually give way to peace and clarity. Darkness encased her, and she suddenly found herself inside a six-by-six tunnel through which she would only move if she kept pedaling. Peace and clarity. Above her, the floor sealed closed. A metallic kiss.

Eventually, she saw a light about five hundred yards down. When she finally landed on the ground, Maria was there waiting for her, wearing pale linens and sandals.

"I know it can be a little scary. But I also knew you could handle it." Zoe beamed. Maria squealed and squeezed Zoe's shoulders, the pressure from her hands going down her arms and then resting finally on her hands, which she held gently.

"I am so excited for you to see all of this. The Mother's given us so many gifts." She took Zoe by the hand. The light in here was from a natural rainy day. Soothing, cloudy. Contemplative.

"I can dim these lights to any level of weather, thanks to the Mother," Maria explained. She brought Zoe to a narrow corridor they had to move through single file. Sliding a door to the left and pulling back a curtain,

Maria revealed a tiny room with just enough space for one person to sleep. There were plush pillows and hand towels. Even a window looking out into a garden, where there was more artificial sunlight.

"This is where you'll sleep. It's cozy."

"What are the other doors for?" Zoe pointed to the doors along the corridor.

"Emergencies," Maria said, "which reminds me." Then she dug around in the pocket of her linen pants. "I need to give you one of these." She handed Zoe a silver key in the shape of a uterus. It was warm in her hand.

"Zoe," she said, "you've come so, so far." Zoe blushed. "Carmen's doing so well. The people you've brought to me, to us—you've gone beyond." She held on to her shoulders.

"I mean, where is that scared little girl I met in Naperville, Illinois?"

Zoe looked down and let out a bashful laugh.

"She's still in there," Maria said, pointing to her chest. "She's useful. Don't forget her. She's part of you." Maria opened her palm. "The dormitories can be cramped, so I wanted to give you this."

Zoe looked at the key in her hand. "Where does it go?"

"It's a master key," Maria said. "It opens up any of these doors. So you can come here and have a moment to yourself." Everyone at the Woman's Stone slept together, ate together, worked out together. And now Zoe could be alone?

"I'm only doing this for you," Maria said. "I know it must've been hard, lying to your sister."

Zoe lowered her gaze. It had been hard. But she knew that everything led to a common goal: a present that they couldn't yet imagine.

"It'll be worth it," Zoe said, clutching the uterus key to her chest. "I'll cherish this." Maria squeezed her shoulder.

They kept moving until she hit a staircase, which led to a glass-covered room with pool tables and chairs you would find in a college dorm room.

Opening another door, Maria held out her hand. Maria was the creator of all things, showing her expansive, indoor, artificial land.

"This is the garden."

Zoe forgot she was several stories underground. Members of the Woman's Stone were watering plants as big as cars while light flooded the room.

"Abundance will come," Maria said, holding up a plump red pepper that a member had just plucked. She handed it to Zoe. "Everything's coming together." Zoe was dumbfounded, once again, at the abilities of Maria, and of women. She hadn't seen the bunker since she came here, when it was merely the remnants of MBTA tunnels, old shoes and cans strewn across the train tracks, one hundred years' worth of dust and grime blanketing the walls. But Maria always put her mind to things, and a year later, with all this effort, and the help of the unhoused people who had been squatting in the tunnels, she did it. She saw them all for who they really were and transformed them, cleaned them, helped them by making them help. It was remarkable.

Maria led Zoe out of the gardens, to where, years before, there was an intersection of tunnels, where trains would pause their journey, waiting for the other to go through. In the middle of the platform was a large bed. Women were knelt all around, arranging flowers. The light around the bed was soft, comfortable. Zoe wanted to fall asleep there, wake up new.

"This is where it will happen," Maria said, hands clutched together. Zoe felt a sharp anxiety in her stomach. She remembered her sister thanking her as she left her apartment, not knowing what she had just done. Sometimes you have to lie to people to get them to do what is good for them. This is how Zoe would be a sister. How she would care.

"She'll be okay, right?" Maria had told her the extent of her sister's history. Shown her the files from rehab. How much she and her family had suffered. Addiction was an ailment because of what this world had done. It wasn't her fault. But she was beyond her own help at this point. The baby, and the world it would bring, would ultimately be good for her, good for everybody else. Maria placed a hand on her shoulder. They would right all the wrongs of men. They would make something better.

"The medication we gave her will alleviate every symptom. She won't feel any pain. And when the time is right, she'll come to us. And we will make this world open."

BIANCA

A breath escaped Bianca's mouth, a hot, angry ghost struggling its way through her gritted teeth. Blue put their hand on her shoulder.

"It's okay," said Blue, who had come back from the kitchen when they heard Bianca screaming. "You'll get it back. In a way, it was a gift." Bianca screeched. She sounded like a bird being struck by a car. This had only happened once before, when her mother had deleted the oral history project she had done with her. She was so mad at her then and had been continually upset when putting together research for her project in Guatemala. It would've been so helpful! It would've saved her so much work. Julian closed the curtains and checked his phone.

"My phone's still working," he said. "How about everybody else?" Blue opened theirs. Yes. Bianca looked through hers. Yes.

"So, they got into your hard drive but not our cell phones. Interesting."

"They?"

"I think it's pretty obvious what's going on here." Julian looked to Blue and Bianca, expecting them to be following his lead, for all three of them to say in unison, on the count of three:

"We're being tracked by the government."

Bianca groaned. "Julian, no."

"Bianca," Blue said, "how do you know this man again?"

"My computer's memory card's shot," Bianca reasoned. "I can probably still access it on the cloud." She logged into her cloud account, searching. She started picking her nails.

"I'm saying, only the government has access to this kind of deus ex machina, main frame shit," Julian said, his eyes wide and his hands in the air, as if he were grabbing the main frame itself.

Bianca rolled her eyes. "The government is not interested in my work at all."

"Okay," Blue said, "I'm leaving again." They turned away, but it was like neither of the others noticed.

"Well," Julian said, "The CIA *did* have a hand in starting a coup in Guatemala. You should know your history better."

"Shut up." Bianca saw that her cloud was completely empty and turned around in her chair, "I was researching something completely innocent. It was a group of artists who were killed during the earthquake that were trying to make the world better through art and mutual aid, as I said." She glared at him wondering if that would make him shut up. "Earnest and tragic."

"Why is that earnest?" Julian looked offended.

"I'm just saying the CIA doesn't care."

"Clearly," Julian said, "they don't want you to figure out whatever happened with Fernando. And probably your uncle. And whoever Sylvio is."

"Sylvester." She let out a big sigh and put her fingers to her eyelids. Julian sat on the floor.

"Did Fernando have a copy of the recordings?" Bianca curled her top lip into her teeth.

"Yeah."

"Could we track them down?"

"In theory." She shook her leg up and down, and it was like Candy was in the room with them.

"Where are they?"

"On his hard drive. At his house."

"Oh . . . he was married right?" Bianca's bowels moved and she had the urge to empty out her entire self on her toilet in her bathroom, to excavate every organ and be left as one sack of skin. She was on the floor, curled in a ball, moaning, because Fernando was somebody with a widow.

She felt pressure on her back. It was Julian. He had his face with one cheek on her spine, like he was listening for something, but she realized he was afraid to touch her but felt like he needed to.

"What are you doing?"

"Trying to help?"

CANDY

There was something about terminating a pregnancy that made you hallucinate and gave you a penchant for flesh that really made you want to start over. Candy was putting her entire life into perspective. *Dang,* she kept thinking, drawing eyeliner onto her giant eyelids and hearing the squawking of her neighbor's toddlers next door followed by the parents screaming, *that really could have been me.* It was time to recalibrate everything.

"Hey, Garfungus," she said, holding the button down to leave a voice note while throwing a scoopful of collagen into her smoothie. "Look, this isn't working for me anymore. I know we weren't officially together, but I have goals, a lot of them actually, and you are keeping me from them. My life's about to start, and you're an obstacle. I love you." She turned her NutriBlend on, the sound buzzing into the recording. "But I love myself more." Then she hung up, poured her smoothie into her mug, and chugged it. She had such a way with words sometimes, she thought to herself, genuinely moved, wiping her mouth and shaking her head, even though what she said was partially stolen from Samantha's speech to her boyfriend at the end of *Sex and the City.*

At work, Candy's coworkers noticed a change in her.

"What's with you," Jenny said, pouring oil into the popcorn machine.

"Nothing!" Candy sang, squeezing Jenny's shoulders and making her flinch. "Isn't that incredible!" She had so much energy. She didn't know where it was coming from. She signed herself up for a creative writing class at a community college for the spring. She started writing down ideas for a script: a memoir-esque coming-of-age kind of movie about a fuckup who kind of gets her shit together after an abortion. *Obvious Child* but with a Guatemalan Colombian former addict!

She even wrote a thoughtful text to Bianca.

Hey bitch!! 🐣 I'm sry I'm been such a cunt puta pendeja perra ass ho 😈💣😮💨😮💨 I forget that ur sensitive because ur face never shows any emotion and it makes people uncomfortable 😄. But I love that about u. Why show anyone what you're feeling when they can use it against you? 🤟🫶 Bianca, ur the only person who knows me ✋🫶. I know I'm a fuck-up and a dumb ass & I deserve to be thrown tomatoes at in the middle of a prominent square of culture 🏰 but I think it's stupid that we don't talk 💔. Probs should have told u this a while ago, but, I was embarrassed💩. K here it goes: I had an abortion 🐚lmao. It's kind of this whole thing 😄. Paola/Zoe helped me??? She's in this wellness cult thing that I do not fuck with, but she's doing okay🤪. Still haven't told Mom about her 👤🙁. Think she's been through it. Some stupid part of me thinks it would be sweet if we were all together again 👩👩👩👩. have a Christmas together. Make tamales. Make Abuelita tell her stories. IDK I miss you. 👿 I lub you. 🤠. Text me back. 😊

That should do it, she thought. It had been about five months since they spoke—the longest they had ever gone. Candy checked her phone after thirty seconds. That's okay. Bianca was still processing it. She left her room and did jumping jacks in front of her TV screen, where a David Cronenberg movie was playing. She waited for the movie to end and then she checked her phone again. Well, okay. At work, she kept her phone locked in her cubby and rushed to it on her break, tugging on the lock and desperately swiping her phone open. Interesting. A week passed. Another. Bianca never responded. Candy tried to wrack her brain through what she said, and if it really was so bad that her sister would never, ever speak to her again. Her message was really vulnerable; Candy was humiliated beyond belief for putting forth so much feeling. Candy deleted Bianca's number from her phone, though she had it memorized.

She tried not to let this get her down. She kept visiting her grandmother, bringing a pastry with her from Flour bakery each time. She'd sit there with her and Mauricio watching *Seinfeld* reruns, wondering if either of them actually understood what was going on. Her grandmother would feed her those soups Candy would never learn how to cook. She also noticed a change in her.

"Hueles raro," Candelaria said, putting her nose into her granddaughter's armpit.

"Really?" Candy gave herself a whiff. She smelled like the aluminum-free Dove deodorant she stole from CVS.

"Are you pregnant?" her grandmother asked, looking up at Candy mischievously and then squeezing her knee. They both began to cackle. Her grandmother almost had tears in her eyes, she thought it was so funny. Pregnant? Candy? Hilarious.

"Si, estoy embarazada," Candy joked, "con el *diablo*." Candelaria's mouth dropped open. She made the sign of the cross and then howled.

"¿Escuchaste eso?" she said, pulling on Mauricio's arm hairs. "Did you hear what she said?" And then Candy had to repeat it, but then Mauricio didn't understand, so she had to say it again, but then he couldn't hear it so she had to say it again, and then he thought she said something about *Seinfeld* so Candy found herself yelling, "DIABLO!" at the top of her lungs in her grandfather's ear. It was the kind of thing she wanted to talk to Bianca about, because it was the kind of thing that only she had context for, only she would think was equally funny. The stupid joke, the reaction, the yelling the joke over and over again so that it lost its spark but then came to life again in a new context. She would totally get it. Candy checked her phone. Just the schedule at the theater set for the next week. Just a text message from the fucking Woman's Stone asking if she wanted a membership.

Was Bianca or Zoe here, appreciating these little moments? No, they were off being selfish, trying to find something they could never find. Lost in the fucking *sauce*. And Candy? Candy had risen above it. Wiped it off her hands. Started anew.

One morning, close to Halloween, a few weeks after deleting her sister's number, Candy woke to rain. Candy loved thinking that she was somebody who loved the darkness; the shorter days and the colder nights. She wanted to feel at home in the dreariness. The creepiness of it all. But often it made her mood tank.

Opening her fridge and sighing, she saw that she was out of almond milk, which meant that she would skip out on her regular smoothie. She was getting kind of tired of them, anyway. Briefly, she had a moment of self-awareness. Were the smoothies just a phase? Was she as reliant on them as she was with other substances? She briefly recalled the packages of raw meat from a few months prior, and how tasty they were, and how those cravings just stopped. *See?* she thought. *I can grow. I can change.*

Never really one to be frugal or practical, Candy decided to spend $12 on an artisanal egg sandwich from the local organic deli on Center Street and eat it on her way to the bus, the rain pattering on her hands and changing the temperature of the sandwich.

Why did she feel like crying?

The cheddar cheese would make her gassy at the theatre, but she tried not to let herself care. Her cheese days were her off days when she could fart in peace. Sometimes she would get this sandwich without the cheese, but it seemed so bare. So dry. She let herself relish in the way the aioli wrapped over the cheese, the jamminess of the egg yolk. She finished the sandwich and crunched the aluminum foil into a ball.

This rain was giving Candy a headache. Her hands smelled like eggs and garlic. She rested her head on the bus's window pane. Were the only people in her life really her mother, grandmother, and Zoe? *Who cares*, she thought, *everybody fucking leaves me anyway.* Her stomach twanged slightly—the cheese was fighting with the lack of lactose enzymes in her gut. She would just deal with it. Be bloated all day. Maybe the smoothies were a good idea after all.

Why couldn't she focus?

Jenny greeted her as she entered the theater.

"Hey, miss," she said, mopping the floor.

"Shut up, Jenny."

Jenny scowled. Candy took a seat behind the ticket counter. The customers arrived and then the customers left.

"Fuck this job," she said, a little too loudly, handing a ticket to a teenager who had just coughed into his hand. She was thinking about how a few months had gone by without seeing anybody she knew when she heard "Candy?" Her name came from the mouth of Rebecca Polkinghorn, the girl from high school whose parents' room she had passed out in.

"Wow, it's been forever!"

"Uh-huh," Candy said into the speaker. "What are you here to see?"

"I'm here with the kids, they have today off. *Indigenous Peoples' Day,* I guess we're calling it now."

Candy pressed the speaker button again. "That's crazy."

Rebecca smiled at her. Two small children were hugging her legs. "What have you been up to? It's really good to see you looking so well." Rebecca grabbed a child and held her on her hip.

Wasn't she kind of young to have two children? Or was Candy getting old? *So well,* Rebecca said. "Yeah, things have been pretty good since I got an abortion," Candy said, matching Rebecca's smile, which quickly faded. "The last time I felt this good was when I got out of *rehab.*" Candy looked directly at Rebecca's children. "Yeah, it was for super heavy drug use. Remember? How I almost died? In your parents' room?"

Rebecca protectively put her hands over her kids cherubic heads. Then Candy was smacked by a wave of nausea. "Enjoy your movie. I gotta vom." She ran downstairs to the bathroom where she retched out her breakfast, annoyed that she couldn't just enjoy something even a little bit artisanal. Fucking dairy. Fucking Big Milk! She wiped her mouth and washed her hands then went back to the ticket stand, thinking about how vomit was at least more graceful than diarrhea. She went behind the concession stand and took a can of ginger ale out of the fridge, chugging it and feeling the bubbles foam around the walls of her upset stomach. Her headache became more intense. Her vision started to blur.

"Hey," Jenny said, her furry eyebrows and long ponytail pissing Candy off for a reason she couldn't place, "you have to write items off that you take. You can't just take the food because you're a manager." Candy narrowed her eyes, trying to focus on what Jenny was saying. A bell was ringing in her ears. But it wasn't a bell. It was a heartbeat. She could hear it. It was coming from Jenny. A loud and luscious fifty-six-year-old heart pumping inside her chest. The smell of the sweat from underneath Jenny's large breasts filled Candy's nose, pies cooling on a window.

"Jenny," she said, wrinkling her nose and wiping saliva from her mouth, "get out of my fucking face."

Jenny put her hands on her hips. "It's your turn to clean theater three." She walked away, muttering something about addicts—Candy knew her employees talked badly behind her back.

The theater still held the energy from everyone who had just come in to see the new Marvel movie palpable in every seat. Theaters always felt haunted because of this: the perspiring and screaming and laughing with strangers in a room that had no windows. Stuff like that just stays. Candy tried not to let it get to her.

She started at the front aisle, closest to the screen, trying to focus on the broom in her hand. Everything was so blurry that it looked like a mosaic painting. She was sweeping ferociously, banging the broom against the seats, when the red curtains parted, the lights turned off, and the screen turned on.

"No!" she called, but to who, she didn't know. "I'm not doing this again!" She turned, and there she was on the screen, in black-and-white.

"I fixed it!" she yelled up at the ceiling, at whoever was running the projection booth, which was dark, because nobody was running it. She was all alone. "I got rid of it!" On screen, Candy stared back, smiling widely, and continued sweeping. A voice began to speak to her again. It felt as though it were her own, but someone was using her words. She, but not she, was narrating this new life.

> *Back where we left you.*
> *Our protagonist.*
> *There you are, the popcorn scattered around. The small wrappers*
>   *with the special Halloween slogans on them. Go on, don't let me*
>   *interrupt. You were doing so much work.*
> *You never know what you might find in between these seats.*
> *Don't cry.*
> *There's nothing to cry about.*
> *Keep going.*
> *Now, what is that, Candy?*
> *You kneel.*
> *The camera moves behind you as if held by somebody else.*
> *Over your shoulder, you can see what she's seeing.*
> *And then, you merge. You are just one Candy.*
> *Something small's under the seat. Tiny.*
> *Move closer. Aren't you curious?*
> *It's no bigger than a cat.*
> *Go closer. Come on.*
> *Squirming and transparent.*
> *A small, embryonic sack of fluid, breathing in and out.*
> *Why is this still happening, Candy?*
> *You back away quickly, instinctually, as whatever was inside the*
>   *bag begins to move toward you, fighting with itself as it gains*
>   *velocity.*

It punctures a hole in its sack. A bit of air comes out. Some red liquid.
Is that a tiny little arm?
You stand on the seats, jumping from arm handle to arm handle.
It slithers toward you, without any limbs.
Don't scream.

Candy came to. The figure slithering toward her wasn't an embryo-creature but a knocked-over package of Welch's Fruit Snacks. It was just Candy inside of the theater. Nobody was on the screen. The curtains were shut. She picked up her broom and set it by the entrance, then walked down to the bathroom. Outside, through the glass windows, she could see that it was nighttime. But how? Wasn't it just the afternoon? Wasn't she just talking to Rebecca about Indigenous Peoples' Day?

Beetlejuice was at the bottom of the staircase with his hands out and his mouth grimacing and Candy jumped at the sight of him. In the bathroom, which was covered in spider webs, she took a few deep breaths. She was just dehydrated, probably, from throwing up her breakfast earlier. She stuck her hand beneath the electric faucet and splashed water on her face. Normal. Normal, still, normal. Breathing. Candy looked at herself in the mirror. Then, a sound behind her. Creaking. Something moving back and forth on its hinge.

You turn and the stalls move blink at you.
Look down.
Your hands are covered in blood. Scary, Candy.
Look in the mirror, Candy. Tell me what you see.
How did so much blood get on you?
You stick your hand under another faucet, which also spouts out
  blood. Another sink, more blood.
You tear out paper towels and wipe down your hands and your face,
  the towels staining quickly.

You feel nauseous. But by now you know it wasn't the artisanal egg
*   sandwich, don't you?*
Opening up a stall, you throw up in the toilet, as the stall door
*   continued to bang behind you.*
The lights flicker.
Worms crawl out of the toilet, and you use your boot to kick the
*   handle of the toilet repeatedly.*

Then the stall door opened and there was Jenny, plump Jenny, with her stomach folding over her pants like dough and her thick arms underneath her Coolidge Corner Theater polo. Jenny held out her hand, and it was so soft, so pillowy, and Candy took it and let herself be lifted. She was inches away from Jenny's face. She was making Jenny blush.

"I thought I told you to get out of my fucking face," Candy snarled, and the smell of Jenny just got stronger, and Candy moaned again. Jenny backed away slightly, but only slightly.

"Are you okay?" Jenny said, her breath reeked of the Dunkin' Donuts pumpkin spice cold brew she was always drinking, "We couldn't find you for six hours." Her teeth were graying and had flecks of yellow on them. Candy wanted to lick each one. She stumbled and grabbed onto Jenny's arm and rubbed it.

"Candy?" *No, no,* Candy thought, *she couldn't. She wouldn't. Don't think about that.*

"I've been going through a lot," Candy found herself saying, *oh, no, oh, no,* "Can I have a hug?"

"What?"

"I just need a hug."

Jenny held out her arms. "Oh, sweetie, of course." Candy found herself in Jenny's armpit smelling the flakes of her deodorant, hearing her heart pounding in her ears, a sickeningly sweet song she didn't want to stop listening to.

"Honey?" Jenny said, because she could feel the wetness of Candy's tongue as she wet her shirt, and the soft moans leaving her mouth, and before Jenny even had a chance Candy had pinned her down on the floor.

There it is.

You can feel it, can't you?

You have finally arrived. You've pulled into the station after a long, long ride where you fidgeted and you distracted yourself with other things that you thought could fill you up. But that was just to keep you going. That was just to get you here. This is what you have been trying to reach your entire life, the hole of it all, filled by the blood shooting out of Jenny's neck as you dig your teeth into it, the way her body wriggles underneath you like a kitten's heart. You are so strong in this moment, so very filled up, Candy. You snap off her arm as if it were a tag on a piece of clothing and the skin slips off the muscle in between your teeth. And the best part of it, which is so much different and better than the cold packages of meat, is that you can see all of Jenny's life, her father teaching her how to ride a bicycle in 1979, her lack of interest in men and crush on her neighbor Miranda, who fell in love with her high school sweetheart, who became a postal service worker, and the solace she took, like you do, in the movies, and Jenny's loneliness, which wasn't too different from yours because you can see, as you take her heart into your hands and bite into it like the buñuelos your father used to bring you from East Boston, Jenny and her gerbil, alone in her apartment in Roxbury, the routines she had in the morning, and the best friend who lived in California she called every Sunday to talk about nothing, and as you move on to her organs, you begin to cry, because it is all so beautiful, Jenny's life. And you got to live it and, for as long as it took to finish her, be somebody else.

Candy burped, collapsing against the bathroom stall. Her headache was gone. She felt new. When she was finished with Jenny, she came to and saw the mess around her. The shell she left behind. The life she had taken to feed herself and whatever was growing inside her. Shame began to set in.

"Shit," she said. "Shit!" She locked the bathroom and pulled open the sink cabinet for the proper cleaning tools. She had never felt so full and complete. She grabbed a garbage bag and tossed the remaining bits of Jenny inside—her uniform, her Adidas, her knockoff Apple watch, her bones. She poured bleach on the floor and mopped up in a panic, grabbing paper towels and violently scrubbing away the blood.

With the sack of remains in a black garbage bag over her shoulder, Candy made her way upstairs. She still didn't understand how it was suddenly midnight, how time had just frozen, sped up, and brought her somewhere else. Everyone had gone home for the night. Thank God. She opened the door outside and looked around her, popping open the dumpster and then thinking about how the sack of remains was evidence. Oops. She would have to walk with the garbage bag home. Something soft rubbed against her leg. She looked down.

"How did you get here!" she demanded. The cat got on her back and showed her white belly, showing off her gummy worm nipples. Then she sat up, stuck one leg in the air and started licking her butthole.

"Girl, you are nasty." Candy turned away from her and began her journey home.

She was afraid to look at her phone. She would've Googled *failed abortion* or *how to sue Planned Parenthood* and come across bunch of botched at-home abortions, women's untimely graves and far-right websites. But the phone would've meant more visions, more of that voice in her head, and she didn't want that again, she thought, Jenny's remains banging against her back.

At home, she rummaged around for a lighter and some vegetable oil. She went out into the yard and gathered all the items, poured oil over them, and set them on fire. As the bits of Jenny burned to a crisp, she began to think about what she had done, and if she had control over doing it again. She was a bad person. She deserved the worst. *Give it to me!* she thought. *Somebody come and torture me, somebody come and make me beg for mercy.*

The fire died down. Jenny and her things were just a pile of ash. She looked down at her hands and her nails that were caked with blood. Maybe it was biblical. Maybe the purpose of her life—this series of fuckups and thousands of hours of movies—was to have a child.

In her bathroom, she searched for one of the pregnancy tests. She peed on the stick and waited, curled up in a ball and moaning. After enough time had passed she looked at the stick and the two lines creeping across it like veins that formed over eyelids.

There was something growing inside of her, and it was now several months old. But there was still no belly. She lifted up her shirt and patted her flat stomach, where she was digesting Jenny. She touched her breasts. Still flat.

Thoughts began collecting in her head, bad ones, coins clinking together at the bottom of a vase: she could throw herself down the stairs. She could find all the pills in her house and take them. She could go to the bar and ask for a whiskey and then another and then another. She could do a lot of jumping jacks?

Candy stuffed herself into the corner of her couch, wanting it to swallow her, to become part of its yellow innards and never come out. "FUCKING CUNT PIECE OF SHIT ASS DICK HELL!" she yelled. She took a pillow and screamed into it. What was she supposed to do now? Why was this happening again?

She dialed Zoe-Paola but she didn't answer. She bit her lip until it bled. A hangover without the alcohol. Food poisoning without any good clams. She took out her phone and looked through her call log and found Fernando. She sent a string of messages.

Hey u fucko I'm pregnant with your strong as hell seed.

Literally it's too late for an abortion so I have to have it

Do you know anyone who wants a baby

Fuck you.

With each message, an automated message back with a red exclamation point: *This number is no longer in service or is a landline.* Did he get a new number? Did he get girls pregnant a lot to spread his seed and then just ghost?

Perhaps it was finally time to look up Fernando Moreno on the worldwide internet. Yes, she had avoided it for months. Looking him up would have made the whole thing real and Candy didn't want to take responsibility, just like she didn't want to take responsibility for eating up her coworker.

He was old enough to not have any sort of profile, not even a poorly edited photo of a mountain on vacation or a child's crayon drawing. But searching Instagram, she found a hashtag.

#FernandoMorenoRestinPeace

There was Fernando, with his arms around his colleagues, hiking boots and long socks on, smiling from ear to ear, the volcanos of Guatemala in the background. Bianca was even in the photo, mad toothy for no reason.

Rest in peace, the post read. Rest in *what*?

Googling his name, she found an obituary.

Fernando Moreno, 45, of Washington Heights, beloved professor
at NYU, passed tragically on March 21st, 2023, while working on
an archaeological site in Guatemala. He is survived by his wife,
Felicity Moreno. Donations can be made toward building schools
in Guatemala at the GoFundMe link in the bio. A service will be
held at the library.

Candy got up and began pacing her apartment, holding her phone like a torch. Did he go to Guatemala the same night they had sex? Maybe he had an early flight? What was he doing in Boston again? She never asked him. She just thought he was stupid. She was just trying to get laid. And get back at her sister. Did he have a twin brother? Was his body so disfigured that they actually couldn't tell who it was? Then her phone started showing her something else.

> *Candy. Don't you remember what happens with screens?*
> *You have to be careful. But let me show you something.*
> *There is a man in a cave. Do you recognize him?*
> *Yes, it's him.*
> *There is a light on his head.*
> *He is afraid.*
> *Now, you are there with him.*
> *In here, it feels like you're inside a great big mouth.*
> *He moves further and you follow him into the darkness.*
> *He gets out a shovel.*
> *He starts to dig.*
> *He hits something.*
> *He squats and lifts something up.*
> *A squirming stone.*
> *A woman, who is that?*
> *What is she doing with her body?*
> *Then, light all around you.*
> *Coming out of your eyes.*
> *Leaking from bones.*

BIANCA

The plan was silly. What were they, on the Disney Channel? This was childish. They were grown-ups. They were people whose hangovers started feeling like lethal poisoning, who needed to stretch in the morning to keep from throwing out their back. They had to start worrying about their pelvic floor soon and how much money was put away for property or children, not putting this half-baked plan that involved Bianca in a waist-length red wig and pretending they were environmental journalists.

After Blue's last client, Bianca sat down in their chair as they begrudgingly applied a wig cap to Bianca's skull. Bald, she was able to look at all her features, all eyes, a tight mouth. She felt like she was really looking at herself for the first time, or like she had reverted to infancy. Her little soul. Her tiny life. She hated it. Blue smothered Bianca in foundation, accentuating her cheekbones with highlights. Completely made up, Bianca was unrecognizable. Finally, they applied the long, red, wavy wig that went down to Bianca's waist.

"Do you think I look better like this? Just be honest."

"You look like you're about to do something *really stupid* but obviously I've done an amazing job." Bianca smirked.

"Julian's kind of ridiculous, right?"

"He's just one of those Brooklyn boys who age colossally slow and will be in nursing home one day and suddenly be like, huh, I feel really bad for taking up space in 2017."

"Yeah, I get that."

"But he could just be earnest."

"Do you think I should just forgo this?"

"This just took me two hours to do. You better fully do this."

"Okay. Thank you."

"Be careful, okay?"

Julian met her outside of the salon. "Wow," Julian said, taking in Bianca's new look. "You look like if Reba was a mermaid."

"I don't know who that is."

They stopped by the café and Bianca ordered an oat milk latte. She had not had enough sleep the night before because of anxiety. The barista with the mushroom haircut and the very wide smile was there.

"How's work?" she asked, her teeth seemed to start at her eyes.

"It's good."

"Who is your favorite coworker?"

"I only have one."

"Did he do this to you?" She gestured at Bianca's wig.

Bianca touched the ends of her wig. "Yes, they did."

"And how does business work over there? Is it just you and him?" The woman was so friendly that Bianca found herself answering.

"It's just me and them. We only take cash and Venmo. And then we split it seventy/thirty."

"Huh. How much for a haircut?"

"It's scaled," Bianca said. "Your hair *is* kind of funny."

The woman shook off Bianca's insult with a laugh, which was not meant to be an insult. Just then, Julian came over holding up a bag of coffee beans.

"You know this farm is on strike right now?" he said, the beans rattling.

"I didn't," the woman said, smiling, almost giggling.

"Something to think about," he said, putting a dollar in the tip jar.

Bianca and Julian took the J at Kosciuszko and switched at Fulton to the A, even though Julian insisted that they just bike there.

"I really just don't like feeling immobile," he said. "Like I'm stuck."

"I'm wearing a wig," Bianca said.

Passing an unconscious person on the subway platform, Julian started going on a rant about how people should always carry Narcan with them. "It's a citizen's responsibility," he said, not looking Bianca in the eye as the A train came barreling toward them.

"Did you bring Narcan?" Bianca asked. Julian didn't answer her. Bianca sipped the latte. The oat milk was made in-house and tasted of canola oil and wax. She made to toss it into a trash can but Julian held out an arm to prevent the drink from going in.

"I'll take that. Don't be wasteful."

"How many people have you saved, exactly? With Narcan?" Bianca asked, watching Julian stubbornly sip from the waxy latte. They were surrounded by subway posters for Grubhub with somewhat nauseating slogans, the Thai takeout looking crisp and high-definition, people's mouths open wide.

"It's not about the number," Julian said, his voice rising, fully ready for a debate. "It's about principle." They still hadn't brought up Candy. Or the fact that they lost their virginity to each other. He was wearing a simple blue jacket, a used pair of Doc Martens, gray slacks, and a messenger bag that was meant to bring to mind someone who was serious about the environment. Bianca found this all funny. It was so easy to make anybody believe in who you are. Julian absentmindedly ran his fingers through his long hair and continued to talk.

"Once we have this all figured out, I'd love to pick your brain on how we can use archaeologists to further our cause and probably save more lives."

"And how archaeologists can help addicts?" Bianca was so bored by this.

"Anybody can help anybody!"

"Can we go over what you're going to say?" Bianca scratched the back of her wig. This was completely ridiculous.

"I am going to say that we're here to talk about passing an environmental bill in the Upper West Side. She is going to give me the time of day, because I am a man. And then you're going to ask where the bathroom is and find those files, then we'll leave."

"This is not going to work." Bianca let out a sigh.

"Trust me," Julian said.

CANDY

Before Candy took the bus to the Planned Parenthood in Allston, she sniffed out a rat scuttling in the middle of the street, stepped on it as it was about to dive into a bag of recycling, and ate it whole, able to see its entire vermin life as she chewed. The cat, of course, was nearby, purring its approval.

"You sicko," Candy said to her, spitting out the rat's spine. "You like this, don't you?" The cat purred. She didn't know why she didn't, or couldn't, eat the cat. The rat was enough to hold her over on her way to the Planned Parenthood, where she was determined to get another abortion, free of charge. She had made an appointment over the phone, lying and saying that she was experiencing heavy bleeding and not a relapse into a craving that made her eat her coworker.

There was a long wait to see a doctor because a lot of scared out-of-town young girls were in with their various chaperones: older sisters with driver's licenses, boyfriends in their parents' cars, volunteers who hosted girls in their living rooms, tired fathers who used their sick days to drive their daughters across state lines.

Candy filled out the sheet calculatedly. She checked off "pregnant" and counted on her fingers—she was five months along. Apparently, the doctor was on leave. *Probably on leave because she is particularly unskilled at scraping babies out of people*, Candy thought. Sitting with her arms crossed in the waiting room, she glanced around her. She was nervous the symptoms would begin again and that she would have to describe what was happening to her. Describing it only made her feel crazy and bad, like someone who shouldn't be around any living thing ever.

The nurse who called her was a tall woman with a neat black bob that lined her skull like a mushroom cap. She wore a wide smile that didn't come from joy; it was just the way her face was shaped. She must have always been smiling, even if she didn't want to, Candy thought. She must have smiled inappropriately to so many moments in her life: the news of death, or somebody telling her that they were allergic to grapefruit, or felt afraid of dogs.

"So, what's going on today? You said you're pregnant but also experiencing bleeding?"

"Kind of both?" Bleeding of course, was a euphemism for being sucked into screens and chomping on your coworker's fingers like baby carrots.

"Interesting." The nurse typed something down on the computer.

"Well, Candelaria, it says here in your records that you received abortion care with us."

"Yeah, that's the thing. I don't think it worked."

"Why don't we do a little exam?"

The nurse told her to lie back and relax as she applied the cool jelly to her stomach. On the ultrasound screen, Candy saw the nurse hovering above her, her smile widening across her face like the Cheshire Cat's, then expanding so that she was one big mouth.

There you are.
You touch your stomach and sit up, making blood marks on
the bed.
You say something to the Mouth Nurse.
Her mouth expands until it looks like it could swallow your head.

"Look." The nurse pointed to a screen, where Candy's empty womb was, the color of the underbelly of an elephant. "There's nothing." The nurse turned on the lights and handed Candy a paper towel to wipe the jelly off.

"What did you say your symptoms were?"

"Nausea," Candy lied.

"Have you tried CBD oil? It's natural. Could calm you down."

"Yeah, maybe." Candy felt like an idiot. "Thanks."

"Collagen helps, too." Candy had to look away from the nurse's teeth. "Maybe in the morning with a smoothie."

"Oh, I actually do that. But I was getting a little sick of it."

"Studies show that it's very good for you."

"Huh. Okay."

"I can give you this painkiller, if you'd like."

"What kind of painkiller?"

"It's all-natural." She took out a bottle of ointment from her bag and handed it to her.

"Where did you get this?"

"An insiders' nurse thing."

Candy held the bottle of ointment in her hands.

"Trust me," the smiling nurse said, "just put two drops under your tongue."

Candy complied. It tasted like nothing.

"Is there anything else?" the nurse asked.

"Yeah, where's the doctor that originally did the abortion?"

"She passed, unfortunately." The nurse flicked on the light and Candy flinched.

"Passed? Like away? How?"

"Yes. A week ago. And I think that's private." The nurse opened the door and kept her hand on the handle. Her saliva was glittery on her teeth. "After you." Candy jumped off the seat and grabbed her bag.

So, she wasn't pregnant. She was just an insane psychopathic cannibal who thought the TV was talking to her. Maybe she did need to rest radically.

She took the 57 to the 1 to Nubian Square because she forgot she was supposed to take her grandmother to get her cortisone shot. Mauricio answered the door, greeting her with a bulky hand. He told her once that whenever it was that he died (she found that old people were always talking about death like it was a change of weather), he would give her his car, purposefully forgetting that she wasn't allowed to drive.

Candy escorted her grandmother down the stairs while holding her cane. Her mother always said that her abuelita was faking it. She could walk miles and miles, actually. She could walk the entire city if she wanted. The cortisone shots just helped a little bit. Made her go even faster. Candy didn't really care. Let her grandmother lie, she thought. Maybe she just wanted somebody to touch her.

You are scratching a ticket you had in your bag and your daughter is talking to people, offering help with torn clothes. She had brought her needles, of course. Her thread. Or maybe she just wants to keep busy.

You watched her work quickly, her hands almost blurry as she sewed patches on pants and coats. A soldier asked if she could do any adjustments and she half-jokingly said she would, for a fee.

Creations by Lucia was successful from the very start. Every day, from nine to five, a rich woman from across town would stand behind the curtain Lucia had fashioned and talk to her about something that Lucia would pretend to know about, her brow furrowed as she concentrated, pulling down rolls of fabrics, making their dresses and trousers fit their tiny frames. They all looked so cold, bracelets bunching together at their bony wrists. Yes, your daughter worked so hard. Too hard, you think. Not enough time to enjoy. To laugh a little. Did your daughter even love this? Or was it just what she knew how to do it well?

You keep scratching with your lucky nickel, matching the numbers together. You hold it up to the light. You blink and look closer. No way.

"Lucia," you say, hobbling over to her, where she's hemming the bottom of a pant for a young white girl with green hair.

"What?" she says, her face fully concentrated, her hands almost moving on their own.

"Can you look at this?" She peers at your scratch ticket.

"Okay," she says. "What?"

"Look at the numbers." She takes the card and hands it back. Then she grabs it again.

"I won, didn't I?"

She is speechless. You've been scratching cards since you arrived here, almost thirty years ago. The most you'd ever won was one hundred dollars, which you then spent on more scratching cards. Your daughter stands up and whispers to you.

"Don't let anybody see." Because you, Candelaria, just won $100,000. It's there as clear as day. You start to laugh, Lucia lets out a chuckle.

"We can discuss what we will do with it," she says, walking you back to the cart.

"What do you mean? It's my money."

"Yes, Mamá, and I don't *trust you with it*."

"Why? I'm not a criminal."

She doesn't say anything and asks for the card.

"No," you say, holding it close to your chest. "It's mine." She opens her palm. You feel like a little girl, but you are her mother. You tuck it into your pocket, defiantly.

"Listen?" you say, "What if I can trade it with them? For the Jeep?"

Lucia rolls her eyes. "You are out of your mind," she says, holding on to your shoulders.

"No, I'm not." Just then, a soldier takes a megaphone and makes an announcement. Everybody begins to sit down.

You whisper to Lucia, "What is he saying?"

A girl with green hair comes to sit next to you.

"¿Necesitar ayudar traduciar?" the girl asks. Her eyes are big and warm.

Your daughter responds to her sternly, in English. The girl with the green hair nods and sits still there on the cot, smiling up at you. What does she want?

"I hope everyone is feeling safe and warm." A small murmuring throughout the crowd. "We have heard from Washington and help is on the way!" Cheering roared throughout the tent. "We will keep everybody posted soon." Lucia marched over to the soldiers to ask them a question, and you are left with the girl with the green hair.

"Where are you from?" she asks, in Spanish. She can't be more than fifteen years old.

"Guatemala," you tell her.

"What part? A mother mine work there." Her Spanish is just as good as your granddaughters'.

"Chiquimula," you say.

"Does it like barriletes festival?"

Que linda. Gabo was just a child when you met Victor. Or did he have another name? Names erode, lost in the washing machine of your memory and popping up at random like socks—*Loreto!* Or getting a cortisone shot—*Victor!* Whatever his name was, you were selling tortillas in the city during the barriletes festival when he appeared to you, tall and dark-skinned with a heavy brow and a guitar strapped to his back. The man asked you about yourself and you liked this, it was as if he knew you already and you liked this too, you didn't *have* to explain anything to him. Gabo brought his kite up to the apartment while you walked around all night with This Man, who told you he was from Belize, that he would only be here for a night, and you were lonely, Canducha, but you weren't going to give yourself up. Still, that loneliness made you open up to him in a different way. The things you told him! All your worries and fears, your hopes and your dreams. You were still behaving like a child, telling a man all of those things. You let your guard down. All that information. And what did he tell you? Something about the world changing and dying, and how time just stopped?

He told you to wait for him at a spot in the city, next to the mechanic shop. And you almost did but something had changed: you were no longer young and stupid. You had a child. You were not going to wait for some-body anymore. You got up, made Gabo breakfast. You went to work. Your life continued. You eventually met ese desgraciado Pedro, and Lucia came and so did another festival, and another, and Gabo left this world and Lucia left your country and then didn't talk to you for fifteen years. You never saw Victor again.

"Yes," you tell the girl. "I like it."

The tent shakes slightly. The huddled crowd inside is shaken but comforted by the soldiers standing at the entranceway with their rifles. Everybody is in a relatively good mood. Somebody is coming soon. It was just an earthquake. And some freak weather. But soon, they will all be taken into somewhere even warmer, with cell service, and be able to communicate with their loved ones, and the power will come back on.

Lucia comes back, looking like she needs to tell you something.

"We need to go," she says, looking around her. You let out a little mariachi hoot and clap your hands.

"¡Eso, hija! ¡Vamos ya!"

"Quiet. Listen to me. We're not going to the Old Country Buffet."

"But—"

"I need to find the girls."

"We are in *danger*," you try to say, and finally, is it coming? Here it is? The truth, finally? Just say it! Say something!

"My girls are in danger. Candy could die."

"They are adults! They made their own choices."

"You would rather just leave them behind? Like you left me?" Come on. She really needs to get over that.

"*You* ran away,"

"Do I have to remind you why?"

"Lucia, you don't know anything about what's going on!"

"And you do?"

"We need to go to the Old Country Buffet. It's a matter of life or death."

"Are you hiding something there? Why do you lie so much?"

"Something Gabo made me. Before he died." Was that so hard?

"You never told me about that." Lucia's face is so unchanging sometimes, it can scare you.

"There was no need to."

"What really happened to Mauricio?" Around the tent, people talk among themselves, paying you no attention.

"Are you telling me the truth?" she asks. "Be honest with me."

You just know she won't understand. She will call you crazy. She will leave you behind. But what's the point of lying at the end of the world?

"I killed him," you say, and it's just as dramatic as it sounds. You are a movie star, your hair being tousled by the wind in a car with the top down. "Just like I killed Gabo." But Lucia looks at you as if you were saying you found your insulin in the flour, which you did. She squints at you like a map at golden hour.

"We need to get you to a neurologist after this."

"It wasn't really Gabo. And it wasn't really Mauricio. So it's okay."

She sits on a cot and puts her head in her hands. Maybe she really is ready to believe you.

"Can you tell me why?"

"Yes. He came to me after we saw the army. Do you remember that?"

Lucia nods.

"Mirna said he was dead, but he wasn't dead yet." She takes her hands away from her face.

"You saw him, too?"

"What? Yes, that's what I'm saying."

"I saw him that day, too. He was outside our house. And then I ran and ran and opened the door and it was just you."

"Yes, well, that's because I had just killed him."

"And . . . why did you do that?"

Her blood is boiling. You can hear it. You cannot say what you are about to say. "Because. He was . . . acting strange. But it wasn't him!" You are shaking, the memory hurts too much, an iron on the hand, a needle through a finger.

"Strange how?" Well, if she's so willing to believe you, if she's so ready to ask questions, you might as well keep going.

"He tried to touch me—"

"ENOUGH!" Lucia screams, making the whole tent turn. "You're a liar. You're a monster. You tried to *sell me* to get out of poverty. And what did I do? Take care of you. Pay for your doctor's visits. I came to *rescue you* and you're still like this! You're never going to change." Lucia begins to sob and the people in the tent politely looks away. But she's not listening now. The girl with green hair just tapped her on the shoulder. Lucia turns around wildly.

"Sorry," she says, "I don't mean to be nosy, but were you talking about Candy?"

"Yes," Lucia puts her hands on her shoulders. "Do you know where she is?"

The girl with green hair looks uneasy. "My mom was her doctor, I think." Lucia begins to pace.

"What do you mean?"

"No era regular doctora." The girl is still trying to speak in Spanish.

"What does that mean?"

"I think these people got her. And . . ." The girl's eyes begin to well up with tears. "I think they killed my mom." Lucia grabs her.

"Do you think you can take me to them?" The girl looks around the tent. She whispers.

"¿Qué dijo?" you say, interrupting both of them. They'd been speaking so low you couldn't hear them.

But you'll never know what she was going to say, because just then, the tent collapses and everybody begins to scream. Another quake. Just as everyone was starting to feel hopeful! Just as everyone was picturing their Christmas cookies and the captions on their pictures about this out-of-the-ordinary day.

I'm sad to say that the man who put up the Christmas lights did not survive. He was thrown across the tent, hit a pole, and landed on the ground with a gash in his head and no life in his eyes. Very sad. The cot shot up into a kind of triangle that protected you and Lucia and the girl with green hair. Somehow you were protected. The shaking was brief but just as disastrous, just like last time. When you creep out from the cot triangle, you and Lucia see destruction everywhere. You look to each other and gather your things. The wind has stopped howling. The tent has blown away. The cold is starting to escape your bones. The sun is shining bright.

Things are leaping through the snowbanks and into the tent. Things that you can't describe, unlike any animal or person you have ever seen. Your brain adjusts and sees something like large, wriggling cats. You can't focus on their faces. One of them has a torn Flour bakery shirt on its chest.

"Ay, no," you say, covering your eyes and then uncovering them. Your daughter shushes you. The beasts devour those who survived the quake, sniffing the dead and stepping over them. Why? Lucia opens her palm.

"I'm not giving you my ticket!" you tell her.

But she lowers her voice and says, "No, the food you have. Did you bring any salchicha?" You rummage, quietly, trying to see which tin foil contains what.

"Quietly!"

"Do you want me to find them or what?" You find the salchichas at the bottom of your purse, you can smell them, and hand them to Lucia. Lucia whistles through her teeth, a trick her brother taught her, and flings the sausages to the corners of the tent. The beasts follow, scrambling, desperate for flesh. Your daughter acts fast, grabbing the guns the soldiers dropped. She throws a pistol to the girl with green hair and hands you another. You step over the bodies as the beasts eat your salchichas, and then, suddenly, sniffing the air, they retreat and exit the tent, as if summoned.

"I don't know how to use this," you say to Lucia, and she rolls her eyes. She knows you do. She empties the other rifles of their bullets and dumps them into her bag. You have already thrown your pistol into your purse along with the military blankets. You have a feeling you won't need those much longer. It's getting hotter and hotter. You hear people moving about. The snowbank is still too high to climb through and snow has collapsed around the brown tent. And outside? The bridge you crawled over has collapsed and a strange shimmer covering the river as it slowly begins to dry up. The sky is a deep bloodred.

Out of the corner of your eye, you see the kind soldier brushing off his shoulders. He is still alive. He was knocked out by the blast, but did not die.

"Mijo!" you say, waddling toward him. He's still on his knees. "Thank you so much." You remember his Spanish isn't very good. "Very beautiful!" He smiles up at you, then you take out the pistol, pointing it at his forehead.

"Jeep," you say. "Thank you so much." He looks taken aback. Lucia was right. You are dangerous. No one else is alive, and his weapons have been tossed aside. He has to listen to you.

He puts his hands up, the gun to his back as he walks to the Jeep.

"Mamá?" Lucia is on her way to another Jeep with the girl with green hair. Does she even know where to go? You can't help her now. You must get to the Old Country Buffet, no matter what.

"Help me into the car!" you scream in Spanish. "More sugar!" you say in English. The soldier confusedly helps you inside, and you know the reason he isn't fighting you is because you are so old. How could anyone kill an old woman?

"Drive!" you say, pointing east, along the river, which is slowly disappearing. "Drive!"

You point the gun to him and tell him to drive, zooming on the sidewalks of Mass Ave, where you see people who chose to die in their cars. This is bad. You know they will wake up soon.

CANDY

At the doctor's office, they had her grandmother move her leg up and down and walk across the room. They held her veiny, spotted knee in their gloved hands. The attendants always loved her. The doctor came in and gave his handsome smile. He seemed a little older than Bianca, with dark eyes and cropped shiny black hair. He could've been an actor or a gameshow host, but instead he was here to tenderly tell a family that her grandmother's knee was quickly deteriorating, and would continue to, that the cortisone shot was only a temporary solution, that she and her family should strongly consider what would happen once she needs to be in a wheelchair. Candy didn't tell her grandmother this. Instead, she said that eventually she wouldn't need a cortisone shot. That she was exceptional when it came to women her age. Mauricio, who understood more English, stayed silent. Watching her grandmother slowly make her way back into Mauricio's car, Candy realized she wasn't hungry anymore, at least not like that, and she was so thankful that she wouldn't hurt these precious people in the car with her, that she began to cry.

"What's wrong?" her grandmother asked, "¿Estás enamorada?" It's what she said every time any of her granddaughters were crying, as in, *I hope it's not because you're in love, because there are worse things in this world to cry about*, or, *There's only one thing that can make a beautiful girl as sad as this.*

Candy shook her head. She wished her Spanish were better, so that she could articulate the nuances of everything she was feeling, so that she could tell a story slowly, detail a cartograph of her emotional logic, let her grandmother give her the advice she needed. But all she could say was, "Siento estresada, Abuelita." Estreseda, a made-up word for displaced Latinx Americans that she used to describe the fact that she ate a coworker.

Her abuelita nodded her head and said, "Sí, mija, el estrés te mata. Por eso es bueno resar y quedarse en la casa." It's good to pray and stay inside.

Candy would've been sad that this was all she and her living ancestor had to say to each other but thought that this was the language of care sometimes: the words were impersonal and recycled, but they came from someone who wanted the best for you. If only Candelaria knew English and Candy knew Spanish and they could wax poetic on life, speak in simile: life is a torn dress, a cup of vinegar holding dead flies, a shoe of a coworker, splattered with her own blood tossed underneath the toilet.

"Un funerario," said Mauricio, hitting traffic. "We just have to sit here and wait."

"Que pecado," said Candelaria, lowering the window to see what was going on. The funeral was a sea of mostly women dressed in green. Something clicked in Candy and she told Mauricio and her grandmother that she would walk home.

At the funeral home she saw the abortion doctor, Gabriella Linden's face plastered on a large poster on the door.

GABRIELLA LINDEN
1975–2023
DOCTOR, MOTHER, FRIEND.

There were women of all ages there, holding each other and crying.

"I had no idea she was suffering like this," one woman said, holding on to a cracker dressed with salmon. "And to think she changed all of our lives for the better. I never would have gone to law school if it weren't for her."

"Depression finds a way," another woman responded, shaking her head. A girl with blue hair interrupted.

"My mom didn't kill herself." Her eyes were bloodshot and her hair looked stringy, like she hadn't washed it in a few days. The women glanced at each other, unsure of what to say. A tall woman with a clipboard came up behind the girl and whispered something in her ear.

"I'm not going with you," she said, almost screaming. "She's only been dead for two days, can you not force foster-care options on me? She probably put that I was supposed to live with her friend in the will."

The woman with the clipboard said something else in a lower voice.

"I don't know you! I've never seen you before!" The girl stormed away, and the woman with the clipboard followed.

Candy stepped away, finding her way to the funeral home bathroom and squatting above a toilet to pee. Feet appeared beneath the stall. A pair of Vans and a pair of simple white sneakers.

"Your mom's will clearly stated that she wanted you with us."

"She would've wanted me with a friend. She's never mentioned you people in my life."

"We are an organization that will look out for you."

"You're full of shit."

"Where else are you going to go? You're not eighteen yet. The government will put you in a foster home."

"Leave me alone," she said, closing the door. The white sneakers lingered for a while. They turned and faced where Candy was in the stall. Candy felt, for a moment, that she was being stared at through the beige door. She flushed the toilet. The white sneakers stayed there. Candy flushed the toilet again, and the shoes left the room.

ZOE

After class one day, Maria called a meeting. Zoe sat in the front with Carmen, their legs crossed. Everyone was silent when Maria entered, her linen pants swishing by her ankles. She lit a candle and sat in the front of the room, where one hundred women were proudly holding on to their new bellies. They had all sought out men in the Boston area to procreate with, being sure to agree to dates when they were ovulating, and keeping in touch were the consummation not to happen. While she knew it wasn't her fault she couldn't have kids, Zoe still felt guilty.

Like she wasn't trying hard enough. Like she could have done more if she wanted. Maria brought out the bell attached to the white box. Nobody had asked Maria where she acquired the bell. They just respected it.

Maria closed her eyes and hummed. The entire room hummed back. They followed the rhythm of the bell. They meditated for about an hour, with Maria giving everybody a shoulder rub as they hummed and the bell rang. To Zoe, Maria's touch felt like a voice in her ear, telling her that everything was alright. She selfishly never wanted her to stop. But then Maria did, and Zoe opened her eyes and saw her at the front of the room, where she turned off the bell.

"I have an exciting announcement to make," Maria said, as everybody came out of their meditation. Frances, a woman with a shiny black mushroom cut, came wheeling something in a large crate.

"I had my doubts but then I sat with my doubts, and I fought them," Maria said, slowly pacing the front of the room. "And now, the Woman's Stone is really here." She nodded at Frances, who had a large smile that just seemed to be the way her face was shaped. Frances pulled on a rope and a side of the box fell, revealing a simple stone.

"Just looks like a rock, right?" Maria said, clapping her hands. "We are all just rocks, if you think about it, spinning around a big rock. Soon? It won't spin anymore. Something new will happen. Something"—and Maria gently touched the bell again—"will open." The stone began to hum to life, it squirmed and bubbled, not holding one distinct shape.

"This is the Mother." The entire room gasped. A few women began to cry. "Like the SCOBY in kombucha. We are the bacteria that comes from this." Tears began to well in Maria's eyes. "It's just so beautiful." It was remarkable. They had all been hearing about the Mother, and some of them had even thought it was just an idea, something that kept them all together. Something to do with Maria's will and all of their determination to make the world new. But it was real, Zoe was seeing now. It was actually a thing. A living, ancient thing.

"On one of my visits to Guatemala I took a part of it and used it in some of my harvests. I've made new vitamins and treatments, as I've told you. I'm sorry it's took me this long to show you all." Zoe was entranced by it. She couldn't tell what color it was.

"Make sure to not touch it," Maria said, wiping her eyes and straightening herself up. "A beauty such as this has consequences."

Zoe looked at Carmen, who wiggled her eyebrows and laughed in disbelief. Zoe felt so light suddenly. And hungry.

BIANCA

Bianca had seen her face before, of course. She had fallen asleep staring at it on her phone: the Google-searched image of a beautiful middle-aged woman, an editor at *New York Magazine*, the cursor hovering over her name. Felicity had let herself grow gray, and Bianca felt it accentuated the youthful pinkness in her cheekbones and the dark shape of her eyebrows. She had a skin-care routine, Bianca thought. Probably Pond's every morning since she turned thirteen. Was it time for Bianca to get one? Felicity was wearing a white, billowy blouse and a turquoise necklace decorated her neck. Her eyes weren't red, there wasn't any trace of crying. She looked remarkably calm, Bianca noted. At peace with something.

"Come in," Felicity said, "I was just making myself a snack." She didn't look sad. There was no sign of sleep or weight loss. She almost seemed happy. Felicity walked them over to an island in her kitchen, where she was chopping up a hunk of Brie and spreading it on homemade bread.

"I made this myself," she said. Julian sat down, comfortable but not too comfortable, gauging the situation, and helped himself. "This is really delicious," he said, sounding like somebody in a TV show with a full mouth. A trained actor, a deceiver. A performer. Bianca also knew he was really good at talking to middle-aged white women in a way that she did not, because those were his parents.

"Your home is fantastic. What kind of marble is this?" Felicity sat next to him, scooting closer on a stool.

"Actually, a lot went into it," Felicity said, going into a rant about the intricacies and bureaucracy of everything it took to install and wax the marble. Bianca stood up and politely, or so she felt, asked if she could use the bathroom. Felicity pointed absentmindedly to the left where the staircase was and Bianca followed. She was shocked at how trusting she was.

She took in the second floor of their brownstone. Fernando had never let her come over. It was too risky. They used desks, Airbnbs. Going on to the second floor, there were photos of Felicity and Fernando up on the walls. Their wedding day. Photos of ancestors, Felicity's, black-and-white portraits of older women in gray with tight-lipped smiles sitting on chairs next to their bearded husbands. No photos of Fernando's parents. They were estranged. But for Felicity, it was important to remember where she came from. Bianca felt a pang of guilt.

She looked around and found a room with a computer. Instantly, she smelled Fernando. His skin cells were all over the books nestled in the shelves and the Post-it notes on the desk. The black leather chair she was now sitting in. His smell. Its own particular woodenness. A freshly refurbished floor of a man and his sweat. How do you mourn someone who left you before they died? Was it painful for him when he left this world? Did he think of her at all? Bianca wondered why this private room was just left open, why Felicity was so trusting. Maybe she never bothered to look Bianca up. Out of sight, out of mind. Still, she felt like she was moving into a trap. Fernando had never let her come to his place.

She started the iMac and it sang to life. There was a password. She tried a standard 123246—nothing. She tried his last name: MORENO. Nothing. Then she typed in *Antigua*, and immediately got in. No wonder his wife found out about them. Idiot.

She went into his email. Spam from funeral homes and life insurance, credit card cancellation fees. She clicked into his sent emails. There was an email to his wife, asking about some house-related errand, but it was after they had broken up.

Feli,

Hi baby. Just wondering if you could send me the password to
the joint account when you get a chance.

Yours,

Fernando.

He sent this when she was on the plane back to New York. He had lied.
Felicity had no idea who she was. Bianca caught a glimpse of herself in her
red wig in the desktop reflection. She was a fool. She kept looking, and
found another sent email, to an address with a series of numbers.

Hi—

Going in tomorrow. Not sure how safe it's going to be? Will get
you the results soon. Let me know if you got this.

F

She remembered what she was here for. All this time and she still had the
instinct to snoop. She had never done it, of course. Because she had deeply
trusted Fernando. She heard Julian still talking downstairs, very loudly, so
that she could hear, about recycling. She closed the browser. She searched
for *Sylvester Leon* on his desktop and found it, finally. The conversation.

ANTIGUA HOTEL, GUATEMALA

BIANCA: The subject is here. Can we talk about this after? Hola,
mucho gusto.

SYLVESTER LEON: Hola! What's goin' on, nice to meet you. You
want a drink? I think it's happy hour right now.

FERNANDO: Agradezco este tiempo que esta pasando con nosotros.

SYLVESTER LEON: I'm sorry, I actually don't really speak Spanish!

She emailed it to Julian, as he had instructed, in case people really were
looking through her email. She continued searching the desktop.

Bianca clicked on a file labeled TENURE. Bianca clicked on it. In this folder, another folder labeled STUDENT FEEDBACK. It was innocuous enough. She clicked on it. Another folder labeled BOOKS. Click. Another folder labeled ACCOUNTS. Click. Another folder. Another. Another. She was twenty folders in before she actually found it. Various files. MP3s? She clicked on one labeled, vaguely enough, FILE__1. She turned on the speaker and began to hear her mother's voice.

LUCIA: He came back to the house covered in dirt.
BIANCA: Why?
LUCIA: I think he was in a cave. Some tunnel.
BIANCA: And what did he say?
LUCIA: He told me to stay away from Juan Leon, he was bad.
BIANCA: And did you?
LUCIA: Yes.

There was her mother's voice and hers, so tiny and teenaged, a little bell on a door. Not possible. Her mother had told her she had deleted the files. Years and years had passed since this conversation. Candy hadn't been to rehab yet. She hadn't met Fernando. How long had he known about her? She looked at herself in the reflection of the window in the office. She was a fool in a wig on the case. She clicked on FILE__2.

BIANCA: Tell me about Christmas.
LUCIA: Fine. No money. We had more food. Gabo gave me a small wooden model that he made. He knew I liked sewing.
BIANCA: Did he make it himself?
LUCIA: Yes, he always liked doing that. Very creative.
BIANCA: When did you discover you liked to sew?
LUCIA: I stuck a needle into my hand. Right into the carne between my forefinger and my thumb. Painful. Gabo gave it a kiss. I think he was magic. I made a dress from scratch the next day.

There were ten files, recordings made on Bianca's device and uploaded to the family's computer. And now they were here? In their conversations, Bianca would often tease him about their student-professor dynamic, and he would bristle. "I'm much more than a university professor," he would tell her, smile crooked and teeth a little, too, and Bianca would giggle. Fernando was so much more than a university professor. He was never who he said he was. She felt rage at the back of her neck, and she cherished it, because its prickliness was so much more welcoming than the depression that had encased her in herself for the past few months.

She took out a mini hard drive she'd purchased at Target, which drunk up the files, and went downstairs, where Julian and Felicity were enjoying pita chips and goat cheese and some kind of artisanal jam. Felicity was sipping from a mug of green tea, and she was so calm and sturdy, that Bianca needed to interrupt it, break through the glass of it all, make shards fly.

"I was having an affair with your husband."

Julian was still chewing on a cracker and seemed to be debating on whether or not to swallow.

"He was a liar. Also, Julian isn't really a journalist."

"That's right, I am *not* a journalist. I'm here to pass an *environmental* bill that would help the city have better recycling tact—"

"That's upsetting to hear." Felicity's eyes looked like she was gazing out at a grand landscape of colorful trees and not at two almost-thirty-year-olds. "People aren't always who you think they are."

She wasn't upset. She hadn't mourned the way Bianca did. She wasn't thinking of the clock of Fernando's facial hair, the shades of it through the day, the eruption at the end of the night, the mustache she would poke her fingers through.

"That cheese was great," Julian said, wiping the crumbs on his shirt. "Delightful. And the hints of lemon?"

Felicity smiled. "I'm glad you enjoyed them."

Julian looked over at Bianca, who was still staring at Felicity like she was watching a snake with a top hat sing.

"Aren't you sad? Or mad at me?"

"A feeling leads into an ocean of understanding. I am less than a drop of water. We all are."

"I really am interested in talking to you about recycling in this neighborhood," Julian said, trying to jump through the tension. He also was legitimately interested.

"Sure," Felicity said, lovingly scraping the leftover bits of the charcuterie board into the trash, the blade facing out.

"A journalist? We went over the plan so many times."

"Sorry, I got caught up in my *emotions*." The last few months, in fact, had been a time of emotions upon emotions. They were all rising up in her and she felt sick with them, practically feral.

"Deeply. You don't know if she's involved with whatever's going on!"

"What was wrong with her? Why was she acting like that?" Julian walked her to the A. Bianca was almost shaking.

"People react to grief in all kinds of ways," Julian said, "I honestly think you didn't need to share that."

"You're being extremely judgmental right now."

"No, I'm just saying in the future, don't blow up like that."

"I didn't even want to go there. This was *your* idea."

"Well, did you get what we came for?" The train had stalled between stations. They were deep in the belly of New York, a capsule stuck in the city's intestines. Bianca gathered herself. She was beginning to feel embarrassed for exploding and almost forgot what she had learned.

"He had old recordings. From before I met him. Recordings I hadn't seen in years."

"Weird. You got that guy right? Sylvester whatever?"

"Yes. I sent them all to your email."

"Okay. We'll go to him next."

"What?"

"We need to figure this out."

"Why?" Bianca felt very strange. It was the same feeling she had when her sister had FaceTimed her on her bike and she was on the floor of Blue's studio. Something was off. Something felt very wrong.

"Because I want to help."

"Why?" Could she trust Julian? Fernando had betrayed her and her sister, too. Why should she trust this earnest man who cared too much about recycling?

"Because."

"Why are you laughing?"

"Sorry, I'm just nervous."

"You sound like a little girl."

"I don't want you to hate me, Bianca."

"That's a stupid reason to do anything."

"No, I don't want you to keep assuming I'm doing the worst. I'm not. You know, I've been meaning to tell you something." The train conductor came on the loudspeaker, saying they would be stalled in between stations for fifteen minutes.

"I'm really glad I got the shits that day."

"Julian, what?"

"No, seriously. I feel like seeing you put me back in my place again, I don't know. Reminded me about a lot of stuff." Was he ever going to say it? Julian was silent but looked like he was going to shit his pants again. He was squirming and clutching his stomach. This pained him.

"I was such a fucking loser in high school," Julian said, letting the sentence out like a tire running out of air. "Nobody was into me. I felt really ugly, Bianca!"

"Is that it?"

"And I feel like we found each other in that white pressure cooker."

"What do you mean. You ignored me."

"I know, and well, let me—" Julian looked like he was on the verge of tears. "I was just like, obsessed with Candy. I mean everybody was. And then, you know, you ask me, really deliberately, to have sex—" Bianca shushed him.

"And then I guess I was like, well, why was that so easy but Candy wasn't?"

"I was easy?"

"No! I don't know! I just wanted it all. And then she asked me to get her those drugs, and like, I had connections, and I told her no, I said no, I don't want to do that for you but she kept begging me in this way that made me feel like it would get her to love me?" Julian was clenching his fists.

"And I'm just really sorry. But I don't think there's anything I can do for it to be undone. So, I guess I'm just helping you with this stupid thing because I feel bad. And I want to make it up to you. So, I'm all yours. Boss me around." Bianca nodded and looked away. The train began to move again, and their thoughts were drowned out by the belly of the city, squeaking and whistling them home.

CANDY

One sneaker in front of the other, Candy made her way down Washington Street all the way through Roxbury and into Jamaica Plain. Blasting the same four Mozart songs once more into her ears, she replayed the conversation in the bathroom between who she assumed was Gabriella's daughter and somebody from some foster program. She felt so much empathy for the teenager. Somebody telling you what to do with your life while you're trying to deal with loss. That does something to you. If it was okay to mourn somebody she had only met once. Was it okay for her to mourn somebody she had met once? She hadn't even seen Gabriella on the day of her abortion. But she had done her a huge service hadn't she? And what about her daughter? And oh my God, her daughter? That's horrible. Imagine doing that to your mother? To your very flesh and blood. A sudden flash of her mother's distraught hand over hers in a hospital bed sped through her head. A bullet train of a memory. A rat sliding its body through a skinny gate.

After the funeral, Candy walked home. The Bible-thumpers must be having a field day, she thought. The person responsible for killing babies has now taken her own life. Suicide was so tricky to Candy. On the one hand, you leave behind a lot of guilt and suffering for the people who loved you. On the other hand, you don't have to deal with it.

Okay, she thought, *maybe I have done something like that before.*

The ointment she had was good for a week. And then what would she do? Would the visions keep happening? Would the cravings? What or who would she kill next? It was dark out all around and Candy was nearing her apartment. She took out her keys and fingered a charm meant to look like a hotel key from *The Shining*, the only thing she allowed on her keychain besides her keys. She didn't like clutter. Behind her, she heard a car door shut. She turned around instinctively and saw a shadowy figure walking behind her. Normal, Candy thought. A lot of people live on this block. Families. Mothers and fathers. Teens. She quickened her pace regardless. The person kept following her. He was going to kill her, Candy could feel it. This was going to be the end of it all. But then the man just went into his house. He was nobody. Or at least he was nobody who would hurt her.

Arriving at her porch, she saw a package addressed to her. The cat sat on top of it, purring again.

"Get out of here," Candy said, grabbing the cat and throwing her off the steps. "I don't fuck with you."

Opening the package with a knife at the kitchen sink, she saw that it was the collagen for her smoothie. Had she already ordered it? Maybe Candy was good at planning. Maybe she was good at thinking ahead.

BIANCA

Blue picked up a pair of scissors. "Goddamnit," they said. "Can you call the sharpening guy?"

"You all right?" Bianca asked, sweeping up yellow strands of hair.

"I'm getting fucking audited," Blue said, throwing the scissors down.

"How did that happen?"

"I have no idea. I'm so good about everything, too. Like, I'm so careful. I have to be!"

"When did you find out?"

"This morning. I have to go through every appointment now and every transaction. It's gonna take me so long. I think I have to close the shop."

"You don't have to do that. We can figure it out."

"I already canceled all of the appointments for today. You can go home. Don't worry about it."

Bianca texted Julian asking him if he wanted to come over to listen to the recordings.

Oh, definitely! I just baked one of my loaves!

K., Bianca texted back.

He came over within the hour, holding a tray with a dish rag over it.

"What is that?" Bianca asked, letting him in.

"It's my tea loaf," Julian said, defensively.

"Did you want tea?"

"No, it's just called a tea loaf. You don't have to eat it with tea. It's just made with tea."

"Okay."

Julian cut the tea cake up into little pieces. He took out his laptop and then set it on their dining room table.

"Shall we?" Bianca gave him a thumbs-up.

FEBRUARY 22ND, 2023, ANTIGUA HOTEL

FERNANDO: My wife looked through my phone.

BIANCA: Even with that disappearing app? No, that's impossible.

FERNANDO: Well, I guess there's an app that finds
    disappearing apps.

Julian paused the recording.

"Can I ask what the disappearing app was?"

"BeDoneFor."

"That one's really encrypted. I've used it for organizing. She couldn't have found that. That's the whole point of it. You'd be done for."

"I know. He never told her at all." Bianca used her finger to pick up the remaining crumbs from the napkin and pressed play.

BIANCA: The subject is here. Can we talk about this after? Hola, mucho gusto.

SYLVESTER LEON: Hola! What's goin' on, nice to meet you. You want a drink? I think it's happy hour right now.

FERNANDO: Agradezco este tiempo que esta pasando con nosotros.

SYLVESTER LEON: I'm sorry, I actually don't really speak Spanish.

BIANCA: What? I thought you lived here.

SYLVESTER LEON: No, I wish! I won this amazing raffle, though. Thanks for meeting me at this hotel, by the way. Isn't this nice? Being treated like a king! Really different from Jackson Heights.

BIANCA: Could you tell us about your father? Juan Leon?

SYLVESTER LEON: I actually don't know him.

FERNANDO: Bianca, I think this meeting isn't actually necessary.

BIANCA: We need to cover our bases.

SYLVESTER LEON: How did you find me, by the way?

FERNANDO: Facebook.

SYLVESTER LEON: Huh, okay.

FERNANDO: It's okay, we don't need to do all of these interviews.

BIANCA: It's part of the entire project.

FERNANDO: This isn't an oral history project. It's an excavation.

BIANCA: So you won't continue them when I leave?

FERNANDO: Bianca, I think this conversation is over.

"This recording is so pointless." Bianca leaned back into the couch and looked over at Julian, who had his mouth stuffed with cake. "Fernando found the guy and then didn't want to talk to him at all. But he could've helped us!"

"He won a raffle? So he just happened to be there while you were there?"

"Yeah, I guess. Look, I never looked into this because it kind of ruined my life." Bianca was starting to realize that she had, in fact, been very emotional about everything.

"Who was Juan Leon?"

"He was this guy my uncle knew. Hold on, I think I can find a recording of my mom talking about it. Fernando had those recordings, too."

"Why did he have those?"

"I don't know."

"He *really* honks. Bianca."

FILE_ENCRYPTED: FEBRUARY 1ST, 2008, 7:02 P.M.

LUCIA: Okay, how long you need for this?

BIANCA: I'll let you know. Can you tell me about your brother? What was he like?

LUCIA: He was an artist. He made little toys out of wood. Ships, animals, dolls. Todo eso.

BIANCA: . . . Is there anything else you wanted to say?

LUCIA: Nice man. Mustache.

BIANCA: Do you have a nice memory of him doing something for you?

LUCIA: No.

BIANCA: What?

LUCIA: Well, one time I was sewing and the needle got stuck in my hand.

BIANCA: Like in your skin?

LUCIA: En el carne, si. Blood everywhere. Gabo he took it out, and all he did was give me a kiss where it had punctured, and it was all better. Then after that, I am better with sewing.

BIANCA: Better?

LUCIA: Really good. Almost magical. Pero fue yo. I practiced.

BIANCA: Did Gabo have any friends?

LUCIA: Yes, all losers.

BIANCA: How do you mean?

LUCIA: They were all *artists*. Musicians. Machistas, too. He had one named Juan Leon, he always was follow me around. Trying to take me somewhere. Said when he saw me, time stopped. So desperate.

BIANCA: And what happened to him?

LUCIA: He died. They all did.

"No, there was one where she was saying he was *bad,* hold on." Bianca looked through the laptop. "Here it is."

FILE_8

LUCIA: One night, Gabo came back to the house covered in dirt.

BIANCA: Why?

LUCIA: I think he was in a cave. Some tunnel.

BIANCA: And what did he say?

LUCIA: He told me to stay away from Juan Leon, he was bad.

BIANCA: And did you?

LUCIA: Yes.

"So, Juan Leon, bad. Okay." Julian almost put his feet on the table but Bianca glared at him. He tucked them under his legs. They sat in silence for a little bit. Bianca stared at the ceiling. Finally Julian asked her a question.

"What made you want to study this?" Julian said. The pointedness of this made her feel stupid.

"Why does anyone study anything?"

"Cop out." Bianca crumpled up the napkin.

"I thought it was beautiful that a group of artists came together to make things better. And that one of them was my uncle. And then something natural destroyed all of that. It's like, no matter what you do, no matter how hard you try, you're still at the whim of the earth."

"Hot take," he said. It was so boring and dismissive, but it was also familiar. It reminded her of her sister. "Should we listen to the rest of your mother's interview?"

FILE_4

LUCIA: It woke us up at three in the morning. I was holding three sapotes and they started to get very hard in my hands and then delicate and then they burst and three cats came outside of them and they were all mine and I kissed them. Then they started to run from me they started to crawl on the walls one of them left through the window and the other went down into the floor boards but one of the cats stayed and became a lamp and that's when I was thrown out of my bed.

BIANCA: You really remember that dream well.

LUCIA: You think I am lying?

BIANCA: No. What else?

LUCIA: I was thrown out of my bed. Abuelita, too. She was on the floor. I ran into Gabo's room. He wasn't there. The ceiling had fallen on my sister. She was screaming from the other room. Abuelita and I lifted the rubble off of her. There was a gash in her leg. I could see her bones.

BIANCA: Oh.

FILE_5

LUCIA: After the second quake we take her to where they have set up the tents. The Americans are here already and we take

Sandrita to them and your abuelita drop to her knees, crying and praying to la Virgencita for bringing us the Americans. Gabo is nowhere to be found. We ask for him. We see his girlfriend, Mirna, and we ask her and she says no, he is nowhere, she says she saw him last night and then went out with Juan Leon to their little artist group.

BIANCA: What do you think they were doing?

LUCIA: I even looked out for ese perro Juan Leon. But he was nowhere too, and then I start to worry, I start to panic, but Gabo cannot be gone, he is my brother.

BIANCA: Are you okay, Mami?

LUCIA: Yes, I just have to burp.

LUCIA: So then Abuelita takes me to the place where they're giving out food. Disgusting food. But I'm so hungry I eat it. I hear someone yelling for us. My mother takes me to the food distribution line and we help pass out what the Americans have brought us. Then Mirna is running to us. And then it's like I can't hear anything or see anything. Abuelita is on her knees, screaming. I throw up. Gabo was dead.

Bianca looked over at Julian, who had tears running down his face. She pressed play on another file.

FILE_7

BIANCA: And then what happened?

LUCIA: I run away. It was so bad. Bodies. Crying babies. I ran to the river. I fell asleep crying there. I forget who I am, where I am, what Guatemala is. I fell asleep. Then I woke up. I make my way back to our home, our little grocery. And I see something so strange.

BIANCA: What was it.

LUCIA: It was an angel.

BIANCA: What do you mean?

LUCIA: It was Gabo.

BIANCA: But Gabo was dead.

LUCIA: Yes, but he came to visit me.

BIANCA: Huh?

LUCIA: I screamed, and he did not look at me. He knocked on the door. He went inside. I run and I run. When I enter, it's just your abuelita, sitting in a chair, the rubble from the ceiling all around her. Was Gabo here? I asked. Then, she takes her shoe off and throws it at me. I put my hands over my head. No, tonta, she said, he's not here. I'm sorry, I say. It should have been you, she told me.

BIANCA: That's so awful.

LUCIA: Uh-huh.

"Do you need a break or something?" Julian said, tears streaming down his face. His hands were covering his cheeks. Her mother told everything so matter-of-factly, like it had happened to somebody else. It was too much for Bianca, too, but she saw no way out but through. She pressed play.

FILE_6

BIANCA: How was it after the earthquake?

LUCIA: Bad. Hardly no food.

BIANCA: How long was it before you left?

LUCIA: Maybe a month.

BIANCA: And what happened?

LUCIA: I don't want to talk about it.

BIANCA: It's an important part of the oral history project!

LUCIA: Who you showing this to?

BIANCA: Nobody, it's just for my research.

LUCIA: Fine. Your abuela invited somebody over. A man with a mustache. She told me to go outside. So I sat in the dirt, sewing Sandra's dress. Sandra comes to me. She looks nervous. What, I ask her. What's going on. She doesn't want to tell me. She shakes her head and tells me to be quiet. She put a finger over her mouth. That is when I hear her. My mother. Negotiating. With this man. She's making a deal. The deal is me. My body. Not even marriage. He will give her enough quetzales not to bring the stand back together but to survive. I didn't even cry. She did not deserve that. When I am allowed to go inside I am nice to her. I make her tea. I sweep the floors. Then I make a plan with Sandra about how I am going to leave: in the middle of the night with enough money to get me into the city. Sandra gives me some money she's been putting aside. We push it back and forth to each other. But she knows I will give in. Entonces, I leave in the middle of the night. I take the road through the woods.

BIANCA: That's awful.

LUCIA: I survive. I don't know why I brought her here, to be honest with you. I should've left her in Guatemala to die.

BIANCA: Do you ever miss Sandra or Gabo?

LUCIA: Of course. Why you think I'm so crazy and depressed?

Julian stood up and paced. "So, your abuelita tried to human traffic your mother?"

Bianca nodded.

"But she's such a sweet old lady."

"Yeah, it's kind of hard to wrap my head around," Bianca felt a little nauseated, "I feel like I understand why she deleted these files now."

"I mean," Julian said, "maybe by today's standards it's abusive, but should today's standard's be universal?"

"I don't care," Bianca said. She truly wanted to stop thinking about it. "Why did Fernando have these on his computer?"

"Maybe we can talk to Sylvester." Julian sat down next to Bianca. "Are you okay?" Bianca moved her eyes but not her head.

"I'm fine. I'm sure this happened to a lot of people."

"It's good that you asked her those questions. I know you think it was difficult, but I think it was good. We need to talk about these things." Julian looked like he wanted to touch her but didn't. She knew Julian was there to talk to her about this, but she also knew that all he could do was react, not actually understand. But she had already had time to sit with it. The past was full of suffering, but wasn't a little suffering kind of good? Did any drive exist on its own, without some ghost at the wheel?

Bianca had lost all of her information on Sylvester along with the recordings. He wasn't on any socials and wasn't coming up when Bianca searched his name and *Queens*. She had one last resort.

Her mother rarely talked to Sandra, anyway, right? She sent her money here and there but did they really talk? She used WhatsApp to call her aunt, who answered after two rings. Bianca kept the camera off.

"¿Aló? ¿Mija?"

"Hola, Tía."

"Bianca divina, linda, criatura hermosa, ¿cómo estás mi amor?"

Bianca stretched her brain for her best Spanish. "Good. You?"

"Here with your Tío Lucas and your cousins. We just celebrated our anniversary actually."

"Congratulations."

"It's a blessing. We wish you were all here." Did she? She barely knew her. Bianca never understood the unrelenting familiarity of Latin blood relatives, but she was about to use it to her advantage.

"Tía, I was wondering if you could do me a favor?"

"How could I forget! You're in Guatemala right? Your mom mentioned something. Come and we can all celebrate together!" *So they do talk*, Bianca thought, panicked.

"I had to leave, actually," Bianca panicked. "It was a family emergency."

"What? Did something happen to your abuelita? Is your mother okay? Your sisters?"

194

Bianca misspoke. She also realized that Sandra knew nothing about Paola. Which was good.

"No, no, they are fine. Everybody is fine. It was actually me. I started having really bad allergies so I had to come back because all my doctors are here." Bianca thought about what her grandmother said once, about the bad luck of lies. Would Bianca one day need a hospital with American doctors? She continued. "Yes. And, I haven't told my mom yet because, you know, she worries, so please don't tell her anything about this." There was some commotion on the other line. "What is that?"

Her aunt let out an animated whoop. There was laughter. "Sorry, sweetie. They surprised me with marimbas! Can I call you back?"

Bianca was getting frustrated. "No, listen, this is important. I'm in trouble." Her aunt was silent on the other line.

"Can you go into another room?"

"Yes, yes, yes." It got quieter.

"What's going on?"

"There was a reason that I left. Um, this man. This American man, he hurt me. In a bad way. And I need to get his information, but I don't want to get the police involved. The hotel has his information. The Antigua. If I send you four hundred and fifty dollars, do you think you can use some of it to bribe the concierge so that I could have his information."

"Oh, my God, Bianca. Are you okay? Your mom should know this." She sounded so much like Bianca's mother. The same tilt of voice. The same particular cluckiness of Guatemalan Spanish.

"No," Bianca said, "I am getting the *American* police on this. I don't want to deal with the Guatemalan police." While a relatively evil statement, Bianca knew this would instill a specific kind of shame in her Tía Sandra and the fear of living in a corrupt third-world country. Her aunt breathed on the other line.

"When do you need it by?"

"Um, as soon as possible." Blue rapped on the salon's glass windows. The phone was ringing off the hook and Bianca had been letting it. She held up her forefinger and mouthed that she would need a minute.

"Okay. I can send Hector."

Bianca stifled at the name. "Hector?"

"Yes, that's my son. Your cousin?" Now Sandra was instilling shame.

"You named your son after my dad?"

Sandra laughed. "It's a common name, amor. Anyway, he does construction work for them, I'm sure he can figure something out. No need to send me money, either. We're just fine here."

"I'm sorry." Somebody walked by her on their two-speed bicycle holding a carton of Trader Joe's eggs. "I didn't mean to be rude."

"No, you weren't. I'm just happy to hear you. And I'm sorry, my love. I'm sorry that happened to you."

"Thank you," Bianca said, pulling on her hair. "That means a lot. Please don't tell my mom."

"Si, si, claro," her aunt said. Bianca tried to picture the marimbas chattering behind her aunt, but she was the kind of person who, when trying to imagine a purple apple, just saw the words *purple apple*. The image of her family at a party on a finca kept inflating and deflating in her mind. All she had was her aunt's voice and the music. Her mind was stranded in a cellphone tower between Brooklyn and Guatemala. Blue rapped on the glass again. They looked frustrated.

"Gracias, Tía."

"Un abrazo grande y un beso. Que la Virgencita te bendiga, mija."

"Igualmente," Bianca said. After all that all she could come up with was "Same." Later, her cousin called with the information. He didn't understand Bianca's awkwardness over the phone and said, "You don't really speak Spanish, do you?" Bianca was silent, and then he finally gave her Sylvester's phone and address.

Approaching Sylvester's building, Bianca spotted a head that looked like a round hat was placed over it, but it was a mound of black hair. She took a right into the courtyard of the building.

"Hey!" Bianca said, and the barista with the mushroom cut turned around.

"Oh," she said, her smile cutting her face into a semicircle. "Do you live here?"

"No," she said. Julian held up his hand.

"What's up." She took it and giggled, like a little schoolgirl. Julian awkwardly pulled it back. They stood together, the three of them, in the doorway, until Bianca buzzed the number they were going to and were let in.

The barista stood in front of the elevator with her hands loose by her sides, like she was ready to turn on.

"We're gonna take the stairs," he said, taking Bianca's arm as the elevator doors closed.

"It's eleven floors up," Bianca said, wrenching her arm away from him.

"Yeah," he whispered, "but that girl is weird."

Bianca panted behind him, clutching the railing, as Julian climbed confidently, holding his messenger bag above him to make a weight, the muscles in his thighs pushing his body forward, tiny beads of sweat forming underneath his armpits, his breath never becoming sharp, but more full. When they finally reached the eleventh floor, Bianca was beet-faced and fearful of a heart attack. She clutched her chest and thought of her father, the lengths his heart went to before it finally gave out. Julian helped Bianca up the last step and readjusted his messenger bag. Reaching apartment 11R at the end of a freshly waxed, checkered hallway, Bianca pushed on the black doorbell. Nothing. Julian knocked.

"He knows we're coming," Bianca said, "I already spoke to him."

Julian tried the doorknob, and it opened.

A painting of the Eiffel Tower hung above a modest white couch. Photos of family members holding each other at graduation events and sunsets rested on a mantle. A faint smell of cigarette smoke.

"Hello?" A male voice from somewhere inside. The wooden floors mumbled. Bianca grabbed Julian's hand and held her breath as Sylvester turned the corner, beaming. He was wearing tight yoga shorts and a muscle shirt.

"Sorry, I thought I heard somebody say, 'Come in,'" Julian lied. Sylvester had a duffel bag over his shoulder.

"I leave my door unlocked," Sylvester said, beaming, a thick Queens accent blanketing his speech. "Why be afraid of anyone coming in?"

"I agree," Julian said. "It makes communities stronger."

"We spoke over the phone," Bianca said. Sylvester's jaw clenched and unclenched.

"Oh, *right*!" he said, "Guatemala-girl! How are ya!" He opened up his arms, as if for a hug. Bianca did not oblige.

"Were you on your way out?" Julian asked.

"Sorry, I thought I was letting in UPS. I got the times mixed up! Was just on my way to yoga. My bad." He sat down on the couch, motioning for both of them to join him.

"That's great," Julian said. "How long have you been doing yoga, Sylvester?"

"Call me Syl," he said, putting out a hand for him to shake. "Where ya from?"

"Well, I was born and raised in Massachusetts, but adopted from Guatemala," Julian said, full of practice.

"Ah, *Harvard Yahd*," Syl said, a finger fun pointing at Julian, who chuckled. Bianca did not laugh at all.

"The last time I saw you," Bianca said, "I was asking you a little bit about Tierra Nueva."

"Terra Cotta?"

"The group that your father was in?"

"Ya know people don't think I'm Spanish because I can hardly speak it, but I could've had a scholarship on these arms alone," Syl said, showing off his chestnut-colored arms.

"Really?" Julian said.

"One thousand percent." It was like Bianca was in the Eiffel Tower painting and not in front of them.

"Tell me more about yoga."

"It's just wonderful. I feel so at peace. So calm. And my butt looks incredible." Syl let out a huge laugh and clapped his hands. "Seriously. A beautiful loaf of bread!"

"Totally," Julian said. "So anyway, we're here because Bianca was doing this project—"

"My dissertation," Bianca said. "For my PhD."

"And in her project, she came across your dad, Juan Leon. Could you tell us anything about him?" Sylvester squeezed his own chestnut-colored arm tightly.

"Look, I thought I told you before. I don't really know the guy. He died before I ever met him."

"What?" said Bianca.

"Yeah. My mom was on a missionary trip and he knocked her up. I guess he was really charming, though. Really waxed poetic about her. He wanted her to run away with him. Said stuff about how she made time stop. He still knew about me though. My mom would write him letters."

"Did he ever send any back?"

"Who knows what that guy was up to!" Syl shook his head, smiling and then looking out the window, where a lonely pothos dangled.

"Always wonder how different my life would be if I had a father. But what are you gonna do? Sometimes people just don't have dads." Julian put his hand on Bianca's leg, and she slapped it away.

"I guess he had a will, though, because I received all these papers when he died."

"Papers?"

"Yeah, just bunch of junk. But I kept it all, you know? All these years."

"Is there a chance you would be willing to show us the papers?"

"I gotta go to yoga!"

"Maybe sometime soon?" Julian said, desperate. Bianca had her arms crossed. Syl waved them over to his meticulously kept, economical room, where a golden Buddha sat on the windowsill with a blue elephant holding incense. He opened up his desk drawer and took out a bloated manila envelope.

"Can we take this?" asked Bianca.

"Uh, sorry, no."

"What about a picture?" Syl scratched his head.

"No," he said, sucking in his teeth, "sorry. Too personal." He put the folders back in the desk drawer.

"Why didn't you ever look into him? Julian asked.

"Listen, I really should go, now. Let me know if you need anything else, okay?"

"You live around here?" Syl asked as they all padded down the eleven flights of stairs.

"No." They both responded. Syl's duffel bag swished passed Julian's arm.

"So, PhD Guatemala Girl!" he continued. "When do you graduate?"

"It's not really about *graduation*," Bianca murmured, looking at her feet.

"But there's a finish line, right?" Syl said, beaming, as they reached the first floor. Bianca didn't answer.

"Nice to meet you all!" Syl said, turning the corner.

They began walking in time, following Syl's bald head. They followed him all the way into a yoga studio with giant windows on the ground floor of a building. They watched as Syl greeted fellow yoga attendants, all with the same exuberance, hugging. Most of them were women, and pregnant. Syl removed a towel and yoga mat from his duffel bag. He began stretching. The woman at the front said something, and then they all said something back—Syl had a giant smile on his face.

"Man, he really loves this," Julian said.

"Yeah. Did he say anything weird?"

"I can't tell. I feel like he's not telling us everything."

"How long are we going to keep watching this?" Bianca asked. They ducked into an Indian bridal store. Julian fingered the garments and Bianca examined a mannequin's missing finger.

"Are you looking for anything?" the attendant asked, somewhat begrudgingly.

"Just browsing," Bianca said.

"This is a bridal store," the attendant said. "Have you been to an Indian wedding before?" Julian slipped on a vest.

"I'm sorry, we'll go. Julian, take that off."

"Sorry." They ducked back out, where Sylvester was leaving. A woman was talking to him. They walked all the way to the end of the street and she gave him a card. He shook his head and gave it back. She handed it to him again, folding his hand around the piece of paper. He didn't want it. The woman walked away.

CANDY

Garfield came back around. He usually did. He was a tedious constant: like flossing your teeth or clipping your nails. You might as well find peace in something like that. A consistency. A meditation within a pathetic man.

He arrived a Saturday afternoon before Thanksgiving to watch *The Leaf* together on YouTube. Candy pulled down the projector and turned off all the lights. She hadn't had a vision or craving in two weeks, even after having finished the ointment. She was all better—it really worked. Life was normal.

The movie began. The man encountered the leaf. Garfield began to chuckle. It was a movie they had found together, clutching their abdomens from laughter at its earnestness. Garfield sat in the corner of the couch, making a concave opening with his arms for Candy to come into. He felt so familiar. An old blanket. A well-worn boot. The leaf showed up at the man's doorstep, with a warning written on itself.

"We should get the leaf tattooed," Garfield proposed. "I mean, that would be so sick."

"Totally," Candy said, not meaning it. The leaf killed the man's girlfriend, who then reappeared, covered head to toe in leaves.

"Are you hungry?" Garfield asked. "I might order something." The leaf woman began to have sex with the man, who was also the director, as a song that he had written played.

"I have food here."

"Oh, you cooking for yourself now?"

"Shut up." Candy got up and went to the kitchen. "You don't have to pause," she said, "I'll be right back."

"'Kay, babe." She opened up her microwave which had spots of red grease dripping on the insides. She would clean it once Garfield left. Or maybe tomorrow. Or maybe never. She moved through her cabinet, looking for popcorn, and saw that it was next to the vase that now held crinkly dead flowers. She reached up to get it, and the vase smashed on the ground.

"You okay?" Garfield called as the man began stripping a tree of its leaves.

"I'm fine," Candy said, gathering the pieces into a paper towel, and picking up a tiny camera that was lodged at the bottom of the vase. She looked toward Garfield, who was still enraptured by the stupid movie. She stuffed the camera into her pocket and tossed around her smoothie ingredients, looking for another. Picking up the collagen, she noticed that the sticker that said VITAL PROTIENS was spelled wrong, the E and I switched.

"Do you need help with this mess? You're barefoot, you could hurt yourself." She turned around and there was Garfield. He looked behind her then back at her quickly, the way people flick their eyes at a pair of tits encased in a tight tank top. Just a quick, innocent glance—how could you help it? What was he looking at?

"Nah," she said, smiling at her kind of boyfriend, wondering if he could see the pulse in her neck. "I'll get it later. Popcorn?"

BIANCA

The pizza place reminded Bianca of the one she grew up next to. The plastic red booths. The smell of ginger ale on the floors.

"Let's go over what we have."

Bianca wrote down *WHAT WE HAVE* in her notebook.

"Juan Leon was his dad." A bell dinged. Their slices were ready.

"And Juan Leon left him these papers, even though he never met him."

"And Fernando was in two places at once."

"And Sylvester is really into yoga."

"Maybe those were divorce papers?" Bianca scoffed.

"We just have a bunch of dead ends," Julian sipped his ginger ale and burped. "Excuse me. Sorry."

Bianca rolled up her pizza so that the oil spilled onto the paper plate, a habit she learned from hot girls in middle school. Then she got up to douse it in oregano and pepper before biting into it. The pizza burned the roof of her mouth and her tongue shot up to comfort it.

"And then what about that woman who was following him and gave him that card?"

"Maybe she is going to evict him. Maybe the people behind this are landlords." Julian finished up his crust. "Is Sylvester like . . . important to all of this?"

"I don't know," Bianca

"Why don't we go back? And try to look at the papers?"

Bianca folded her paper plate. They were already this close. "Do you think he'll be home?"

"He said he didn't lock his doors."

Julian turned the doorknob once more. Inside, all the lights were off.

"What if he's still here?"

"Then we say that we forgot something," Julian whispered, "a water bottle."

"But you're holding a water bottle."

"Exactly. I'll be like oh, *there's* my water bottle. And then pretend to pick it up from the floor."

"Right."

"Okay." Julian closed the door

"This feels weird."

"This whole thing has been weird."

"I don't think we should be here," Bianca said, and that feeling oozed back to her, the one that made her feel like the skin of reality was slipping away and something was very, very wrong.

"We already are." Julian grabbed her hand and they made their way through the dark. "It's okay to be afraid. I'm kind of freaked out, too, to be honest." That made her feel better. It took away the anxiety of being afraid alone and feeling like a small pathetic little baby. The floors creaked from just ahead of them.

"Sylvester?"

"Shh!"

"Someone's here." They made their breath small, afraid of making their chests rise anymore than they already were. The creaking stopped.

"Can we just turn on the lights?"

"Yes." Julian felt around in the dark for the switch. "Bianca?"

"Yes?"

"Fuck, fuck, fuck." Julian said.

"What?"

"That's not you to my left, Bianca?"

"What do you mean."

"I thought . . ."

"What?"

"I thought I just touched a nose? Your nose?"

"WHAT?"

"Shhh," Julian said, "Let's just keep going toward his bedroom. It's to the right."

"Why isn't there any light in here?"

"I can't find the switch. I'm gonna use my phone light."

"Okay." Julian's phone lit up the photo of Sylvester at a graduation.

"We're okay," Julian said, "we're okay." Bianca couldn't tell if he was saying that more for himself. "I think I found a light, one second. Don't let go of my hand." Bianca didn't. "There." The overhead light drenched the bedroom in reality. Sylvester's desk was overturned, drawers empty and thrown on the floor.

On a hook hanging from the closet's open door, Sylvester hung from a checkered tie.

"Shit!" Julian said, backing away toward the wall. Sylvester's eyes were half-open and his head was turned down, his body slack, a piece of meat swaying at a butcher shop. Bianca gagged.

Julian used his elbow to turn off the light and gripped Bianca's hand. "Let's go."

CANDY

Candy met Garfield during a showing of *Tampopo*, that ramen movie with the couple dripping raw eggs in each other's mouths between scenes. She felt very aware of him the entire time, how he crossed and uncrossed his legs, the sound of him happily sucking up his blue slushy. When the movie ended she bumped into him, spilling popcorn.

"Why did you do that?" She was accusatory and deliberate.

"I didn't."

"Why are you lying?" She assumed he was in an in-between phase of not knowing if he was scared of her or turned on by being scared of her. She pursued *him*, she thought, this fool who made skateboarding videos, lived with six roommates, did one semester of community college, loved virgin picklebacks, which was just drinking pickle juice from a jar. How well did she really know him? Bianca and her mother had only met him once, and were extremely judgmental, of course. She had never met his parents; he said he didn't get along with them. He didn't have any social media, but was that because he was hiding something or because he was a luddite?

"What are you doing today?" she asked him the next morning, gripping the collagen smoothie she had just made.

"Dunno, applying for some jobs."

"Cool," she said, squeezing his arm. "Do you want some of this?" she said, holding the container up to him. Garfield wrinkled his nose.

"You know I think that stuff's gross."

"Try it!" Candy said, smiling, more friendly than she usually was, "It's good for you!"

"I should go, baby," Garfield said. "Have a good day at work!"

"Love you," Candy said. She watched him walk away, his frayed jeans kissing the sidewalk. "Loser," she said. Clutching her smoothie on the bus, she saw a woman with a scarf tied around her head flicking her eyes up at her. Candy looked away. The bus arrived at the theater and she got off. The woman with the silk scarf did, too. She ran across the street. The woman stayed there. Was she watching? Candy walked into the theater, where one of her coworkers asked her if she had seen or heard from Jenny recently.

"She's supposed to cover for me on Friday for this wedding."

"Don't know," Candy said, pushing past them. "If you don't find coverage, that's not my problem."

"But . . . you're the manager." Candy was already in the bathroom, where she opened her container and dumped the smoothie down the toilet.

In theater three, she waited. If she was wrong, if she was crazy, nothing would happen. If she was right, Garfield was poisoning her. She put down the red broom, the one that was so satisfying to click open and close. She settled in the seat, continued to wait. Yes, she was afraid. But she needed to know.

After five minutes, the screen blasted to life. Candy swallowed. She breathed in and out. Okay. Okay. The curtain opened. The voice again.

There's a man sitting next to you. Do you see him?
You hug yourself.
The man kisses you on the cheek.
He pulls at your clothes.
You stare into the audience.
He pulls at your clothes, he takes off your bra, he rubs your nipples with his thumbs.
A small smile from you.
The man is grunting.
His eyes glow red.
Fumes come from his nostrils.
He grabs you by the head and kisses you, big and sloppy.
You keep your eyes open the whole time, the whole time looking at the audience.
He passes you something through his mouth.
You swallow it.
It balloons down your throat.
The man keeps slobbering at you, giving your neck pecks.
He is a beast.
You are a meal.
Your shirt pops open.
A round, full belly.
Something wriggling underneath.
You begin to moan and scream, dipping into the chair, legs spread.
The moans of the earth.
The screen shakes.
The film whirs.
The curtains close.

BIANCA

After crashing down the eleven flights of stairs and through the lobby, and then for three straight blocks, their panting and crying turned into hysterical, helpless laughter. Their eyes looked distressed but their mouths were open and hollow, letting out animal sounds.

"Oh no," Julian said, as their laughter died out, "I forgot I have a show tonight."

At Elsewhere, Julian loaded equipment and Bianca stood in the crowd with twenty-year-olds with color in their hair and outfits from Beacon's Closet, trying not to think of the recently deceased body she had run away from. They probably all got their hair cut by Blue, she thought. She rubbed her VIP sticker on her pant leg and went to the bar, where she pulled out her phone and texted Candy.

> **Hi. Don't know if you got my other messages.**
> **I'm at a show right now and having a lot of social anxiety.**
> **I really need to talk to you.**

The messages had been delivered. Maybe her sister would text her back finally. She grabbed a whiskey sour and decided to text Blue. She hadn't heard from them all day.

> **You doing okay?**
> **How's studio stuff?**

Blue texted back. **Bad**.

Julian went on and the crowd erupted. Bianca was in the back, not wanting to draw attention to herself or think about what she was wearing, which, if she had to be honest with herself, looking around the Bushwick crowd, was basic. A crewneck sweater? L.L.Bean jeans that didn't show off her hips or waist? Hiking boots? A lot of people sang along and seemed to know the words. A few times Julian let the crowd sing instead. The music reminded her of the Beatles, but maybe because that's the only band she had ever really heard of. That's what her dad used to listen to and she didn't want to think about her dad. She hadn't realized how popular Julian was. Was he famous? Another whiskey sour, please. She grabbed the plastic cup too hard and now its shell was digging into her palm and her face was hot but if she thought about that too much she'd think about Syl and his face which was bloated with blood like a fucked-up balloon and if she thought about dead bodies she'd think again of her Dad, and anyway she had packaged those memories into the storage of her psyche, perfectly labeled and perfectly sealed shut and who was that in the crowd with black hair like a helmet? The lights blinked, the people sang. Bianca turned and there was that fucking barista and her awful smile, growing wider and wider. Just as soon as Bianca saw her, she was gone. Her drink finished and they were still jamming. Somebody was jumping up and down. Everybody knew the words except Bianca. Of course, Bianca was always out of the loop. Bianca was a nerd. Bianca was not as pretty as her sisters. And now the set was over, and the lights were flickering off, and Bianca was pushing her way outside and feeling the cool air on her cheeks and remembering why she never went out.

Outside, two girls were discussing Julian's relationship status while waiting in line at a taco truck. Maybe he was queer, one of them reasoned. Maybe his girlfriend is long-distance and they're open. His girlfriend moved to Boston. *Who cares*, Bianca thought. *Who cares about any of this?*

Bianca and Julian hadn't really talked about romance, save for Fernando, the sun they kept revolving around. Fernando was a code for everything that had happened with Candy, with their shared experiences in their hometown, their loneliness in this city. They should probably quit it. Something was nasty about the whole thing.

"Hi," Bianca said. Julian was sweaty from the stage and beaming. She could tell that he was energized by this, that he felt close to something unnamable when he was up there, the same thing astronomers feel when the skies go beyond equations or reason.

"Thanks for coming. I really appreciate it."

"Yeah, you did good." She was surprised she wasn't honest. She was kind of tipsy. She didn't really think anything about music in general. Sometimes a jingle from a commercial would get stuck in her head and she'd hum it. Julian just looked so like a child showing her his day's drawings in crayon. Look what I did! Look at all that I can do!

"I feel like . . . I could use a drink. Do you want to hang out with the band? Talk about something that isn't Fernando Moreno? Or a dead body?" Bianca's social battery had completely tanked. She wanted to go home and sleep this off but she was afraid of seeing Syl's face when she closed her eyes. Bianca saw Syl's head flash through her head again and shuddered.

So Bianca followed him to a local bar where they did tequila shots together with his bandmates.

"No, I don't have a savings, are you kidding me?" one band member said.

"Like, not at all?"

"We are all gonna die in fifty years no matter how old we are."

"That's still a long time away."

"Yeah but there will be some new flesh-eating disease, dude. Or some mega tsunami that's just shit water."

"Like bad water?"

"Water made out of *shit*, bro."

"Yo . . ."

"And even if I survive, do you think I'll need cash? Nah, it's about my wits! How good you are with a knife!" He fake-stabbed Julian in the chest with a cardboard straw.

"Are you good with a knife?"

"Absolutely not," Julian said.

"Exactly. I'm fucked. We all are."

"What do you think, Bianca?" She was thinking about how she almost agreed. Why be hopeful when you could just be ready? People either die or disappoint you.

"Yeah, aren't you a climate scientist?"

"I'm an archaeologist." Bianca's phone buzzed. Blue.

Can you come home?

Bianca sighed under her breath and rolled her eyes, snatched her beer, and swallowed it in one gulp.

"I guess whenever I've held an object like hairbrush or something that's been buried deep underground on the site of a building that's about to be made, I remember that people existed long ago, and that's comforting, because I'm going to die eventually, and I have no control over what I leave behind."

"Shit, that's so beautiful. Let's do more shots."

Another text from Blue. **Please let me know if you're seeing this.** Bianca downed another shot of tequila, sucking on the lemon and feeling the alcohol in her eyes. She leaned into Julian, who caught her.

"I'm gonna get home."

"I'll go with you and walk from your house," Julian said, looking dis dainfully at his roommates.

"I'm in the opposite direction as you. And it's a forty-five-minute walk."

"Exactly. That's a long time. And you're a woman alone at night," Julian said, lowering his voice as his bandmates started to fart on each other, "And we just experienced a *trauma*." They spent the car ride giggling again. Manic laughter, unstoppable, evil snickering.

"I need to throw up," Bianca said, and the driver slammed on the breaks so Bianca could open the door and retch on the street. Julian patted her head, still laughing. When they arrived, the laughter stopped.

"Can you come inside?" Bianca said, her hands wrapped around her knees. "I feel scared."

Inside, Blue was on the couch wearing their teal silk robe, their feet in the fuzzy slippers that they only wore in dire times.

"Blue?" Bianca said, stumbling in with Julian. Blue looked up at them with bloodshot eyes.

"What's going on?" Bianca said, falling into their couch.

"I have to leave," Blue said, "but I wanted to say goodbye first." Julian fell over.

"Sorry," he said, "I need to pee really bad, I'll be right back." Blue shook their head.

"No," Bianca said, putting her hand around theirs. "You don't have to go. We can live here together forever!" The room spun.

"Did you get my texts?" Blue asked.

"Are you mad at me?" Bianca said, her voice squeaky.

"I need to leave," Blue said. "I'm not safe here. And I don't think you are, either." They pulled out their phone, where there were photos of Blue's studio, which they had fundraised to get a lease for, spent hours scrubbing the floors and arranging plants by the windows, spraying homemade perfumes in the morning so that the place would have an unforgettable scent, completely destroyed. The pots for the plants were shattered, clots of dirt all over the floors. The seat had been stabbed multiple times, cotton coming out of its insides. On the seat was a gutted cat, and the mirror, in the cat's blood, presumably, read *STOP LOOKING*.

"What do you think it means?" Bianca said, squinting. Blue stood up. She had never seen them this way.

"What the fuck do you think it means? It means whatever you're doing, you need to *stop*. Before anything happens. To anybody!" Julian came out of the bathroom, adjusting his belt.

"Everything cool, my brothers?" Julian said, his eyes half open.

"Blue's just freaking out about something again." Blue looked from Bianca to Julian and shrieked. They stormed into their room, and when they came back, they were wearing blue pants, a blue puffer jacket, and a blue scarf around their head, a giant blue suitcase rolling behind them.

"My car is here."

"Why are you leaving?"

"I'm not safe here anymore!" Blue said.

"Yes, you are," Bianca said. "You're with me."

"You have made it so that I'm no longer safe!" they screamed.

Bianca flinched. "You're upset with me. I can tell."

"Bianca," Blue said, "you're selfish. You think everybody babies your little sister, but you baby yourself. I've been babying you. I'm literally employing you! I told you to stop digging around in this Guatemala shit, and now my business, my baby, has been murdered."

"Are you still being audited?"

"Did you not see the mutilated cat? Something bad is going on. And you don't want to see it! You keep searching and searching, but for some reason, you don't want to *look*. You think you were doing some anti-colonialist archaeology but guess what? You can never divorce colonialism from like, anything! And you're never going to fill the Fernando-shaped hole in your pussy. He's gone." Blue's phone buzzed. Their car had arrived. "And so am I!" Blue dragged their suitcase to the door and Julian leapt to help them put it in the car as Bianca watched from their door. Blue stared at Julian for a moment, then gave him a hug. Julian patted their back. Julian walked back up the steps and sighed.

"Do you think they hate me?" Bianca said. Julian looked at her and shook his head. Julian sat awkwardly on the floor next to Bianca's bed while she threw up in the bathroom. Crawling on the floor, she arrived at the entrance of her room.

"My sister never called me back. My whole family hates me." Bianca started crying. Julian put a hand on her shoulder.

"She will."

"How do you know?"

"Because she's your sister."

Bianca moved away from him and to her bathroom, where she began to brush her teeth. Her reflection was fuzzy in the mirror. She didn't like getting like this. She didn't like being out of control. This is how her sister had been. But maybe she was just like her. Maybe she shouldn't have been so judgmental. And now her sister was never speaking to her again. All because she had set a boundary!

When she came back, Julian was still sitting on the floor, looking out into space. As she changed, Julian politely looked at the ceiling. She wiggled underneath her covers.

"What do you think about that message on the mirror?"

"Probably related to Syl hanging from his tie."

"I fucked up with Blue."

"You didn't know."

Bianca set her glasses on her nightstand. "That was scary today." She turned to him.

"It was." He lay down next to her. They were voices in the dark again.

"And he was really nice."

"Seemed like you hated him."

"I didn't like that you two were talking over me. It was rude!"

"Bianca, you have to butter people up if you want them to tell you something."

"I don't *do* that. I'm not *like that*."

"I like that about you."

"Who do you think has those *fucking* papers?"

"Someone with a lot of resources."

"You think it's a conspiracy. You think it's the government?"

"I just mean they have a lot of money. Did anyone give you funding for your project?"

"It was from an anonymous donor!"

"Hmm."

"I think I need a break from thinking about this, 'cause I feel nuts!"

"Okay. We can reconvene tomorrow. Good night."

"Buenas NOCHES."

"Bianca?"

"Yeah?"

"What did you think about my band?"

"I already told you. Super good."

"But you were lying. And now you're drunk and I want to know the truth."

"Honestly, I don't really like music."

Julian laughed and found himself rolling over so that his hips were almost touching hers.

Bianca remembered how her mother said she had found her father when they were both lonely. He needed his pants taken in for a valet job and her mother worked at a dry cleaners in Roxbury. Her father only went there because everybody spoke Spanish. She measured his waist and the line from his groin to his ankle. She was professional. She was not thinking about what her back looked like as she bent over, or of the gracefulness of her wingspan as she stretched the measuring tape. They were both twenty-four and lived with strangers. Sometimes all you need is something in common.

"It's okay," Julian said, gently shaking her shoulder, "I'm not offended. Sorry that was coach-y of me. Good job, buddy!" Bianca laughed. He kept his hand on her shoulder. It was a handshake that never died. He didn't move it.

"Are you scared?" Bianca asked him.

"I just don't know if somebody's going to come for us."

He moved his hand to her neck. Could he feel her tendons? Syl and the gutted cat darted past her mind. How long did it take for them to die? How could it be so easy to lose a life? Bianca kissed Julian, him, her hot mouth on his, and he kissed her back, their lips smashing. But his head wasn't moving. Bianca broke away.

"You don't want to."

Julian touched his lips. "That's not true."

"Then what is it?" Bianca started to cry. "Nobody wants me. I'm ugly and boring." Julian put his hand to her face. Julian gently turned her around and put his arms around her hips. A backward middle school dance. Two people in a boat.

"Bianca, you're very drunk."

"But I know what I *want*!"

"Let's talk about it tomorrow."

"Not fair," Bianca said, and she began to nod off as her phone lit up, sending a blue signal to her ceiling, and she thought she could see an image in the blue, a face, almost, a body, somebody familiar. But then it was dark again, and she fell deeply asleep.

The next day, Bianca woke up to ten missed calls from her mother and called her back.

"Hello?"

"Bianca, you need to come home."

"I can't just hop on a plane and go home. I'm in Guatemala, remember?" Julian had already left. Thank God. He had understood that it was just this one time. A much-needed release after a long night of talking about doom and seeing a dead body. Then she remembered that they hadn't had sex at all, and she made a humiliated noise.

"What is that?"

"That was me."

"Why you sound like that? You sick?"

"No."

"It's Christmas Eve. Where are you?"

"What? No, it's not. That's not for a week." Bianca checked her phone's clock. An entire week had passed. How was that possible?

"Your sister is gone."

"What?"

"She never came to make tamales. I can't reach her for a week. You all abandoned me."

"A week? Mami, we didn't abandon you. I'm in Guatemala and things are really busy right now—"

"You are lying. Sandra called me. She told me. She said someone in Guatemala did something bad to you? A man?"

"That's not what I said. She misunderstood me. You know how I am with Spanish."

"Why are you lying?"

"Where is Candy?"

"Rehab." She heard her mother gulp.

"Oh no."

Her mother started to sob audibly on the other line.

"Does she have insurance?"

"She said she got someone to pay for it. She left a note. I'm afraid, Bianca."

"Afraid of what? She's an adult." But Bianca, too, was afraid.

"What if she does something?"

"She's not going to do anything. I mean, it's good she's going to rehab. She's been honest with herself."

"Come home." Her mother hung up.

ZOE

Zoe knocked on Maria Santiago's office door, where a painting of an Indigenous Guatemalan woman nursing a newborn hung. Zoe had just had an acai bowl with chia seeds and blueberries and mushroom coffee. It was settling uncomfortably in her stomach, but she might also have been nervous to see Maria Santiago.

The night before, Maria had given her the papers to study, saying that she would be an "integral part of the process." The papers were slightly yellowed, with drawings and small stick figures as people gathered around a bed where another stick figure was. There were no verbal instructions: just these drawings.

"Come in," she heard Maria say. She opened the door. Maria's office was minimal. The desk and floors made out of wood she had imported from Guatemala. On the desk were tiny fertility statues she had collected. And of course, there was the bell, in the middle of the room, where Maria was seated cross-legged on a yoga mat. Zoe felt the pull of it as she opened the door and then was immediately returned to herself when Maria turned it off.

Maria started stretching on her yoga mat, bent over with her ass sticking out at Zoe, like a cat in heat. "How are you, Zoe?" Maria said from between her legs. She was barefoot, no paint on her toenails.

"Good, Maria. Thank you." Zoe placed one hand on her stomach.

"Any luck?" Maria asked, changing positions to sitting on the floor, and crossing her legs. Zoe shook her head. The other members had already conceived. They were waddling all around the studio with full bellies, perfect, feminine Oompa Loompas. It was almost time for the ceremony.

"That's okay, Zoe. Our role in this next process doesn't have to birth."

Zoe nodded. She took a deep breath. She was going to ask the question. "I need to know a little bit about the process, actually. I read the documents."

Maria nodded enthusiastically. "Fantastic, isn't it? So ancient and yet full of purpose." Maria patted down her yoga mat, indicating Zoe to sit with her.

"I don't think I understand the papers, Maria," Zoe admitted. She felt ashamed. Was she just stupid? Was she not worthy of the Woman's Stone?

"What didn't you understand?"

"The fourth and fifth steps." Maria got up and Zoe did, too. Maria rolled up the yoga mat and grabbed the white box that held the bell. She set it carefully on her wooden desk and took a seat in the cashmere chair behind it. When a member asked about the exorbitance of the cashmere chair, Maria said that it was important for all women to be comfortable. Coziness is close to godliness. Zoe hadn't seen that member in a long time.

"Remind me again what you've been learning throughout the years. The core of the Woman's Stone." Maria looked out the window. The weather was dreary. A hurricane from Florida had blown up the cold weather. The sun hadn't even come up that day.

"The world is finite, but women are forever," Zoe recited, "Creation can only come with destruction, and what we put in our bodies is holy."

"Yes, Zoe." Maria breathed in through her nose and out her mouth with her eyes closed. Then she opened them. "What did you put in your body today?"

Zoe told her: some dates, pumpkin seeds, the acai bowl, and the mushroom coffee.

"And how does it make you feel?"

"Good," Zoe said.

"You're lying." Maria blinked and turned to Zoe. Her eyes were so piercing and blue. "I can tell. You look a little bloated, your hand is on your stomach." Zoe shook her head and smiled. How did Maria know everything?

"You're right. I'm gassy." Zoe rolled her eyes at herself.

"You need some carbs to balance out all that fiber. Don't slip back into detrimental habits. Why don't you check with our nutritionist and see what works best for you?"

"That's a good idea."

Of course. She was so concerned about not gaining weight, still. That toxic mentality of not taking in any carbs had yet to be wrung out of her brain. Progress is lifelong. The work is never done. Still, Maria hadn't exactly answered her question.

"Sorry, I don't quite get it," Zoe admitted, "What does this have to do with the fourth and fifth step?" Maria stood up noiselessly and locked her fingers behind her back.

"I was hoping you would understand by now." Another disappointment. She would have to do better. She would have to go back and study the papers.

"I'll go back and look through the papers again."

"No, no. I'll explain." Maria still had her back to Zoe. "In times of struggle, in times of desperation, humans turn to the unimaginable in order to survive. In order to bring forth a better world."

"Okay," Zoe said.

"This world has made it so that we are terminally the consumer, and without thinking, all of a sudden, we have become the consumed."

"Right."

"Candy was given a remarkable gift."

"Yes."

"Do you feel envy?"

"I am sitting with my envy to see how I can make it more useful."

"That's good, Zoe. What Candy has is a gift that will make us start over. The Mother has been waiting for her."

"How did you know that Candy's was the gift? I mean, what were the signs."

"Zoe, tell me what is recommended of mothers to eat after they give birth?"

Zoe thought for a minute. "The placenta. Because it's rich in nutrients that will help the mother recuperate, so that she can give proper nutrients to her child through her breastmilk."

"Candy is like that placenta." Maria turned around, fingers still locked behind her back. She was so comfortable in this silence. Could wade in it forever. Zoe hated it. She just wanted to know what was going on.

A knock on the door.

Carmen was there in the doorway holding a ceramic bowl of soup.

"Maria? You wanted to see me? I brought you some PCOS stew."

"Thank you so much, Carmen. Zoe, thank you for the conversation. I'll see you later today." The lentils and peppers wafted into Zoe's nose as she closed the door, and suddenly, she understood.

CANDY

The cat puffed out her chest, as if she had just brought a dead rat to Candy's bedside. "This cat is so cute," Garfield said, holding out his hand to her. "She followed me here."

"She's not allowed inside," Candy said, shutting the door. He came inside carrying pizza and set it down on the counter.

"I missed you." He took his two hands and cupped them around her face and gave her a sloppy kiss. He had just been away for a month with family that she had never met. Convenient.

"Sit down," she said. He opened up the box of pizza and took out a slice of pepperoni, the cheese dripping down his hands.

"Help yourself, baby." She had put a blanket over her TV and turned off her phone. Garfield ripped a napkin and set it below his slice. She settled next to him and watched him eat. He was bluffing, she could sense it. He was trying to seem like he didn't know what was going on, but he did. She had to play along with him.

"I've been thinking a lot about us," she said, making her eyes bigger and her voice a tilt higher.

"Really?" his eyebrows raised. This is exactly what he wanted her to say.

"Yeah," she said, "And I think you're right. I think we should try to start a family." Garfield almost choked on his pizza. He set it down on her coffee table and gave her a hug.

"I'm sorry I've been so, you know"—he motioned to his pants—"bad about that."

"That's okay," Candy said, "I can help you." Then she straddled him and his hands flew up.

"Where is this coming from!" She kissed him and he kissed her back as she grinded into him with her hips and he held onto the small of her back. She pinned him down with her weight. She whispered into his ear, "I know exactly what you've been doing."

"Yeah," he said in between kisses. "I mean, I'm really close to finding a job." She had her hands wrapped around his throat. "You're kind of hurting me."

"I stopped taking my collagen."

"I told you, you didn't need that stuff. You're so beautiful!"

Candy snarled, the back of her throat trembling, making her neck vibrate.

"Whoa," Garfield said, blinking rapidly because some of Candy's saliva had plopped into his eye. She could smell the pizza disintegrating in his stomach. She whimpered. He found the strength to lightly shove her off him.

"I don't really like this game," he said. "I dunno, I feel like there's other ways to get turned on." Candy panted. Garfield brushed a strand of hair out of her face.

"Can we talk about this?" His hand hovered by her face. He was trying to trick her. "Please?" She was breathing rapidly, sounding like a heater in an old building coming to life. He traced a finger on her shoulder, as if he were about to massage it.

"Your mouth looks a little funny." He blinked. "Like it's going all the way to your ears." With one last huff she grabbed his wrist and took a bite out of it. Garfield screamed as blood gushed all over the pizza. In the moment that she savored his flesh, he managed to get away from her, running toward the door. Candy caught him by the feet and dragged him to the bathroom as he banged his fists on her floor shrieking for help.

You are digging into him now with teeth and nails. You are seeing all of his life. His apartment building in East Cambridge. His first ride on a skateboard. The scrapes on the pavement. Corn flakes with 2 percent. The bathroom with his father, the sound of pants falling to the floor, his mother, her pills, their yellow kitchen, skipping class, getting high, getting sober, the sense of security and love he felt, sitting next to his friends in the dark playing video games. Biting into his gangly arms, his screams dying down, you see the first time you met, how he saw you. So taken by you. You feel so in love, seeing the way somebody who loves you sees you. You were new. Electric. There was glee when you shoved him. The hour he spent picking out the vase for the flowers he bought you. You search and search for a conspiracy, sucking on his bones, getting to the marrow. There is nothing. He really just loved you, Candy. You've done it again, haven't you? Given in to something just to remember the feeling.

Without time to think, she took down her shower curtains and wrapped up his remains, this poor man who fell into her trap. She put his beanie into a little bag, along with his one dangly earring and his Vans.

She needed to do something. She needed to get rid of whatever was inside of her so that she would stop hurting people. She found herself at CVS, Garfield's blood still caked on her mouth, muttering to herself. She purchased eight packets of Plan B. By now, the baby was eight months along and viable outside the womb. Maybe she could push it out of her and drop it off at a fire station with a cute little note and the demon baby could spend its entire life making art and music about being abandoned. She purchased a bundle of oregano and a large bottle of oregano oil and a turkey baster, remembering something she saw somewhere about abortifacients. She couldn't get rid of the pregnancy but she could get rid of the baby.

Candy locked her door, pushing several chairs in front of it. She took a baster and inserted oregano oil inside herself. She then swallowed eight Plan B pills and began tearing into the bundle of oregano. Something had to give at this point. Swallowing the pills, she realized she would need help, were she to bleed out while pushing out the parasite. God, she couldn't even DIY-induce herself. She didn't know who to turn to. She took out her phone and voice dictated a text to Zoe.

Zoe can you come over? I can't get into it but it's an emergency.

She waited for the oregano or the pills to hit. She felt nauseated and dizzy, a sudden, otherworldly cramp hitting her abdomen. The TV shook and sparked. The lights blinked wildly. She got into a ball and found herself chanting, humming to a heartbeat she couldn't hear.

A knock on the door. So quickly? It had only been a few minutes. Candy opened the door. Zoe had her hair pulled back. She looked like she hadn't slept in a while. Zoe glanced toward the bathroom, where the light was flickering.

"I'm not on drugs," Candy said, panting, noticing a splotch of blood on her sneaker.

"Okay."

"Is it snowing outside?" Candy said, pulling at her own hair.

"Yeah."

"What's up with you?" Candy asked, her eyes completely dilated and blood making a ring around her mouth. Zoe looked behind her.

"Can I come inside?"

"Yeah, yeah, of course, come in come in," Candy said, suddenly a gracious host. It was all so overwhelming. All at once pretending she hadn't just eaten her boyfriend, and also Zoe's very nervous demeanor, and also the cocktail she had just put inside of her.

"I think I did something stupid." Candy cupped her hand around her mouth. Was she going to heave? She wanted an ice-cream cone. She wanted a Band-Aid with Spongebob on it. She wanted her mother.

"What did you do?" Zoe sounded faraway, like she was listening to somebody she didn't know talk about their dream from the night before. Maybe the oregano oil was working. Maybe she would throw up a baby, stomp on it with her boot and move on with her life.

"I'm being pursued by something, agh!" Candy slapped her head with her palms. "It's my fault," Candy pointed to her chest. "It's my fault. I *fucked* that *guy* and I think he put some kind of like, *chip* inside of me because, because I'm seeing all of these things and then this *nurse* gave me this ointment so it went away and then," Candy took the tiny camera out of her pocket, "someone's been *watching* me and then I ate my boyfriend and I'm gonna be a mother I guess!" Candy started retching onto her floor, her body moving like toothpaste being squeezed of itself. Zoe crouched, holding back Candy's hair. The door opened. The blanket over the TV shook off as it turned on.

"And like, right now, I see all these women in white and they're all pregnant, but I know that they are not actually there! It's just like, I thought my subconscious was working with this chip that my boyfriend put into my brain and—"

Two women in white took her by the arms. Candy didn't resist.

"It feels so real but it isn't real. It's an *interpretation* of what's real. You just have to let it happen to you." Candy was trying to make it all make sense. Maybe she hadn't actually eaten Garfield. Maybe that was a vision. She felt herself getting through to her sister, who looked at her with sympathy.

"You don't see them, too, do you?" Candy said, not yet having put it all together, what had already happened, what was about to happen.

"Yes, I see them." The women beside Candy were so still, toy soldiers awaiting instruction.

"That's amazing. I mean, maybe it's something genetic. I bet Bianca is having these visions, too. It's probably intergenerational trauma or something. Like how water retains memories and we are ninety-eight percent water." Candy was babbling, she knew it. But she also had a feeling that if she stopped talking, something bad would happen.

"What do you think, Zoe? Do you think we're all fucked in the same way?" Zoe got closer. Her eyes were watering. Candy looked at the people in white and back at Zoe.

"Zoe, what's going on." Candy started wriggling from their grip, kicking her legs out. Their grip tightened.

"The world is ending, Candy."

"Obviously, that's why I don't want to bring another person into it. But so much for that!" Zoe nodded at another person in white. How many were there? Why were they so emotionless? Where was the movie magic?

"Why did you just do that with your chin. What did that mean." Zoe uncrossed her arms. It had never been Garfield. It was her very own fucking family.

Candy broke from the women in white, kicking one of them in her round stomach. The woman doubled over and fell to the floor. Candy punched another in the jaw and she stumbled, holding her chin and gasping. Zoe grabbed her by the wrist.

"It'll be so much easier if you don't resist," Zoe said, "please." Candy wrenched her hand away and yanked open the door, and ran.

Air filled her lungs. Her heartbeat was in her hands. Candy was running for her life and hoping the half-formed one inside of her would soon expire. The TVs in the homes around her began to hiss with static as she ran past them. She could feel them. She was watching people watch sitcoms. Crime serials. Romantic comedies. She would run to the Orange Line and hop on a train and then get to South Station and take the next train to New York City. She didn't care how much it cost. Why hadn't Bianca called her? She knew her address. She had it memorized. She would show up on her doorstep and say, *Surprise, bitch! You're a tía!* Bianca. Know-it-all. Smart ass. Mrs. Stoic Poofy-Ass Hair. Secretly a little fucking freak who porked her professor. Little slut! Ah-ha! She was almost proud of her. She didn't think she had it in her. Oh, she missed her.

Candy felt something cool spread in her neck before she collapsed in the middle of the street. The oregano oil? No, a needle. They'd gotten her before she escaped. The TVs were all so loud, the static kissing her ears. She kissed it back. She took out her phone and dialed Bianca, her last chance. The number was disconnected. They had blocked her from Bianca, somehow, Candy realized. Because Bianca would've always picked up. She would've texted back. She wouldn't have just ignored her. *My sister,* she thought, *my sister never would have fucking done that!*

And then they surrounded her, their faces all meshing into the other. Zoe was there, too, suddenly standing above her.

"I'm sorry,"

"Please, Paola," Candy said, her eyes closing against her will. "You fucking cunt, please." She kept saying *please* over and over again, a hurried, useless prayer, as darkness came over.

IV

EARTHQUAKE

BIANCA

They gathered themselves into Julian's blue Volvo, which was constantly breaking down and he was constantly fixing.

"We should probably talk about last week?" Julian plugged his phone in and searched Candy's address. The purple flowers on his yellow knitted sweater looked so earnest to her, singing musical numbers to her about moving to the big city. Bianca didn't want to talk about last week, which to her felt like last night.

"I haven't been that drunk in a long time."

"Can I be honest with you about something?"

Bianca's headache pounded. "Sure, what."

"I think we should just establish where we are with each other."

"Your car."

"How do we *feel* about one another."

"Julian, I was drunk. It didn't mean anything. I don't want to do this tender checking-in thing with each other. It weirds me out. Blue and I have gotten into fights because I just don't do that. I was wasted and I came on to you. That's the only reason."

"Okay." Julian blinked his heavy lids and turned onto Green Street, where somebody was taking a shit in the middle of the road. Bianca shifted, her shoe grazing against an empty Zapp's Voodoo chips bag.

"You are probably the last person on earth I would have sex with normally." Maybe that was too mean. But she wanted to be honest.

"Well, we did have sex once." Julian looked over at her and gave her a wink.

Bianca groaned into the window, her breath fogging up the glass.

"We don't have to make this a whole thing. Sorry I'm so dramatic."

"Sorry I'm being a fucking cunt right now."

"You're not a cunt."

"I'm too pushy. And judgmental. My sister won't talk to me and I sent her down a spiral and now she's in rehab again. I was pushy with Sylvester, and now he's dead. I was pushy about doing this investigation, and now Blue is gone."

"Can I just mention one more thing about last week?"

"Fine."

"You said nobody wants you. Do you really think that?"

"Sometimes."

"I don't want you to think that."

"It's okay if it's true."

"It's not." She felt an aura wrapped around her like a blanket that did not belong to her. A blanket in the shape of someone else. Someone Julian thought she was. Bianca wrapped her actual coat around her, feeling self-conscious about the outline of her waist and breasts. What was Julian about to say? Was he about to confess something to her?

"You're really special. And smarter than anyone I know. And your face looks like it belongs in a painting where everyone's trying to figure out what that woman was thinking. I don't know anybody like you." She grabbed a tote bag from the backseat and retched.

"That was disgusting," she said, using the handle of the tote bag to wipe her mouth.

"It's just vomit."

"No, what you said."

Julian laughed. "Well, I'm kind of glad that happened, anyway."

"Me vomiting?"

"No, you coming on to me."

"Can you just stop?"

"No, because now," Julian said, turning onto Bushwick Avenue, where a mangy cat had narrowly avoided getting hit by a car, "we can just be friends."

"We're friends?"

"Yeah, I regret to inform you, we're totally buds now."

"Were we ever friends?" Once Julian came over to make tamales with her family. His moms were awkwardly there, writing down exactly how to make the recado and the masa in a Moleskine notebook. Candy was on a stool mixing the masa, corn flour and milk splattered on her little arms, moving the dough around unhelpfully. Paola and Bianca were chopping up peppers. And Julian sitting on a chair, kicking his knees out and hitting the table with his feet. His head was in his hands. He looked bored. Bianca's mom was stressed about the white American women asking so many questions. *I don't like having strangers in my home*, she said later to her father. Bianca had the whole conversation transcribed into her notebook. Her father said, *The kid is lost. They can't tell him who he is.* Bianca felt proud then. She knew who she was. *No more*, her mother said, *this is the last time*. And it was.

You could move to a different city, you could try to make something different of yourself, you could try to prove some unnamable thing, and still end up fulfilling your parents wishes.

It's all circumstantial, Bianca reasoned, trying her best not to be sentimental, but the hangover was making her tender. She could've not had an affair with Fernando and then been sent back to New York and then work at the salon next to the plant store. She could've not been interested in archaeology. Actually, when Bianca thought about it, what she really cared about was preservation. Archiving, not archaeology. Maybe after all this was over she could go to library school. She realized something that felt equally important and stupid: you need other people to help you figure out who you are. Julian made a fist and waited for Bianca to join hers with his. She did.

"Hell yeah, brother."

The soldier does not seem afraid of you. The pistol pointed at him, held up by your spotted hands, is not what seems to be driving him forward. He is looking ahead, and following your finger, as you point down the Charles River toward Arsenal Street. Something has changed in the landscape since you've been inside the tent. Out of the corner of your eye, a beast scuttles away. They are not interested in you anymore. You do not know why.

There's a crack in the sky, as if the earth has been hard-boiled and is about to be peeled of its shell. And as it grows, parts of the city fade. The outline of the river remains, but the skyline has disappeared. Beyond the bridge and the dried-up river, there is no CITGO sign or John Hancock Center. There's just space. Stars shine from the other side.

You understand the soldier has given up. His fellow soldiers are all dead. The world is disappearing. It's just him and this old lady at the end of the world.

You pull up to the Watertown Mall, where a sign about holiday sales is ablaze. As you pull into the parking lot, Arsenal Street falls away, in one big *whoosh*. All the cars and the signs and the new Arsenal Mall, and the roadkill, and what was once a Bugaboo creek, and the 71 buses, and the Boston geese. The ducklings. All gone. But reality remains at the Watertown Mall. The soldier pulls into the parking lot, but he doesn't stop.

"Mijo," you say, "déjame aqui. Thank you so much." But he can't hear you, and Candelaria, how did you not notice that he fell asleep?

Or is he asleep? Oh, no. You should've been paying better attention. His head falls on the steering wheel, which you turn with your hands so that it doesn't jam into one of those red balls in front of the Target.

"¡Despiértate mijo!" The Jeep crashes into the Target and slams into the returns desk. You climb out of the steaming car and open the door on the soldier's side. His body falls out, blood gushing from his forehead.

"No," you say, falling to your knees and holding his head in your hands. You feel bad. He was just a kid. A baby who had fallen asleep. You have been allowed to get older, Candelaria. Sometimes you feel like it isn't right. What did you do to deserve this much life? Your granddaughters are lost in their youth. A few more years and things won't seem so crazy to them. They won't be so overwhelmed. They just have to get there. And you have to help them.

And then the soldier opens his eyes.

You were sitting in the kitchen when the knock came, staring at the fallen-in ceiling and all of the rubble around it. You opened the door, and there was your son. His body wasn't crushed to death. His face was intact. He was your boy, who you grew inside of your body. An organ of yours with legs.

"Gabo," you said, "mi hijo tierno," holding on to his chest, taking in the smell of his striped shirt, which did not smell of the soap you'd washed it with yesterday before the earthquake, but nothing at all. He held you back, but he didn't speak. You broke away from him. He moved toward you. Your instinct was to back away.

"When I look at you," he said, "the world goes away. Time stops."

"Thank you, mijo," you said. He kept moving toward you with his hand out. You could feel it, how much he was not your son. He put his hand on your shoulder and rubbed it like a lover would. You reached for the knife you kept in your skirt and gutted him. He didn't react. He turned into this pus, melted in front of you, his body dripping away into a horrible neutral, eraser-like mold, and disappearing before your eyes.

And now, as the soldier rises again, the same look in his eye, you hold up your gun. He looks hungry for you but you will not be consumed. You point it at his head and hit the trigger, and see his brains scatter on the window, beautiful twenty-three-year-old brains that had grown up watching cartoons you didn't understand, and as he falls you let the memory wrap you tightly, this suffocating embrace, remembering how it was to see your son die again at your own hands, how it only confirmed you would never see him, in his physical form, in this world, again.

"Perdóname," you say, as the young man falls to the Target floor. You think of your daughter, the way she helps you out of cars, how she bought you the new coat you are wearing even though she said it was because everything you own is old, and how despite it all, you have become a woman who needs to be taken care of.

CANDY

Asleep, she went to the place she always did in dreams. This time, she was the forks on the table. She felt herself pierce the fruit, the juice pushing against the seeds. Ecstasy, almost. Relief. Maybe she could stay here forever, in this nightmare that felt good in a perverted way. She was cutting open the feast. She was slipping in and out of the mouths of the attendants, being licked by their tongues. There she was on the table, asleep. *Wake up*, she said, as the fork, *wake up!* But it was too late. She was diving into her own skin, cutting through bone.

When she woke up, she was on a hospital bed, with doctors all around her. There was an IV in her arm. She smelled vomit—her own. They made her throw up the Plan B pills. *What about the oregano oil? Damnit*, she thought. *All that did was make my pussy smell like salad.*

"Can someone tell me what's going on? Please?" she asked the masked faces around her, who all had large bumps underneath their scrubs.

"Something special," one of them said, squeezing her leg.

"I've been aching to meet you," another said.

"Me?"

"You must be hungry," one said, and Candy touched her stomach, which was still flat. There was a rumbling underneath. She was hungry. Had they seen what she had done to Garfield?

"Why don't we get you something to eat?"

"Yeah, would love something to eat. But first, can someone explain why I was drugged and kidnapped?"

The doctors looked at one another and one of them said, "You were being saved."

"Saved," Candy repeated.

"Yes, and now we will take care of you."

"Somebody put a shot in my neck. I don't think whoever did that is looking out for my well-being." Nothing from them.

"Where's my sister?" Nothing.

"I would like to leave."

"I'm afraid we can't let you go."

Candy groaned. What kind of hospital room was this?

"Why don't we get you something to eat."

"Can I see my phone?"

"No screens."

So the screens did have something to do with this. And they didn't want her looking at them. Whatever they didn't want, Candy thought, was probably something she wanted. She was silent, thinking. She would comply. She would gather information. When she saw an exit, she would make a run for it. They blindfolded her and led her to a cozy room. There were pink pillows and plush towels, even a little toilet.

"We'll come back with your food." And the door was shut. Candy went to every corner of the room, looking for answers. The floors and walls were a calm, green color, and marble-like, cold to the touch. She pushed on the walls, and they didn't give. She looked under the bed. She opened the drawers, where she saw comfortable night slips to dress into, pajamas. She was still groggy from the drugs. The attendants knocked on the door again and came in, but with no tray. She worried about what she would do.

"Can you get me a burger? Maybe raw?"

But then she heard a small whining sound. Another attendant came in, with a chihuahua on a leash.

"What do you want me to do with that?" Candy was trying to be coy. After all, this could have been a trick.

"We'll leave you alone." The chihuahua went to the corner of the room. Did they have a shelter down here? She reached out to the small animal, who was shaking. How could she do this? But she had a huge headache. And she felt herself on the brink of another vision. She reached out with her hand. She had done it before, so why did she feel so bad now?

"Come on, little guy," she said, gulping, "I'm not going to hurt you." But you can't run away from who you really are. Or whatever somebody made you. The dog, shaking, came closer to her. She held its small body in her hand and its fluttering heart. Her stomach growled.

"I'm sorry," she said, and she did mean it. But can you ever truly be sorry, if you still do the thing you are apologizing for?

"I have to," she said, and the dog yelped.

Every day there was a new animal. Cats, more dogs. Sometimes mice. There was even a baby goat once. Blood dried around her mouth and then she cleaned it off with wipes provided by the attendants. They were all encouraging this behavior. They wanted her to stay here, in this monstrosity, eating innocent beings. Despite all the animals she still thought of the way Garfield's arms tasted, how she could feel his entire sad life inside of her, and how beautiful that was. The animals had lives too, of course, but they hadn't been as electric.

What happens at the end of cult movies, she wondered? In *Rosemary's Baby*, she is free, but the baby is Satan. The directors' wife was later stabbed to death, in real life, by a real cult. A cursed movie. She had always loved it. In *Suspiria*, the ballet school burns down. Nobody wins. In *Martha Marcy May Marlene*, nobody dies in the cult, but Elizabeth Olsen sees them everywhere she goes. They are inescapable. Pathogens in the air. Mood swings so fierce they are caught by other people.

And the baby? She still couldn't feel it. She couldn't even see it. What would happen when it came out?

She tried feeling emotional toward it. She tried imagining a squirming small human and the natural pheromones that would arrive. The way milk would leak from her breasts with motherly love.

Nah.

Maybe she could give this baby up to the cult and they could do whatever they wanted with it. *Hey, can I have this baby and bounce?* Then she would stop having cravings for flesh and just be a normal girl.

"Can I see my sister?" Nothing. She had no idea where Zoe was. The next time she saw her, Candy swore, she would beat the shit out of her.

So she didn't have to eat Garfield after all. He wasn't part of the cult, he was just kind of a traumatized dumb ass. Their relationship wasn't a lie, just a bust. She should've known.

"Can't I watch a movie or something?" Candy said to the attendants. "I'm so bored in here."

The attendants shook their heads. "No screens," they said, sweeping up fur and tendons of a few squirrels.

She tried to make a run for it the next time they came in with food, but was then drugged and dragged back to her room, then denied food for a day and a half. Her visions were awful. She was then given a piece of paper and a crayon (no sharp objects allowed) with a note that said, *Express your wishes and desires here.*

Candy wrote, in the red crayon, *FUCK OFF*, and slid it under the door frame.

What was she gonna do? Write a poem?

At some point, she wondered if they were doing some *V for Vendetta* shit with her. Alone in the room, she was faced with herself. There was no stimulus at all. She did push-ups again. Stretches. Planks. She was fitter than ever in here. On day five she had a panic attack. She threw the bed around and tore up the pillows with her teeth and nails. This was so unfair. Why was she being punished like this? Because she had indulged, more than once, in the worst way. She remembered rehab, the older people in there, how she never wanted to be like them, always in and out because they couldn't get a hold over themselves. She always just thought she was being lazy, that she didn't have the ganas to get out of something. Maybe being kidnapped by a wellness cult and being subjected to isolated torture was the only way for her to get ahold of herself.

The next day, an attendant arrived. Candy had a thought. A small one. But alone, you have to savor every morsel of hope before you consume yourself.

"Hey, what's your name?"

The attendant paused.

"Carmen."

"Carmen. Like the opera. Love that. What's your favorite movie, Carmen?" Candy hoped she didn't sound too fake or that her smile wasn't too beaver-like.

"I don't know."

"Sure you do. Tell me." Carmen's eyes darted around the room and she peeked behind her.

"I'm not gonna try to escape," Candy said, "I just want you to tell me what your favorite movie is. That's it."

"*Across the Country with Me*," she said, sheepishly.

"I've never seen it," Candy said. "Can you tell me about it?"

Carmen began. "There's this woman who wakes up one day and doesn't know where or who she is and she's wearing these gloves. Inside the glove is this note with an address. She looks in her purse and she has enough money to get across the country. So she finds the nearest train station, and she goes there." As Carmen finished describing the movie, Candy could see the ending in her eyes. Then it happened: she was in the movie, she was the woman with the gloves on. She moved through the train, where she saw another woman. It was like she was lucid dreaming.

"Can I use your phone?" she said, and the woman turned at her, shook her head. There were no phones here. The movie was old. Then Candy came to, but this time, she wasn't on the floor passed out. She had only been gone for a little bit.

"Do you have another one? Maybe post-9/11?"

"I guess I liked *Blanche*."

"Yeah, what's that about?" Candy found herself in an office space, looking at the back of a woman's head—probably Blanche. Blanche's crush was on the other side of the room. Quick, she thought. Quick, quick. She found someone to the left of Blanche's cubicle, an extra making Z's go across the screen to seem like she was busy. Candy felt slightly short of breath. Drowning in the dream again, but not quite. She could talk. Talk, Candy! Talk!

"Can I use your phone?" But the extra couldn't hear her. The air started getting very tight. Candy reached toward the keyboard and tried to type in a letter. But then she was out again.

"Are you okay?"

"Yeah, I think I just need some water." She had figured it out. And even though the vision was over, she knew that, somewhere, in whatever building she was in, there was a phone. Or a TV. Or some kind of screen that she could tap into. Asleep, she thought of a normal, recent movie. *Scream 6*. She went through the scenes in her mind and tried to visualize them as she slept. One of the characters was using a phone. When she got to it she would wake up. *Eventually*, she thought. *Eventually I'll get to them. They'll have to find me.* They'll have to.

BIANCA

Her mother was outside of Candy's place, parked on the porch, crying. Bianca held on to the handle of the car's door. She thought she was going to vomit again.

Julian got out and opened the door for her.

"Come on." She held on to his arm, like they were going to prom together, except prom was her very upset mother.

"Mami?" Lucia looked up at her with red eyes. She was holding a note. Bianca sat down next to her. Julian did the same.

"¿Y este?"

"He drove me." Julian stood up and put his hands in his pockets.

"Puedo ir. No hay problema." Lucia looked at him without expression— Bianca's. It was the way bears or lions had ears and noses and mouths like humans, how they could even look like they are smiling at you, and make you forget that they could end your life with the jaws they were given, the claws at the end of their fuzzy paws. Julian bowed away respectfully.

The silence that Bianca sat in with her mother made time stop. They were at a stop light that never changed. Laundry held captive by the spin cycle. A beachball twirling as a computer died.

"I'm sorry I lied to you," she said, finally. "I just didn't want you to be disappointed in me."

"I really needed you. The business was suffering. Your abuela's health is getting worse. I have no one to help me. And now your sister. You left me alone." Bianca didn't want to have this conversation. She wanted to sleep until a comet came. She wanted to step in front of a bus.

"I'm sorry." Her mother's eyes were puffy.

"I need your help now."

"Okay. That's why I'm here." Her mother handed her the note.

"Look at this."

Mami,
I'm not in a good place right now. I've been using again, and it's
been bad. I have been given the opportunity by an anonymous
donor to start again. I'll be back soon. Don't worry about me.
Love,
Candy

Bianca examined the note. The handwriting was bubbly. The *i*'s were circular and cute.

"What do you think about this?"

"I don't think she would have just done this. She would have come to me. She would've come to you. Where have you been? She told me that she text you, she call you, and you say nothing to her. Nothing. You can't do that. You are sisters. You need to be together. Because when I am gone, what will you have?" Her mother's eyes brimmed with tears again.

Bianca felt horrible. Her mother was, indeed, being dramatic but Bianca felt awful. "She never texted me."

"She said she did."

"I texted her. I called her. She never reached out." The porch squeaked. A gray cat stared at them with button eyes and was loudly purring.

"They disconnected us from each other," Bianca realized. She wasn't horrible. She hadn't pushed her sister away. She had been yanked away from her by other forces she was just starting to name.

"Do you remember when I went through Paola's diaries, trying to figure out where she was?"

"I don't want to talk about Paola. There has been enough tragedy in my life."

"Well, I remember her handwriting. Because it was really girly. Bubbly."

"Why you talking about bubbles?"

"Paola is alive. And she's with Candy." She opened up the map on her phone and typed in *Woman's Stone*. She looked at reviews—all glowing. She opened up their local website and clicked on *Instructors*. There she was. Paola. With blond hair now. Completely toned, muscular. Her legs were extremely defined and her ass looked like it hurt to touch. She showed her mother. She needed to show her mother.

"No," Lucia said. "No, not her. She's dead."

"She's not, Mami." The cat got on her back and showed off her stomach.

"And you knew this?"

"No," Bianca lied. She didn't need to reveal another thing to her mother, who was still processing that Bianca was never in Guatemala and that her oldest daughter was still alive. Lucia put her face in her hands, breathing into them, choking back a tear. If she had stopped dyeing her hair it would be completely gray. The stress of mourning her daughter and her husband had made her go through menopause in her forties and given her hair loss. Bianca remembered seeing clumps of hair in the trash can, and her mother wearing baseball hats, like somebody in disguise. She went on strange diets, ate a lot of things with nuts and oils. After two and a half years, her hair came back, but never again in all its luscious glory. It was muted, flatter. But it had returned. A part of her had come back. And that is all you can hope for. A small, beautiful piece.

LUCIA

Her daughter's face had grown slightly thinner. When she was her daughter's age, she already had two babies. Bianca still hid her body in big sweaters and jeans that Lucia used to wear when she first arrived in this country. Why did she like that? She had a beautiful body. She was the opposite of Candy, who had always shown off her body like a parade, waiting to be ogled at, offered something.

The first day Lucia gave birth was the first day she had ever truly known fear. And Lucia had felt afraid before. Arriving somewhere, shaking and small, in a country where everybody was already looking down on you because you don't speak the language. But the moment the being she grew inside of her was wriggling around in her arms was the same moment every horrible possibility became real. With Paola, she never wanted to be away from her. She was jealous when other people spent time with her. *She's mine*, she would think. *She is only for me.* The first two years were sleepless because Lucia could only sleep if Paola's face was nestled on her breast, snoring.

Bad things had happened to Lucia. She became an adult too quickly. She didn't get to be a mess. There was no coming of age. There was just arriving somewhere breathless, with everything you owned in your arms, thankful she made it at all. And because bad things had happened to Lucia, bad things could happen to Paola.

And so Paola was not allowed to do anything.

Lucia smothered her, she admitted to herself, only recently. She had not loved her in a way that let her grow. She just wanted to keep her close. Keeping her inside made Paola lazy, snacking on things that weren't good for her, growing fatter by the day. It was American laziness to her. It was something that you just needed to snap out of.

When she met the boy, there was a shift in Paola. She was always smiling to herself, a glint of something in her eye. When she disappeared, it was two years and a week after Hector had passed away. The grief groups always talked about how the second year was the hardest, but once you passed it things would slowly start to get easier. What happens when grief mounts on top of grief? How many years to get over your husband and your daughter?

Instead of turning back into the pit she had emerged from, Lucia found a light in anger. Paola had abandoned her. She abandoned their entire family. She sat with her mother on their couch, her mother who was trying, not very well, to give her advice.

"How could a daughter ever do this to her own mother?" She picked her mother's hand off her own like a piece of lint.

"You don't know anything about my daughter," Lucia told her. "*You* were the one who made her feel so bad about her body."

Candelaria looked aghast.

"You were a horrible mother to me and a worse grandmother to the girls. You don't know anything about taking care of anybody because you're ignorant trash."

She locked herself in the bathroom for two hours, huddled in an angry ball staring at the water accumulating in the Garnier Fructis shampoo bottle she and the girls all shared. She couldn't deal with the mystery of wondering where her daughter was, alive or dead. Or knowing that Paola was happier away from her. And why did she run away? Because she had made a few comments about her weight? It was honesty. She was doing her a favor. She wouldn't have survived a day in Guatemala. With real honesty.

She didn't think that she was retraumatizing her children with a funeral. To her, it was a message. A sense of finality. No more looking for Paola. No more wondering where she was. She placed a silk lavender dress in the coffin, one that Paola hadn't lost enough weight to fit inside of. Candy walked up the empty coffin with a toy skunk she had that, when squeezed, would let out a farting noise.

"Somebody should make her laugh," Candy said, her head bowed and her eyes red. Bianca was stone-faced, as she had become after Hector had died. But Lucia could tell that she was just thinking. She was putting it together. She always was.

Lucia had started questioning her choices the day that Candy overdosed. She hadn't been there enough for her youngest daughter. Tragedy after tragedy. She decided to make it up to her by getting her richest client, Rhonda, to pay for her rehab, in exchange for free dry-cleaning and adjustments for the rest of Rhonda's life. *You need to thank her*, Lucia told her daughter, *she saved your life*. To which Candy responded: *I don't know that bitch*. Rhonda moved away shortly after that, and sometimes Lucia would email her with updates about her daughters. Bianca was going to get her PhD in New York City. Candy was now a supervisor at a movie theater. Rhonda always responded with flourishing sentences. She was always traveling, though. Lucia missed her. Rhonda would really listen to her. Have so much empathy. Lucia almost told her too much one time. Lucia was embarrassed about it. She didn't want Rhonda to pity her. To feel bad. Rhonda stopped responding after a few emails. *That's okay*, Lucia thought. She was being too much.

Sandra had called her, as she did periodically. They were starting to reconnect, sending grainy photos back and forth to each other. How did she make daughters who would lie to her? What did she do to be lied to?

Sitting on her daughter's porch, she wondered if Rhonda had come back somehow. She was like her angel, Lucia thought. Maybe God sent her. Maybe that's where she was traveling. Helping other people.

"Mami?" Bianca said, holding the note in her hand. "I need to go."

"Where?" Lucia said, so very tired. *Hold on to your daughter's hand, Lucia. Come on.* She went for her wrist. Bianca flinched a little bit.

"I'm sorry," Lucia said, choosing the words carefully, "if I wasn't a good mother." Bianca's face, still made of stone. Did Lucia do that too? Make her afraid to feel anything?

"You are not a bad mother," her daughter said to her, not moving away from her touch. "There were things that you couldn't control."

"I'm sorry I never looked for her," Lucia said, the emotion sweeping into her face, a harsh wind. She let out a sob.

"I'm sorry I lied to you," Bianca said, "I didn't want to tell you I messed up."

"Everybody makes mistakes. You didn't want to see me?"

"There was a man. He kicked me off the site. But I was stupid, Mami. He was married. I'm so stupid, Mami," Bianca cried. "I've been so, so stupid." Her mother hugged her.

"No." Her daughter shook beneath her, and she could feel her tears pattering on her neck.

"How can you say that about my Bianca?" she squeezed her. "You are my smart girl." She took in the smell of her daughter's hair.

"You smoking?"

"No. I went to a show."

"A *show*?"

"Julian."

"He smokes?"

"No."

"Be nice to that boy." Her daughter held on to her neck, and she remembered the nights she had taken her to her bed and took off her glasses, watched her sleep peacefully without the sorrows Lucia had known, but soon to be with her own. That was inevitable. What this world brings. Bianca broke away from Lucia. The warmth from her started to fade.

"I have to go." Again.

"Where?"

"Candy is in trouble. She isn't in rehab. I think I know where to find her." Her daughter hugged her again.

"I'm going to fix this." And her daughter got up, the porch sighing from the weight of her, and moved away from her, her body shifting underneath a winter coat, opening a car door, and the boy she was with, Julian, started the car, and he backed out of the parking spot, turning the wheel, leaving the street, taking her farther and farther away.

BIANCA

"Let's hear it."

"We need to go to the Woman's Stone. It's where Syl was doing yoga. And it's where Paola is doing spin. Paola has Candy. I'm not sure why. But she does."

"What does this have to do with Fernando?"

Bianca squinted her eyes. "I don't know yet." Suddenly, she didn't care.

"How's your mom?"

"She's okay." Bianca picked at her nail.

"Good," Julian said, "That's good." Bianca's phone started to ring from an unknown number. She answered.

Now playing in theaters everywhere, Crazy, Stupid, Love*! Starring Steve Carell . . .*

Bianca hung up.

"Didn't Fandango go out of business?" Julian shrugged. Her phone rang again.

"Hello?"

Two sisters find themselves in trouble when they try to break a mysterious curse in Practical Magic.

Bianca hung up again. The phone rang again.

My Sister's Keeper, *starring Cameron Diaz and Toni Collette.*

"Annoying," Bianca said, putting it on mute.

Bianca pushed open the glass doors of the spin studio. Classical music was playing. She saw her sister on a poster on the wall, and a painting of a pregnant woman with a bunch of people dancing around her hung next to her.

"Can I help you?" the woman at the front desk beamed. Bianca clutched the note in her pocket.

"Just looking around."

"Happy to tell you more about this, but there's also a pamphlet here with details if you're curious about anything." Bianca thanked her and grabbed a pamphlet. She sat down in a pair of plush beige chairs. Looking through the pamphlet, she read her sister's bio again. She had changed her name and her hair color, but Bianca would know her everywhere. She read.

Started in 2010 by Maria Santiago, the Woman's Stone is an organization dedicated to holistic wellness, made by women, for women. Led by expert instructors, we offer spinning classes, cooking classes, rehabilitation meetings . . .

Bianca peered at the photo. Maria Santiago. She exactly looked like her mother's client. Rhonda Heffing. The one who sent Candy to rehab. Her mother's richest client. Old money that just kept growing. She had also paid for Bianca's archaeology camps. Bianca's mind whirled. Fernando had mentioned that his student loans weren't forgiven because they were all private. That his inheritance had just dried up. How did they get to Guatemala again?

Rhonda was Maria. She had changed her name. Yes. *She wanted something*, Bianca thought. *She wanted something that only Bianca could find.* Her whole life, she had been working toward something for Rhonda to steal. But to do what with? Did it kill Fernando? The door opened, a little bell ringing with it. Julian looked around, looking very out of place in his Carhartt and skater shoes.

"This place is off," Julian whispered, sitting down next to Bianca and making the chair creak. The woman picked up a phone.

"Did you find Paola?" Bianca put her finger over her mouth. She took out her phone and went to her notes.

anonymous donor runs this place.

She handed him the phone. His eyebrows went up.

how do u kno
same woman who put Candy in rehab. I think she was emailing
fernano.
R we ever gonna find out why F was in 2 places at once

Bianca shrugged. Bianca asked to fill out a form for her and Julian for registration, giving a fake name, as Paola and Rhonda had done. The woman shook her head.

"Sorry, this is strictly a women's facility."

"That's kind of fucked up," Julian said. "You don't know if I'm a woman or not."

"Well, are you?"

"I'm not telling you that information." Julian put his hands on the counter, his fingers gripping the edges. Bianca pinched his waist.

"It's just part of our policy."

"Listen, yeah, maybe I am cis, and male, and white in certain situations, but that's a pretty fucked-up policy."

"Oh, my God, stop talking."

"Has no one complained about this? You know anybody can be a woman, right?" The woman was refusing to answer him. The door jingled again, as blue and red lights filled the air.

"Bianca Castillo and Julian Woodward?" The pair turned around, facing a pair of police officers, one with a blond ponytail and the other with a bob.

"Don't answer them," Julian said underneath his breath.

"You're under the arrest for the murder of Sylvester Leon."

CANDY

Candy was in every movie from her childhood, spinning through the scenes and trying to find a phone, training herself like a deep diver holding her breath. She would make a call and then wake up. She didn't know what was happening or if the calls were going through, but she had to keep diving in and pulling at the doors of her consciousness until she couldn't anymore. She had only been in here for a few days. Carmen came again.

"How long am I supposed to be here?"

"Until it's time."

"Is there a doctor? Like, how am I supposed to get this thing out of me?" Carmen stood by the doorway.

"Yes." So they wouldn't leave her to die. A week had passed when the door opened and the attendant let her out. She had a round belly and copper hair, and each time she had come to her, she had been very bubbly. But this time, she was a little serious. Almost somber.

"Today is the day, Candy." And she offered her hand to Candy's, small and stubby, dry. She followed her down the corridors, groaning.

"You okay?"

"Yes. I just started my contractions, actually." That explained her somberness.

"Uh. You nervous at all?"

"I've thought about this moment for a long, long time." Candy didn't know how much she could be herself here. If she should choose kindness or keep being a fucking bitch. What did it matter? They had kidnapped her.

"Well. Hope it's chill."

Carmen squeezed her hand. "Thank you for saying that."

She led her through a corridor and then another one, until they approached a bed, surrounded by fruits and candles. Candy's heartbeat went up.

"What is this?" Because she had seen it before of course, for the last decade or so. It was what she would wake up with a sweat from, all supposed to be a reflection of her childhood trauma.

"Stay here."

"Am I going up there?"

"Not yet." Candy looked for an exit, but more and more women were coming in through every entrance, their hands on their round bellies. Carmen winced and put her hands on the edge of the bed. She then disrobed, her hair falling over her breasts. She squatted, like she was about to take a dump. In the crowd, humming began. It sounded like yoga humming. A steady breathing and chant. Carmen groaned. An older woman walked through the crowd, one bare foot in front of the other, smiling broadly. She had turquoise necklaces on her neck and her hair was down to her back.

Next to her, was a woman with a mushroom cut, following her stride. That bitch from the abortion office.

The woman placed her hands on Carmen's hips and told her breathe in and out, like she taught her. The woman with the mushroom cut kneeled behind Carmen, ready to catch the baby. Carmen's groans were now screams, and the sound of them made Candy want to hurl.

"Save me!" Carmen shrieked. "Save me! Sweet salvation!" The humming. Blood leaked from between her legs.

"It's coming," the woman with the mushroom cut said. "One more push." And then Carmen pushed again, and a head emerged, a large marble stretching against her. The woman grabbed the head and slid the gray baby out, who was wriggling and screaming, getting ready for this new world. Carmen lay back, exhausted. Her eyes looked like they were else-where. The woman with the mushroom hair took out a knife to cut the umbilical cord, and then she gave Carmen her baby, and Carmen had tears running down her face as she touched the baby who looked like she was covered in parmesan cheese. She kissed its head and then the woman with the mushroom cut took the baby away, placing her in a small bed next to the giant bed. Then she grabbed a knife from her pocket.

"Good job, Carmen," said the leader of them all, "thank you for all you have done." Carmen smiled. Then the woman with the mushroom cut came up behind her and slit her neck.

"What the shit." Candy's hand flew to her mouth. Candy thought she saw Carmen smiling through the blood. The leader opened a white box and tilted Carmen's blood inside of it. A strange bell started to ring, and Candy could feel it in her stomach.

"It's time, ladies," the woman said, holding up the bell. The mushroom-cut woman took Candy's arm. Candy tried to wrench herself away.

"No way, Toad," Candy said. "I'm not doing that."

"It's different," she said, like she was pointing out that chamomile tea was not mint tea. "Carmen was just preparing us."

Candy looked all around her for exits. There were none. Where was her sister? The women all around her started their humming again, holding on to their bellies with their eyes closed.

"Please, Candelaria," one of them said. "Look underneath the bed."

"It's Candy and you all need Jesus."

"We need you to touch what's under the bed." The mushroom woman tightened her grip on her shoulder.

"First look, now touch? Take a bitch to dinner first!"

"You have to trust us." Carmen's eyes were vacant. She wasn't a woman anymore. She was a discarded vehicle, a receipt stepped over and over again on the street. The bell was so loud. Candy covered her ears. She could feel it throughout her, making her body convulse. She collapsed on the floor. The humming grew louder and louder. Candy realized all these women were giving birth. She tried to resist the sounds of the bell, but she found herself lifting up the bedsheet and looking under the bed.

There was something squirming. It sounded like macaroni and cheese being moved around with a fork. Was it fungus? Mold? A subway rat with a lot to prove? She couldn't make out, exactly what it was. Colors flashed but they weren't close to colors that she knew. Groaning, humming. Groaning, humming. Her hand moved out, shaking. She moved her hand back. The bell was so demanding. She found her hand shooting toward it, like a magnet, and before she could name what it felt like, a sharp pain hit her abdomen. Candy shrieked. Did she just piss herself? Water had shot out between her legs. The women kept humming. Breathing. It hit her again. And from up above, the ground started to shake.

BIANCA

The police car took them through Charlesbank Road and into Cambridge. Their phones had been taken away and Julian and Bianca had been trying to communicate via eye signal. Their eyes kept winking back and forth at each other to no avail. An eyebrow wiggle could mean *What should we say?* But also *Of course they are woman cops.* A few, rapid blinks could mean *Do we get a lawyer?* But also *There's something in my eye.*

The car pulled in next to an abandoned MBTA station. The officers got out of the car and took them by the shoulders.

"You have the right to remain silent," one of them began, and then stopped.

"Why are you reading me my rights now?" Julian said, breaking his silence, "I thought you guys didn't do that anymore." The cop with the bob opened a door and shoved them inside an abandoned building.

"Our police station is under renovations," the blond one explained, leading.

"This is illegal," Julian said. "I don't know how, but it is." Opening a door, they led them down a series of moldy staircases. Finally they reached a corridor, and then went all the way down. Then they were led into a room with warm, radiating light. In this room, in a chair, was Bianca's mother's client.

"Rhonda?"

"It's Maria now. Bianca. It's so good to see you. You've been doing so well." The cops set them in a chair, their hands steadily on their shoulders. Out of the corner of her eye, Bianca saw a gun.

"Where's my sister?" Maria rested her head in her hands, like she was watching a show.

"Safe. She was falling off the deep end again, I'm afraid. Seems like she didn't learn anything from her first stint. But there's no shame in that. Life is a lifelong journey."

"Did you hear that?" Julian said. "That didn't make any sense, right?"

"Safe? In rehab?"

"Yes."

"Why did my older sister leave the note?"

"I have the feeling these aren't *really* cops," Julian blurted out, too late.

"We have a rehabilitation facility here. Your sisters had become a lot closer since you were gone." She felt jealous. Did they really get closer? Were they hanging out without her? Talking shit? Having so much fun without her because Bianca was such a drag, selfish, like Blue said?

"Can I see her?"

"Not now," Maria said, her mouth moving into a thin-lipped smile, "but eventually."

"I want a lawyer," Julian said unhelpfully.

"The problem is, you two were involved in a murder." Maria said this as if they were toddlers in preschool painting on eggs and one of the eggs had broken, fell between them on the floor.

"I don't know what you're talking about," Julian said.

"Sylvester Leon was full of life. He never would have killed himself. But witnesses from across the yoga studio saw two people following him down the street. A man and a woman. Both a little short."

"That's really low." Julián squirmed underneath the weight of the cops, who were pushing down on him very heavily. "You're holding us illegally," Julian said.

"Suddenly you're a man of the law?"

Julian released himself from the grip of the cops only to have them both put guns in his face.

"Sit down, Julian," Bianca said, staring at Maria unflinchingly, her emotionless face serving her well. The cop cocked her gun. Julian obliged, scowling.

"I'm proud of you, Bianca. Standing up for yourself. You've always been so much smarter than your sisters." Bianca had to ask something. The gears in her brain were spinning. She was finally putting it together.

"What happened to Fernando?"

"Bianca, I've been so excited to share this with you."

"Share what?"

"I needed your help. And only you could have gotten me so close."

"What?"

"When I was younger, my father took us on a trip to Guatemala. He didn't want to deal with me. I asked too many questions. Just like you. I went on my own to the Candelaria caves, and, don't know if you've ever been, but the darkness. You can feel it in your mouth. And the tour guide told me, this little frightened thing, about a legend. A stone that was not a stone and people who worshipped it. The Tierra Nueva. Sound familiar?"

"You're not answering my question."

"Bianca, what you need to understand is that this world cannot last."

"What do you mean?"

"How many children are killed in shootings a year? All because the men who run things feel like they need guns to keep them safe." A gun was still pointed at Julian, who was shaking slightly. Maria continued.

"Tides recede. Babies are born with plastic inside of their bodies. Catastrophic floods. Warm weather in December. Inevitable dust bowls. Politicians making their way to Mars. It seems endless. But we can end it."

"What are you saying?"

"Something new has to come. We need to start over. But I can't share with you just yet what it is. And I also can't let you go. So you'll need to wait. Just a few more hours. I promise. You'll be safe." The cops who were not cops did not say anything, taking them both to a corridor with a lot of doors. They opened one door at the end and then threw them in.

"This is kind of what those Swedish prisons look like," Julian said. Bianca sat on the bed, putting her head in her hands.

ZOE

"How can I trust you, right now, Zoe?"

"I brought her to you, didn't I? And we saved the baby."

"But you tried to take her away. Carmen told me. She said she had to stop you outside of her house."

"Loyalty has to be proven constantly, you taught us that," Zoe said, fingering her satchel. "This was just another test for me."

Maria stroked a small fertility statue.

"This is my family now," Zoe said. "My blood is here. Please forgive me for being scared."

"Do you believe the process? Do you believe the Mother?"

"Of course."

"The documents are ancient. They've been passed down for centuries. I had someone who was an expert in ancient Latin American scrolls to interpret it. It's all backed up."

"Right," Zoe said, rising and wiping her palms on her gym pants.

"I'll see you later."

"Yes," Zoe said. "Later. For the ceremony."

"One more thing, Zoe." Zoe turned around.

"Yes?"

"I'll need to have that key back."

Zoe stared at Maria for a moment and unzipped her satchel, from which she took her ring of keys and unhooked the master. She handed it over to Maria, palm facing up.

"Your car keys, too."

Zoe faltered.

"Do you need a ride somewhere, or . . . ?"

"Like you said. Loyalty."

BIANCA

"HELLO?" Bianca screamed, banging on the walls. "LET US OUT OF HERE!" Julian joined her, his fists pounding against their strange cell. He climbed on the bed and balanced on the posts to see if the ceilings moved at all. They did not.

"Maybe they're watching us somehow," Julian said. "Look for a camera." They tore through the simple room, ripping up pillows and examining the fluorescent light.

The room was starting to feel smaller and smaller. Bianca rubbed her knees and then her arms. What if they never got out? The air felt tighter around her.

"We're going to figure it out," Julian said, sitting down next to her and putting his arms on her shoulders. "They have to feed us at least. Right?" Bianca clutched the quilt on the bedspread, studying the pattern. There were two red circles, colliding like a Venn diagram. She patted her hand on each of them.

"What are you doing?" Julian said, as Bianca patted.

"Maybe the circles mean something." She continued patting, as if she were playing the drums.

"Goddamnit," she said, bunching the sheets up in her hand and screaming into them. "What the fuck did I get us into?" What if she never studied archaeology, she thought. What if she never fucked Fernando? What if her sister never disappeared and her father never died? It wasn't her fault she was born!

"I should've been an accountant," she said.

"But then," Julian said, "what if Maria found out who you were and became your biggest client and then blackmailed you or something?"

"My mom really loved her. She made us feel so guilty about her helping us."

"It's nice that she helped you I guess?" Bianca glared at him.

"I don't know," Julian said. "I have so much guilt all the time."

"Not this again."

"No, we gotta talk about it."

"You don't have to say sorry anymore," Bianca said. "Don't you understand that the more you apologize, the more work it is for me? For anyone?"

"Yeah, but—"

"No, Julian, I've already forgiven you. You don't have to keep hunting down an acceptance. It's already happened okay? You are fine. You are *good.*" Julian opened his mouth and closed it. Bianca shook her head. It would never be enough for him, she realized. Slamming her head down on the bed, she remembered that it wasn't enough for her, either.

"I feel guilty all the time, too. I feel like I swapped grief with guilt and then swapped it again for grief about Fernando. And now I just feel ashamed and stupid for wasting all that time. And now we're underground and probably gonna get killed by my mother's client's cult."

"Do you ever think it's enough to just say stuff out loud?" Julian said, sitting on the floor.

"Julian, why are you on the floor? This isn't a dorm room."

"Feels like it," Julian said. "Like those Swedish prisons."

"Sometimes," Bianca said, still examining the quilt, "I feel like if I say it out loud, it'll just make me a better person or something?" The circles had to mean something! Psychopaths loved hiding their shit in plain sight. "But you still have to make changes. And not wallow."

Julian's eyes were big and almost wet with understanding. Bianca couldn't stand it. "Yup."

She rolled her eyes. The door creaked.

"Maybe that's dinner," Julian said, like they had just ordered takeout and weren't in a cell underground. "I'm fucking starving." The door opened, and there, after fifteen years, with strong dark roots taking over her bleached hair, was Paola.

ZOE

Zoe shoved the copy of the key she had made into her sports bra and closed the door. There was still so much she didn't understand. So much that was glossed over until it rose up and stared back up at her like a rabid, slobbering dog. She'd gone to Candy's the night she realized that they were supposed to eat her, but was stopped by a very pregnant Carmen, who had mentioned her husband's mysterious death and how it was still open for investigation. How did she know that? "Creation can't happen without destruction," Carmen had chimed. "Your sister is a miracle. She will be remembered for the rest of the new world. They'll make a statue of her. There'll be schools and holidays named after her. She'll be so alive." She thought she was doing Zoe a favor. She thought she was saving the world.

The ceremony was about to start. She was going to get Candy, get into her car, and drive to Canada, where she would dye her hair again and the two of them would start over. But when she opened the door, it wasn't Candy. It was Bianca. And a short Guatemalan man.

"Bianca."

"Are . . ." Julian said. "Have you come to sacrifice us?"

"No," Zoe said. "What are you doing here?"

"Paola," Bianca said, her face just as hawklike as it had been when she was a child, and her hair styled but still frizzy. "Where is Candy?"

"She was here," Zoe said. "She was right here!"

"Well," Bianca asked, "where is she now?"

"Oh, no," Zoe said.

"What's going on, Paola?" Zoe pulled on the handle but it wouldn't move. She tried the key but when she stuck it in, it melted.

"FUCK!" She pulled on the handle. It came off.

"Well," Julian said, "I guess we're not getting food anytime soon." The room began vibrating. The bell started ringing. The heartbeat everywhere. Zoe clamped down her ears.

"Cover your ears!" she said. "Don't listen to it!" Bianca ripped open the pillows and stuffed cotton in her ears, handing some to Julian and Zoe. Above the heartbeat was the distinctive sound of breaking, buildings falling, people dying, people running, and a room full of women giving birth.

CANDY

Of course, when Candy touched the stone, she thought of her favorite movie. She was smarter than that. And she realized who that woman was. How rude she was to her when she came to get her things fixed at her mother's shop. It was a subtle rudeness, in her stiffness and quick smile.

All the ways she said, *I am better than you*. When her mother had asked her for money to send Candy to rehab, she had the gall to make her feel bad about it. She made a little show of it, saying, "Lucia, I'm happy to help you, but I can't do this all the time," and Lucia, pleading with her, needing help for her daughter, had Bianca write up an extensive email for why Candy needed help and what she would do once she was out of rehab. A fake life plan for this woman who, for her, this amount of money meant nothing.

When Rhonda would see her later, she would ask her how she was doing, and Candy would only give her one-word answers. She didn't want to seem grateful. She wasn't. She was annoyed that she had to be taken care of at all. That she couldn't just do it herself. That after her overdose, she was being carefully *watched*. Her mother kept telling her that she needed to pay Rhonda back, go to college, get a good job with a salary to pay back the $15,000 she had loaned. But Rhonda moved away. Oh well, bitch. Too bad. Pulling up the bed sheets, she remembered how much Rhonda had assumed she was nothing but an addict who could be led any way she wanted. She thought she would just look. Dumb bitch. No way.

While the light caused her contractions, she was already in the world of Wes Anderson, moving through the carefully crafted, symmetrical sets, putting on a coat she found in a character's closet, and running. But the outside was reflecting her inside. As she moved through a street, the sky burst open, and she was back on the table, staring up at a ceiling, with unbelievable pain. Another movie.

She scrolled through her archive desperately, trying to find something to watch to keep herself from ruin. *Long Island Expressway*.

She was on the bridge staring down with Paul Dano. No, too tragic.

Step Up.

She was on a dance floor, cheering Channing Tatum on, when the dance floor broke open and creatures came out of it, crawling all over and trying to get to her. She switched again. On to the next. *28 Days Later*. That one was fun. She felt like she was in a video game, killing zombies and hiding underneath cars. But she got bored and switched to *Mad Max*.

Jaws. Toy Story 2. Die Hard. When Harry Met Sally. She went further and further into her archive, going into her childhood collection. *The Lion King. Jumanji.* But each time she switched, it became harder to move. She felt herself moving through the air as if it were a pool. But then she was no longer in the movies, she was in the screen as well.

She saw herself as a small girl, with Bianca, in their room the day their father died. Bianca had popped the DVD into the TV and told her to watch. She was holding her farting skunk and wrapped up in the movie. She was watching herself watch. And all around her, the ground was moving open. The found family was clutching onto themselves. She remembered how confused she felt here. How much worse it would have been if Bianca were not there. And then, the ultimate comfort, the screen. It captured her. Stimulated her. How could they make everything seem so real? Candy crouched and looked down at the TV. She looked so sad. Her hair so poofy. Poor thing. She touched the screen and it zapped her into *Far and Away*, which was playing on the hospital's TV screen the day she was in a coma. Tom Cruise and Nicole Kidman were running around in a field, and in between the large pieces of grass, there was a television. Candy kneeled and peered. The wind around her whirled. Peering at the television screen, she saw herself in a hospital bed. Bianca and her mother and her grandmother were gathered around her, like she was some kind of saint and not a dumb teenager who wanted to experiment with drugs to cope with the loss of her father and the feeling of being abandoned by her sister.

"Wake up, you loser," she yelled at the screen, cradling the device in her lap. "You need to wake up or your whole family is gonna get fucked from all of your bullshit!" The doctor came in, and he was saying something about how she was brain-dead, how she would never wake up from this. Her mother was sobbing, trying to shake her awake. Candy cried, too. This is what she had done to her family. She had fractured them further. She made a choice, and now she was staring at it.

"Wake up! You're gonna be better soon, I promise," Candy said, tears streaming down her face, because was she better? She hadn't let anybody really close to her in years. Garfield was a prop. A sex doll who wouldn't have sex with her. She replaced one thing with the other, the spirit of addiction floating from one thing and captured in the next. It was endless. It was never-ending. She screamed and found herself in the hospital bed, which turned into the birthing bed, and there she was, the dream that was forever there, and the people all around her with knives.

"WAKE UP!" she demanded, and all around her there were cameras, and she was behind all of them, filming herself, and she hated it, she hated the pain of it, the wretchedness of understanding who she was, who she had always been, and the things that she could not change, but the scream and the cameras made her eyes open. She was watching it happen. She had saved herself.

ZOE

The shaking had subsided. They were all holding on to each other, still alive.

"What was that?"

"It started."

"What did?"

"The ceremony."

"This is a fucking *cult*," Julian said.

"Paola, can you tell me what is going on?"

"I go by Paola now," she said, trying to stand up straight, then corrected herself, "I mean Zoe." Her sister was making her self-conscious.

"Okay," Bianca said, as if Zoe were telling her that the store they were in was closing in fifteen minutes.

"Do you remember Julian?"

"Hey, Zoe," he said, awkwardly holding out his hand. She remembered him smaller, his head in his hands at the kitchen table.

"So, um, what the fuck is going on?"

"Candy was chosen."

"By who?"

"The Mother."

"Whose mother?"

"*The Mother.*" A pause.

"Can you explain what that is to me?"

"It's an ancient stone that's the beginning of all humankind. The start of us all." Bianca raised her eyebrows.

"And you've seen this?"

"Yes, it's real."

"And it chose *Candy*? To do what?" Bianca was a woman now. The last time she saw her she was an awkward teenager who she walked in on recording her phone conversations.

"It . . ." She looked from Julian to Bianca. "It got her pregnant."

"Oh my God." Julian cupped his hand around his mouth.

"Fernando."

"Fernando is an ancient woman?"

"No, Julian, *shut up.*"

"Just trying to understand."

Zoe squinted her eyes. "Who is Fernando?"

"Her ex-boyfriend," Julian explained. "And he slept with your other sister, too. But it turns out he was actually dead the whole time."

"What happens then," Bianca said, looking her sister up and down. "After she gives birth?" Zoe put herself into child's pose.

"Zoe," Bianca said, pushing her lightly with her foot, "What happens?"

"They're going to eat her."

"The baby's a girl?"

"No, I don't know the sex. None of us do, yet. They're going to eat *Candy.*" Bianca sank to the bed again. Julian stood up.

"Okay, so just so I understand what's going on here: your ex-boyfriend, by way of an ancient magical stone got your sister pregnant with a baby? And maybe your uncle worshipped this stone?"

"My uncle wouldn't do that shit." Bianca was looking at the quilt and the sewing work on it. What uncle were they talking about?

"What if the Mother was activated by your uncle, and then he died?"

"What happens after they eat her?" her sister said, emotionless.

"Creation can't happen without destruction," Zoe said, a ball of fear shooting through her stomach. She realized she had been selfishly ready for it, and whatever it would bring: oblivion. Maria wasn't subtle about it. There was only so much willful misinterpretation she could do.

"What does that mean?" Bianca clenched the quilt.

"Oh, fuck," Julian said, "it's a rapture baby." Bianca started hyperventilating.

"We can still stop the ceremony," Zoe said, "I can get us out of here."

Bianca looked behind Zoe and it made Zoe's arm hairs stand, because it was the way dogs do when nobody is in the room.

"Has that TV always been there?" Bianca walked to the screen that was now floating in the middle of the room. She looked behind it. It had a normal backing. Something that would be very popular in the early 2000s. Then, the TV turned on. It was static at first, and then the screen squirmed and belched. Finally, it showed them something.

"What are they doing to her?" Julian said. On the screen, Candy was convulsing on a table covered in food and flowers, her eyes rolled into the back of her head, surrounded by very pregnant women who were chanting.

"How are we seeing this right now?" Bianca asked Zoe. "Do you know what this is? Don't you live here?" Zoe shook her head. Bianca approached the TV like it was a giant horse.

"Does it look funny to you?" Bianca asked Julian.

"Maybe it's sped-up HD. Like you know when you have a fancy TV and makes everything look like you're on a film set?"

"No."

"Oh, okay."

Bianca peered at it and touched it. Her hand went through, as if it were air, and not a screen.

"I think we have to go inside of it." They three of them moved the cot directly underneath the television screen. Bianca looked at the quilt. They rolled it up and tied it at the middle and the ends, to form a rope.

"Help me up," Bianca said. Julian and Zoe grabbed on to her ankles and hoisted her into the television screen, so that she was sitting on the edge of the screen.

"Okay, put me down," she said. "If we jump, we might break something."

"It's fine," Julian said, peering down. "I think we could make it."

"We have to act quick," Zoe said, "We need to destroy the bell." Zoe explained to them what that ticking bell sound was, and how it activated the Mother, because it was being fed human blood.

"What the fuck," Bianca said. "So how do we destroy it?"

"I think kind of like," Zoe said, making swinging motions with her hands.

They decided that Julian should go first (he had a history of parkour in high school), then Zoe, who was agile from all her spinning, and then Bianca, whom they would plan on catching, because she was clumsy.

First went Julian, crawling all the way down the quilt rope and then somersaulting and landing on his feet. The pregnant women were all still in deep meditation. Then came Zoe, who landed on her ass. Julian helped her up.

"Actually, I don't know." Bianca gripped the rope.

"You have to, Bianca!"

"Come on!" Zoe had her arms wide open. Zoe looked back as her other sister convulsed with her eyes rolled to the back of her head. "She needs us!"

"Why did you leave us!" Bianca yelled down. "Why did you leave me alone?"

"I wish I had a good reason!" Zoe yelled back. "But I just don't! I wish I hadn't! I wish I could've seen you grow up! I . . . !" Zoe felt the past clogging up her throat. "I can't believe I don't know you anymore! I can't believe you're a stranger!" Zoe had her hands cupped over her mouth. "But who knows, maybe when this is all over, we can all try again!"

"Do you love me?"

Zoe's hands fell to her sides. "Of course I love you, Bianca!" Her arms reached toward the screen, "I wasn't supposed to be a wife! Or even a mother! I'm your sister. That's the only thing that's ever made any fucking sense! I'm back now! I promise!"

Bianca nodded and closed her eyes. She jumped, sliding awkwardly down the rope that was tied to the cot and through the television screen that led them into this underground bunker.

"Quickly!" Zoe said, and they ran to the center of the room, to their sister, stepping over women who were starting to give birth, liquid bursting from their legs on the yoga mats. She saw Maria and the box by her feet, Carmen's body tossed aside now, too. What had she done to Carmen? Maria's plan the whole time had been to kill her, to feed her to the bell, to the Mother. Zoe saw her baby wriggling around in a basket. Did Maria even know what she was doing? Why make Carmen get pregnant at all if she was just going to kill her? There were so many gaps in Maria's plan. She could see now, clearly, that she had messed with something she wasn't supposed to. She thought her money and her will and her charisma would be able to control anything. She wasn't working *with* the Mother. She was just feeding her. Bothering her. And destroying the world in the process.

"Hey!" Julian yelled, going up the steps. What was he doing?

"Julian," Zoe whispered, "not yet!" She still needed to grab the bell and destroy it. She figured she would overturn it and kick it aside. Bianca was out of breath, catching up with him still. Zoe grabbed the white box, could feel it vibrating, its heartbeat rhythm that she now understood was Carmen's heartbeat, in her hands. She opened the box and there was a squirming, kidney-like stone, covered in blood. Zoe shook it out of the box and it landed at her feet, where she was still wearing her spin cleats. Just then, Julian grabbed a hold of Maria's hand, prying it away from the woman with the mushroom cut. Maria opened her eyes.

"Julian," she said, "it's dangerous to take up space like this."

"You're the dangerous one," he said. Candy was still convulsing. Zoe wondered, exactly, what the other stone was. Would she destroy the Mother if she stepped on it? Or all of humanity?

Bianca finally reached Julian and Candy. "Get away from her," Bianca breathed heavily.

"After all I've done for you?" Maria asked, so calm. "You don't want to let me do something for the world?" Zoe raised her foot and stomped on it. Maria turned around, in shock. Zoe was screaming, her spinning cleats crushing the stone, which seemed to be made of nerves and flesh. Maria laughed.

"It's not that easy," she said, and then she reached around to her pocket, where she took out a knife. The woman with the mushroom cut did also, and now she had Julian by the throat.

"Get off me," Julian said. "You are so creepy!" Maria kneeled down to the stone and gathered it in her hands. "Why are you smiling! Why is your face like that!" Carmen's baby was still cooing in the basket. Maria held the stone to her face and cooed to it.

"There, there," she said, as the stone wriggled back to itself. "It's all right." Zoe lunged at Maria, trying to wrestle the stone away from her, but a pregnant woman got to Zoe, moving her hands around her back. Bianca made her way to it, but then Maria got to her, putting her knife to her throat.

"The Mother needs to be fed," Maria said, "or all of this will have been for nothing. Now I must ask you to make a very hard choice, Zoe." Zoe tried to wriggle away from the pregnant woman, but she couldn't. She was somehow giving birth while putting her in a death grip. Maria was digging her knife into Bianca's neck and the woman with the mushroom cut was digging her knife into Julian's. Carmen's baby was still in the basket, sleeping peacefully, her small chest rising and falling. Zoe shook her head.

"You aren't the only one who had fertility trouble," the mushroom-cut woman said, "but that's not everybody's destiny. It's time to make a choice." Candy's eyes were rolled to the back of her head and she was twitching back and forth.

"You're nervous," Zoe said, blood rushing to her head as the pregnant woman's arms dug into her neck, "because the ceremony isn't working. She would've been giving birth by now. You lost her, didn't you?"

"You need to choose." Maria was furious but still composed. "It's either your sister you don't know anything about anymore, this man you hardly know, or a new baby who was just born. What's one small life?" Zoe looked to the baby, and then to Julian, and then to her sister, who she had spent all these years without. How did it get like this? *She can't kill her,* Zoe thought. And what if this is the man Bianca loves? And the baby—the baby didn't do anything wrong. All it did was become. *Still,* Zoe thought. *I don't even know that baby.* It had no thoughts or experience or memory. But she knew Maria was bluffing. She knew that her sister, her grumpy rude sister with issues, who loves movies so very much, managed to get away somehow.

"Now!" Maria said. "Or I'll make the choice—" And then a shot rang out through the bunker, overcoming even the loudest of the birthing screams, and Maria held on to her stomach, full of surprise and shock. She looked at her hands and her blood, dark and blooming. This is where her life ends. Julian wrestled away from the woman with the mushroom cut, but she was strong, she got back to him, slicing his wrists so he couldn't use them and stabbing him repeatedly in the neck. Bianca grabbed the gun that Maria was holding and shot the mushroom woman through the shoulder, but then started screaming immeasurably, horribly, a gut-wrenching vomit-inducing screaming, because she had somehow just shot her grandmother.

Julian clutched his neck, his own blood squirting from it. He made the noises of somebody who is very afraid and still desperately thinks it can be reversed. But Zoe was not paying attention to any of that. Not her sister's screaming or Julian bleeding out on the floor or her grandmother's body. Zoe was still looking over at where the shot rang out. She was in a daze. She was thinking that there was nothing ever so glorious as the sight of her mother with a gun.

You walk through the Target, finding the entrance to the mall. There are fake Christmas trees at the entrance. Where have all the people gone? Now you are really all alone. Behind you, the Target has fallen. You cannot say where. But it is not in this earth anymore. And all around you, are stars. You run as the ground disappears, jumping from tile to tile. And there it is, the Joy Garden. A.k.a. the Old Country Buffet.

The ceiling windows that once let in light now shroud the mall in a deep red, are starting to crack, just like the sky. You open the doors to the Joy Garden and see how much it has changed. The Buffet is still there, but the booths are gone. The place where you collected Mauricio's plate of macaroni and cheese and wet green beans. Oh, you had romance, Candelaria. Not everybody gets that.

I admit, I was a little jealous.

You walk through the Buffet, moving chairs as the lights blink and you hear growling again, but you don't know where it's coming from. You are afraid that it's for you.

Before you quit the Old Country Buffet, you hid something in the booth, right under where Mauricio's foot would have been, in his shoes that he polished every morning, the ones for winter and spring. Underneath the floor there was a latch that led into some piping, and after hours, you knelt down and hid it there, because you knew that if anything happened, you would come here. You feel around; they can't have dug up the floors already, could they? Finally, you feel the latch. You pull it with some effort and it opens, you move your hand around on the inside. There's no way people would go looking for things that they cannot see, would they? You pull it out, the stone wrapped around string and held together by a necklace. You hold it to your ear. Faintly, you can hear it cry.

Your son woke you up the night before the earthquake.

"Mamita," he said to you, "I've been involved in something bad," and you thought it was a gang.

"If anything ever happens to me, promise me you will swallow this."

"What?" You stared at the stone, thought you could see it pulsing.

"Promise."

"Why, hijo?"

"It's the only thing that can stop them, if they try to do something wrong."

"How will I know?"

"You will not recognize me anymore."

"What?"

"And you'll have to kill me, mother."

"No, hijo. What are you talking about? I could never do that."

"You will," his voice shook. El pobre. He knew that there was only so much time left.

"And you have to send Lucia away," he said, solemnly.

"Why?"

"Because they want her. And they will get her."

"What are they going to do to her?"

"They want to destroy her. So that everything can begin anew again." You waited for everything to make sense. Was he drunk? Really, it had just made so much sense to him but he had no time to explain it to you.

You unwrap the stone from its thread and sniff it.

Smells like nothing.

You pinch your nose. What if it smells like nothing but tastes like shit? You open your mouth and stick out your tongue, placing the stone on it, and you've never felt so much nothing in your life. You spit it out because all of that nothing tastes so bad. A black hole of a morsel. Worse than despair. It was the loneliness and realization that there was almost nothing beyond your mouth and this stone and this mall. You try once more and spit it out again. You have to do this, Candelaria. You have to try. You can't just give up.

But then, what is that?

One of the TV screens has turned on, above the chairs. Something looks strange about it. Because it's hanging in the air, not attached to anything else. A TV hanging in the air, in the middle of the Buffet at the end of the world. Que ridiculo. You walk around and look behind it. The same TV, showing you the same thing.

"¿Alo?" you call. "¿Alo, alo, alo?" The TV throbs in response. The stone in your hand lights up and beats along with it. You wonder if maybe everything Gabo said to you all those years ago was wrong. Perhaps he didn't know what he was talking about. Or, he had an idea. But nobody can know everything. You can try your hardest to protect yourself and the people you love, but sometimes your imagination cannot account for the actions of other people. Or events. Or things.

You tie the stone around your neck and feel its heat against you. You stop and wonder—did you make this entire day up? Did you collapse on your way out of the apartment building and has everything moving forward been a kind of hallucination? You touch the stone next to your heart. Whatever the hallucination is, you think, you need to find a way out of it. You look behind you, knowing that the TV won't be open for long and you see Mauricio sitting at the booth. The booth! It's there again. You run to him, and there's a tray of food in your hand. Macaroni and cheese with green beans. You're wearing an apron that says Old Country Buffet and a pin that reads CANDELARIA.

"My name is Candelaria," you say once again. "Thank you so much." And he says, just as you remember, "Un nombre divino." And then you serve him the tray—but wait, Candelaria, isn't this a buffet? Didn't he have the tray to begin with? You just collected plates. You didn't serve them. Still, you hand him the tray, and as he eats, something changes in him, his eyes turn yellow, he gets ravenous, when he finishes the macaroni and green beans, he eats the plate, when the plate is done, he goes for the table. Wood chips fly everywhere and then he looks at you, the way a bad dog would if they knew you were taking them out back, or a child when you're dropping them off at preschool, or a lover when you know you are never going to see them again, and he begins to eat his hands, finger by finger, and this is your goodbye.

"No!" you cry, "don't!" Though I'm not sure why the plate and the table were so okay with you, but anyway, he continues. The man is still going, despite it all, and you see all of it disappearing, the chairs, the floors, the windows, the mall itself, until it's just you and this booth and this man, and his mouth.

You had a good hunch, Candelaria. It was just a little wrong. Do I have to remind you?

You hadn't told your daughter yet or your granddaughter, and she has mostly been distracted this year. You wanted to deal with it yourselves, at your own pace, instead of being treated like children who don't know what to do with themselves. He had stage four liver cancer, and you were making him take you to the beach! On Christmas Eve! When he came in that morning, it was from the doctor, Candelaria. Not the store. He smelled like the hospital, which smells like death, not nothing. But you smelled what you wanted to smell. You saw what you wanted to see.

And then, the news. The stillness in the air. Yes, that was the sign that you were looking for. It was more in your bones than in Mauricio's. The memories were all colliding with each other in that moment, to tell you something that wasn't truly there, but to still keep you safe. Because, Candelaria, realistically.

He would have never made it.

You did not want to see him suffer.

You did not want to be that old woman, who crouches over her boyfriend, not even a husband, who has not taken care of himself as much as you have, has not had enough water to drink or good sleeping patterns, or was just susceptible to some cruel thing like mold or circumstance that you had no control over, and had cancer slowly eating away at his body for who knows how long, multiplying until it would eventually kill him. You did not want to see him struggle to walk with you as the undead came running, or him to tell you that he couldn't go on anymore.

So when you stabbed him, it was, in a way, a mercy, but also a way to keep the slow fade of love at bay, the soft edges that can fray the ventricles of your heart that are somehow much worse than the immediate bluntness of a terrible accident. It was more for you, than anyone. You are a monster, just like Lucia said. But shouldn't she have learned by now? This is what women must become.

Mauricio is chewing at his clothes, ripping them to shreds.

"Adios, amor mio," you say, looking up to the ceiling, that is coming in, the tiles twirling into Mauricio's mouth. You feel that Mauricio, or not Mauricio, this manifestation of your heartache and your lost love, will come for you soon. "Mi companía," you say. Someone to cook for, to wake up next to in a fellow twin bed. To talk about nothing.

Whatever is behind this TV, it will take you away from here. You stretch out your hand, managing to put a pinky through it, and it feels like whatever you put in your mouth, whatever was on this stone, just nothing. But behind you is slowly turning into nothing. So, what if you just embraced it?

You have to climb up into the nothing, as Mauricio devours himself. Another mouth waits for you. There is a ledge you have to step into that is made up of the world you are in, a block of reality that you must jump over. So you push a chair next to it, and climb on in. You take out your gallon of water and step on it. It's not enough. You grab your Virgen candle and place it on top of the gallon of water, and yes, you knew she was the one who was going to push you through. La Virgen. Impossible that your weight didn't crush the candle, but miracles happen, don't they? You jump and dive in, gasping as your knee hits something hard in all of the nothingness, and you shut your eyes as Mauricio, or the vision of him, or just something you needed to see, goes on to his legs, and then you shut the door behind you and hurtled into the nothingness.

A heartbeat all around you. Whose? Not fast or slow. Just regular, healthy. Your eyes adjust to all of that nothing and you start to see your hands. Maybe in this existential plane of existence, between these doors of life and not life, it is possible to see things. What was it you and Mauricio talked about? The neighbors. Candy. Your long life. Stuff that didn't matter. What if all that stuff that didn't matter is in here right now? Everything that slips the mind like a fork falling from a plate of cake? Just nothing. Boring. Who cares. Whatever was said as he sipped on a Corona Light. The cap of the beer. What is that? Your feet. Yes, Candelaria, keep thinking about it. Tell me more.

Plátanos that aren't ripe enough yet. Socks that need to be ironed. Red Sox winning. Red Sox losing. Your daughter calling. Unplugging your phone. Your dead phone. Look, your arms! More, more. The apartment you and Mauricio made together. The altar you made for la Virgen. The plastic flowers from the dollar store. A scarf you tell your granddaughter to wear so she won't get a cold. The fact that she never wore it. And then, what is that? Your torso? You hug yourself. You are still here, fading into reality.

Now, you are in a fourth space: not work, not home, not a café, but something different: a casino. Lucia is there, playing a game with frogs. They shoot up each time she hits a knob, and knock back down when they hit the top, fluttering down and spilling coins out of their mouth. Your daughter is very concentrated.

"¿Hija?" you say. "Where are we?" She doesn't look at you.

"No se," she says, "Probably dead. In hell. With you." You look around. There are no attendants. Nobody serving drinks. No beautiful women draped over handsome men smoking cigars. You used to come to the casino all the time with Mauricio, relishing in the game of money.

"¿Y la niña?" Lucia shakes her head. After all that, she's dead?

"Should I play?" Your daughter shrugs.

"If you want." You sit down next to her and look at her very concentrated face. She looks more like her father, ese hijo de puta, the way she narrows her brow in conversation, that slope of the nose. Her profile is so pretty. It has survived years and years, stayed up and tight, a painting hung on the wall.

"How did you get here?"

"The TV."

"Me too!" You put your hand in the pocket of your skirt and find a token. You pop one into the machine's slot, and it lights up like a parade.

"How long have you been playing for?"

"I don't know." She still hasn't looked at you. You stop and wonder about what will happen if you also play. All day there has been calm before the storm. You want to be prepared. Have you died? There is an exit sign above another television, hanging in the middle of the room. Will that lead you back out? Something is wrong. You can't be here.

"We must leave."

"No."

"We have to go now."

"It's bad out there. Safer in here." You look at your daughter's hand. It is starting to melt onto the knob she's been pulling. You snatch it off. She grimaces.

"Why did you do that? I was playing a *game*." She sounds like a child.

"You have to come with me," you tell her, yanking on her arm. She yanks it back. "You were a bad mother," she tells you. "You didn't take care of me. You tried to sell me. I was only fifteen. I was a virgin. How much money was he even going to give you for me? How much was I worth?" She is not crying. Your daughter is stronger than that. The bouncing frogs start making a thunking sound, making the screen they are behind crack. They are becoming rounder, more pronounced.

"That's in the past," you say. "We have to move on, now." All around you, things fall.

"I don't forgive you," your daughter says, looking you straight in the eye. "I can't. And I won't. You are not a good person." The nothing starts eating up the walls of the casino. Soon it will envelop your daughter and then you.

"We have to run," is what you tell her. Not that you love her, or that you are sorry. Not about what was taken from you. Not about how you were shaped by men on horses or men at desks in their empires, by power whirling from one raised hand to the next, and always out of your grasp. "We have to run."

You take all the strength that's left inside of you and yank her, as the frogs leap out of the game, littering the room, and together you run, her with one hand around your waist, running and running, and holding her you are holding you, arms outstretched to the exit sign, which could be a door to the treacherous outside and you push together, releasing yourselves into this new room.

I feel you, Candelaria. You are so, so close.

The room is not a room, but once again, the outside. Or is it? There are others here. Pregnant women, all moaning. The sound is so awful. Perched above on a bed, there is a young woman vibrating, her eyes rolled to the back of her head. Another woman holds on someone who looks like Bianca by the neck. And is that the boy who used to be around? ¿Este indito? Held on by knifepoint by some woman with a strange haircut?

Your daughter takes out the gun she stole from the soldier and she doesn't even think, she shoots and the woman collapses, and Bianca breaks free, but at the same time the woman with the strange haircut turns the young man around and they begin a struggle, a back and forth, he pins her down, he is pretty muscular, but then she bites his face and he screams and Bianca has grabbed the gun that the woman was holding and is, admittedly, somewhat uselessly holding it as the woman pins him down and the two of them are struggling for power, the knife squeezed in between their hands. She wins power, just from a small slip of the grip, she slices his wrists, she stabs him repeatedly in the neck, wildly, messily, trying to open him up.

"Candy!" Lucia screams, for the young woman on the table is your granddaughter. You yank on her wrist, tell her to wait, you are screaming it so hard, how much you need her to stop, to listen to you, just this once. Because now, you finally know where it needs to go. You rip off the necklace and hold it to her. She scrunches up her nose.

"¿Qué carajo es eso, Mamá?"

"This will save her. Save *us*." The screaming just won't stop. It's accompanied by new sounds, baby sounds. The sounds of life entering the world, or whatever is left of it.

"Put it in her mouth," you say. She takes it from you just as the woman with the mushroom cut drags that boy's body to a white box. She is scooping blood from his wounds into it, as he groans, when Bianca grabs the gun from the other woman, and shoots her chest, and she hits the ground, and you are so caught up in the drama of it, the spectacle, that you don't realize the bullet has gone through her and lodged in your arm. Right in the artery. You grab yourself and fall to the ground, like a glass of wine, like the last of the cherry blossoms.

"Abuelita?" Bianca runs to you, taking your scarf and tying it above where the bullet is, trying to make a tourniquet, but it's too late.

"Por favor," she says, her face red, tears in her eyes. "Por favor, perdóname, no sabia que estabas alli, por favor, no te mueras, por favor, no te vi, no te vi." She is wailing, the middle one, who grew up to dig up dinosaurs, who has read so much, has developed such a deep, inner world fueled by existential listlessness, questions upon questions that are never answered.

"Bianca," you tell her, touching her face with your gnarled, spotted hands. You point to the stone Lucia holding: "En la boca."

"¿Que?" You are fading away, all your blood leaving you, a beautiful crimson river.

"No entiendo." She shakes her head, and your mouth tries to swallow air.

"En la puta boca," you say, and then everything goes dark, and then, there is really nothing.

BIANCA

The bell chimes and her mother falls to the floor. Bianca looks at Julian and her grandmother bleeding and begins to shriek. She makes more noise than she ever has in her life. She is every mythological screaming woman, every banshee, llorona, every scorned ghost funneled into one body.

Julian's breath comes out in short, bloody bursts. Candy continues to convulse, foam forming at her mouth. Bianca turns her on her side.

"KEEP HER LIKE THIS!" she instructs Paola, who complies. Bianca kneels to where Julian is.

She puts pressure on the wounds—there are so many. The blood beats out beneath her palms. Julian tries to talk, but his mouth is full of blood. He holds on to her hand. He is looking off behind her and mouthing something, but what is it? She puts her ear to him. She cannot hear. Her sister's face is almost gray, with veins stretching against her like roots. She has to think fast.

"I'll be right back," Bianca says, to Julian, who is not responding to her, "just hold on for a little longer." She grabs the stone on the floor and instructs Paola to turn Candy on her back again.

She can almost hear it breathe, the little stone. Looking to her grandmother's body on the floor, she wondered exactly why she told her to do this. If she should've, this past year, just come home, asked her abuela more about her life, instead of diving into the past the way she did. All the people dead because of it. The friendships lost. Just from trying to figure out who she was.

Her sister looks eviscerated and shiny, chupada, her stomach moving as if a hoard of bugs were beneath about to burst out and bite.

"We have to open her mouth," Bianca says to Paola, who is in shock at the bodies on the floor.

"Paola," she says, the hot stone throbbing in her hand, "Come on, I need help!" Paola pries open Candy's mouth and screams.

"She *bit* me!" Blood leaks from Paola's fingers. Paola tries again as Bianca holds on to Candy's jaw. Paola sticks her fingers into her mouth to keep them open, and it's so frightening, seeing her sister like this, an animal being studied for science. Bianca drops the stone in, like a roll of dice, a pinch of salt, and then Candy's mouth clamps close. Bianca kneels again by Julian.

"Julian?" she says, holding him like a stack of books on the first day of school, "Julian?" She kisses him on the cheeks, blood getting on her own, she puts her nose into his neck, she breathes in the last of his scents.

"Do you hear that?" Paola asks her sister. They are coming through the tunnels, now. Snarling. Growling. Paola and her sister hold on to each other, waiting for whatever they were told to do and without explanation, without reason, to work.

CANDY

Once again, Candy found herself in an empty theater. She put her feet up and sighed. All of this movie-hopping was tiring. But maybe she could do it forever. Jump from one thing and then to the next until the world ended or she did. The curtains opened.

"Sick," Candy said, clapping her hands, "here we go."

And on the screen, of course, was Candy, stretched out on a table, food all around her. But there weren't any Garfields or members of NSYNC or cults surrounding her with forks. She was all alone and she was awake.

"Yup," Candy said, "makes sense." She looked down at her hand and saw that she was holding a knife. She sighed again.

"What do you think this means?" asked the Candy on the screen.

"I don't know," said the Candy in the audience. "I don't care anymore."

"I think our family is here."

"All of them?" Candy said.

"Yeah. I can feel them." Candy shook her shoe against her thigh. "Don't you want to leave?" Candy on the screen propped herself up with her hands.

"Nah. It's bad out there."

"Hmm."

"What?"

"Nothing, I just feel like . . ."

"Say it. You can say it."

"I think maybe if you don't leave . . . you'll die."

Candy groaned. "I don't want to have a kid, okay? I'm not made for taking care of something. Bianca was never going to have a kid. Zoe can't have children. I was totally fine being the last one! This is who I am! All of those generations of suffering amounted to me in the end! Sorry!"

The Candy on the screen bit into an apple, indifferent.

"I'm not perfect!" Candy in the audience said, "I am an addict. I'm traumatized. I've hurt people."

"Ate your boyfriend."

"That was one time!"

"And what about Jenny?"

"I couldn't control it. Whatever it is inside made me do it and I don't want to deal with it. My family can. Whatever. Fuck them."

"Do you hear yourself?

"Obviously."

"What if it's not a kid?" Something was changing in the theater. Either Candy was getting bigger or the Candy on the screen was getting smaller. She felt closer to her.

"Then it's some alien parasite thing that's gonna make me explode."

"So, you'd rather die? And leave that with your family?"

"Why is this whole thing some anti-abortion commercial?"

"It's not." Candy on the screen spit out her apple core, and it landed on Candy in the audience's cheek. "This wasn't your fault."

"But it is. *I* fucked Fernando. *I* chose to do that."

"At least you're taking accountability."

"Shut up."

"Anyway, like I said. This isn't your fault. They got you. And you were vulnerable. And they knew that." Candy on the screen was now Candy on a stage. Looking behind her, Candy saw that there was a packed house.

"They're all watching us."

"Uh-huh."

"What do they expect me to do?" Candy lied down and scratched at her eyes. She was tired, too.

"I think they want you to leave." Candy touched her stomach. She felt like she was going to throw up.

"They fed you the stone."

"What, the *Woman's* stone herself?"

"I guess so."

"Goddamnit. Do you think they're the ones who stole my bike? And then went to Zoe's stupid spin studio? And then ended up calling Bianca? Which made me fuck Fernando's body snatcher ass? Oh, God. It's all *connected*."

"Probably. Or you forgot to lock it up." The stone wriggled around in Candy's stomach.

"I feel bad," Candy said, crouching down, clutching her stomach. The audience sighed with her. All the lights were off. "For eating people."

"It's what you wanted. It was a symptom."

"But it was wrong."

"They made you want something you didn't."

"Still. I can never take it back."

"It's not your fault. It's not your fault."

"Whatever, Robin Williams."

"You love that movie."

"I really do." The Candy on the table ate another apple.

"I guess I can't make you feel better about any of it." Candy looked at her reflection in her knife.

"Should I just go through my life feeling guilty?"

"Nah, nobody wants to be around that." Candy spit out the apple core again. Candy was getting queasier and queasier.

"What's supposed to happen now?" A director, who was also Candy, ran onto the stage and showed Candy the script. Candy peered at the audience. They were all Candys, all watching her.

"Why?" Candy said, handing it back.

"You gotta consume or be consumed, babe." Candy lay back down and the other Candy, our Candy, started retching the stone, which bounced on the stage, covered in her bile.

"It's just a rock?"

"Yeah."

"So, if I do this, everything will be okay?"

"Of course not." Candy looked at her knife. "It's just the first step."

"Will it hurt you?"

"I'm you, bitch."

"I know, but. We just started getting to know each other." Candy on the table rolled her eyes.

"Don't be dumb."

"So, it's the first step and then what?"

"And then don't worry about what comes next. You just have to do this first."

"You sure? What if I get out of here and I end up being a middle-aged piece of shit who everybody hates?"

"You're already a piece of shit. And life is really long, actually. Until it's not."

"How would you know?"

"I guess I don't. But I think you will. You should. Come on."

"Don't you mean *we* will?" Candy on the table shook her head.

"No. I mean you."

"But you're me."

"Yes and no. Come on." Candy on the table's lips were trembling.

"I don't want to."

"You have no choice."

"Come on!"

"I don't know."

"NOW!" Candy on the table shrieked, and then Candy dug the knife in, and began to eat herself, and as she ate, she saw her entire life: milk bottles in the microwave, the taste of the saltine crackers and jelly sandwiches her dad used to make her, walking with her abuela to the park as she told her something about never trusting men in vans, receipts in her mother's shop, spools and spools of yarn, the sound of her mother yelling that often blended in with the music Candy had been blasting, her sister Bianca, and the way her laugh sounded like a beautiful bell ringing in a very solemn church, her sister Zoe, who ran away for her love, it turns out, just for love, and how pathetic Candy thought it was just because it was vulnerable, and how actually, that was the hardest thing, to be soft enough to cut into, and how lucky it was that her sister got to feel that way, open to the world, and how if she, Candy, wasn't the last of her family, then maybe there would be someone else, who could do it, all of it, all of this around us, a little bit better.

We came because we were hungry. Starving young. Dying elders. The future was where I'm from. El más allá. In a way. But I landed in your past. In the places that you look back and call to, feel in your dreams.

Landing, I became part of this earth. Broke into three pieces and lived.

I know all the history. I can feel it in the rocks that move every millennia or so. Fish you can't even imagine because they're so deep down.

Your people almost understood it all. About what's beyond this. About why you're here. You were close.

We were, too.

I am made up of the same things as you are: the moon, the stars. Just a bunch of hot gas set to a personality. But accelerated and turned backward.

Some thought I was some kind of god. When they interacted with me, I gave them powers. They just found themselves *better* at things. Sometimes it was hunting. Sometimes it was art. A lore formed around me. Documents were written. The authors of those documents discovered that a ritual, summoning me, they would—and forgive me for being so rude—create a piece of me, in a specific way. The way your men carry billions of pieces of themselves inside. Do not make me spell it out. They believed if I, in a shadow of them, a copy, impregnated one of their women, a new world would come forth.

And the impregnated women would be endowed with my kind's strengths. They would be telepathic. Become hungry in a new way. Our way. The price of a new life. We all kill to live, don't we? They realized I needed to be fed. They gave me blood from animals. Sometimes from their own people. The Tierra Nueva believed that a muse was necessary. They believed they needed to find her, make her pregnant, and end the world to begin a new one. When somebody finds a secret, they do what they want with it. A secret can change, based on who it's told to.

People died trying to figure it out. Because it was just an interpretation of what was happening. When you make a wish on an object you don't know how the object will morph. I feel them wherever they are. I felt you. That man at the Bariletes festival? Victor. He was so bad at it! I started giving all of them little gifts, here and there. He became better and better. He was about to be so good. And when they sent him to you, well, I was changed forever. Time stopped for me. My seed was hit by a bus before the deed could be committed. Also, you never showed up.

I left so fast, went back to the caves and didn't wake up until your son and his friends arrived. I kept one face on my mind to keep me sharp. Your face, Candelaria. While I haven't had a body, I have been able to find you. In the screens. The ones you watch and the ones you don't even see. What was it about you, Candelaria? All my thoughts have been with you. Just a brush of your hand on his and I could feel every part of your life. I can't say why it was you, specifically. Sometimes things just click. Sometimes people just stay.

You are rising up above them all. What do I look like to you? I tried to make myself look like a man.

The boys continued the tradition. One heard from the other. A kind of gossip. I saw them. I felt them. I called them to me. Can you blame me? I needed to eat. And they came. One by one.

And the woman. Maria? She doesn't know how it goes, exactly. I felt her searching for me, but she did not know what I was. Fernando stumbled upon me with a flashlight and a backpack. He had purpose. Financial troubles.

And Maria—she was there—took part of me attached to a bell. She had a plan for me. A different kind of interpretation.

Shall I talk about how touching me broke his body? How I smelled you from him? Fernando was older. I felt it: all of his thoughts and his fears. Colon cancer would've come for him eventually: a slight, unaddressed pain in the abdomen. A woman in his mind: your granddaughter, Bianca. I found myself there, me but not me. A part of me. A seed. It can make you travel very fast, desire. But then fate put my seed in a different path. It saw her. Oh, she looked just like you. I wondered for a moment if no time had passed at all. They wanted to destroy her. I'm sorry. It was me but not me. Creation needs destruction.

That is clear. They all understood. When their leaders call out to me, that's what I tell them. That is what I know because it's what I learned on the way here.

Or maybe I only told them what they wanted to hear. That is, after all, how you get people to fall in love with you. Or to feed you.

They danced around me. They hummed. I gave them part of myself. It was loose change to me.

How do you feel?

You had a son. Gabo. He was valiant. I admired him. He interrupted the ritual, touching me and causing what you felt was the earthquake to happen, making me erupt and turn his body into a seed. He still killed thousands of people. All to save your daughter.

Yes, that was me, all those years ago.

Not really. A seed of me.

You see, I cannot help myself.

I have a duty. It is in my biology.

I cannot make you understand.

I was always the key they turned.

The earth is dying, that is true. I have felt it for so long. Since I arrived, it has been a place of death.

But that is true everywhere.

Listen.

I don't even want to be here.

They will be fine.

Someone will always begin again.

Something will always be breathing.

A mouth will always need to be fed.

So selfish—to think that I am just one thing. That I belong to no one.

But what if my purpose is to belong to you?

I can see you.

Young and perfect, shiny and new. I can see you, Candelaria. The people you trusted. The lottery tickets you scratched. I can see you, Candelaria. The day your daughter called you. The loneliness you felt, the uselessness, too. Like a fruit peel. A pregnant dog on the side of the street. Invisible. Old. I can see you, Candelaria. Your skin tightened. Your cataracts melted. Your spine stretching. The veins burning away from your smooth legs. I can see you, Candelaria. Matured and baked, legs bowed and knees swelling. The hair on your head dyed crimson. I see you. I know you better than anybody.

Won't you come with me, Candelaria?

Forgive me.

I could be a better man. I could be a man.

Yes, yes you are listening.

I know you are listening.

You understood, you knew to give that part of me to your granddaughter.

It won't make everything right, but it will save them.

And we can see beneath the earth together, drop out the bottom, and fly.

We can go into the sky and find something else. Something no one has ever known.

Something better than this, that you can compare to everything else.

You can get bored with it.

You could leave, eventually and become endless.

What do you say?

Come and find out.

Maybe you will see.

Maybe it could be all you've ever wanted.

JULIAN

The first time Julian was on TV was during a record snow day in Boston. His mothers had taken him sledding at the Casey OP Park on the border of Watertown and Newton. The newscaster from channel 7 was interviewing his mother Patty about how she felt about the snow fall while his other mother, Katherine, was going down the hill with him. He was bundled up in blue, his brown cheeks flushed, laughing with his mom's arms around him. His mother Patty had said to the newscaster, "We're just trying to make the most of it!" Katherine squealed behind her and Julian did, too, his tiny arms up, the flakes flying everywhere.

Julian found himself in that field of snow now. He was the cameraman, holding up the camera and having snow cling to his beard like a packing peanut. The newscaster wore a tweed coat and his mother a green L.L.Bean jacket that was still hanging in their mudroom at home. He always thought his mother could have said, *My partner and son are trying to make the most of it*. That she could've acknowledged that they were a family. For all their liberalism, Julian thought, they still were cowards. It was the early 2000s. It wasn't legal for them to be married yet and they were worried about Julian being taken away. They were a *we*. His mothers had recorded the clip when it came on at 6:00 P.M. and then labeled it perfectly SNOW DAY W/ JULIAN, THE NEWS, and they placed it in a shoebox for memories somewhere in their spacious living room. Julian would be able to look at it whenever. His mothers probably wished he would ask. They were always proud of him even when he was reading Lenin and walking around with a Che Guevara military hat.

Holding the camera, he realized that Patty had actually said more. That actually, she had spoken too much. She was proud and excited. Nervous, but not afraid. She said, "My partner and I just moved here from California, so this snow is definitely new for us. We're both lawyers and we've had Julian for a year now." His mother started tearing up then.

Julian had always thought her eyes were watering from the cold. "Sorry, it just. Took so much to get him. And we can't believe he's here. Anyway, it's beautiful out today. We're just trying to make the most of it!" They had cut out what she said either for time or for content.

His mother turned around and joined him and Katherine. Julian felt a sharp pain in his neck. He set the camera down in the snow. The newscaster did not turn around. He touched his face. The beard was gone. He was himself again. Despite the cold he felt very, very warm. The newscaster spoke to him, but her voice seemed to be coming from the sky. She was still turned around.

"What are you doing here?" the voice said.

"I've been hanging out with your sister."

"That bitch."

"Can you tell me where I am?"

"Pretty obvious. It's the day you went sledding with your gay moms." *Gay moms* echoed throughout the field, shaking the trees and the football posts.

"Right, but why?" The newscaster sighed and the sigh became part of the wind. Snow flecked her raven hair. She still hadn't turned around. Julian picked up the camera and turned toward the newscaster. Her hand was frozen around a microphone. Her lips were icy. The snow was static around her. He knew it was her talking to him, even if she wasn't opening her mouth.

"So Bianca pulled you into this?"

"Not really. She didn't want anything to do with me. I kind of insisted."

"Oh, so you deserve this, then." Julian didn't answer.

"I'm sorry. I'm just kidding. But something bad must have happened if you're in here with me." Julian recalled the woman with the mushroom cut and her freakish smile, how she had stabbed him messily, hitting his jugular vein and then pouncing on him to stab his stomach. It was quick and sloppy, but she had been successful.

Behind him, his mothers and himself were sliding down the hill over and over again, in an endless loop. He began to see the lines around the scene, as if the film were wearing from use.

"Are you okay, Candy?"

"No, ha-ha." *Ha-ha* was in the wind now, too. Candy was laughing everywhere.

"Stupid question, my bad."

"I really fucked you up, didn't I?"

Julian felt the instinct to hold up the camera, to record her. So he did. It began to whir. Looking through the viewfinder, he saw that she was still frozen, but her hair had started to whip around.

"If you did," Julian said, "it's my fault."

"What? So masochistic, Julian. Why do you want to feel bad forever?" He saw her pinky twitch around the microphone.

"Guilt isn't always useless," Julian said, the camera growing heavier on his shoulder. He had to hold it up with the other hand now. "It can motivate."

"What if I told you I forgive you? And that I don't want you to feel bad anymore?"

"I guess that would make me feel better." The newscaster's lips moved. The static frost around her melted. She shook her hair and laughed. She was Candy from the hallways of high school, as he had loved her, wild and electric, uncompromising and mean.

"I was so in love with you," Julian confessed. In love enough to let her convince him to hurt her. He was now using his knees to balance the camera. He was afraid to let go of it, to move his gaze elsewhere. *Candy? Candy?* he had said, when he found her on the carpeted floor of some rich parents' bedroom where they probably only had sex every fourth Wednesday. He was just a kid. He had just lost his virginity to Bianca the night before, and yes, was secretly hoping to have sex with Candy that night, thinking that it was good for him to now have experience. The party was still murmuring downstairs, young people being young, other formative traumas probably taking place. Julian remembered feeling like he was inside of a stomach, rocking back and forth with chewed up bits of food and enzymes as the world raged on beyond the walls of this bedroom. "Your sister overdosed," Julian said into the phone, looking at Candy's crumpled form, "I don't know how," though he did, and Bianca did too. "I don't know what to do." When the EMTs arrived, he said he was her boyfriend and that he had no idea what was going on, a thing he had hoped for, a thing that absolved him from guilt. At the hospital, after she miraculously woke up, Lucia called him a hero. "You saved her," Lucia said, embracing him with force he wasn't expecting. "What would we have done if you weren't there?" Julian looked to Bianca, who led him into the hallway, and told him to never speak to her family again. *You're dangerous*, she said.

This had echoed throughout Julian's head as he ran away into the valleys of his late teenagehood and early twenties, dropping out of school and getting his GED, then moving to New York City. *You're dangerous*. Julian was so very aware of the way he could cause harm that he had spent most of his time in New York trying to undo all forms of it: advocating for free injection sites, delivering groceries to neighbors during the pandemic, building free libraries next to public housing, collecting compost scraps from all his friends for community gardens. He wasn't sure if he was trying to do good, but he was trying to reduce harm, though his exes wouldn't say that. How many lovers had he not been able to fully commit to or communicate with, because he felt he needed to be as busy as possible doing good? Because he felt like he deserved to be alone?

As severe and moral as he was, Julian still believed in signs. When he first moved to New York, a little cliché on the Bolt Bus with a guitar and suitcase, he sat next to a mother and her child, a small boy playing with a blow-up guitar and saying, *I'll be a star! I'll be a star!* Julian felt that young boy was him, or that the mythical universe was showing him that he was very new and had all the time in the world. Did he ever get to be a star? His band had been reviewed on Pitchfork but he paid it no attention. And now he was going to die.

"Shut up." Candy began dusting off her coat.

"Sorry."

"No, no. Don't be." She threw the microphone to the ground, where it got lost in snow.

"Your family is waiting for you."

"I know." Candy rolled her eyes. "How do we get out of here?" But Julian knew, now, why the camera felt so heavy. Why it was taking up so much space.

"You have to go through," Julian said. The camera was sticking to his legs, and he felt the wires meld to his bones, and the places he was stabbed growing wider and wider.

"You're not coming with me?" He didn't answer. The snow was so loud. Like a million people whispering.

"There's not enough time."

"That fucking bitch." Candy rolled up her fists at the sky.

"What? Who?"

"Never mind." Candy walked closer to him but then fell into the snow.

"Why won't this stop being hard!" He thought he heard her crying. "I didn't mean to get you into this." She was sobbing. "I didn't mean for this to happen." Julian was crying, too. Because he always thought his life would end at the front lines of something, for some reason, for some true purpose. He also felt, that despite all of his criticisms of travel and colonialism, he really wanted to see the world. And he was going to miss it.

"Can you find my moms," he asked.

"I don't want to," Candy said. "I don't want to do this to you. And no offense, but they might be dead." Julian felt his body stretch out, his hands holding on to the edges of the screen. It didn't hurt, to become this.

"You look fucked up, man." Candy said. "I really wish you could see yourself. It's *messed up.*" Julian shook with laughter and wires began taking over his lungs. Candy edged closer to him, touching his stomach, where the screen began.

"I hope everything turns out well for you," Julian said, and Candy touched the wet screen, holding on to the droplet of Julian's tears in her hands. She put it to her own cheek, and then, for some reason, sucked it off her finger.

"I don't think it has to be this way," Candy said, desperately, "I mean, we can figure something out! We can wait. We could both just chill here?" She touched her face to the screen, and Julian felt her warmth, her scent, and together, they buzzed. It was almost a kiss. Julian wanted to say more. He always did. He wished he remembered more. He wished he had recorded more, like Bianca, who had cataloged her entire life. Candy moved away.

"I don't think it does, but I think I want it to be."

"You want to *kill* yourself."

"No, I'm just making a choice."

"I don't want to."

"But you need to."

"You're an idiot," she said. The snow was growing higher and higher. Julian couldn't talk anymore. He simply buzzed back, the knobs on him moving to show different channels. He showed her a live concert of Daniel Johnston. He showed her cartoons chasing each other through mountains. Towers falling. Riots. Marches. Kyle MacLachlan sipping coffee. Oranges being zested. Nirvana's *Unplugged*. Everything he felt, that he couldn't say, that he didn't know he needed to.

This wasn't torture. He knew it wouldn't be like this forever. He finally showed her what he needed to show her.

"They really are all there," Candy said. Julian buzzed. Candy hugged the edges of Julian, embracing him one last time. She stuck her head through him, and Julian grew for her so that she wouldn't have to squeeze through. He made himself wide. And once she was through, to the other side and whatever was left of it, Julian looked around at the scenery, at the loop of him and his mothers, and the way snow made everything so bright.

He had tried very hard, his entire life, to be someone who was going to change things for the better. Despite everything he had accomplished, and all that he had raged against, and everyone he had helped, he realized, as him and his mothers became frozen in the loop, suspended in the air, this was who he always was.

That's okay. That's all right. He had treated life the way it should always be: long and short at the same time. He had tried so hard because he always felt guilty, but he also always felt hopeful. Naively hopeful. Foolishly so. But you had to be, he concluded, falling down into the snow, the wires in his legs smoking. You had to be.

He thought of something silly and seemingly inconsequential. It wasn't very profound. It had nothing to do with helping anybody or making any sort of difference. It was a small, disgusting moment, when he was just a body reacting to what was inside of it. And he laughed and he laughed. And then he shut off.

THE GRANDDAUGHTERS

Bianca is still holding Julian, whose eyes are as blank as a newly painted apartment. She puts her ear to his chest, as he had once done to her back, and prays to hear something. There is nothing. Just flesh, just blood, just bone. She cradles him, she rocks him back and forth. She says something into his ears that is something like a goodbye.

Creatures begin piling into the bunker. Where they came from, the granddaughters don't know. They are indescribable. Their eyes bulge, it is difficult to tell where their mouths start; where their tails begin. They sniff at the bodies. And then the Mother stone—perhaps Maria had just named it that—starts to crawl out from under the table. It was, like the smaller stone, a ball of nerves and flesh, squelching as hands pried out of it to move it forward.

Zoe gags at the sight of it. The stone crawls to the creatures which, it seems, had all been waiting for it. A creature leaps onto the stone, then another. They pile on top of each other, binding to one another, becoming inseparable. Their limbs become wheels and the wheels each hold a pair of eyes, and they, it, whatever it was, hold their grandmother up. And what was that? Is she opening her eyes?

The new mothers gather their babies and huddle, holding them tight. But the creatures don't care about the babies. They never did. They are spinning their grandmother around and around. Bianca brushes the hair from Julian's face. She gives him a kiss on the forehead. She is thinking about how much of her life has been marked by death, and how, if the world goes on, how much more of it there will be.

Then, a coughing sound.

It's Candy, coughing up the stone, which is, unlike the Mother and unlike the bell, just a stone. It falls off the table and rolls to the floor. Candy has a baby in her arms, a normal one.

"Hey," Candy says to Zoe, "can you hold this? I have to tie my shoe." Zoe takes the baby into her arms and has never felt something like this before: unnamable joy; pure, unselfish desire.

"Normal," Zoe said, holding on to the baby's toes. Candy groans.

"I don't really have to tie my shoe."

Zoe doesn't hear her. The baby is so new. Carmen's baby coos from her basket again.

"There are so many fucking babies," Candy says. "Everywhere. What are we supposed to do with all of them?"

Bianca grabs her sister and embraces her. Her hair sticks to her forehead, and for a moment, you cannot tell one strand from the other.

"You're back," she says.

"Whatever," Candy says, closing her eyes and holding on to her arm. "Don't leave, okay? At least not for a while. Your wizard roommate can move to Boston. Are they all right, by the way?"

"I hope so," Bianca says. She realizes she doesn't know what happened to the rest of the country. Or the world. That she would have to be okay with starting small. The bell has stopped ringing.

"What happened to Julian?" Candy asks, staring at his body on the ground.

Bianca helps her sit up. "You fucked my boyfriend is what happened."

"Bitch, that was not a boyfriend."

"I know, he was some alien thing."

"No, he was never your boyfriend. He was married, bitch." Candy looks at her sister and her sister looks at her. One begins to crack up, and the other follows.

"What's so funny?" Zoe says, bouncing the baby up and down. They can't answer, they're laughing too hard.

Lucia, their mother, wakes and leaps up to where all her daughters are, at last, in the same place. She holds them all tightly, her arms around every neck, each of their heads touching, the new baby in the middle of them all.

They break apart.

Candy looks at the thing with the giant wheels and eyes that's still spinning their grandmother.

"What the fuck is that?" Candy asks. Zoe is still holding the baby. Its eyes aren't open but it cries. She looks at her mother, who is staring at her like she's a ghost.

"Hi, Mom." And while there was just that dramatic embrace, they do not touch again. They do not say to each other everything they've always meant to say. Not yet, at least. But now, maybe, there is time.

"That kid is probably a cannibal-psychopath-murderer," Candy says, head still dizzy.

"We don't know that," Zoe says, defensively, because she's already thinking of names for the child in her head. "We have no idea yet."

"You gonna raise it?" Lucia asks her daughter, the first thing she says to her full of reservation and judgment. One eyebrow flicks up in disapproval.

"I don't know," Zoe says, holding on to the baby's head full of black hair, "we'll see." The thing, the giant wheels with eyes, spins their grandmother, who is awake, and alive, higher and higher, but she doesn't seem to realize she's on top of it. Lucia looks up.

"¡MAMÁ!" she yells, her hands cupped over her mouth. "¡Bájate de alli!"

"Is she saying something to us?" Bianca squints, trying her best to make out what her grandmother could possibly be communicating.

"I can't tell," Candy says, taking in the wreck that is the world. "Looks like she's laughing."

"Ya regreso, niñas," I tell my girls, a lie, because the light is about to swallow me and I am going to let it, and life has been a series of I'll-be-right-backs and we-will-meet-agains anyway, each quick embrace stringing together into one final goodbye, and this, this is the last square in the quilt, and I am throwing it over you all so that you can feel a little warmer, and not so alone. "¡Ya regreso!" My skin is hot and cold at the same time, oh, is it falling off me? I'm starving!

Am I all around now?

Am I in the air?

Be good to your mother.

Feed birds when you can.

Dinner is better with company.

Please know that I have tried my best to love you.

More sugar.

Very beautiful.

Thank you so much.

"¡Espérame!"

Wait for me.

A NOTE ON HISTORY

The 1976 7.5-magnitude earthquake of Guatemala killed twenty-three thousand people and displaced and left thousands of others homeless. The majority of people affected were poor and Indigenous. Most national disasters only highlight what is wrong with the current government and how it does or does not take care of its people. There is no Tierra Nueva, but I did base them on the Theology of Liberation Clergy, a religious group started after the earthquake, who believed the earthquake was God's statement to create a "Tierra Nueva" on earth, believing that "a true Christian can only be a revolutionary in our country." The nuns and priests involved were condemned by Guatemala's archbishop and became the target of death squads. The Jamestown dog phenomenon is from a discovery by Ariane Thomas of the University of Iowa. The conclusions in the novel are made by me, and fictional. Dogs are real but all dead.

ACKNOWLEDGMENTS

The phrase "Nothing so glorious as her mother with a gun" is from an Angela Carter story called "The Bloody Chamber."

The quotes in A Note on History are from an article by Deborah Levenson-Estrada, "Reactions to Trauma: The 1976 Earthquake in Guatemala."

The description of the houses in Jamaica Plain looking like crayons is from Jess Rizkallah. Thank you for drawing the Five of Wands for me on that omicron Christmas.

The idea of archaeology being like finding a dollar in your jeans pocket is from Sira Dooley Fairchild, who answered a lot of my questions about archaeology. Thank you.

This book would have no life without Rachel Kim, who kept asking about my idea about a grandmother in the apocalypse. Thank you for sitting with me for hours to map out this story and coaching me through the initial pains of writing a novel, and your notes on my first draft in pink pen that said, "What lol." Thank you, Angeline Rodriguez for taking this on and being so good at what you do. Thank you, Danny Vazquez for believing in this novel and being so encouraging of my vision. Thank you Rola, Rachael, Tiffany, Alessandra, and Ben for all of your incredible support throughout this process and all of Astra House for keeping me in check.

If you've been following me since my viral slam poetry (vomit) days, I couldn't have done this (write a fucking novel) without you. Thanks for coming to my readings, buying my valentines, retweeting my horny sad girl stuff, sharing poems with your niece, thank you. You've made my dreams come true.

I am one of those losers who is obsessed with their family: thank you Mami, for being so resilient, encouraging, and hilarious and for keeping me inside most of my childhood because you were afraid of me being kidnapped. Thank you Papi for believing in me except for that one time when you said, "What if nobody is at the Anna's Taqueira when I drop you off?" and then when we arrived you were right. MJ & Stephanie, my sisters and cornerstones of womanhood, thank you for making fun of me so much: I deserved it.

I could not have written this without the help of my friends who are smarter than me. Thank you, Puloma, for being my constant hotline when I was ripping out my hair about certain plot points and for granting me the extreme privilege of a life-long friend who knows you forever, you bitch. Thank you, Olivia, for our friendship of telling each other scary stories until we pass out or cry, always commiserating with me about the exact loneliness, insanity, and beauty that it is to write a novel. Thank you, Arti, for giving me so many damn books to read, cooking me dinner, and reminding me that art and fun should come first. Thank you, Molly, for being so knowledgeable about fiction, and for reading initial drafts with such veracity and love. Samuel, Chris, Tiffany: you are so brilliant and I don't know who I'd be without your goofy, never-ending friendship, your music, or your art. Will, you are my sister. Hannah & Don—my vintage pandemic roommates and friends forever whether you like it or not: we survived. Jamie, thank you for teaching me what butt-chugging is. El, you are the only friend I've seen perform at Elsewhere, so thank you for rockin', and also? For rollin'.

Thank you to the Brooklyn Public Library and the librarian who showed me books about the Popul Vuh and the Guatemalan Civil War and the other librarian who helped me print 308 pages. Thank you, Lara and the glorious Airbnb where Molly and I finished our books.

Candelaria is inspired by a poem I wrote called "How To Survive the Zombie Apocalypse as an 82-year-old Guatemalan Grandmother," performed at the National Poetry Slam (remember that?) in 2015 as a duo with Jonathan Mendoza. Thank you, Jonathan, Janae, and Portia for seeing so much life into this poem when I was a little baby poet and for showing me how to hold an audience captive.

ACKNOWLEDGEMENTS

Thank you to Paige for your very understanding, last-minute doula-consolation about DIY abortions. Thank you to Ryan Carson and my sister, Mariajose, who both gave me important insight about Candy's journey through their invaluable work in harm reduction and rehabilitation. Thank you, Jonny, for being an incredible booking agent and taking care of logistics while I spiraled—I'm proud of you, buddy.

Thank you, Polly Nor, for being so receptive to doing another cover with me. I love your demon baby brain and I'm so lucky to have gotten to work with you. Thank you, Chimera Singer, for my stellar author photo.

The following people contributed to the life of this book in extreme ways, through conversation, friendship, love, something you said once that you didn't know I would remember forever, general sense of community, reading drafts, and just being there for me: Danialie, Paola, Alex, Ari, Marcia, Blake, Koa, Dani, Elliot, Alejandro, Chris, John Manuel, Jared, Oz, Jamie, Hannah R., Priya, Michi, Sai, Matthew P., Sarina, Kyle, Jeremy, Juan Felipe, Matthew R., Sylvie, Christine, Claudia, Ben, Kat, Natasha, and the Specs.

Thank you teachers, thank you abortion doctors, thank you doulas, thank you small movie theatres, booksellers, and baristas. Thank you, Amtrak and the sleepless night I spent writing one scene that I ended up deleting.

There is not that much romance in this book, and that is because I was in love while writing it. Thank you, Miguel Salazar, for being supportive, hot, funny, smart, going over the Spanish with me, hot, helping me see this through, and making the corny (time stopping when I look at you) true.

Thank you, Fransisca Villeda, my stylish, hard, funny, scammer, amazing cook of an abuelita who can still shimmy at ninety years old. There is nobody like you in the world.

Thank you, Candelaria. I don't remember you, but I know you prayed for me. I will take your good with your bad, your harm with your love: I'll remember you.

ABOUT THE AUTHOR

Melissa Lozada-Oliva is the child of Guatemalan and Colombian immigrants. She holds an MFA in poetry from NYU and her writing has been featured in *PAPER*, the *Guardian*, *The BreakBeat Poets Vol. 4*, *Wirecutter*, *Vulture*, *Bustle*, *Glamour*, *HuffPost*, *Muzzle Magazine*, *The Poetry Project*, Audible, and BBC Mundo. She has worked with Armani Beauty, Instagram, Google, Espolon Tequila, and Topo Chico Hard Seltzer. She is from Massachusetts and lives in New York City. Her debut novel-in-verse, *Dreaming of You*, was published by Astra House in 2021.